Broken People Duet

Vi Carter

Copyright © 2023 by Vi Carter

No portion of this book may be reproduced in any form without written permission from the publisher or author, except as permitted by U.S. copyright law.

Contents

OTHER BOOKS BY VI CARTER

Other Books by VI CARTER

WILD IRISH SERIES

FATHER (NOVELLA)

RECKLESS # 0.5

VICIOUS #1

RUTHLESS #2

FEARLESS #3

HEARTLESS #4

THE BOYNE CLUB

DARK #1

DARKER # 2

DARKEST #3

PITCH BLACK #4

THE OBSESSED DUET

A DEADLY OBSESSION #1

A CRUEL CONFESSION #2

YOUNG IRISH REBELS

MAFIA PRINCE #1
MAFIA KING #2
MAFIA GAMES #3
MAFIA BOSS #4

MURPHY'S MAFIA MADE MEN
SINNER'S VOW #1
SAVAGE MARRIAGE #2
SCANDALOUS PLEDGE #3

WARNING

This book is a dark romance. It contains scenes that may trigger some readers and should be read by those only 18 or older.

BLURB

Jared

They say love and hate dance together along the same line.

My feelings for Layla don't dance on the line; they destroy it.

It's been seven years since she disappeared without a trace.

And now she's back, but things have changed—I've changed.

I'm no longer the Jared she remembers, the boy who wanted to protect her.

I'm very much my father's son, and I take what I want, and what I want is Layla.

But this time, I'm keeping her forever.

Layla

Seven years—that's how long it's been since I've seen him.

After painstakingly putting myself back together, I'm finally ready to start a life without his memory chasing my every step.

Imagine my surprise when my new beginning leads me straight back to him.

Only he's not the boy I remember.

He's angry.

Damaged.

Hiding secrets that want to destroy him.

He hates me. He wants me.

I'm not sure I'll survive the man he has become. His demons threaten to destroy us both.

Part One of the Broken People Duet

Deceive Me

Broken Peple Duet Part One

PROLOGUE

JARED

*P*OVERTY.

It's something I'm not accustomed to, not anymore. Not since my father took me from the slums and brought me to his billionaire mansion. He told me it was all mine and that I needed to buck up and be the son I was destined to be.

I don't think I can ever live up to his expectations.

The car slows as I approach Woodview Estate. It gives me the fucking shivers. I'm not afraid; it's more of an old memory, like a fire burning in my mind. One I extinguish as I park my new BMW along the curb. This place is devoid of life, not even the grass has survived. The wilted shrubbery hangs over the side of the curbing. This is Ireland, so it rains all the time, but this place is forsaken. Even the rain doesn't bother to piss on the landscape. As I stare around me and study a little closer, I start to notice signs of life.

In front of me is a large row of houses, and at the corner of the end house, shadows of movement catch my eye. Behind drawn curtains, light seeps through the small cracks. I'm sure some watch me from the windows.

My presence here has not gone unnoticed. I get out of the car and lock the doors. Shadows creep closer. Most of the men have their faces camouflaged inside hoodies. I focus on house number six. I'm apprehensive of the guys at my back, circling closer to my car. The moment I push open the gate to number six, they murmur.

Their whispers reach my ears. "He's with Chester. We'd better scram."

Like rats, they scurry. Chester must be the man I'm seeking. Warren only gave me an address, no name. I knock on the door three times before someone answers. The guy who opens it isn't looking at me, so I'm faced with his profile. Tribal tats rise from the collar of his jersey and wrap around his neck.

He draws a drag of a cigarette, side-eyeing me. His hands are coated in tattoos too. "What do you want?"

"I'm looking for Chester."

This fucker is a wolf, but I'm no lamb. He faces me, flings the cigarette past my shoulder, and grins. "What for?"

"Can I come in?" I ask, and I take a step closer to him.

His grin transforms into a sneer, but he steps back. "Sure."

I don't like that he's at my back, but I continue to keep a relaxed posture as I walk into the dingy entrance. The smell of smoke and something stronger clings to everything.

"I didn't pick up what you wanted." He passes me while lighting up another cigarette. He shoulders a door to our left open, and we step into a sitting room that's full of guys who are sporting tats just like his. I unquestionably have the right house.

He plops down between two other men on the couch. All eyes are on me.

"I didn't say what I wanted." I point at the empty armchair to my left. The guy, who I assume is Chester, nods, and I sit down, opening my jacket.

R&B music plays in the background. A fog of smoke floats close to the ceiling.

A guy near me offers me a rolled-up cigarette. It doesn't smell like smoke, and I decline before facing Chester. "Could we talk somewhere private?"

He glances at the other men, who laugh, before he faces me. "No. If you have something to say, say it."

I'm not telling him shit in front of everyone. They all move when I reach into my pocket. I raise one hand as I slowly withdraw the envelope of cash with the other. "Three grand for a word in private, Chester."

He jerks his chin, and I toss the envelope to him. He catches the cash, shreds it open, and starts counting. Once he's satisfied, he passes the stash of cash to the guy beside him before standing.

"You've bought yourself five minutes."

My five minutes are in the entrance hall. I assumed it would be someplace more private, but I take the time I'm offered. "I need a gun."

"What makes you think I can get you one?"

"Warren O'Reagan gave me your address," I explain.

Something shifts in Chester's stance. "You don't look like a friend of Warren's."

I smirk. "Neither do you."

Chester jerks his chin again. "It will cost you."

"Name your price."

He thinks about it. "Ten grand."

For a fucking gun? "I want it wiped."

"It'll be untraceable. But it will take time."

"How long?"

He takes a drag of his cigarette before stepping to the front door. Opening it, he flicks the cigarette outside. He pauses before looking back at me. "Is that your car?"

"Yeah." I stride toward him.

He lets out a whistle. "Touch the car and you die." He issues the warning to the group outside and closes the door. "I should have asked for more money since you're driving a car like that." He grins.

I don't smile. "I'll give you five grand tomorrow and the other five grand when I have the gun."

He nods, and I hold out my hand. Chester hesitates before he grips my fingers. "We have a deal."

I'm ready to go when he asks a question he shouldn't. "What do you want it for?"

I glare at him. "I'll see you tomorrow."

"Just asking, brother. You know it won't end all your problems." He holds up his thumb and forefinger, mimicking a gun.

"It might end one," I say before I take off. My car is still unscathed. Driving out of the estate doesn't make the memories evaporate; instead, I'm yanked right back to my childhood. The very reason I want a gun.

Everything comes full circle. My father once said, "What's meant for you won't go by you. Justice will be served in this life or another."

I say, fuck that. If Justice isn't served the way it should be, then I'll take matters into my own hands and deliver my kind of justice.

Once I do this, my life will be my own again. I'll finally be able to live.

CHAPTER ONE

LAYLA

S O MUCH CAN CHANGE in a moment; a lot can change in seven years. Seven years. That's how long it's been since I've seen Jared. Seven years to the day, when I was dragged from his arms kicking and screaming. He fought so hard to keep me with him. He fought to the point that his violence made me shiver.

The sound of the sliding door opening pulls me away from my thoughts. The swing bench creaks as Evelyn sits down. The smell of her moisturizer on her olive-tone arms consumes me. Glancing up from my hands, I find her deep brown eyes watching me. She brushes long locks of black hair over her shoulder before smiling at me softly. "You don't have to do this."

My heart skips a beat at how much I want to walk away from this, but I can't. I can't walk away, because Evelyn and Carl have packed up their lives and moved halfway across Ireland so I can go to the best college. I'm both nervous and excited at the prospect of starting over in a new place. This is my chance to start a new life and leave the past behind.

"Close your eyes and take a breath."

I do what Evelyn instructs.

"Tell me what you're thinking about." Evelyn speaks in her calming voice. She's a counselor. Some would say I'm lucky to have been adopted by her and Carl, but her voice of reason isn't always welcome. Right now, though, I need her.

"Jared." His name causes Evelyn to stiffen beside me. Her reaction to him always confuses me. She makes it seem as if Jared was the one who hurt me, when he was the one who protected me. I drop my hands to my lap before opening my eyes. "I was thinking about him. How he always protected me."

Evelyn takes my hand in hers. "Now it's my and Carl's turn to protect you." She brushes a loose strand of blonde hair behind my ear. I want to ask her why she gets uneasy when I talk about Jared, but I don't get the chance.

Carl steps out into the backyard with a steaming hot mug of coffee in his hands. His soft green eyes and olive skin make him attractive, even for his fifty years. He keeps himself in shape. "It's time to go." He shows us his watch. I can't read the front face from this distance, but I nod and hop up from the bench. Evelyn stands behind me, placing both her hands on my shoulders. The slight squeeze fills me with the strength I need. I inhale a deep breath and swallow. "I'm ready," I say to Carl.

The smile he gives me is stuffed to the gills with encouragement.

I have spent seven years in therapy trying to erase every slap and thump, every word and memory, and now it's all coming back. For some reason, starting over makes me go back to the start—to Bert and Ronnie. To Jared. Most times, I keep the knowledge to myself that I have never really let go of Jared. I keep that information bottled up.

I want to prove to Carl and Evelyn that they saved me—that they fixed me.

I gather my phone and bag, hurrying to the car before I change my mind. The click of it being unlocked has me climbing into the back. Evelyn and Carl both get in and glance at each other. They share a look for only a split second, and it has me sinking into the car seat. They don't think I'm strong enough.

"I'm ready," I say once again, even as my throat threatens to close. Pulling down the visor, Evelyn glances at me in the mirror with a soft smile that wrinkles the skin around her brown eyes. "We know you are, sweetheart."

Carl starts the car and backs out of the drive. My gaze drifts away from Evelyn's and to the neat rows of houses we pass. Each one is white, and each one is as perfect as the next. It's a far cry from where I came from. Bert's house was unkempt and dilapidated, a bit like its occupants.

"I could have driven," I say, staring out the window.

"We wanted to take you," Carl says. Silence filters in, and I'm waiting for someone to pierce the quietness. "If—and I'm only saying if, Layla—you change your mind, we can always turn back." The softness and kindness in his voice still startles me sometimes. Even after seven years of witnessing what a great man he is, I can't erase the other twelve.

My childhood in foster care was a different time and a different life, one that I dip into for a reference, but I never stay there. "Thanks, Carl. But I want to do this. I mean, it's only college." I force a wobbly smile.

Carl gazes at me in the rearview mirror; I catch my own reflection and look away. My white skin is ghostly.

Another glance is shared between Carl and Evelyn. I pretend I don't see it as I clutch my bag tighter. They are such good people, and I'm the only child they adopted, not being able to have children themselves. I often wonder why people who deserve to have children can't, and the ones who shouldn't be allowed to have children can. Is it God's plan, or is it just a flaw in the body? To me, it's such a shame. Both of them are amazing.

The drive to Kingscourt College feels like it takes forever. I've made this journey a few times in the car that Carl and Evelyn had purchased for my nineteenth birthday only two weeks ago. The red starlet was a lavish gift, but one they both said was nothing. It isn't new, but to me, it's perfect. The car will take me to school so I won't have to rely on Carl or Evelyn to drive me.

"I was thinking when we pick you up, we could stop and grab some Chinese," Evelyn says.

I tense as the large black iron gates loom in front of us. The castle that houses Kingscourt College is set deep in the background and grows larger as Carl continues to drive. I glance up at the monstrous structure where I will spend the next three years studying business.

"Yeah, that would be great." I swallow the enormous lump in my throat as we pull into the parking lot. Food is the furthest thing from my mind right now.

Carl knocks off the car, and I quickly grab the bottle of water out of my bag. After taking a nervous gulp, I replace the blue lid. *Stop delaying. You can do this.*

Repeating this in my head gives me the strength to climb out of the car. I hold on to the door and bend my head to look back in. Both Carl and Evelyn turn to look at me.

"I'm going to be fine," I remind them.

"You can get back into the car." Carl's words have my head dipping as my heart feels like it's shrinking.

"But we both know you're strong enough to do this." Evelyn's words wrestle a smile out of me as I look from her to Carl.

"You are." Carl smiles back, and I release the car door and close it. I don't look back as I drag my bag across my shoulder. Other students gather around vehicles parked across from Carl's car. They glance at me, but I'm dismissed quickly. I take a peek back at Evelyn and Carl, who are still sitting in the car watching me. I give them a little wave and walk across the vast open space that's half-filled with cars.

The grass softens my steps as I leave the parking lot, and I crane my neck back to really take in Kingscourt College. The gray stone of the castle tells a story of time. The closer I get, the more scars I see along the stone. I walk along the footpath and trail my fingers across the harsh ridges. History intrigues me. It's there for us to learn from. We never do, but it's there all the same. My fingers leave the wall as two guys walk past me. One smiles, and I try smiling back. His mouth tugs higher, telling me I'm doing great. I look back at the parking lot, wanting Carl and Evelyn to see my progress already, but Carl's Mercedes is gone.

I turn away and take the three steps up to the main red doors. One door is open, a black chock keeping it in place. The light inside the lobby is dim, and it takes my eyes a moment to adjust.

Chairs are placed all along the wall, where people sit waiting. Some appear dressed more for an interview rather than college. My eyes collide with a girl whose lips remain in a thin, straight line as she watches my progress down the hall. Her high blonde ponytail is something I could never achieve with my hair. My long blonde strands are too fine to stay in place. I tuck a strand behind my ear and approach a large reception desk.

The air in the lobby is heavy and warm, and I find myself pulling at the blouse that Evelyn laid out for me. I matched it with my favorite black skinny jeans and black boots. I ditched the suit jacket she had left for me—it made me appear too formal—but seeing how everyone else is dressed, I regret leaving it on my bed.

"Take a seat." The receptionist doesn't even look up as she speaks. When I don't scurry away, she sighs. "Take a seat." She looks at me from under her red-rimmed glasses, and I step away from the desk and turn to find the occupants of the chairs watching me.

The black plastic chair I sit on is warm. My gaze collides with the blonde girl, her eyes narrow, and I look away and sit in silence as other students filter into the lobby and make their way to their classes. My attention is drawn to the door every time I hear a creak. Each time, my heart leaps as more students filter in and others leave. The receptionist stands and points at the first seat. Time moves slowly. I keep taking peeks at the blonde girl, and she smirks. When she's called, she flicks her hair as she walks past me.

She has the figure that most girls would die or starve for. She leans in on the desk, and the receptionist laughs.

When it's my turn, I gather my bag and approach the desk. The receptionist gives me a brief second of her attention before sliding her glasses up on her head. "How can I help?"

"HI, I'm Layla Masters. I'm new here. I'm looking for the gym." I attempt a smile.

She slides the glasses back down on her face. "Down the hall. On your left you will see a set of Brown double doors. You'd better go before you're late." Her words catch me off guard.

"Thank you." I leave the desk and follow her directions to the brown double doors. I take a final look at my attire before reaching for the handle. I didn't bring my sports uniform in hopes that I could sit this one out. Taking gym class isn't standard for Irish colleges, but Kingscourt has made this class mandatory.

I pull the door open to have every head turn in my direction. If that's not bad enough, I'm very aware that all the men wear shorts, and the girls are in skirts.

"Get changed and join us on the floor," the coach shouts.

"I don't have a uniform." My voice is low.

He shakes his head and walks closer to me. "There are some spare uniforms in the large green locker." The coach blows his whistle. "Hurry up. Let's start."

I want to say no, but the words get lodged in my throat. The blonde girl I saw earlier smirks before leaning into a guy beside her. A guy whose brown eyes are so deep they appear almost black. But, in those eyes, I see a young boy—one I've dreamt of for the last seven years.

Jared.

I've found Jared. I've found home.

CHAPTER TWO

LAYLA

DISBELIEF WEIGHS SO HEAVILY on my heart that I'm looking for a sign that he isn't Jared. His eyes flash with a warning that is soaked with recognition before they flare up. The hate burns the light away, and I'm left staring at a stranger.

A girl's laughter draws my attention to the group, and they're watching me as I stare at Jared. The coach has his back to us as he gathers up a net of balls.

The blonde girl's laughter dies, and she steps closer to Jared. He doesn't seem to notice the motion as he narrows his gaze, and his jaw tightens.

"What are you looking at?"

Oh God, his voice...

The tone is deeper, but I know that voice. The hairs rise on the back of my neck as I continue to stare at his broad chest. I try to comprehend his question, which is stuffed to the gills with bitterness.

The blonde clears her throat, and her small hand brushes against Jared's shoulder. He noticeably tenses under her touch, but I see what she's doing. She's claiming him.

I can't breathe.

My mind can't accept what I'm seeing—his face, a face I looked at every day. One I loved seeing. One I feared I would never see again. Yet here he is, against all odds. His features are the same, but stronger and manly. He's harshly beautiful.

My bag slips off my shoulder, and I can't stop the motion as it hits the ground. This can't be real. His jaw is stronger, his dark eyes deeper, his lips fuller. He's so much bigger, so much angrier. But this is Jared.

I always knew that when he grew up, he would be something amazing to look at. I was right.

My heart tries to burst from my chest as his lip curls into a sneer like the edges of burning paper. I'm trying to stay still as he drags his gaze across my body, even as my skin feels like it's on fire.

He doesn't recognize me.

He steps forward, detangling himself from the girl, and slowly starts walking toward me. The rise and fall of his shoulders remind me of a lion. I should run. I hold still, reminding myself that I have nothing to fear from him.

"I asked you a question. What are you looking at?" The cruel sneer remains on his fiercely handsome face. The closer he comes, the more my certainty of who he is wavers. He's so much bigger than I am. His width seems to block out the world behind him, and it's like a dark veil falls over me.

"Jared." I say his name as my throat burns.

His jaw tightens, pain twists his features, and soon it's all swallowed with a hate I don't understand.

"Ms. Masters, why are you still standing here?"

The world snaps back into focus. The coach approaches me.

"Get changed now," he barks, and he blows his whistle, which pierces the space. "Everyone, let's go." He claps his hands, and Jared jogs backward away from me. He spins when he reaches his group of friends, who all glare at me.

"Ms. Masters!" The shout from the coach has the heat across my cheeks flaring up as I gather my bag off the floor and turn to find a door with a sign for the locker rooms above it.

I'm trying to get my breathing under control as I open the green locker to find a stack of sport uniforms. I don't find my size until I'm halfway down the pile. I take off my shirt and slip on the baby blue T-shirt.

The longer I'm away from Jared, the more I question if that's really him. If that's really the boy who protected me and saved me. My stomach twists, and my hands tighten on the gray skirt. I take a few more deep breaths and strip off my trousers to put on the skirt. My scarred leg has me sitting on the cold bench as a memory assaults me.

I take tiny baby steps, clutching the pink plastic basin in my hands. The sudsy water splashes from side to side, threatening to spill over. When I reach Bert, I'm proud that I haven't spilled a drop. After placing the basin to my left, I take the towel off my shoulder and spread it between Bert's feet. His laces are always covered in dust and dirt from his workdays in construction. Pulling off his large size-twelve boots nearly sends me falling back, but I keep my balance.

I take off his sweaty, smelly socks on autopilot. He stretches his toes like a cat stretching itself while I put the basin in its place. Bert rolls up his jeans to his knees. I don't move. I wait until his feet are in the basin. He dips his toes, barely breaking the surface of the water. Bert lifts his legs quickly, his eyes growing round and wide. My heart stills.

"You tried to burn me," Bert accuses.

I shake my head in denial, unable to speak, and he plants his feet on either side of the basin. I fall back at his sudden movement.

"You little bitch."

I shake my head again, words refusing to come to me.

Scrambling back, I try to avoid the flying basin as Bert kicks it in a rage. Water sloshes across my legs and onto the wooden floor. I cower, trying to disappear as the basin collides with my side. Keeping my eyes closed tightly, I tuck my head into my chest as my heart beats wildly. The ground disappears beneath me, and I'm airborne. My back roars at the abuse as Bert smashes me against the wall. His large hand encircles my throat, and my small feet dangle near his knees. I claw at his hands, terrified for the first time that I might die. It isn't just his grip around my throat, but the violence in his eyes. My nails sink into his large hands, which tighten at a neck-breaking strength.

I kick and claw as light and strength start to disappear.

As Jared pounds his fists into Bert's head, trying to make him release me, I still can't breathe. Bert's grip leaves my throat, and I hit the ground; the impact sends pain into my hip, but it's nothing like the pain in my throat.

Jared.

I get up off the bench and finish getting ready. I take a pair of gray sneakers that are too big and slip them on. I'm searching for a moment in the mirror where I tell myself how strong I am and that I've got this, but words cower deep in my belly, just like always.

"Ms. Masters, do you need assistance?" a voice calls in.

I scurry away from the mirror, and as I leave the locker room, I meet the coach, who hands me a ball. Everyone is passing them back and forth to each other.

"Alex, you're with Layla."

My fingers tighten around the ball. Alex, the blonde girl, approaches with disdain, twisting her pretty features. Her focus drops to my leg, and she tilts her head to the side. False pity fills her eyes.

"I'm sure the coach would let you wear sweatpants, considering..." She flicks her hair.

Once again, words fail me, and I try to catch Jared's eye, but he's further down, engrossed in passing a ball. He doesn't remember me. His right hand has a dark ink band around the wrist. I think it's a tattoo, but I can't be sure from this distance.

Fingers click in front of my face. "I'd like to get some physical activity done today." She follows my line of sight before a hateful laugh falls from her ruby red lips. "So out of your league. Jay wouldn't give you a second glance."

I fire the ball at Alex, and she catches it quickly.

"Jay?"

Her expression hardens. "That's what I said."

She passes the ball to me, and we continue this as the knowledge that this guy isn't Jared slowly sinks in. He may remind me of Jared, but from his hostile glares, I can assume that the recognition I thought I saw isn't really there. He has no idea who I am.

When class ends, I'm a little less shaky and quickly change back into my clothes. Alex and two other girls talk openly about me gawking at Jay. When their words grow hushed, I hear them talking about my scarred leg.

I leave without looking at the circle of mean girls. That's what they are, mean girls. Most schools have them, but I didn't expect to find the mean girls in college. I've been fortunate enough not to attract the attention of them before. I've always been able to fly under the radar.

Passing through the gym, I can't help but search for Jay. The area is empty.

Taking out my schedule, I check to see what my next class is. Pivoting, I stop as I come face-to-face with a girl who wears a name tag: Ashley. Her tawny skin is flawless, as is her long black ponytail. With eyes not quite green or brown focused on me intently, I shuffle my feet, feeling self-aware. What does she see when she looks at me?

A tall, thin, and pale girl who is staring at her for far too long?

"I've been assigned to be your guide." Her accent sounds Hispanic, which makes sense with her features. She turns on her heel with a slight smile. Her movements remind me of a ballerina. Her frame isn't really suited to that, though, as she's all curves. "By the way, I'm Ashley." She pulls at her name tag as she speaks. "I'll show you where we eat."

I follow Ashley to a large empty room that is lined with benches and long tables. Right now, the space is empty, but I can imagine the activity during break times. This is one space I will avoid. Two ladies dressed in white aprons hustle behind a long silver steam table.

"Great," I say.

Ashley grins, flashing white teeth. "It's not a restaurant, but the food is decent. Trust me, after morning classes, this place is like a haven."

I nod. *Not to me.*

Being around people isn't something I do often, unless you count Morgan, the girl who lives across the street from me. We moved here only two weeks ago and her mother greeted us on our first day in the neighbored. That night I ended up going out with Morgan and her friends just to please Carl and Evelyn.

I follow her out to the bustling hallway. She points a lot as she tells me where everything is. "That's the library. Avoid the back area." She rolls her eyes as she glances at me over her shoulder. "That's where people go for fun times."

I'm making notes. *Avoid the library and the lunch area.* We stop at a gray door.

"So this is our business class. We better go in before we're late." She pushes open the door, and we step into the lecture room. I don't look around me. I keep focused on the steps I climb until I see a row at the back empty. That's where I sit, with my single notepad and pen. Coming to a new college halfway through the year is tougher than I imagined. This college is way ahead of where I left off at my old college. I spend the next few hours going from one class to the next. Ashley never leaves me, and I'm grateful for her constant chatter.

"So, it's lunch now. Are you good at finding your way there?"

My blood heats up in my veins at the thought of being left on my own, but I need to rely on myself. I nod. "Yeah, sure, I'm good."

The heat spreads across my checks, but Ashley doesn't seem to notice as she rolls her shoulders before heading toward the mass of students. I look around and decide to make my way outside. I'm tempted to glance up and make eye contact with people, but after my run-in with who I thought was Jared, my nerves are rattled, and my stamina has dwindled to nothing.

A group of guys have gathered close to the main door blocking me from leaving.

The scent of cigarette smoke surrounds them. All of them have similar features to Ashley's. My steps falter at the sight of the group, but I push one leg in front of the other until I reach the door..

One of the guys, who wears jeans that hang way too low and a T-shirt that could house a few guys his size, grins at me. His eyes travel from my flat black shoes, up to my black jeans, and on to my white shirt.

"You're new?" he says with a wide smirk.

"Yes. I just started today." I'm ready to walk away when he steps in front of me. "Can I help you with something?" I ask, slinging my bag over my shoulder.

"You can help me with a few things."

The suggestive remark has his friend laughing while bumping into him. "Man, you hittin' on whitey?"

I can feel each nerve zing inside of me. I want to run out of the building. I force a smile and sidestep them. My hands roll into fists until my knuckles turn white and my heart hammers.

Don't run.

"Lucas, you dumb..." Ashley gives me a quick look before glancing back at the trio. The one who spoke to me is Lucas.

"What are you doing?" Her hands go to her hips, and she looks fierce. I want to be like her when I grow up.

"Don't be like that, *hermana,*" Lucas says.

Ashley tuts at his words. "Does *Madre* know you're here, *bobo?*"

The other boy snickers. "She called you a fool!"

"You are a *bobo* too, Sam," Ashley says.

Sam's smile melts off his face.

"We are only messing, Ashley. Relax," Lucas says, removing a pack of cigarettes and a lighter from his pocket.

Ashley moves away from Lucas and Sam, who split and go back down the main corridor, but not before calling goodbye to Ashley and blowing her kisses—ones she doesn't respond to.

As they leave, a familiar voice rises up.

Why didn't I say something?

How many times have I frozen in the past? When Bert was screaming a question at me, I'd freeze. Not responding was the worst thing to do, but I always *froze.*

I am such an idiot.

"Are you okay, Layla?"

My head jerks up at Ashley's voice. "Yeah, fine. Why?"

Ashley looks away from me briefly, then her nose scrunches up as she speaks. "You've been staring at the same spot for the last few minutes."

The heat comes again, fast and hard—my face blazes.

"Look, I know Lucas and Sam can be full-on. But they're harmless." Ashley tucks her hands into her shirt pockets while leaning against the wall. Her stance looks so relaxed, but her eyes once again are fierce, making them grow more brown than green.

"I'm just... not good with new people."

She nods like she gets it, but there's no way she could understand what I'm saying, and I'm not going to enlighten her about my childhood from hell.

"Lucas and Sam are my brothers, and they wouldn't hurt a fly. They're Idiots, but they wouldn't hurt anyone." Ashley stands straight with a goofy grin on her face. "Do you have any brothers or sisters?"

It's a simple question that people ask each other all the time. For me, it's one of the hardest. My nerves are frazzled, and I push back on my heels. If I say I do, she'll ask more questions. If I say I don't, I feel like I'm hiding Jared, Riley, and Nelson. My throat dries up and my pulse spikes. "Oh. I better get going. I forgot my purse." She turns away while nodding. "We'll chat later."

I try to mirror her smile. "Yeah. Great."

The moment Ashley is gone, I grip my bag and walkout of the building.

Tomorrow will be better. First days are always the worst. I'll try harder. I won't search for Jared in every set of brown eyes.

My nose and throat burn as I take a peek at the car park. Carl won't be here yet, and it gives me a few moments to pull myself together. I don't get to process much more, as a large hand springs out, and I'm dragged around the side of the building. The moment my back hits the wall, I'm frozen under the heavy stare of a set of dark, angry eyes.

And I'm at it again. All I can think about is Jared.

CHAPTER THREE

JARED

MY HANDS DEMAND I hurt her. I push harder on her small shoulders, and the foolish boy in me screams to take my hands off what's his. What he has spent years searching for, each time coming up emptier and a little angrier than the last. Yet, here she is, staring up at me with wide blue eyes. Her scent seems to envelop me, and I dig a little deeper into her shoulders.

I could snap her so easily. I want to.

She shouldn't be here.

"What the fuck do you want?" I bark and lean in, inhaling her aromatic lavender scent.

Layla.

Anger bubbles through me, and my back arches.

"You're the one who dragged me over here." Her voice is stronger, her gaze more defiant than she displayed in the gym. Earlier, she looked like a victim. I remember how good she always was at playing the victim.

I grin and take some of the pressure off her shoulders but don't remove my hands completely. "Because you were staring at me like some lovesick puppy." I say each word with a mocking tone.

Her lip trembles, and my gaze lingers on her mouth. She's still Layla, just older. More womanly. That fact isn't lost on me, with all the curves she displayed in gym class. She isn't someone who fades into the background.

She always stood out, even when she didn't want to. I don't need her to be here. I don't need the distraction.

"I thought you were someone else, but I was wrong."

I release her, and she reaches up and rubs her shoulders. I don't step back. I don't want to walk away from her. The pull that was always there hasn't eased with time. If anything, it seems stronger.

I hate her.

"Let's hope your drooling over me ends." I fold my arms across my chest. I know my size will intimidate her. I battle with the need to protect her. It's all I knew. All I cared about. She was the reason I got up, the reason I lived. The reason I fought to survive. Until she left, not giving a fucking care in the world about me.

"I thought you were someone else," she says again. Pain drags down her lips.

Fuck her.

"I don't want your sob story." I lean in close to her and dip my head so that she can hear me very clearly. "Stay out of my way, Layla, or I'll make sure you regret ever crossing my path."

Her chest rises and falls faster. My words fully sink in; I've made my point. Her swanlike neck draws my hand to it. She inhales sharply as I tighten my fingers around her fragile throat. Her pale skin is soft. I can imagine pressing kisses along the flesh. I tighten my fingers further, trying to banish the thought.

She pulls away. "Get your hands off me." Her hysteria pierces my anger. The protective boy in me has me removing my hand, and yet I can't step away from her.

She ducks under my arm and flees while I stare at the wall, wondering what the fuck is wrong with me.

I tighten my hand into a fist, and all I want to do is smash it into the wall.

"What was that about?" Alex's voice springs up behind me.

I loosen my fists, and I turn to her wearing my signature *I don't give a fuck* smirk. "I have that effect on women. They throw themselves at me. I was just telling her I wasn't interested."

Alex assesses me for a moment. "It looked a little intense."

I step closer to Alex and let my smirk manifest into a smile. "I'm an intense guy."

Her posture relaxes before her lips tug up. "I can verify that is true, Jay." She winks at me.

I start walking toward the parking lot while looking for a blonde girl who shouldn't be here. Did she search for me over the years too? It really doesn't matter. I want to stay focused, and she's too great of a distraction.

"So, this charity event tonight..." I start.

I glance at Alex, and she rolls her eyes dramatically. "Do you have to go too?"

"Yes. Raising money for starving kids while we eat a seven-course meal and drink our fill seems like such a fitting thing to do." Sarcasm drips from my words.

"You seem bothered." Her words hold an accusation.

I drag back my control that Layla rattled. The last person I want to see a crack in my armor is Alex. She's clever, and she would do anything to climb higher in our social circles. That includes handing me to the wolves if need be. I stop walking. "Maybe I am bothered." I lean into her.

She smiles. "Bothered and intense. I do like that combination."

Alex is striking. Her reasons for liking me are far more calculating than any physical attraction. She knows our parents want us together. We would be a powerhouse. I've tasted her strawberry-flavored lips many times before, and I'd happily taste them again.

"I'll see you tonight," I say once I reach my vehicle. I glance around the parking lot, but I don't see Layla.

"I look forward to it." Alex still lingers at my car as I climb in.

I close the door and lose my smile. She's still watching me as I reverse out of the parking spot.

***

"Jay, today is not the day," Rex shouts as he climbs out of the ring. He's sweaty from training some new guy who waves at me like he knows me. For Rex's sake, I wave back.

"I need to blow off some steam." I remove my sweater and throw it alongside the ring.

"I'm training someone." Rex juts his chin over his shoulder. The new guy is watching us.

"Does he bring in as much money as I do?" I ask as I pick up the tape for my hands.

Rex shakes his head. "Don't be a dick."

"I don't mind," the new guy calls. "Jay, you go ahead."

I smile at Rex. "Problem solved." I hand Rex the tape, but he doesn't take it.

"Stay in the ring, Lenny," Rex fires without looking away from me.

Lenny is halfway through the ropes but does as Rex says.

"Just let me hit the bag at least." Rex has rules—rules that I never break. Only one person in his gym at a time during training. He doesn't want any distractions. That's what makes him the best trainer.

Rex shakes his head again. "Hold out your hands."

I do, and Rex takes the tape from me. "You can work with Lenny."

I tut. "No. That's bollocks."

Rex raises a brow. "That or leave."

I glance at Lenny, who's looking very fucking happy with himself. "Fine."

Rex tapes my hands and slips on my boxing gloves. He hands me a helmet, but I climb into the ring without it. I don't think much is going to happen with Lenny.

Rex jumps up along the side.

"Lenny, I want to see you defend yourself. Don't strike back. All you do is protect your body." Lenny starts bouncing at Rex's words and nods. He smashes his hands together.

I look at Rex. A bag would be more beneficial than fighting Lenny, who won't be able to stand up too much. I bounce, too, warming myself up. Everything fades away. This is why boxing is a lifeline for me; it allows me to peel every emotion back. And today, after seeing Layla, I need this release more than ever.

I dance closer to Lenny. His hands protect his head. I keep my movements slow to test him, and then I strike at his ribs. I don't put much force behind the punch. He bends, lowers his hand, and protects himself.

"That a boy, Lenny," Rex cheers him on. "Keep focused."

"No cheering for me?" I ask as I fire a jab at Lenny's head. He protects himself again and dances away.

"Your ego is too big, Jay," Rex teases. I grin and fire off a few quick but light-handed jabs at Lenny, who blocks each one like a pro.

"You're good," I tell him.

He stops moving and smiles. "Jesus, Jay, thanks so..."

As he dribbles on, I hit him solid in the stomach. The force drives him back, and he hits the ground hard.

"Get up!" Rex screams, and I dance back as Lenny rolls to his knees, trying to catch his breath.

"Get up now, Lenny, or your training ends here for good."

Rex's words get Lenny up off his knees. His face is red and raw as he fights for air while holding his stomach.

"Never lose focus. It can be a compliment, it can be an insult, but don't let your guard down."

I dance around Lenny and take a few gentle swipes, which he blocks. I keep my hits low as he finally gets his breathing under control.

His hands aren't as high; my hit seemed to have knocked his confidence.

"Keep your fucking hands up," I bark at him.

He does.

"One little hit and you turn into a fucking woman," I smirk at him. "Pitiful."

"Jay," Rex warns.

I reach out and tip the side of Lenny's head. "Weak," I tease.

I don't anticipate Lenny's attack. One thing Rex warns us about is that no matter what, don't bring anger into his motherfucking ring. His words. So I don't expect it when Lenny barrels into me with all his strength. His fist cracks into my side, and I'm falling, but not before he hits me with an uppercut. My lip splits open, and blood pours from my mouth as I hit the ground. I recover quickly and bounce back to my feet.

"Didn't know Lenny the pussy had it in him," I tease as I wipe the blood from my chin.

"That's enough. Both of you get out of the ring."

I'm not done. Not even fucking close.

I step up to Lenny, ready to retaliate.

"Jay." The warning in Rex's voice has me backing away from Lenny. I look at Rex for the first time since entering the ring.

Yeah, he's pissed.

I shouldn't have come here.

Words rise up, but I swallow them and get out of the ring.

"You lost your control." Rex speaks to Lenny. "Never lose control. That's my number one rule, Lenny."

"I messed up," Lenny counteracts.

I remove my gloves and start peeling off the tape.

"Hit the showers," Rex orders Lenny.

"Good fight," I call after Lenny.

He glances over his shoulder at me and smirks. "Thanks, Jay."

Rex faces me. "You want to tell me who pissed in your cornflakes?"

Rex knows where I came from, but Layla isn't someone I ever discussed with him. He pulls off the rest of the tape for me.

"Are we still good for tomorrow night?" I ask. That's my official training day.

"Yeah, Jay. You can't just arrive like this again."

I pick up my sweater and pull it on over my head. "I won't."

Rex doesn't move as I wipe more blood onto my sleeve.

"If you ever need me, just ring. Like a normal fucking person." Rex grins as he holds out a fist. I bump it with mine.

"See you tomorrow." I leave the gym feeling more tightly wound. Once I'm in the car, I check my face in the rearview mirror. My lip still bleeds. My tongue flicks out and licks the blood. The cut stings, and I keep jabbing at it the whole drive home. The pain keeps me focused. It keeps my thoughts away from Layla for a short time.

Large white gates start to open. The ivy covers them, not allowing anyone to see into the property. My father values his privacy, especially after the scandal with my mother that still tortures him. I sink my teeth into my cut lip. Blood soaks my tongue, and I swallow the metallic liquid as I drive up to the house. Lights along the driveway have started to come on. It's only four, but it's already starting to get dark. By five, darkness will blanket most of the grounds. I pull into the six-car garage and turn off my car. I dab at my lip as I make my way into the empty house.

My father is never here, but a staff of servants moves around the house without making a noise. They seem to appear when we need them. The hallway is warm; two of the fires along the long wall have been lit. From the heat, I'd say it's been a while. A mirror that hangs on the wall soars twelve-feet high, stopping at the ceiling. The black outline is decorated in twisted metal petals. I take a step closer and examine my split lip. My father won't be happy with me showing up at the charity looking like I've been in a fight. He doesn't approve of my boxing but turns a blind eye to it. For now, that is.

"Good afternoon, Master Jay."

I step away from the mirror.

"Your father asked me to give you this."

I turn and take the small envelope from William's gloved hand. I open it in front of him, and he glances away, giving me my privacy.

Don't be late. We expect your arrival at 8:15. I would appreciate Alexandra being with you.

I push the note back into the envelope. A phone call would have gotten his message here quicker. Why my father insists on leaving me fucking notes is beyond me.

I nod at William, and he gives a bow of his head before I leave to go upstairs and get ready for the charity. I dial Alex's number, and she answers on the second ring.

"I'll be ready at seven thirty," she answers.

"How did you receive your message? By a carrier pigeon?" I ask as I climb the stairs before rounding the landing and making my way to the next set of stairs.

"A letter." I can hear the smile in Alex's words. "Hand delivered today by one of your father's servants." She pauses. "Don't be late." Her words no longer hold a smile as she hangs up.

I make it to my room to find my suit hanging up. The fire has been lit too, and my curtains drawn.

Anger laces through me, and I swallow it down, but it's like a yawn that's already formed. It leaves a lump in my chest.

I take out my phone again and pull up my private PI's number.

He, too, answers quickly.

"Jay, it's been a long time."

"I found her," I say into the phone. I'm picturing his bushy gray eyebrows rising into his fading hairline.

"A full refund will be given," he grinds out. He's a man who doesn't like to lose.

"She arrived at my college. Keep the money and get me her address. She must live nearby."

Some part of me hopes he says no, asks me why I want her address, and tells me that's a line he won't cross.

"Give me twenty-four hours."

My heart trips at the idea of finding out where Layla is living, and with whom.

"I want it by eleven tonight," I say.

There's a pause. "That's six hours."

I grin. "You better get to work, then." I hang up as my mind starts to conjure ideas of what I'll do when I have her address.

I need to leave her alone.

But I already know I can't. The moment she stepped into that gym was the moment I knew everything I had built up here was fucking useless against her.

CHAPTER FOUR

LAYLA

IT'S BEEN THREE DAYS since my first day of college, three days of numbness. I built up all my hopes of having a fresh start, only to have them smashed. To make matters worse, Evelyn received news about one of the kids from the foster home I grew up in.

My chest tightens as I think of Nelson, and I wonder yet again, for what feels like the millionth time, how he died. No one will give us any information about him. I want to attend his funeral, but without a second name and his location, that isn't possible. My mouth dries up at the thought that if the news had been about Jared, I don't know how I would have handled it.

I also came to the conclusion that Jay isn't Jared. Jared would never hurt me. My shoulders are marred by small purple bruises, but nothing feels worse than the fear he pushed deep inside me. So deep that it opened up old wounds.

The clang of Evelyn's knife on the white porcelain plate draws me back to the breakfast bar. I glance at Carl's empty chair. He's staying in Galway over the weekend. I push my cereal around my bowl. Evelyn's soft touch on my arm has my gaze jumping to hers. "He'll be back soon."

My face blazes. *Am I that transparent?* I get anxious when one of them isn't around, and an irrational fear shows up, telling me this perfect life that

I've found myself in won't last forever. Evelyn tells me this self-doubt is normal, and these thoughts will fade. But they haven't.

"I know. I was just thinking about college," I lie, then I shovel a spoonful of cereal into my mouth. I chew, not tasting the food.

Evelyn's smile tugs at her mouth. "Layla, it's okay to worry about Carl. Honestly, he loves when we fuss over him." She rolls her eyes dramatically. "It would break his heart if he thought we weren't pining over him." Her words and batting eyelids have me smiling back at her.

"There's that smile," she says while gently stroking my cheek before tapping me on the nose. "You better get ready for school you don't want to be late."

I quickly check my phone. Yep, I am going to be late if I don't leave soon.

***

I park my car under low-hanging trees and have to run into the college as the rain pelts the asphalt with a violence that sends the water spraying back up. The fabric of my black trousers soaks up the water. I clear the three steps and make my way into the building, dripping wet.

The hallway is empty—I'm late. The receptionist glances at me. Her gaze trails to the small puddle of water that's started to form under my feet. Her nose curls before she turns away.

I hurry and make my way to my business class. I give a quick whispered apology for being late and sit down. I take out my notepad and pen, which survived the onslaught outside, and take notes for the next hour and a half. My clothes have dried out somewhat, but they still feel damp against my skin.

I spot Ashley a few times during the day, but each time, I duck my head. Today, I don't want to talk to anyone, and missing three days of class has pushed me even further back. After the news of Nelson, school didn't seem to matter—until it did. Until I could see the concern and worry in Evelyn's eyes, and I couldn't disappoint her any further.

My body collides with someone, and I stumble back, but I catch my balance at the last second.

Alex glares at me. "You did that on purpose." She brushes off her designer sweater while tilting her head. Her face holds a smile, but her words aren't friendly.

"Sorry, I wasn't watching where I was going," I stutter.

She shakes her head, and two girls who appear as perfect as she does flank her on either side. "Clearly. They're really starting to let anyone into Kingscourt." She speaks to the girls as if I'm not standing in front of her.

Move, Layla. I sidestep Alex and her friends, but she blocks me.

"Watch where you're going next time, scar."

My head snaps up, and her smirk grows while her gaze travels to my legs like she can see all my scars, even though they're covered.

I brush past her and hear their laughter the whole way out of the building. I don't stop until I'm in my car.

The drive home is haunting. Memories of Bert's anger and violence resurface with a vengeance. I push his face away while fighting the tears. Seven years of therapy, then one insult from a pretty girl sends me into a tailspin. The news of Nelson is the real reason, but it always takes that one small thing to tip a person over the edge: the tip of the iceberg, the icing on the cake, the last straw, the straw that broke the camel's back. That is one of Evelyn's favorites. The heaviness lifts slightly as I think about Evelyn saying it; she was so serious, and the saying made me laugh hard even as my body and soul cried from all the pain.

I'm home quicker than I expected. By the time I walk into the house, exhaustion pulls heavily on my shoulders. I take a deep, calming breath before going to the kitchen. Evelyn takes off her reading glasses and glances at me. She has so many questions burning in her eyes. Why am I home early? Was I crying? How was college? Her khakis and loose cotton blouse make her look like she belongs on a beach, not in a kitchen reading some thriller.

She settles on "So how was school." as I get myself a glass of water.

My throat has utterly dried up. I gulp the water until the glass is empty, and only then do I turn to Evelyn. "Interesting." That's the best I can do, but as Evelyn continues to watch me, I have the urge to tug at my ear to give my hands something to do. "I'm just tired. Honestly, it was a lot. You know, missing so many days. But I'll catch up. I'm really enjoying it."

Evelyn tilts her head before her mouth rises, forming a pleasant smile. "Good. That's really good, Layla."

Lowering my gaze, I fidget with my bag, which is still slung over my left shoulder. Placing it on the counter, I glance at Evelyn and nod. "I'm going to take a shower before dinner."

"Okay, sweetheart."

I take the opportunity to leave without any further questioning.

"Layla." I stop at the door, glancing back at Evelyn. "I'm so proud of you."

I inhale deeply, and a weird feeling pulses through me. I find myself standing a little straighter as Evelyn beams at me. "Thank you." The words are low, but from her smile and nod, I know she heard me.

The spray of the water helps my aching shoulders. Lathering my hair, I try not to think about the day I just had, but I can't stop the memory playing out in my mind. Ruminating is something Evelyn warns me about. Yet I can't stop the memory of Jared that assaults me.

It's the cold—the cold that seeps into my back and runs so much deeper than my twelve-year-old brain could truly comprehend.

A coldness that, after seven years, has never left me. I fear it never will. My lids squeeze closed as the memory tears another piece of me apart.

Scorching heat burns my face, and it's no match for the cold slate floor that penetrates through the back of the light, flimsy white dress.

Bert's hand rises again but stops in midair, every finger straight to the point of straining. My eyes shoot from his hand to his red face, flushed with anger and alcohol. I'm waiting for the blow. I'm waiting for a reaction so badly. I want it to happen and for this to be over.

The front door behind Bert is stark white. Why I focus on the door, I'm not sure. It becomes a beacon that seems to grow smaller the longer I lie there waiting. My gaze darts back to him, and his hand connects with my face. The burn seems worse than the first time. My head whips to the side. Darkness clouds in quickly, and I welcome the blackness, only for the veil to disappear and keep me rooted in the here and now. The spindles on the stairs take priority in my mind. My eyes trace where some of the white paint has been chipped off from all the children that have passed through the doors of Bert and Ronnie's foster home. Each breath I take hurts as I force the air into my lungs—lungs that never seem satisfied.

"I asked you a question!" Bert's voice isn't slurred or fueled by the anger clearly displayed on his sixty-year-old face. His words are a command. A prelude. A promise that isn't idle.

When he asked me where his car keys are, a fear developed deep down inside me because I don't know. And if I don't answer soon, he will continue to beat me.

My hands tremble as I try to push myself up from the stone floor. Bert's eyes are wide, and he tilts his head. A threat for me to hurry up screams from his tight features.

"I don't know," I say honestly. All the while, my body curls in as it braces itself for the next slap that Bert plants on my face without hesitation. This one is harder than the last and sends my head snapping back. Blood fills my mouth, and stars fill my head. It takes me a few seconds before my hearing slowly starts to trickle back. On reflex, my hands touch my aching face.

Bert steps closer and leans over me, stumbling slightly. If he falls, his sheer size will smother me. But he catches himself and continues to bend down.

"You think you're clever?" he snarls.

My shoulders hunch forward as I try to move away. It's a movement, a tiny movement, one he won't notice.

He notices. Oh, no, no, no...

He reaches for me, and my shoulders draw closer together as I dip my chin into my chest. His large hands easily encase my small wrist, and he applies pressure that threatens to shatter my bones. A scream that I can no longer keep in is torn from my lips at the same time the front door opens.

He's taller and broader than I am. I can't see his features with his black hood up, but I'd know him anywhere. I know that his eyes will be tight around the edges.

My body sags with relief. Everything will be okay now. Jared is two years older than me, but right now, he's like a giant filling the doorway. Bert releases me and is focused on the door.

"Get away from her." Jared speaks each word through heavy breaths. Bert spins toward him, and Jared's body stiffens. A new fear enters my system; the dread drips slowly down my spine. What if Jared got hurt this time? The thought pulls a whimper from my lips.

"It's okay, Layla." Jared's reassurance is spoken as he stares at Bert. All I can do is nod at him.

"It's okay, Layla," Bert mimics, and he sneers as he lingers for what feels like forever but is only a moment. Then he gives me one final look before leaving Jared and me alone in the breezy hallway. Jared's steps are measured as he walks slowly to me while pushing back his hood. His brown eyes are soft as he kneels down and reaches out carefully to take my hand. His fingers entwine with mine, and all my bones sigh at the contact.

"It's okay, Layla. I'm home."

My lips wobble at his words, and before I can respond, he pulls me into a hug that, at first, is too tight. My groan has Jared loosening his hold on me, but he doesn't let me go, and I let all my guards down and inhale. Everything feels right, and all I smell is Jared.

Even with the blare of the TV and the constant threat of Bert's anger, right now, I am safe. I am home. I am with Jared.

My heart thumps heavily in my chest as if I've just relived that moment all over again. I'm a mixed bag of emotions and try to think of Evelyn's words about ruminating. I need to think about the positives.

"Three positive things," I say while taking water into my mouth, nearly causing me to choke. I move my head out of the spray and let the warmth hit my back so I can speak without drowning.

"I survived my first few days of college. Ashley seemed nice." I hesitate, searching for a third positive. "I didn't look hideous in my gym uniform." I let my head go back under the spray so I can condition my hair.

I feel better when I leave the bathroom and enter into my adjoining bedroom. The carpet under my feet always makes me sigh with contentment. The full-sized bed takes up most of the room, and my desk sits neatly under the window that overlooks the front garden. The best thing about the room is the walk-in closet. I flick the light on and pull out a clean pair of pj's.

Once dressed, I face the mirror to brush out my hair. Even wet, the color still looks light, and the strands reach my waist. Dropping the brush on the dresser, I leave my room and go downstairs.

Evelyn is still reading her thriller. When I arrive in the kitchen, she takes off her glasses and puts her book down. "I'll get your dinner now, sweetheart."

"I'll grab it. Go read your book."

Evelyn picks back up her glasses. "Thanks." She sinks her attention back into her reading. She's such a bookworm; she devours up to three books a week. I place my dinner in the microwave and grab a soda before sitting down at the table. As soon as I'm seated, my phone dings. It's Morgan.

How was your first day at your swanky college?

My fingers quickly glide across the letters. **Great. It's a regular college.**

I turn the phone over as I eat my dinner; the click of the soda can is the loudest sound in the quiet house. My phone dings again, and I ignore it so I can focus on my food.

"Who's that texting you?" Evelyn glances at me over the rim of her glasses. Her glee at me texting someone has me picking up the phone.

"Oh, it's Morgan." I force a smile while looking at Morgan's message.

How boring. Want to go out tonight?

"She's such a lovely girl," Evelyn says.

"Yeah, we're going out tonight."

Evelyn tries to tone back the dial on her sunshine, which beams at me. But it's still way too strong. "Great. No curfew. You go out and enjoy yourself." Evelyn picks her book back up. Her excitement is evidence in her lack of parenting. But I'm not like most girls my age. I never drink, and I always come home early.

I reluctantly answer Morgan's text. **Yeah, where to?**

Just be ready at nine.

I place the phone back on the table while pushing my food around the plate. My appetite just took a run and jump off a cliff.

***

Morgan doesn't arrive until nine thirty. I grab my bag and race from the house while Evelyn stands at the door, waving me off. I can see the girls in the back of the car snigger as I approach. I've met Morgan's friends once or twice, but I always forget their names.

"In the front seat, L." Morgan rolls her window down and waves at Evelyn.

I give one final glance to Evelyn before climbing into the car. I feel like a kid being coaxed into a kidnapper's vehicle—the sweets I'm offered aren't worth the aftermath, yet I go anyway.

For the millionth time in my life, I do something I don't want to.

CHAPTER FIVE

LAYLA

"L ET'S GO." I SNAP my seat belt into place, and Morgan beeps the horn as she drives away. I'm so underdressed, but I always am. Morgan looks presentable from the window. Her red dress has a high neck with long sleeves, but it's cut off, barely covering her behind. Her long tanned legs go on forever. My skinny black jeans and green blouse look so bland and ugly compared to these girls. Both of her friends are dressed to kill in halter dresses.

"So, where are we going?" I ask as Morgan pumps up the music. The thump of the beat penetrates the dashboard. Crossing my arms, I try not to fidget or look behind me as the girls in the back whisper and giggle. The smell of cigarette smoke lingers, the scent making my queasy stomach more unsettled.

"Woodview Estate in Mullagh. A guy I know is friends with a guy who lives there." Morgan looks at me for the first time. The flick of her gaze across my outfit is done with raised eyebrows.

Shifting in my seat, I turn more toward Morgan. At that angle, I can slightly see one of the girls in the back. Our eyes clash, and she winks at me. The car feels too warm suddenly, and I open the top button of my blouse.

"I have a curfew, Morgan," I lie. Woodview Estate has a bad repetition. It's one thing going there during daylight hours but another thing to go there at night. Her vagueness on who is hosting the party causes a tightness in my chest.

More sniggers erupt from the back. Morgan glances at her friends in the mirror with narrowed eyes. "I'll have you back in time. Relax, Lola," Morgan replies.

Wow!

"My name is Layla," I say through gritted teeth. I sit back and face the window this time.

Morgan mutters, "Sorry." The streetlights soon thin out as we leave our small town and make the short journey to Mullagh.

"Oh my God. Les just texted." The music is switched off, and Morgan bounces in her seat, glancing from the mirror to the road.

"What did she say, Bonita?"

"Mindy is drunk and she kissed Deco."

Morgan inhales a sharp breath while both girls squeal in the back with excitement. I don't know who Mindy or Deco are. All I want is for this night to be over so I can go home and climb into bed and tick off this outing. I won't have to do this again for three more months. That's the silver lining.

"What a tramp!" Bonita says, tilting my seat slightly as she pulls herself forward. "I mean, she was only with Kieran, like, last week."

Morgan inhales deeply again at the scandal. "Oh, I thought he was seeing you, Bea?" Silence fills the car as the tension grows. I hide my grin as I look out the window.

Finally, Bea laughs. "No, I dumped him ages ago. Me and Kieran are history from, like, really far back. So far…"

Well, that isn't transparent or anything. Morgan and Bonita overlook Bea's hurt and lies. They start slashing Mandy—or is it Mindy?—instead. The poor girl really takes a bashing.

The house we pull up to doesn't look like one that's hosting a party. From the road, no lights shine from any of the front windows. Morgan turns down the music as she pulls in along the curb.

"Is this it?" Bea speaks up from the back. I glance at Morgan, curious too. Maybe I'll get lucky and the party will be called off. She's scrolling through her phone.

"Does it say number six?"

I wait for one of her friends to check.

"Layla!" Morgan pokes my leg.

"Sorry, I didn't think you were talking to me." I look at the number hanging beside the door. Yep, the gold number says six. I relay this, and we all climb out of the car. Shifting from foot to foot, I clutch my bag.

As Bea and Bonita climb out of the back of the car, I get my first proper look at them. They look like hookers.

"Morgan, are you sure?" I have a bad feeling about this place. The girls giggle behind me while linking arms with each other.

Morgan reaches for the buttons on my blouse and unbuttons two more before trying to wrestle my bag from me.

"You look like a granny. Give me the bag," she snarls at me.

I pull my bag back, having enough of her. "Better than looking like a hooker." I say the words before I can think. Bea drags in a sharp breath. Morgan stands back, and shame burns my face.

"You're just jealous," Morgan seethes.

"I'm sorry, Morgan. I shouldn't have said that."

"I'm freezing. Can we go inside already?" Bea jumps up and down in her tiny outfit, her boobs almost pouring out of her dress. I don't want to go into the party, but standing outside on a dark night in the middle of an estate isn't the brightest idea.

Morgan gives my bag one final look before clicking her fingers. "Let's do this, bitches."

I fall into place behind them. A shiver crawls up my back and prickles my neck. *There's nothing wrong. You're overreacting like always.*

The closer we get to the house, the clearer the music and voices become—my pulse spikes.

Morgan knocks on the door.

"Is my lip gloss still on?" Bea asks Bonita, who pouts her own lips before answering.

"Yeah, you look hot." They bump hips.

Morgan knocks on the door again before pulling down her dress. The action is pointless since every step she takes allows us all to get a view of her white thong.

"You're hot too, Bonita," Bea says.

I'm focused on the door and praying that no one answers Morgan's insistent knocks.

"Maybe we should go," I say just as the door opens.

The scent of something stronger than cigarette smoke seeps through the air. A guy much older than we are leers at Morgan and her friends. His eyes skim over me with disinterest. After cracking his tattooed knuckles, he opens the door wider. His three-quarter-length shirtsleeves showcase his tattooed arms. Some tribal ink rises from the collar of his red-and-white checkered shirt and disappears into his brown hair, which is cropped close to his head. A scar that runs along the left side of his skull is stark against his dark skin.

"Come in, ladies," As each girl passes, he checks out their rears with a smirk. As I pass by him, I quickly glance at him before looking away. I curl my shoulders in, hoping it will discourage his wandering eyes.

The hall floor is concrete except for a few threadbare rugs strewn around the place; no smiling family fills the empty, crooked picture frames that hang over the radiator. A light flickers overhead as we enter the kitchen, where most of the partygoers are. Sweat makes a path down my back. The small room is crammed. I huddle behind the others, and for the hundredth time, I wish I had stayed home. This isn't the usual type of party Morgan brings me to.

"Morgan!" a guy shouts excitedly while jumping off his chair. He nearly topples a girl to the ground who'd been perched on his lap. The girl gets her balance and thankfully doesn't fall. She stands out from the rest because of the pink stripes in her hair. The guy embraces Morgan, his hand groping her behind at the same time. Bea and Bonita get called over by two guys who lounge at a small yellow table. Two ashtrays filled to the brim hold burning cigarettes. Too many cans and glasses litter the table. Both guys wear black wool hats, which gives their eyes a hooded and dangerous look. As I quickly glance around the room, all the boys look the same: tattoos, baggy jeans. They all watch us now.

"Kieran, take your hands off my ass," Morgan says to the guy hugging her. His blond hair and sun-kissed skin look so out of place from all the other males. I feel like I've stepped into the wrong house. Out of the corner of my eye, I see the guy who let us in take something out of his pocket and slip the small bag into another guy's hand. I press my arms along my side, trying to make myself appear small as the guy from the door latches his eyes onto mine. I try to swallow, but my throat is too dry. He looks away, moving on to the next guy and passing him another small bag of powder.

"Hi, I'm Kieran."

I blink at the hand that's held out to me. I take it and follow the tanned fingers to their owner's light blue eyes.

"You want a drink?" he asks. I shake my head, taking my hand back before glancing around at everyone else; they've all fallen into place with someone. The music is a low hum that makes all conversations unintelligible.

"Everyone here is really nice," Kieran says to me. He holds up his hands, and a grin spreads across his face. "Don't judge until you get to know me."

Kieran's lips twitch into a full smile. I want to tell him to leave me alone, but he's the safest bet. It isn't his appearance that makes me think he's the safe bet; it's how he makes me feel. I don't feel unsafe.

Everyone else looks like they're from the wrong side of town, and I'm pretty sure they're all high, whereas Kieran seems to be just slightly drunk. The girl with the pink stripes in her hair keeps watching us. I think it's Mindy, the one the girls spoke about in the car.

Kieran talks and doesn't seem to mind having a one-sided conversation. I nod but keep my eyes on the girls. A few times, the guy who let us in catches my eye; his stare is unsettling. I swallow, but my dry throat can't take much more.

"Could you get me a glass of water?" I ask Kieran.

His eyes light up with surprise. "You talk?"

I force a wobbly smile. "Yeah."

He nods enthusiastically before getting me a glass of water. I force myself to loosen my death grip on my handbag by slinging it over my shoulder. I try to appear more relaxed.

Kieran returns, smiling while holding my glass of water. I examine the contents before taking a deep drink. The glass is empty when I return for air.

"Do you want another one?" Kieran's brows knit together.

"Yeah, please. My throat is parched," I explain lamely. When he returns this time, I drink slowly, my eyes skimming over the brown kitchen and worktops that seem to only hold alcohol and mixers. There is no toaster or kettle—no signs that this house is used every day.

"You have beautiful eyes," Kieran compliments me.

He catches me off guard, and I choke, spewing some of my water on him. "Oh God. I'm so, so sorry." I start dabbing his shirt with my hand.

"It's fine." Kieran smiles. "You don't take compliments well?"

My cheeks heat with embarrassment, making me stop what I'm doing. "What?" I ask.

"I complimented your eyes, and you spat on me."

I drop my hands and try to calm my beating heart. I'm coming across like a nutjob. "Thank you, Kieran."

"You're welcome... You never told me your name."

"Layla."

"What a beautiful name for a beautiful girl." He takes my hand and presses a soft kiss to it.

"Where is the bathroom?" I ask.

Kieran tells me the bathroom is upstairs—the first door straight ahead. He even kindly offers to accompany me, but I decline. Before I leave the kitchen, I look for Morgan. She is very... occupied.

The hallway is empty. As I go down the hall to get to the staircase, I notice a door to my right that I didn't pay attention to when we first came in. I hear voices in the room, and one in particular tickles at my memory. I pass quickly and walk quietly but briskly up the stairs. The bathroom is old and simple but surprisingly clean. I do my business before washing my hands. I look up into the mirror and meet four sets of wide blue eyes. The crack runs in a zigzag down the whole mirror. What caused the crack? A smash of a fist? Maybe something else?

The cut-off screech of a female has me freezing. I listen, but there's only silence. I take a tiny step toward the door, pause, and listen again. I can hear someone whisper. I stare at the door, unable to move.

Pull it together, Layla.

I open the door to a scene that has my body going still, but my mind goes straight into reverse, to a twelve-year-old Layla, who has no scars on her leg. Time can heal so much, but not that. Never that.

"What are you staring at?" The question snaps me back to the present, and my shoulders tighten. The guy who opened the door holds Bea by the throat. The red marks promise to bruise soon. Her mascara runs down her face as she looks at me with a plea for help.

Tattooed fingers snap in my face, and I stumble back.

"Are you stupid?" he barks. I hate that word. I've been asked that my whole life. I shake my head; my words have disappeared again. He lets Bea go, and she runs down the stairs without looking back at me. Now I have this guy's full attention. A tremble builds violently in my hands.

"You don't look right to me," he says as he takes a step closer, his eyes traveling up and down my body. His lips curl into a snarl. "What are you doing here anyway?" His stare is full of suspicion.

I shrug. *Say something, Layla. Please.* I look at the ground, hoping he'll leave me alone. His hand curls around my face, and I whimper. Forcing my head up, he tightens his grip on my face.

"You open your mouth to anyone about me, and I will cut out your tongue."

I nod as fear from all angles builds up inside me.

"Chester." This voice is one I remember.

Chester releases me and glances down the stairs at Jay, who stares up at us with a wrath in his eyes that makes me shiver, and I have no idea if it's directed at Chester or me.

CHAPTER SIX

JARED

Fʋᴄᴋ ᴍᴇ. Sʜᴇ ʟᴏᴏᴋs like a virgin in that getup. I want to defile her.

"What's up, man?" Chester raises his head as he speaks. He's still too close to Layla for my liking. He shouldn't be breathing the same air as her.

I grip the banister. "The boys want you."

Layla hasn't moved. Her chest is still, and I question if she's breathing. What is she doing here?

"In a minute." Chester looks away from me.

My hand tightens on the banister, and it creaks under my grip. "Now, Chester."

His focus is back on me. He grinds his jaw, but he nods as he walks away from Layla, giving me more relief than I should feel.

Chester juts out his chin and narrows his eyes in question as he makes his way down the stairs. I stop him before he passes me. "Don't ever put your hands on her again." My voice is low, deadly.

"If you so say, Jay." Chester doesn't like my request.

I grin. "I do say so."

He fights a snarl, and I let him pass me before I allow myself to do what I really want, which is beat him to within an inch of his life.

Layla doesn't move as I release the banister and take a step up toward her. "What are you doing here?" I growl.

Her chest rises and falls rapidly. Her pink tongue flicks out and wets her lips. Her mouth is small but perfect. I can imagine it around my cock.

"I'm here with friends." Her voice is stronger than I expected.

I continue to climb the stairs. "What friends?" I sneer.

She folds her arms across her chest. "My friends."

I grin as I clear the last step and tower over her. "I thought I told you to stay out of my way." I dip my head while pushing my hands behind my back. They demand I hurt her, but I deny that want for another that is so much deeper. The one that has liquefied in my veins, manifesting as something so primal—the urge to protect her.

I fucking hate it.

I want to defy the need to protect her.

"I'm going." Layla ducks her head and tries to get past me. I don't move, blocking her access to the stairs. Now I'm wondering which waster she's with downstairs.

Anger accelerates my thoughts, and they scatter as I step closer to her, stealing the last of her personal space. She won't look up. She's staring at my chest. The pulse flickers rapidly in her neck.

"You can go when I say you can go."

Her head lifts up to me. Her blue eyes drink me in and pierce something inside me that twists my gut.

I hate her.

My hand leaves the confines of my back, and I'm touching her hair. The strands are as silky as I remember, and I lose myself in my primal instincts and lean in, inhaling her scent. She takes in a sharp breath at my action, but I don't give a fuck that she's watching me sniff her. Everything in me stirs to life, and her lips become my sole focus.

I want to fuck her.

I want her.

My mind becomes consumed with someone else fucking her. Someone else fucking what they have no right to touch. My hand tightens on her hair, and she hisses in pain.

"Who are you here with?"

"I told you. My friends."

I tug a little harder and draw her closer to me. Her legs brush mine; her breasts press against my chest. My body is aware of every single inch of Layla, and my cock becomes a rod of steel. "I want names."

"Morgan and her friends," she stutters.

I loosen my hold but don't release her hair. I like her this close to me. "This isn't a good place to be."

"I've realized that." Her sharp words brush my cheek.

I release her, but I can't step away from Layla. She fucks so badly with my head that I can't even think straight.

"Layla." A female voice behind me should have me stepping away, but I can't.

"I don't ever want to see you here again." I keep my voice low as I issue the warning and step away. I don't go back down the stairs but brush past her. I ball my hands into fists so I don't reach for her again.

She rushes down the stairs. "Are we going?" Layla's voice is panicked.

"Yeah, Bea wants to leave."

More female voices fill the hallway before the front door closes.

"Where did Layla go?" I hear a male voice a few minutes later, and I have to control the speed at which I arrive down into the hallway.

My lips stretch across my teeth. "Who's looking for Layla?" I ask.

A blond guy is holding a plastic cup of alcohol and points it at himself while wearing a fucking grin. "Me. And you are?"

"Kieran, go into the kitchen." Chester pushes Kieran's chest, and he stumbles back, spilling his drink across his shirt.

I need to leave before I allow the violence to pour from me. I turn and pull the front door open. I don't bother to close it behind me.

"Yo, Jay!" Chester calls after me, but he can fuck right off. I've parked my car down a side lane at the end of the housing estate. Chester has warned everyone not to touch my vehicle. They listen to him. Here, he is the king—just not to me. No one rules over me.

I get in, and I find myself driving in the opposite direction of my home. After a while, the group of houses I'm starting to become accustomed to seeing comes into sight. The small white fences all in a row tell me I'm close to hers.

I slow down as I near Layla's home. I have no idea if she's there, but I allow myself to picture her safely inside. The front bedroom is hers, and I watch the dark window for a while. I sit until a light comes on in her room. My heart thumps loudly in my chest as she appears; it's a split second as she pulls the curtains. She doesn't look terrified in her natural habitat. She's Layla. She's beautiful. I find myself smiling, and then her face is gone, the curtains blocking out the light, and I look away as the smile leaves my face. Then I drive home.

***

When I arrive back home, Alex's car is in the driveway. *What the fuck does she want?* I park in the garage and enter the house. Like always, William appears in the hallway.

"Ms. Alexandra is here to see you, Master Jay."

I'm waiting for William to tell me where she is.

He clears his throat, looking uncomfortable.

"Where is she?" I have to ask.

"In your quarters, Master Jay."

I don't linger but make my way to the third floor, which my father gave me to live in. I only use about one-third of the floor that spans across the entire mansion.

I find Alex flicking through a magazine in the sitting area. She's wrapped in a dressing gown.

"I don't recall scheduling a sleepover," I say, holding back my irritation.

She continues to flick through the magazine pages. "We never finished what we started at the charity event." Alex drops the magazine and stands up. She pulls the band out of her fake blonde hair, and all I can do is compare it to Layla's naturally straight blonde locks. Everything about Layla is natural. I grit my teeth as Alex opens the dressing gown and lets the material pool on the ground around her stilettos. The red lacy set doesn't leave much to the imagination. The red stockings cover her legs, and she takes a confident step toward me.

"Like what you see?" She reaches me and pushes up on the tips of her toes to press a kiss to my mouth. I turn my face away, and she doesn't like that one bit.

Touching my belt, I wriggle it open. She grins and falls to her knees. I push my jeans and boxers down and take my cock in my hand, stroking it a few times. I picture blue eyes flashing with fear, and my cock starts to grow. I remember the feel of her hair, the smell of her skin, the brush of her breasts against my chest. My cock is painfully hard. A warm mouth wraps around my shaft, and I groan as I picture Layla on her knees. I grip Alex's head and push her further down on my cock until she gags. I hold her there for a moment before letting her back up.

"You like that, Jay?" Alex's voice pierces any illusion I've created.

I glance down at her as she looks up at me before taking my cock in her mouth again. I nudge her away, my cock dying, and I give it a few strokes and look away. I conjure up the image of Layla again. I'm picturing her sprawled out on my bed in a black lacy set. I grip Alex's head and push her back down on my cock. I approach Layla, and she smiles up at me. All I want to do is bury myself in her. Alex groans and pulls me out of my fantasy. I force her head quicker over my cock so it won't die. I've never had a problem holding an erection, but ever since Layla showed up, the only thing that makes my cock stand is her.

I go back to my fantasy of Layla and fast forward, burying my cock inside her. Layla moans, and a groan slips from my lips. I pump faster and harder, wanting to empty myself in her sweet pussy. I pound fiercely and Alex gags, but I stay with Layla as I grip Alex by the hair to keep her lips locked over my cock as I fuck her mouth hard. I groan again as Layla's face twists with ecstasy, and my seed pours out of me. I give a few final jerks and release Alex's head.

She crawls away from me, coughing and gasping. "What the fuck was that, Jay?" She's wiping my seed off her face with the back of her hand.

"A great blow job, Alex." I wink at her and pull up my boxers and jeans.

She gathers herself off the floor. Alex looks at me, ready to complain again, but no one invited her here. I buckle my belt and don't look away from her.

She stands straighter and picks up her dressing gown, wrapping it around her body before heading to the bathroom. I sit on the couch that Alex just vacated, and it's easy to pull up the image of Layla again. My cock twitches but quickly dies a few minutes later as Alex enters the room. She's dressed and is stuffing her gown and shoes into an overnight bag.

"Not staying?" I tease.

"I'll see you at school tomorrow." She flicks her hair across her shoulder and holds her head high.

I salute her with two fingers, and she leaves me in peace—before it turns into something dark. I get up and leave the room. The farther I walk across the third floor, the heavier the weight grows on my shoulders. A part of me wants to stop this, but I grin as I pull the chain from around my neck and unlock the door with a key that hangs from it.

I step in and close the door behind me. The room bursts into light as I flick the switch. Her face is everywhere, in every available space in the room that once was a servant's bedroom. I step up to my most recent one. It captures Layla perfectly. I had the curve of her nose wrong before, but now she's perfect. Pictures I've drawn of her over the years coat the walls. A lot are from memory, but soon I started to wonder what she would look like as a woman. I didn't get much wrong, just the nose. I touch the most recent picture; it's her standing in the gym, the look in her eyes. So haunted, so tormented, and that's what I drew. That look that I know all too well.

When my father found this room, he looked at me with the most disturbed expression on his face.

"This ends now, Jay. If it doesn't, you are getting help." He speaks while looking at the pictures of Layla. "I have tried to find her, but she's gone. You need to let her go."

The pencil snaps between my fingers. She isn't just a girl. No one will ever understand. I don't think even Layla understood what she was to me. I can't face my father. This addiction is like a cancer that's eating away at me, but no matter how painful it becomes, I don't want it to stop.

I've lived my whole life in chaos, and my father wants calm. I don't know what calm feels like.

"Jay. You bury this here, right now. Jared and Layla don't exist."

My vision blurs. He has no idea what he's asking of me.

"You. Are. My. Son." His hand touches my shoulder, and I shrivel under the contact. "Why do you cower from me?" My father's question carries hurt and confusion. Those emotions are like friends of his when they come to me. He has tried to penetrate the walls that even I can't seem to bring down.

I spin and face him. Anger roils through me, twisting me, and I want to lash out.

He sees it. "Control yourself. You are a McGivney. You do not lose control." He pushes my chest. "You do not cower."

I blink tears that spill as I fight for control.

My father's voice lowers. "We do not seek anything or anyone." He looks around the room, his voice lowering further. "We do not obsess. We are powerful just as we are." He reaches me, and this time, I don't cower as he grips my neck. Pain leaches out of him.

"You are my son," he reminds me.

I'm a shadow of a person—a shadow of his son. I fight a fresh wave of tears as I try to show my father that I am the man he needs me to be.

He releases me and nods, taking one final look around the room. "This ends." My father's gaze is still unsettled, and the longer he glances around the room, the more naked I feel.

"Yes, Father." My admission has him nodding and leaving the room.

I didn't lie that day. I locked up this room and all my pain with it. That is, until she showed back up. Three years of not obsessing. Three years of not feeling. Three years of touching this door but never entering this room. Three years of keeping my promise to my father.

Three years smashed in a second.

CHAPTER SEVEN

JARED

"**H**AVE YOU HEARD THE rumors?"

I don't respond.

"Jay?" Alex's tone holds annoyance.

I look at our group as I sit on the hood of my car. My mind is still stuck on Layla. I spent most of last night obsessively drawing images of her from different times I've seen her on campus. I've scoured my memory from watching her home, and I drew her standing at the window of her bedroom, her hands raised as she grips either side of her bedroom curtains, ready to pull them together. Every time I've seen her, I've drawn the moment, capturing her face perfectly.

"What rumors?" I ask, not giving two fucks as I slide off the hood of my new BMW. I try to keep my Layla watching to a minimum, but I scope out the parking lot and campus grounds for her every few minutes.

"You okay, man?" Mark stuffs his hands into his letterman's jacket pockets. Navy and white stripes run down the arms. The crest of Kingscourt College is printed in bold gold on the front.

"Yeah. So, what rumors?" I ask again and try to appear present. Alex is watching me with narrowed eyes. I grin at her, my gaze skipping to her mouth, which I fucked last night. She's not one bit amused, and that entertains me.

"Coach was caught with one of his students." Mark dishes the dirt with a smirk.

"Who?" Warren asks while lighting up a cigarette. He's the only person in our group who smokes, and he doesn't wear the college jacket like the rest of us. I think Warren likes to think of himself as a rebel of some sort. He's from money, but as far as I know, it's pretty fucking dirty money. He's an O'Reagan, and around these parts, that makes him untouchable, so I'm happy to have him in our group.

"Not sure. I think her name was Lucy or something." Mark shrugs and digs his hands deeper into his jacket pockets.

"Maybe he'll bring her to the dance next month." Alex smiles sweetly. There's nothing sweet about her. I try not to stiffen as she links her arm with mine. "No one will steal our crowns."

Abby and Caroline smile at Alex. She could vomit on the ground, and they'd be in fucking awe of her. How have I not noticed how annoying this group is? For the last three years, I've moved through my day on autopilot. Was I happy? Maybe. Numbness gave me some reprieve from the constant throb that had returned since Layla's arrival, and with it came a huge fucking appetite for pain.

I untangle myself from Alex and rub my hands together. It's cold, and I've had enough of standing around—my eyes snag on a blonde running across the lawn. A guy lingers close to her. Too close.

I'm already walking away.

"Where are you going?" Alex barks after me.

I spin and walk backward. "Some of us have class," I lie.

She knows my schedule. I'm sure William even gave her a blood sample on my father's instructions. Alex doesn't call me out, though. Public appearances and all that bullshit, and I use that to my advantage as I walk toward Layla, who's nearly out of my reach. I have no idea what I'm going to say, but I have this urge to be near her. This constant need to be around her never seems to lessen. Even when I'm close to her, it doesn't go away. I'm not sure what would make the ache stop. My cock twitches. Having her fully might.

She disappears inside the building. The guy who was trailing behind her reaches the main door, but I grip him by the collar of his sweater and spin him around so he's facing me. The front door slams closed as his hand slips off the handle.

"Why are you following Layla like a fucking stalker?"

He tries to pull out of my hold. "Get your hands off me."

I smirk and lean in. "Make me."

He tries to pull away, and I let him for a few seconds, until I get bored and shake him, cutting off his protests.

"Fuck's sake. She's friends with my sister, Ashley. She asked me to keep an eye on Layla."

I don't like his answer. I shake him again. "Why?"

He tugs, and I release him. He shrugs his shoulders. "Ashley didn't tell me why."

I'm watching him, searching for lies.

"You need to relax, man."

Relax? I take a threatening step toward him.

"Mr. McGivney."

I turn to the dean, who raises a brow and two fingers, beckoning me forward. I give the boy a death glare, and he leaves.

"Dean."

He inclines his head. He holds no love for me, nor do I for him, but my father has placed both of us in his pocket, so I do the dance and follow the dean to his office.

"The anticipation is killing me," I say flatly as he opens his office door. What bullshit assignment does he have for me now? Give a speech to the school on the importance of grades? I've made too many of them in my three years at Kingscourt College. I'm sure I could squeeze a few more out, especially since I would be addressing Layla too. If I were addressing the whole college, that is.

The dean's lips tug up, his eyes filled with smugness. I follow his gaze and take in my father. It's my turn to give a smug smile when the dean reacts to seeing my father sitting in his chair.

"Frank called me about your attendance."

My smile would have grown at the look on the dean's face, at my father using his first name, but my attendance isn't something I thought would be brought to my father's attention.

I face the dean. "You could have spoken to me," I say through my annoyance.

"He spoke to me," my father interrupts. "It's one thing paying the teachers for your grades, but with your attendance, we can't make every student not remember you were missing. Having one hundred percent attendance is imperative. So, three days in a row isn't something we can make disappear." He stands.

"It's only three days." I hadn't missed a day in three years. So what the fuck did it matter?

"Where were you?" My father walks around the dean's desk and toward me.

"You could have asked me this at home."

"I was in the area when Frank called."

The dean wisely says nothing.

"You weren't with Alex, because she was here. I've checked."

My heart starts to race. My father is watching me closely. I spent three days staking out Layla's house because she was missing from her classes. My father has no idea that she's even here, and I can't let him find out.

"I wasn't well," I finally say.

My father reaches me and lowers his voice. "You weren't at home. We checked all the footage."

I shrug and try to stay calm. "So what? I took three days off and blew off some steam. I'm sorry," I add at the end.

My father holds my gaze. "Why don't I believe you?"

The dean clears his throat. "We can mark off several students from his class for a three-day field trip."

My father nods without looking away from me. "Whatever you have to do, Frank."

"Don't do that," I say. "They didn't miss class."

"You should have thought about that before you decided to fuck up your perfect attendance." My father's jaw tightens.

I have to look away to control myself.

"I'm going to be late for my meeting. Frank, I will leave it in your capable hands to clean this mess up."

"Of course, Mr. McGivney."

My father doesn't say goodbye as he leaves the dean's office. I'm ready to follow him out the door when the dean stops me.

"What was your business with Lucas Garcia?"

I clench my jaw before I speak. "Who?"

"The boy outside just now. Lucas Garcia. The one you were speaking to."

The one who was stalking Layla. I'm not in such a rush to leave now that I have a name.

"His sister, Ashley, asked me to keep an eye on him. Some kids were bullying him."

The dean sinks down into his chair. "That's very admirable of you, Jay, to look out for people less fortunate than you." His words are sincere. "He and his siblings are here on scholarships—which your father pays for. But I'm sure you already knew that." The dean's words aren't so sincere now.

Fuck him.

"Yeah, keeping an eye on my father's investments."

The dean leans forward in his chair and starts rearranging his desk. "Best to leave him alone."

Is it now?

"Of course, Frank."

He bristles at me using his name. "You can leave now, Mr. McGivney." His words are sharp.

I leave his office. The hallways are thronged, and everyone is moving outside. I can hear the rapid beat of propellers.

I'm making my way outside, but I already know what I'm going to see.

My father is rising high above the school in his personal helicopter.

"Wow, someone has a helicopter here?" a boy says beside me.

"Maybe the president was visiting?" a girl says beside him.

I'm pushing through the crowd. On the other side of the helicopter pad is Layla, shielding her eyes as she looks at my father. If he looked down, would he recognize her from all the drawings in my room?

I'm not sure if Layla can sense my gaze on her, but she looks away from the helicopter that still captures everyone's attention and over to me. Her chest puffs out with a sharp inhale before she shifts back into the crowd and out of my sight.

CHAPTER EIGHT

LAYLA

I'VE BEEN AVOIDING EVELYN since coming home from the party with Morgan last night. But I don't think I can avoid her again today. I wish I could, as I'm extra frazzled after seeing Jared again. He brought up too many emotions in me. Each time I see him, I don't really see this guy—Jay. I see my Jared; I think he's in there somewhere. I'm just not sure how to reach him. Each time Jay corners me, one emotion seems to rise above all the rest, and it surprises me. I want to be brave. Brave for Jared.

After placing my key in the door, I open it slowly. The TV sounds softly from the living room, so I become a coward and close the door gently before tiptoeing up the stairs and into my room. I tie up my hair and enter my bathroom. Running the taps, I splash my face with water as my bedroom door opens. A surprised Evelyn comes in as I dry my face. "How was last night? You broke curfew," she says with a broad smile. Like me coming home later than eleven is great. I have no idea what time I got home, but it felt late.

Guilt has me gripping the towel—*small white lies.*

"It was fun," I say. I keep my back to her while slowly folding the towel and placing it back on the rack. It gives me a chance to gather myself before facing her.

When I turn around, Evelyn watches me carefully. "You know you can talk to me about anything."

I've shared my darkest secrets with Evelyn, and she and Carl have helped me, saved me. But I won't let them down. I *will* be a typical nineteen-year-old. I force a smile. "It was fun. Really."

Evelyn starts picking up the clothes that I dumped on the floor last night. "If there was a boy there, you could talk to me about that." She glances up, a smile playing on her lips. Once again, I don't want to let her down.

Taking a deep breath, I smile. "Well, there was this one guy."

My clothes hit the floor as Evelyn claps her hands. "I knew you were hiding something. Tell me."

Am I really going to do this?

"His name is Kieran." I tell her all about him, only I place him in a fancy house with friends who look just like him—the surfer kind and not ones who look like they would rob you. Everyone laughs and dances, and it's all fun and games.

Evelyn takes my face in her hands. "I am so happy for you. *You* deserve this, Layla."

My eyes burn, and my throat contracts. Turning away, I move to my bed.

"Thanks. I better get started with homework," I say as I climb onto the duvet and drag my book bag closer to me. I open the flap of my bag and start taking notepads out. When I glance at Evelyn, she's smiling. I fidget with the notepad, wanting nothing more than for Evelyn to go. She does, giving me a kiss on the forehead before finally departing. She pulls the door closed, and I'm alone. My mind wanders to the dark place, where it tells me I'm not worthy of Evelyn and Carl. I'm lying to them.

Small white lies, I remind myself. I get off the bed and walk to my window. I often think I see a car across the road watching me, a car very similar to the one I've seen Jay drive. Right now, no one is there. Another thing I'm sure I'm imagining.

I return to my bed and throw myself into my work. This is how I spend the rest of the night.

∗∗∗

Only a handful of cars dot the parking lot; it's still pretty early. Facing Evelyn this morning wasn't something I was up to after lying to her. My focus had been consumed with my schoolwork, but once I stopped, guilt churned painfully in my belly most of the night, making sleep come and go in broken spells.

I get out of the car and am surprised when I meet Ashley halfway down the hallway. I avoided her yesterday, but today that doesn't seem possible. She grabs my arm and steers me down a small corridor.

What have I done?

Ashley lets me go and swivels around to face me. "Look, I'm going to be really straight with you." She takes the same stance she had with Lucas and Sam only days ago—one hand on her hip, her head swaying to each word.

I force myself not to take a step back. My bag's strap slips slightly off my shoulder, and I push it back up.

"What you do with your free time is your business," she continues, "but I know you were at Chester's over the weekend." She pauses while lowering her head slightly, as if egging me on to answer but not giving me a moment to gather my thoughts. "Those guys are into some really heavy shit, and I don't want to see you getting hurt. You getting what I'm saying?" With furrowed brows, she stares at me.

"I'm going to make a lot of assumptions. Like Chester is the house owner?" I pause, and Ashley nods. "I'm also going to assume the heavy stuff is drugs?" Another nod. "And you think I would take drugs? Just to make it perfectly clear, I would never." As I speak, my voice lowers. I'm trying to defend myself without letting anyone else hear.

"You look like a really nice girl, Layla. I'm surprised you were even there. But looks can be deceiving." Her tongue runs along her teeth.

"I was surprised too. But you have nothing to worry about." I want to get to class. I don't need thoughts of Chester swirling in my mind. There's a tense moment of silence between us, which consists of her staring at me and me clutching my bag strap and trying to stand still without fidgeting. Finally, we both relax, and the tension breaks.

"I'm on cafeteria duty today, so I'd better get started." That ends our awkward conversation. I'm ready to bolt, but she's been so good to me.

"Want some help?" I ask.

She smiles. "I'd appreciate that. It's just preparing for the morning rush."

Ashley doesn't mention Chester again, and we spend the next hour getting the cafeteria ready. I never thought cleaning could be so relaxing. But the silence of the school and the soft overhead music relaxes me. We finish early, and Ashley comes over to me as I'm putting away a brush. Ashley is really nice; she smiles a lot as she speaks. I'm a bit surprised to hear she has a baby, considering she isn't much older than I am. Her love for her son, Nicco, shines through her words. He's twenty months old. She never mentions the father, and I don't ask.

As we gather our bags, I feel relaxed enough with her to ask the next question. "How did you know I was at Chester's?" Saying his name feels wrong, like saying Candyman in the mirror. I find myself glancing over my shoulder so that I can look back at Ashley. Her whole demeanor has changed at the mention of his name, and I regret asking.

"Sam was there. One of the other guys was asking about you."

It must have been Kieran, but why was he talking about me? I find myself smiling. Maybe it wasn't an untruth I told Evelyn after all.

Classes go by quickly, and no matter how many times I tell myself I'm not looking out for Jared, I know it's a lie down to my core. I finally spot him outside with a group of people who seem captivated by what he's saying. His profile has me entranced. His wavy black hair is cut short, showing his tanned neck. The black T-shirt stretches across his muscular back. My heart thumps as I think of a boy from years ago. His jeans are faded on purpose and not from being washed too much. He's over six feet tall. The boy he reminds me of causes a pain in my chest.

I continue to watch as he rocks from heel to toe. I used to make fun of him for that, and he never got mad at me no matter how much I teased.

The bang of the main door drags my attention back to here and now. Ashley slings her bag across her back and looks up at me.

"Are you okay?" she asks for the tenth time today.

"Yes. I'm just tired," I answer. The daylight is starting to fade, and the evening is slowly crawling in, throwing a dusting of darkness across everything. The shadows look like bottomless pits, and I shiver while shoving my hands deeper into the pockets of my red jacket. It was one long day at college.

Everything in me stills as Jay walks toward me, his face tightening the closer he gets. It transforms him from someone I used to know with dimples and light eyes to an angry god.

"Hi." I sound breathless as he stops in front of me.

He glares at me and rubs his jaw before speaking. "The three days you were missing... Where were you?"

He's angry.

My throat aches again; my heart beats rapidly as I stare up into the dark abyss that wants to consume me. I need to speak, but for the first time with Jared, the words are lodged in my throat.

His large hand touches my jawline, and my eyes flick up at him. His stare has darkened even further, and I'm not sure what prompted him to touch me. He looks revolted by the action, yet he hasn't let me go. When we were younger, I knew exactly what he was thinking, but right now, that unknown is scaring me.

His hand travels down to my neck, his thumb flicking back and forth. His touch burns into me. I swallow.

"Where were you?" He looks at me with haunted eyes.

CHAPTER NINE

LAYLA

"J ARED." My VOICE SOUNDS like a plea, and he drops his hand from my face, but the depth in his eyes doesn't disappear. It feels like I've just woken up as I look up and notice Alex. Her lips are pursed.

"So, I'll see you tomorrow?" Ashley's words are drawn out, making me acknowledge her. A brow rises with a question, and I don't blame her. I pivot toward her so I don't have to keep staring at Jared. She glances between him and me.

Heat burns my cheeks. "Yeah. I'll see you tomorrow."

"Three whole days is a long time," Jared says, and my attention reverts to him. He still stares at me with a thousand memories. He rubs his jaw as the tension grows.

Alex folds her arms across her chest. Her nostrils flare, and all I want to do is walk away, but I can't seem to make my feet move.

"Are you going to introduce us?" Alex's words are clipped.

But once again, Jared stares at me. "This is Layla," he blurts.

My lips twitch.

"Yeah, I remember her from gym class. But how do you know each other?" Alex's gaze trails down to my trousers, reminding me of my scarred leg.

My chest caves in. I need to leave. I dip my head, not able to keep Jared's stare much longer. "I better go." Pulling the strap of my bag up, I glance at Jared and regret it almost immediately.

His jaw is tight, his eyes narrow. I can't stand how he's looking at me, so I walk away.

"I asked you a question." His angry outburst seems to surprise Alex as much as me. Her eyes widen, and I find myself hurrying away.

Racing to my car, my hand searches my bag for my keys, and when they land on the cold metal, I yank them out.

"You're running away from me?" He's right there, his voice controlled, like I had imagined his earlier eruption. I stop to take a calming breath before turning to him. His hands are jammed in his jeans pocket, and I can see the thirteen-year-old Jared. There's a small vulnerability underneath his hard surface.

"No, I'm not running. But I don't owe you an explanation. You said..." I look behind him at everyone who watches us. "You said to keep out of your way."

He steps closer. "Now I'm asking you. Where were you those three days?"

"What does it matter to you, Jay?" My voice lowers to a painful whisper. "You aren't him."

He takes a step away from me. His jaw clenches, a muscle working away. He doesn't leave.

"You're you, but you're not."

"Jay?" Alex calls, and he glances at her over his shoulder before looking back at me.

I'm standing in front of someone who said we were forever. That no matter what, we were stuck with each other. But now I'm a stranger to him, and I don't know why he wears such a look of hate.

"Jared," I say softly as memories have me wanting him to be Jared.

His sneer rattles not just my hand, but it bounces and throbs right down to the core of what made up Jared and me. My hands shake as I try to get my key in the door.

He's still behind me, and my hands continue to rattle, but I manage to unlock the car. I climb in and grip the steering wheel, and his large frame bends so he can look in at me.

"This isn't over." His words are said like a promise. He reaches in and pries the keys out of my fingers. I'm waiting for him to drag me out of the car and demand that I answer him. Instead, he slides the key into the ignition.

He closes the door, and I put all my focus toward the windshield as I watch his departing form from the corner of my eye. My stomach twists as I turn the key. I reverse, and my eyes lock with his. All I see is Jared. Pain latches on to my soul, and like a vulture, it tears strips off me. Pulling away from him is the second hardest thing I've ever done in my life. The first was losing him to begin with.

You can cry now, I tell myself, but no tears come. Instead, laughter bubbles up my throat and passes my lips.

"Jared," I say. "Jared." I speak lower this time. My throat burns; my eyes sting.

The ringing of my phone cuts through the silence. I rummage in my handbag with one hand while focusing on the road.

"Hello," I answer.

"I was worried about you." Evelyn's voice is a wake-up call.

"I got caught up on campus," I tell her while hitting my indicator for the next left-hand turn. "Sorry, I should have called," I add.

"That's okay, sweetheart. You're on your way now?"

"Yeah. I'll be home in ten minutes."

Evelyn says her goodbyes, and I throw the phone down on the passenger seat.

Pulling into the driveway makes me question everything that has happened since I started college—believing I had found Jared, agreeing he was Jay, and now knowing it's him. I don't linger in the car; I'm already late.

After opening the front door with my key, I call out a hello and get two in response from the kitchen. My chest tightens. Should I tell them? Something in me says not to. I remove my red coat and hang it on the white freestanding coat rack that was only delivered last week. It finishes off the hallway nicely—oak floors and beige walls, while the small hall table and now the coat rack are white French furniture. The walls are decorated with so many photos of us. From the zoo to just random days at the house, Evelyn seems to capture every moment. I feel like a traitor.

Evelyn stands at the island, making a sandwich. "Take a seat. I'm making you one too." She points the knife at my usual spot in the kitchen. I take a seat, letting my bag slip off my shoulder and onto the arm of the chair.

Carl joins me, giving me a cup of tea. Sugar and milk already sit on the table. Why do I feel like a stranger all of a sudden?

"How was your day?" Carl asks while stirring his tea. His freshly shaven face has a gleam to it. I thought the beard suited him better, and so did Evelyn, but neither of us ever said it to him. He thinks he looks younger, which he does, but a beard just suits him more.

I sugar and milk my tea, giving myself a moment.

"Good. I had lots of classes. I had to stay late to catch up on some notes," I say as Evelyn slides the plate across to me before sitting herself down with a steaming mug in her hand.

I take a bite, and while I chew, I decide what to disclose. They don't seem to like Jared, and right now, my emotions are all over the place. I need to assess them and be more stable before I speak of him. I can't bear them being negative toward him, and I also don't want to disappoint either of them.

"I made a friend." Volunteering information is always a good tactic if I don't want them to ask questions.

Evelyn raises an eyebrow. "Well, is he or she in one of your classes?"

"Yeah, and she's really nice." I find myself smiling, thinking about Ashley.

"Do you have class tomorrow?" Carl asks. "I want us to have a family day."

"Could we move it to Monday?" Evelyn requests. "I have a lot going on tomorrow."

My phone buzzes in my bag, and my heart jumps. I tell it to calm down. After taking a few bites of my sandwich, I look up to find Evelyn staring at me, a smile on her face.

"Aren't you going to check that?" she asks, clearly delighted that someone is contacting me. When I don't, she continues. "It might be Kieran."

Heat scorches my cheeks, and I actually groan while glancing at Carl. Yep, he's going to have the talk.

Getting the phone out of my bag, my chest hitches. I have a message from an unknown number.

I want answers.

I'm staring far too long at the three words.

"Kieran?" The hope in Evelyn's voice has me looking up. I glance again at Carl.

Tiny lines form around his eyes as he smiles. "It's okay, Layla. You're a young woman now." He pats my hand, and I want to crawl under the table for so many reasons. They both wait for my answer. I look down at the message again. I close my phone.

"Yeah, it's Kieran." I've never seen Evelyn so excited. She covers her mouth with her hand as she continues to smile.

Carl gives my hand one final pat before getting up. "Just... Evelyn will have a chat with you." And there it is—the chat about the birds and the bees. I don't look at Carl. He sounds as embarrassed as I feel.

"Going to catch up on some football," he says.

"Okay, love." Evelyn removes her hand as she watches him leave. Her nod to him tells me he's mouthing something. I turn just as the door clicks.

Picking up the second half of my sandwich gives my hands something to do. I have no appetite now. The feeling of betrayal causes a thickness in my throat.

"It's okay, Layla."

My head shoots up at Evelyn's words. Does she know I'm lying? Am I that obvious? I can feel the blood drain from my face. "What?" I ask, finding it hard to keep her gaze.

Her eyebrows furrow. "I'm not going to have 'the talk.'"

The fact that I wasn't caught has me releasing the sandwich back onto the plate, and I force a smile. "Oh. Thank God."

Evelyn observes me carefully. "You look really pale."

"I'm always pale, Evelyn," I say with the lamest laugh ever. My hands hug the mug.

Evelyn nods, the tension leaving her shoulders. When she smiles, the crinkles around her eyes appear. "When do we get to meet Kieran?" I must have paled more, because Evelyn laughs. "I'm joking," she says while standing and taking her mug to the sink before coming back to me.

"We'll see how it goes?" I say, and she nods before looking down at my half-eaten sandwich.

"Are you finished?"

"Yeah, thanks." I pass her the mug before taking my phone off the table. "I'm going to take a hot shower, get some studying in, and maybe have an early night."

"Okay, sweetheart." Evelyn speaks from the sink. A part of me wants to walk across the kitchen and hug her, but I don't want to alarm her. I slip out of the kitchen, and when I have my foot on the bottom step of the stairs, my bag slung over my shoulder, and my hands gripping my phone, I realize I should say good night to Carl since I didn't intend on coming back down.

I push open the door to the den, and Carl looks up at me. His dark eyes hold mine for a brief moment before he quickly returns to the TV.

"Just wanted to say good night. I have lots of studying to do, and then I'm going to get an early night in," I say.

He looks relieved, as if I might be here to ask questions that would make both of us uncomfortable. "Well, good night."

He opens his arms, and I walk over to where he sits, bending at the waist to hug him. Closing my eyes, I relax, and a lump forms in my throat.

"Night, Carl," I say before leaving the hug. I don't want to start bawling all over him, but it's not until now that I realize how much I needed a hug from someone I know who loves me.

Finally, in the safety of my room, I sit on my bed and open the message again.

I want answers.

My fingers trace the message. It's Jared. Funny how I found him. Tears burn my eyes, but they don't fall. I want to say so much, but words sometimes aren't my friend. They get lodged in my throat, and afterward, I would kick myself for not saying something.

I miss you I type and then delete it.

Thank you for always saving me. I delete it.

I'm only here because of you. I delete that as well.

I don't send anything, but I save his number. Something tells me to save it as Kieran, but Evelyn and Carl never look at my phone. Secondly, lying to them isn't right. I'll leave it for a few more days, then tell them it all went south with Kieran and tell them about Jared. My stiff shoulders relax, and I start to feel less guilty about lying to them.

"Come here." I hang my head, letting my hair cover my face as I make my way to Bert. His friend's eyes follow me as I cross the room. "Get up here." He pats his knee like I knew he would, and I don't hesitate to sit on it.

My legs touch the ground. I focus on Ronnie's black boots. They remind me of something from the movie Hocus Pocus. The toes curl up at the ends. She would fit in perfectly with a bunch of witches. Her large frame and constant laugh make people see her as harmless and jolly, but behind the smile is a witch. One who doesn't like children, just the money she gets for them.

"Sing a song for Richard." Bert's breath brushes my hair, and the alcohol fumes are enough to make me look away. I flick a glance up at Richard, who leers at me. My skin crawls.

"Sing 'As She Moves Through the Fair.'" I don't want to, but I know better than to say no to Bert. In front of his friend, he won't hit me, but he will humiliate me. Then afterward, he'll hurt me. Closing my eyes, I picture my favorite person in the world. I wish he was here right now. If he were, he would stop this. With one eye open, I take a quick look at all the horrible faces, and none of them are Jared.

"Don't drag it out," Ronnie says, her eyes narrowing. She hates any attention that Bert gives us. Her jealousy is unfounded, but she justifies it somehow in her twisted mind.

"Shut your mouth," Bert shouts at Ronnie. I curl in as much as I can, my heart picking up pace.

"Sing!" he barks, and I close my eyes and picture Jared while I sing. The room is silent until I sing the final note. I open my eyes, and everyone claps.

"Fucking brilliant, isn't she?" Bert slurs his words. His praise makes me never want to sing again. He takes the good out of everything. But it is my own fault. I should have never allowed him to hear me sing. I thought the

house was empty as I cleaned, but he was there listening, and now this is my punishment every time his drunken friends come over.

"Off to bed with you." Ronnie speaks then and takes a deep gulp from her beer can. "You've school in the morning." I don't move until Bert bobs his knee—that's his permission to leave. I do, with my hair hanging in my face.

"You're good people taking in a simple minded kid." Richard speaks before I'm out of the room. My face burns. "But she can sing," he adds.

I take the stairs two at a time. The green carpet is worn down; the small red flowers that once were vibrant are now faded. I enter my room quietly. Two single beds face me, both covered with the same patchwork cover. Riley is usually asleep in bed long before I am. Her long brown hair splays across her pillow. She's two years younger and doesn't really speak. She goes under the radar in the house, and it annoys me. I'm jealous of how invisible she can become. Maybe one day I will be too.

I take off my clothes and hang them on the large wicker chair at the end of the bed before taking my nightdress out from under my pillow. After getting dressed, I slip into bed, the cold sheet a welcomed sensation on my still-burning skin. Pulling Jared's sweater out from under my pillow, I close my eyes and say my prayers, thanking God for Riley, Nelson, and Jared. I pray that I will find a better home, maybe somewhere with trees. I love trees.

With that thought, I fall asleep and dream of wild forests and running through long grass, while the smell of Jared makes me feel safe.

CHAPTER TEN

LAYLA

MORNING COMES QUICKLY. I spend too much time sitting in the parking lot rereading the message.

I want answers.

I want answers too, but I don't think I'll get them—all the answers to too many questions. I can assume the answers will be painful, anyway.

Why did you not try to find me? Maybe he had finally gotten rid of me, and he was glad that he didn't have to save Layla again. I'd been a noose around his neck that he was free of.

I squeeze my eyes shut before opening them, like I can erase that last thought, which terrifies me. Jared is better off without me. I seem to bring pain to the people I love most.

I shake my hands out as I get out of my car and make my way to the main entrance of the college building. Once I make it all the way to the back hallway, my shoulders slump as a bitter smile moves my lips. *He wants answers.*

I tell myself I'm overreacting and need to calm down. Maybe the message isn't from him.

"Morning."

I jump at Ashley's voice.

Ashley holds up her hands at my reaction. "Wow. Jumpy, are we?" she questions while dropping her hands.

Yep. I need to relax. Five minutes in, and already I'm acting like a nutjob. "Sorry. I didn't sleep well," I say honestly. The large dark circles under my eyes are my evidence. I follow Ashley out into the main corridor. My gaze darts around the space, searching for the large frame of Jared, but no one is here yet.

"So... yesterday?" Ashley makes her way to our first class. She moves her notebooks from one arm to the other. She doesn't glance at me as she speaks, and I'm grateful as a flush creeps across my cheeks.

"Yeah, that was awkward," I blurt out.

Ashley turns back to me, her eyebrows raised. "That's an understatement."

My toes curl in my shoes as the tops of my ears burn.

"How do you know Jay?" Ashley narrows her eyes slightly, her lips puckered as she hugs the notebooks to her chest while waiting for my answer.

I shake my head. "I don't." A puff of laughter escapes my lips.

"You really don't know him?"

"Yes, and no. I knew Jay from a few years back, but we were kids then." It's hard using the name Jay. We were kids who lived with abusive people, who damaged young children to a degree that functioning in our adult life is still a challenge.

"It looked pretty intense." Ashley doesn't shy away.

A heaviness settles on my chest. She has no idea.

"What about his parents?" I ask.

Ashley's hands tighten on the notepad, her stance more rigid now. "Honestly, everyone knows Jay's father, Mr. McGivney. He practically pays for the school. My family and I are so grateful to him. I wouldn't be here without his scholarship program."

My stomach sinks. What are the odds for me to arrive at a school that Jared's father owns?

"His mother?" I ask.

"I'm not sure. Rumor has it that she's dead, but that's not definite."

A fluttering starts in my belly as Alex stands in front of us.

She's alone.

Her gaze is fixed on me. Her hair flows down her back in thick blonde waves. The cut-offs she wears showcase a pair of long, tanned legs. She wears deep red lipstick that defines her mouth.

"Alex," the warning in Ashley's voice has me wanting to run.

"I'm only here to say hi and introduce myself properly." She glances at me now. Her gaze is hard, even as she smiles. "I'm Alex. Jay's girlfriend."

My lungs constrict, making breathing difficult. She's beautiful, and they're perfect for each other. A stunning couple.

"Hi," I manage to say back without sounding as devastated as I feel. There's an expectation heavy on my chest, like I should say more. But that's the best I can come up with.

"He told me he knew you when you were younger."

A wash of dizziness makes me reach out for the wall I'm standing beside. I nod my head as I stare at my hand touching the wall like the paint is the most interesting color of magnolia I've ever seen. He spoke about me—confirmation that he's Jared. He's really Jared. That knowledge hits me harder each time. The weakness in my muscles steals me of any remaining strength.

"I get it. You're like his little sister." Alex continues to twist the knife. "I'm cool with that."

I nod again. "We don't really know each other anymore." My voice sounds squeaky as I remove my hand from the wall.

Alex tilts her head with a sly smile on her lips. "Are you calling Jay a liar?" Those red lips continue to rise, and she appears gleeful that I would call Jared a liar.

"Alex. She's not calling anyone a liar. All she's saying is she hasn't spoken to him in years, so leave her alone." Ashley moves in front of me. "We have a class to get to," she says to Alex before turning to me. "You've missed enough already." She raises both eyebrows while nudging her head to the left, telling me to go now, and I do so without glancing back.

Slumping against the wall once I'm out of sight, I let my rattled heart settle.

Here is Jared, with a girlfriend, a family, and friends. I don't wish I had never met him because I honestly don't think I would have survived, but I hate messing anything up for him. I push off the wall. Ruminating isn't allowed—number one rule of Evelyn's.

Classes go by slowly, and I find myself not being present during the lectures. No matter how many times I read the text in front of me, I can't fully comprehend the words. The moment the class ends, I make my way outside. The air is crisp, and I don't want to go back into the building for afternoon classes. I throw my bag in the passenger seat of the car.

"Are you hiding from me?" At the sound of the male voice, my heart threatens to come right out of my chest. The first thing I notice is Lucas's slightly damp hair, as if he just showered. The second is the brown paper bag in his hand. A large silver watch catches the light, getting my attention for a moment before my eyes travel to his soft brown eyes.

"No. Why would I be hiding from you?"

He holds up the brown bag. "Okay, correction. Are you hiding from Ashley? She's worried."

I exhale. "I just needed fresh air."

I want to ask what's in the bag, but Lucas smiles.

"You are avoiding my sister, and I get it." He walks a few feet away and sits down at a bench. "She can be a lot at times."

"I like Ashley."

Lucas grins and unrolls the bag. "Sit down. Join me."

I don't have anywhere else to go, and I don't want to be rude. I slide in across from Lucas and stuff my car key into my pocket.

"Peanut butter sandwiches," he says, holding one out. "Take one."

I'm staring at the sandwich.

Lucas laughs. "I didn't make them—Ashley did. So you won't get food poisoning."

"I'm okay." The smell of peanut butter is strong, and a thousand memories assault me.

"Please? It will make Ashley happy if she knows you ate one of her sandwiches."

I swallow the lump and reach out and draw up a sandwich. I've avoided peanut butter. It isn't exactly something that was an intentional decision, but more on a subconscious level.

I take a bite, and it's everything I remember. Each bite is painfully joyful. So many memories of Jared smiling at me as I waited at the table for him to bring me my sandwich. He would cut off the crusts achingly slow, a grin on his face, knowing he was torturing me. Peanut butter sandwiches were food for our battered souls.

The bread grows heavy in my mouth, and my vision blurs as I look up at Lucas.

He looks horrified. "That bad?"

I try to swallow, but the bread is lodged in my throat. I don't have a minute to compose myself as a shadow looms over our table.

I can't process anything as Jay reaches out and grabs my arm, pulling me from the table. I'm ready to protest, but I'm so astonished as he continues to drag me further away from Lucas, who sits there with a look of pure shock on his face.

No words pass my mouth as Jay yanks me across the lawn. A few students glance our way and whisper, but no one intervenes.

"Get off me." My words have no impact. Jay doesn't slow down. A brand-new BMW that I know is his comes into view. He spins me just as we reach his car.

"Are you ready to give me my answers?"

I try to pull my arm out of his hold, but his fingers are too tight. Jay towers over me, and my words get swallowed up.

His eyes darken further, and his lip drags up. "You want to make this hard?" He looks past me at the school. "Fine." His grin stretches; it's like watching a shark circle blood.

We're moving around his car, and before I have a second, I'm in the passenger seat, and he's getting into the driver's seat.

"What are you doing?" My brain catches up with the situation as I reach for the door handle. The lock snaps into place, and my head turns back to Jay, who has started the car. "What are you doing?" I shout louder.

A booming bang grabs my attention. Alex has slammed her hands on the hood of the car, her gaze on fire with rage. I pull at the door handle again, but it's still locked.

"Let me out," I demand. Jay ignores me and revs the engine. I sit back as Alex removes her hands from the hood.

Her mouth moves. "What are you doing?" She asks the same question I did; only hers is said with a snarl. Her gaze leaps to me and pierces me with heat. If the sharpness were real, I would bleed out right now in the passenger seat.

Jay revs the car again, and Alex jumps to the side. He doesn't give her a second before he slams his foot down on the pedal, and we launch forward and out of the school gates.

CHAPTER ELEVEN

JARED (Eighteen hours before)

WHEN I ARRIVE HOME, it's not the silence that makes me pause in the grand hallway; it's William's absence. He normally materializes like a phantom with some update or request. Today, there's nothing, and that makes me edgy as I make my way to the top floor of the mansion. I'm still disturbed by my father's earlier arrival on campus. I'd been stupid and careless, but Layla's disappearance had burned so deeply that I needed to douse the flames and find out where she was. I dump my bag on the floor and make my way to my bedroom. After pulling my sweater over my head, I hit the double doors with both hands, and they swing open.

I stop advancing into the room and pull my cell out of my jeans. I got Layla's number when the dean was out of the office, and I grin as I stare down at her name in my phone—where it belongs. I write a text.

I want answers. I hit send and slip the phone back into my pocket. I'm ready to continue into my room. I'm not sure what makes me pause; the draft on my bare flesh, perhaps. I step away from my bedroom and pull my sweater back on. My father stands with his back to me. His hands are shoved into his black suit trousers pockets. He hasn't entered the room, but his head bobs from side to side as he takes in all the new artwork of Layla. "She's at your school."

William's vanishing act makes sense now. Fear strikes hard and fast and makes my steps falter.

"Layla Masters." My father glances at me and wears a look of fondness on his face, which fucking confuses me. "Silly of me, really. I should have known she would come for you eventually."

What happens now? That's the question I want to ask. Guilt weighs down my shoulders as I step up beside my father. "I kept my word for three years."

"Three years? Is that how long it's been?" My father's voice sounds foreign to me; it's the undercurrent, something I've never heard before.

"Father..." I start to explain, but the words die on my lips.

"She's beautiful. I can see the fascination." He looks at me with that odd fondness in his eyes. "Beautiful and dangerous."

"Layla isn't dangerous." I defend her straight away and regret it immediately as his spine straightens.

"I had my son for three years, and I knew recently, I had lost you again." He points at a picture of Layla on campus, hugging her books to her chest. Her hair is loose, and her eyes are wide and filled with fear. "To her."

He turns away and steps out of the room. I don't follow him. I'm fully aware he hasn't taken more than a few steps before he stops.

"She knew where you were all this time. She knew your name. She knew the college you attended. Layla might come across as innocent, but she's very dangerous."

Pain oozes into my being, and I turn to my father, wanting him to take back his lies. "Don't hurt her," I plead.

His gaze hardens. "She was missing the same three days you were. Was it because of that boy?" His anger heightens his words.

"What boy?" Is Layla seeing someone? The thought is fuel to my veins, and it only elevates my rage. I have no one or nothing to fire it at, so the rage boils in my blood.

My father turns his back on me. I want to scream and demand he tell me all about this boy.

"You look like a man possessed." His voice is low.

I relax my fists and stretch my aching fingers.

"She only wants your money, Jay."

"I don't have any. And Layla—"

My father swings around to me. "Don't be so naïve. All this..." He swings his arms wide. "It's all yours—no one else's. You are the sole heir to not millions but billions. You have to see what's at stake here. In four months, you turn twenty-two, and I plan to pass it all over to you."

He's making Layla out to be a gold digger, a vindictive one. Could she have known that I was here? What took her so long to find me? The thoughts of this other boy start to consume me again.

I blink and look up, but my father is gone. I have no idea how long I've been standing here fighting with the demons in my head.

"Father?" I call. Silence bounces back to me.

A throb along my neck has me looking back at the room filled with images of Layla. I walk inside, and with a lot of willpower, I close the door and turn the key. I want to look at her, but I also need the distance before I explode. Placing the chain around my neck, I know this room isn't sacred anymore. My father has a key and I never knew.

***

The next morning, Alex is waiting for me. I already know it's about Layla. I think I left everyone wondering what was going on with my outburst yesterday. Maybe that's what tipped my father off. My display was stupid and out of character. I'm sure Alex ran to my father.

I bury everything—all the hate I feel for Alex that tries to consume me—until there's an odd silence in my head. The habit from years of training myself not to think or feel returns like a blanket across my shoulders, and I get out of the car.

"Good morning," I greet Alex.

"I need to know what's going on with that girl. Layla?"

I lock my car and walk to Alex. With a nod, I speak. "Layla and I knew each other as kids. She moved away, and our friendship ended."

Alex folds her arms across her chest with a look of satisfaction. "When you were kids?" She smirks.

I continue to walk to Alex. "Exactly."

Alex's smirk turns into a full smile, and she links her arm with mine. "For a moment, I thought it was something more."

There's a question in her statement. I grin at her. "I was just surprised to see her."

"Where did she live?"

I thought my replies would have Alex losing interest, but clearly, she hasn't. I stop walking and face her fully. Digging my hands into my pockets, I lean in close to her face, only an inch between our mouths. My lips drag up. "Don't tell me Alexandra is feeling threatened?"

She scoffs as her gaze travels to my mouth. "Hardly. She hasn't got anything on me."

I step away. "Then you have nothing to worry about." I walk off, and Alex doesn't fall into step beside me. I move through the hallway taking fist bumps and pats on the back from guys while I return the smiles and shy *hellos* from girls. It's not until much later, when I see Layla sitting with Lucas Garcia, that my facade cracks wide open, and I lose all composure. I forget every trick I learned to conceal what I feel; I forget everything. All I see is Layla.

She's looking at Lucas with wide eyes as they share fucking sandwiches. My control shatters, and I reach the picnic bench and drag her from the table. I want to grab her face and make her soak up all my rage, but I pull her across the lawn. A few students glance our way. I fire a warning to each set of eyes I meet, and they stay fucking seated. I need to let her go. I need to gain some control.

"Let go of me." Her voice is strong. Too strong.

I spin her around so she's facing me. "Are you ready to give me my answers?"

She tries to tug away from me, and I tighten my hold on her. She knew where I was all along. She's looking up at me with fear etched into her stunning face.

I dig my fingers a little deeper into her arm. "You want to make this hard?" Someone walking toward us catches my eye, and I look past Layla, my gaze snagging on Alex. This should be my warning to calm down, but I can't. I want answers. I turn away from Alex and continue to my car. I try to be gentle with Layla as I place her in the seat. She's stunned, and her shock buys me time as I run around the car and get in.

"What are you doing?" Fear grows thicker in Layla's voice, and she reaches for the door. I push down the lock, stopping her from leaving, and she faces me. "What are you doing?" Her words are filled with dread, and I soak them up.

A bang grabs our attention as Alex slams her hands on the hood of my car. She's pissed. She knows this is more than what I told her.

Layla starts pulling the handle again, but she can't get out. "Let me out."

I ignore her and glare at Alex as I rev the car.

She narrows her eyes but removes her hands from the hood and stands straight. "What are you doing?" Her lips form a thin line. She swings around to Layla, and the way she looks at her has me revving the car again in warning.

Fury flashes across her features, but she still has her wits about her and steps to the side. I don't give her a second before I floor it, and the car roars out of the parking lot.

"This is madness." Layla's words grate along my heart.

I grip the steering wheel as I push the pedal to the floor. We lurch forward as the car tears down the road. "Slow down." She grips the overhead handle.

Without thought, my foot lifts slightly from the pedal, and the car slows down, but we still make it to the lake in record time.

Layla's silence the rest of the journey worries me, and when I pull up at the lake, I can't look at her. I get out of the car and leave her in the passenger seat. The veil of vexation starts to lift, and I glance back at Layla, who's paled further as she stays seated in the car.

I'm walking back to her. Each step I take has her breathing growing more irregular. I pull open her door.

"Those three days... Where were you?" My patience snaps. "Who's the boy?"

Layla closes her eyes, and I'm ready to reach in and shake her when they flutter open.

"I had some bad news and needed time off." Her voice shakes only slightly, and she unclips her seat belt. I wasn't aware she had put it on. "Can I get out, please?"

I'm crowding her, but I step back and let her out.

Once she stands outside the door, she speaks. "Nelson died. I'm not sure you heard." Sadness floods her blue eyes.

I take a step away from her and watch her from the corner of my eye. "How?" My heart beats wildly.

She wraps her arms around her waist. "I don't know. They wouldn't tell me."

Bile bubbles in my stomach, and I take another step away from Layla.

My father's words about the boy make me feel sick. He knew. He knew Nelson died and didn't tell me.

"Jay." Layla steps closer to me, reaching out like she's ready to offer me her condolences.

"Don't fucking touch me."

She jerks back; her features tighten before she explodes. "Why do you hate me? What have I done?" Her voice shakes, and she points a finger at me. "I'm sorry. I'm sorry you had to keep protecting me. I'm sorry I destroyed your life." Her lip trembles, and she battles the pain that fills her eyes. "I am so sorry, Jared."

"Shut the fuck up." I can't breathe.

"You left me." Her words break and crack.

"I said shut up," I growl.

She doesn't hear me, but I start to walk away from her, from my past, from the emotions that are clawing at me. I keep walking until I reach the end of the pier.

"I searched for you." Her angry words are hurled at my back. "You leaving destroyed me."

I spin around and face her.

"I..." Her mouth opens and closes, but not one tear that glazes her eyes has escaped. "Jared." She says my name so sweetly, and it undoes me.

I clear the distance and slam my mouth down on hers. She doesn't respond as I taste desperation and peanut butter. I break the one-sided kiss abruptly.

"You were eating peanut butter sandwiches with that little prick?"

Her tongue flicks out and licks her lips. My brain is still analyzing how it felt to kiss her. Fucking amazing. Her lips are softer than they look, warmer. Her scent has stolen my ability to smell anything else. Nothing can compete with the scent of Layla.

"He offered me one."

My temper flares, and my fingers grip her. She spins so easily in my hands as I face her toward the lake.

"Jared, I can't swim!" she screams as I push her into the lake.

I know.

CHAPTER TWELVE

LAYLA

WATER GUSHES OVER MY head. The last image I have burned into my brain is Jared standing on the edge of the pier with a perplexed look on his striking face. The world turns to green and brown as the lake swallows me whole. Pain burns my lungs, pain that isn't just from being oxygen deprived. Betrayal is a new kind of pain as my brain keeps repeating on a loop that Jared pushed me into the lake with the knowledge that I can't swim.

My arms and legs kick out. My thoughts are not with the action, but I'm aware of the flailing limbs that try to erase the growing distance between me and the surface. The world shatters as something breaks the surface and zooms toward me. I can't see through the murky water as an arm circles my waist, and we're tearing toward the surface. Light glitters off the rising water, and just as my lungs burn for what feels like the final time, the water snaps and bends, and I'm staring at the sky as I gasp for air.

"Slowly. You don't want to choke."

Through the veil of fear and sheer panic, I glance down at Jared, who holds me solidly against his chest with one arm. The other arm moves in my peripheral vision, keeping us afloat.

"In through the nose, out through the mouth." He speaks with a slight smile.

I hate him at this moment, but I'm drawn to the old habit we established for calming me down.

"Take a larger one. Let it fill your belly," Jared says, and my breathing evens out as a new type of hurt digs its talons into me. At this stage, Jared would tickle my stomach, and I would laugh instead of cry, and the crisis would be over.

"Feel it down to your toes," he continues.

I shake my head as my throat and eyes burn. "Stop."

The slight smile he wore disappears, and he continues to keep us afloat in the middle of the lake. Jared hasn't looked away from me, and his arm around my waist is a promise that I'm going nowhere.

His gaze drops to my lips, and more confusion floods my system. Why did he kiss me when he clearly hates me?

I focus on the pier that seems far away. "Take me back to the shore."

"No." Jared's tone draws my attention back to him. "I don't want you around that boy anymore."

I don't ask who. I know who. The one he dragged me away from. But I don't understand why. A breeze dances on the surface of the lake. The water shivers under the caress, and I lean in closer to Jared's solid chest.

I'm aware of how solid, how big, how different he is.

He's a man.

"Fine. Take me back to shore."

His lip twitches, and he leans out so I have to lie across his torso as he swims closer to the pier but not the whole way. He stops and straightens up. His hand pulls me closer, tightening around my waist.

My fingers dig into his wide shoulders. "You knew I couldn't swim." I allow the hurt to pour into my words.

Jared doesn't flinch or wear a look of guilt that anyone else would. His shoulders lift under my touch. "I wouldn't have let you drown."

"You're my fucking hero." The angry words lash out.

They don't cut Jared at all. In fact, they tickle him as he barks out a deep laugh that twists my core.

His laughter dies, and something dark passes his gaze and deepens the brown to a startling black. He dips his head, and I think he's going to kiss me again. He passes my lips, his cheek pressed against mine, and I swear he inhales. Shivers break out across my skin and find their way throughout my body.

"Keep kicking your legs, Layla." His whispered words have me kicking again, and it's funny how my legs move at the same speed as his. We are in sync with each other.

His closeness is doing something funny to my heart, and he still has his face buried in my neck as he sniffs me.

"When did you learn to swim?" I ask. It's what breaks him away from my aching flesh, and he's dragging us back to the pier. The moment he reaches the dock, he turns to me, and I'm airborne as he pushes me up with one arm. I grip the edge and haul myself up. Water spills out on the wood, and before I have a second to process anything, Jared joins me. His T-shirt is plastered to his chest. I spot a chain around his neck; it's not the first time I've noticed it.

"I learned to swim after my father found me." Jared's words are spoken as his gaze travels across my blouse.

Looking down is so pointless. The fabric is glued to my body, and nothing is covered. My cheeks blaze, and when I glance back up at Jared, I don't know what I expect, but his anger isn't it. "I made sure I eliminated every weakness I had."

His large hand that I stare down at is another reminder of how much bigger he is. I swallow more confusion and loss as I look back up at him. "You were never weak to me, Jared," I admit as my vision blurs. Words bubble up and pop before I get to tell him what he meant to me.

He's standing, and I'm being dragged to my feet. "Everyone and everything was stronger than you, Layla. So nothing would seem weak to you." His words are driven with each step we take to his car.

I was weak then, and I still am now. I feel so small as he releases me and moves to the trunk of his car. He returns with an oversized letterman's jacket.

I take it from him, but I can't look at him right now. The old Jared would never say such a thing. He steps closer and reaches out; his hand burns my flesh as he tilts my head back. I swallow so much loss that it's choking me. He's here in front of me, but he's not. My own brain can't seem to process all the emotions that speed through me.

Jared's transfixed on me. His lips move, and his eyes soften. I can almost imagine that he's ready to take back his words. Maybe he wants to apologize for pushing me into the lake. Maybe he wants to tell me he missed me too.

"That boy, Lucas, is only at Kingscourt on my goodwill. I can take it back anytime I want and have him removed." Jared's fingers tighten on my jawline. "You understand?"

It takes my brain a moment to catch up with our conversation. How did we get back to Lucas? Why did he care about Lucas?

"He's harmless—" I start, but Jared's fingers trail up and press firmly against my lips, cutting off my words.

"You will have lunch with me each day at school." He steps away after issuing his bizarre demand. "Get out of those wet clothes." He walks a few feet away and stops, keeping his back to me.

I don't hesitate and start to peel off the wet clothes. The material clings to my body, but I manage to get the shirt over my head. I don't remove my bra before wrapping Jared's jacket across my cold flesh. I could wrap it twice if I wanted to. When I glance up, Jared is facing me. He grips the bottom of his T-shirt and pulls it off over his head. My heart dances wildly in my chest. His body speaks of hours at a gym, his physique in peak condition.

Why did my mind think that all that muscle was created as a product of his childhood, our childhood? My focus is snagged on the chain that hangs around his neck. On the end is a key. I want to ask about it.

Jared throws the T-shirt into the trunk before closing it. He doesn't walk around to the driver's side but returns to me looking ridiculously handsome, with water dripping down his chest from his darkened hair. I get another look at the key before he speaks.

"Trousers too, Layla."

My cheeks heat against the cold. Jared's eyes light up as he takes another large step toward me. He grips the band of his trousers, "I mean, I can take mine off first if it makes you more comfortable."

The teasing in his voice has me almost choking on the pooling saliva in my mouth. "No. Don't. And don't you have a girlfriend?" I say, sounding as jealous as I feel.

I hear his soft laugh as he walks around to the driver's side. I kick off my boots, and a small stream of water pours out beside the tire of the car. I check the pockets of my trousers first and am surprised to find my car keys still there. I take out the key and peel my trousers off, dragging them down they burn my skin, but once I have them off, I stripe off my socks too. The window rolls down.

"I don't have a girlfriend." There's no humor in Jared's voice now.

I hate how happy that makes me feel. "My clothes?" I ask as I gather them off the ground so he can't see the truth in my face that the news makes me happy.

"Throw them in the back."

I do as Jared says before sliding into the front seat. The leather isn't cold but heated under my bottom. I don't look at Jared as I buckle in, and slip the car keys into my pocket. Once I'm done, and we haven't moved, I take a peek at him.

His focus is on my leg. My scarred leg. I'm tempted to tuck it under me. The scar is a reminder of the worst day of my life.

"I'd never heard anyone scream like that." His words are low and haunted.

When I look at Jared, he takes a gulp of air. His hands crumble on his knees as he stares at my leg. The dark ink band around his wrist is another part of him I'm curious about. Why did he get that tattoo?

"I want to know everything," he says, and our gazes crash again. This time, my heart stalls before galloping.

Jared shifts and rests his chin in his hand, two fingers covering his mouth. The intensity in his eyes burns my soul. I swallow all the emotions and clear my throat. I'm not ready to relive that night, but looking at the tension in Jared's shoulders and how still he is, I know this is important to him.

"I was taken straight to the hospital." My voice sounds so weak, and I clear my throat again.

Jared shifts closer to me, and I'm momentarily frozen solid before warmth rushes through my body and thaws the coldness. Jared slowly and carefully takes my hand in his, and I'm dumbfounded as I stare at his tanned one entwining with my small, pale one. A part of me knows our holding hands isn't right, not when Jared has a girlfriend. Yet, I don't pull away. He said he doesn't have one, but Alex seems to believe they're together.

"I had third-degree burns and some nerve damage." My heart jumps with how he's looking at me. His brows furrow, his hand still covering his mouth but tighter. "I'm so sorry." His voice is soft, which doesn't match the hardness of his posture right now.

I'm shaking my head as he speaks the words. "You saved me," I say, squeezing the hand that still holds mine. His thumb moves lazily in a circular motion, and he closes his eyes, letting out a breath. My stomach flounders from each small touch.

Get a grip.

Jared finally opens his eyes. "Keep going." He doesn't sound sure, but a soft tug of my hand has me nodding.

"I also had a fractured leg from the fall. But the worst—" I pause while taking a sip of air as if it's a painkiller. Why is this so hard?

"You can tell me." Jared's voice seems deeper now; his low words have me glancing at him.

"They had to rebreak two previous breaks that never set correctly."

Jared's nostrils flare, and he lets go of my hand.

Heat burns my cheeks. "I'm sorry," I say quickly while he rubs his face.

At my words, his head shoots up. "I'm not mad at you, Layla."

God, why did he sound so angry, then?

He's beside me before I can blink. My heart races as his arm brushes mine. The heat from his naked torso touches my flesh. The position is so intimate.

"I'm mad because I should have reported it a long time ago. I should have stopped it." He ducks his head, not allowing me to see his face, his forehead so close to mine.

"Jared. Look at me," I tell him. He does. "You were just a child, just like me. Please, it hurts my heart to see you blame yourself." My phrase 'hurts my heart' wrestles a smile out of him, and I knew it would. I used to tell him this all the time if he wouldn't dance with me or read me a bedtime story. It was the line that got him every time.

He takes my hand once again, his touch soft, but the violence in his eyes has me wanting to stop.

"What happened next?"

I'm shaking my head.

"What happened next?" Anger snakes and courses through his words.

I skip a lot, as I can see I'm agitating him, so I skip to the happily ever after. I can't bear the way he's looking at me right now.

"They got a counselor for me—Evelyn. She spent weeks listening to me and finally let me meet her husband, Carl. They took me in." I can't stop the smile as I remember that moment Evelyn told me she was taking me home. *Home* was so foreign to me, but I could tell that this time, things would be different, and they were.

Jared does the most bizarre thing. His lips turn up, and it's a real smile. Dimples that I haven't seen in years make an appearance. My chest tightens, and I have to look away before I crack and split in front of him. It's all too much.

"I asked for you, but no one knew anything." Looking up at Jared, I can see my own pain reflected in his eyes. Suddenly, I'm in his arms. My head rests against his chest. The frantic pounding of his heart fills my ear.

No words are spoken between us as we hold each other. It's a past that doesn't deserve a place in the future, yet it seems to have wormed its way in after being buried for seven years.

Jared pulls back. The loss of his arms and warmth has me looking up at him. He no longer appears happy as he moves back fully into his seat.

"Everything turned out fine for you." His words are hollow.

I get an empty feeling in the pit of my stomach as I watch him transform from Jared into Jay in a matter of seconds.

I can feel the coldness in the air and almost taste it as he drives away from the lake with too much anger in his tightening fingers.

"What about you?" I ask.

"You already know, Layla." His words are bitter.

"I don't. So tell me."

His sneer confuses me. "Yeah, I got my happy ending too."

I tighten my hands on my lap. Cold water drips from my hair onto the jacket. "Then why don't you sound happy?" I swallow a lump in my throat.

"Because, Layla"—Jared fires me a sideways glance—"you're here."

His words make no sense, yet they hurt so much. My temper flares. "You brought me here. I didn't ask. You dragged me into your car. You pushed me into a lake."

Jared doesn't respond but continues to drive past the campus.

I'm watching as the college disappears in the side window. "I need to get my bag. I need to call Evelyn."

Silence.

"Jared."

That gets a reaction out of him. "My fucking name is Jay."

"Where are we going?"

"To my home," Jared responds, and I get this horrible feeling, like I'm stuck in an alley with someone I don't quite trust.

CHAPTER THIRTEEN

JARED

CREAMY LEGS CATCH MY attention too many fucking times. Having Layla beside me wearing nothing but my jacket makes me want to keep driving so this time with her doesn't end. It's a new kind of torture having her close but not touching her the way I want to. I take another glance in her direction. She's gnawing on her swollen red lip, and my cock hardens in my trousers.

"I don't want to go to your home. I want you to take me back to campus." Her voice is weak, and she won't look at me.

Like fuck am I taking her back. I'm keeping her close because she's the enemy right now. My father said that she knew where I was all this time. Yet she acted too innocent, like stumbling into Kingscourt was just a coincidence.

Each time I close my eyes, I see her sitting with Lucas, sharing a sandwich.

"How did he know about the peanut butter sandwiches?" I grit out.

She takes a sharp inhale. "Lucas?"

I glance at her, not liking his name in her mouth—a mouth I want to kiss, a mouth I want to fuck. I can't answer as anger keeps my lips glued together.

She frowns. "Other people eat peanut butter sandwiches, Jar—Jay."

I grip the steering wheel and take one final look at her legs, which she tries to tug closer to the seat like she can hide them from me. I refocus on the road.

I don't want her to hide. I want every single tiny piece of Layla. I slow down as I near my home. My father isn't here; he's off in London at a meeting, so I'll have the place to myself.

I keep an eye on Layla as we pull up to the white gates. She ducks her head and glances out the front windshield to take in the house. She doesn't say anything as I drive up to the mansion. We wait for a moment as the garage door silently rolls up, and I park in my usual spot, and still, she doesn't speak. Her hand shakes as she unclips her belt. That's the first sign that she's nervous. That is, until she glances in my direction. Her blue eyes pierce the darkness in me; her light burns in the worst kind of way, and I drink in her gaze.

"I would have eaten lunch with you every day, Jay. You just had to ask." Her voice is soft. She pulls down the jacket so the material covers her knees.

"I'm not asking, Layla. I'm telling you." I grin in delight as her cheeks heat. Her blue eyes cloud over, and her lids flutter closed, cutting me off from all kinds of torture.

I get out of the car before I reach across and kiss her again. She hesitates only for a moment before she gets out too. She doesn't follow me immediately but gathers her clothes from the back of the car. "Is there somewhere I can dry these?"

I nod and turn away. She looks terrified. We enter the foyer and William materializes.

"Master Jay." He nods and hands me a piece of paper that I don't open. William acknowledges Layla with a bow. "Miss."

My home holds the most exquisite furnishings. Marble that is carved into statues, painted portraits of my father, and items that my father acquired from far-off lands. But nothing looks as foreign as Layla at this moment. I take a step toward her. A smile springs and steals my frown as I reach for her. I have to pry the clothes from Layla's hands. "I'm not going to steal them," I tease.

She doesn't smile, but color seeps beautifully into her cheeks, and instead of stepping away from her, I reach up and touch her pink cheek. The heat radiates into my hand and fills me up.

I must still be smiling, because her eyes are smiling at me.

William clears his throat.

The coldness returns as I remove my hand from Layla and pass William the wet pile of clothes. "Can you dry these, please?"

"Yes, Master Jay." William leaves, and I turn to find Layla glancing around. I reach out, and she startles as my fingers graze hers. I should stop, but I entwine our fingers together. Her blue eyes zero in on our hands, and I give her a tug, leading her toward the stairs. I feel the strain on my hand as she hesitates, but it's too late for that. I pull her easily, and we climb the two flights of stairs until we stop at the third floor.

"Can I use a phone?" The pulse flickers wildly in her neck.

"Who do you want to ring? The Gardaí?" I ask and release her hand.

Layla frowns. "Evelyn. My phone's at school. I'm sure she has called me and is worried." Layla folds her arms across her chest.

Even in my letter jacket and nothing else, she's the most beautifully destructive thing I have ever seen.

"You're not good for me." I take a step closer to her. "You shouldn't be here," I say as I tilt her head back using the tip of my fingers under her chin. Bringing her here was a bad idea.

"I agree," Layla bites out, but her gaze lands on my lips.

I let them rise, and she shivers before looking up to mine. "Take me home."

Home. Is that what she's calling it?

I release her and walk away, entering the sitting area. I open a drawer and power on one of my spare phones. The other one got lost in the lake. Once it powers up, I turn to find Layla standing close to me. She's checking me out. I hold out the phone. She reaches out, and I pull it back, forcing her to look at me.

"You ring only Evelyn," I warn.

She doesn't answer, and I keep the phone held away from her. The want to touch Layla has me stepping closer. She cowers in front of me. I don't want her to cower.

"Make your call." I push the phone into Layla's hand and leave her.

"Hi, have you been trying to call me?" Her voice shakes, and I pause in the hall. Why is she afraid? Is Evelyn hurting her?

"I'm sorry. I left my bag in class." Her words are stronger. I can't hear the voice on the other end of the phone. "No. Ashley, my friend, invited me to her house to study."

Of course, she won't mention me.

I don't shower but change into a fresh pair of jogging pants and a black T-shirt. I towel dry my hair and return to Layla. She's standing where I left her, the phone still clutched in her hand. I want to know what she's thinking. When she glances up at me, defiance flashes in her eyes, and I wonder if she rang the Gardaí, saying I kidnapped her. I clear the space and swipe the phone from her hand. I flick open the dial log and can only see one number.

I look at Layla. I've seen that look in her eyes before. The defiance is fucking prepossessing.

"Remember when you pushed Ronnie's doll pram down the stairs?"

Her eyes light up, and she unfolds her arms from across her chest. The jacket gaps slightly, and I see a glimpse of white flesh. My heart thumps, my cock grows instantly, and the memory evaporates as I take a small step closer to her.

"It was the best feeling ever." She smiles, and I'm back there with her again.

My lips drag up. "It hit every step with a bang." One push sent the pram sailing down the stairs. The rattles sound distant as I recall the memory. I remember the satisfaction in Layla's eyes that day; they shone with the defiance I saw only moments ago.

I laugh. "It was the ugliest pram."

Layla folds her arms across her chest, dragging the jacket back into place, hiding all that tempting skin. "Blue. The doll pram was like an egg blue velvet material. It was her pride and joy. Her father had bought it for her, and she said it was mine. Like I wanted anything from her." The smile melts off Layla's face.

I take a step back as her face tightens.

When I left Layla that day, I was smiling. Bert and Ronnie were out, and no one would know what she had done. The pram showed no signs of damage.

"How did you get it back upstairs?" I ask as I think back. I had left to go hang out with Fintan and Keith.

Layla drops her gaze. "I didn't. Ronnie did."

I dip my head to make Layla look at me, but she won't. "Ronnie wasn't there." Is this another lie? Just like the one she was telling me, pretending she didn't know where I was all these years. Like the lie she just told Evelyn, saying she was at Ashley's.

Layla finally looks at me. "She was asleep in the conservatory. The noise must have woken her. You had just left when she arrived in the hall."

I'm shaking my head. "She and Bert were gone. I remember."

"She was there. I remember that day clearly." Layla unfolds her arms, showing me some skin again. Is she doing it on purpose, trying to distract me? "I want to go home."

"No." I'm not ready for her to leave yet.

"You can't stop me." Layla spins, and I see the panic in her eyes.

"I mean, you can't leave wearing only my jacket. Your clothes should be dry soon. But I'll get you some fresh clothes while you wait."

She turns back and blinks several times at my logic. "Fine."

I take her to my bedroom. The door at the end of the hall is like a beacon. A warning. What would she think if she saw inside that room? When I glance back at Layla, she's followed my gaze. I'm tempted to reach up and touch the key that dangles around my neck.

"What happened with Ronnie?" I ask as I enter my bedroom. I take a moment to look at Layla standing close to my bed. How many times have I pictured her here—lying on my bed while I fuck her? I switch on the light in the closet and enter, getting a T-shirt for her. When I step back into my room, she's glancing around, and I wonder if she ever fantasizes about me the way I have obsessed over her all these years.

I walk to her, and she swallows. "Tell me what happened." I keep the T-shirt out of her reach.

"It doesn't matter, Jar—Jay," she bites out.

It fucking matters a lot. Every single detail about her existence matters.

I don't speak but glare at her, and it does the trick.

"I ran upstairs into my room, and she followed me. She was beyond angry." Layla's blue eyes darken. "I pressed myself against the wardrobe. I just knew I had really messed up. She didn't slow down when she entered the room. She slapped me across the face." Layla takes in a large breath. "I kept waiting for her to stop, but with each slap, I soon realized she wouldn't. So I screamed."

My fingers tighten around the fabric in my hand. A throb starts in my gut as I watch her torture herself with each word I make her relive.

"I didn't stop screaming until she was dragged off me. I've never seen Bert so angry." She blinks several times, and when I move closer, she doesn't even notice.

"He was fucking livid. She was afraid of him. Really afraid. Like the fear we felt." Layla peeks at me then. "He forced her to stare at me, and he was shouting at her to look at my face. That she had marked me."

Layla breathes heavily again, and it's like she's stepping out of the memory.

How had I not noticed that her face was marked? I noticed everything about Layla.

"You didn't look hurt the next day," I say, and I'm touching her cheek. She flinches under my touch but settles at a second.

"Bert had placed cold washcloths on my face that whole evening and night."

My gut twists painfully, and my heart starts to hammer. My brain tries to force thoughts I don't want, and I can't take much more of them. I grip Layla by the back of the neck and drag her face to mine. Her eyes widen as our noses touch. "I've dreamt of fucking you," I confess.

She tries to pull herself out of my hand, and I clamp down on her neck. "In the most delicious ways," I continue.

She pales further, and it isn't my desired effect. I just want to speak my truths that cover up other truths. I inhale her openly, not shying away from how I must appear.

She whimpers, and the hairs rise on the back of my neck.

"I would never hurt you," I whisper against her lips. They shake before I press mine against hers. The kiss is soft, but my thoughts are disturbed. Fucking her is all I want, but I keep my hand on her neck to keep us rooted to the spot so I don't force her back onto the bed. So I don't take every single piece of Layla for myself.

Her mouth doesn't move under mine, not even when my teeth graze her lips or when my tongue prods against her mouth. After a few torturous moments, she turns her head away from me. Her breaths are fast and hard, and I'm staring at her pink cheeks. I press a hard kiss against her face before I release her.

She won't look at me, but I'm not leaving until she does.

I hold out the T-shirt. "You need to change."

She shakes her head. "No, thank you. I'll wait for my clothes."

"You can wait in my bedroom if you want."

Her head snaps up toward me, and I grin.

"I'd prefer to wait in the living room."

I give a sweeping gesture toward the door, and she scurries past me. Her long legs move fast, and I'm snagged on her scar again.

We enter the living room, and her clothes are folded on the chair. I didn't hear William enter. Layla doesn't miss a beat but starts to drag on her trousers, then her socks. Her shirt is in the trunk of my car. I walk to her and reach around. She freezes as I place my T-shirt on the arm of the chair.

"I'll give you a moment," I say, and I don't turn away as she shrugs out of the jacket. Her skin is flawless, her back begging to be touched. I can imagine running my hand down her spine, making her bend over. My cock grows quickly, and I turn away from her.

"Thank you." Her voice has me turning around.

My T-shirt falls down to her knees, the material swallowing her up. My jacket hangs across the arm of the chair. Layla pulls on her boots, which can't be dry. "I'm ready to go."

"I'm not ready to let you go."

She tilts her head. "Please, Jay."

CHAPTER FOURTEEN

LAYLA

AIR IS RARER THAN gold dust right now. I'm struggling to find enough to satisfy my lungs as Jared towers over me. He's larger than life. He's angrier than a storm. He has a savage beauty about him that makes being in his presence hard to bear.

Jared steps back to the chair and gathers up his jacket. I'm frozen to the spot as he returns, and with such a tenderness that sings to the most humane part of me, he drapes the coat over my shoulders, and my pain wants to howl his name.

"Let's go." His words are hollow, and the echo of them has my pain burning up faster than dry paper. I follow him quickly out of the mansion. Taking snapshots in my mind of the architecture that under normal circumstances I would admire, my mind reels. I can't believe this is where he lives. It appears that Jared has everything. Appearances can be and are deceiving, though. I've never seen another human so empty at times.

I shiver and wrap my arms around my waist as I follow Jared into the garage. He unlocks the car and slides into the driver's seat. When he looks up at me, my heart thumps. Walking around the car makes me aware of how I'm holding myself, how I'm walking, as his gaze soaks in everything about me. I get in and focus on buckling the belt.

The car hums under us as Jared reverses out of the garage. He's gone silent, and I don't want his silence right now. His confession about thinking about fucking me threw me for a loop. I have no idea how to feel or what to make of his honesty. Falling in love with Jared wouldn't be good for my heart. Falling in love with Jay would be so easy but so dangerous. I don't think the damage would be just my heart, but my mind, my body, even my soul. My traitorous heart thumps away in my chest as I replay his words.

We pull up to campus, and now I'm the one who's not ready to go. I'm confused, and some part of me wants Jared for a moment so we can figure this out. Jared would be levelheaded about this. Jay is too unpredictable.

"Jared…" I start the moment the car stops. He isn't facing me, but the words get lost as a shadow looms over the passenger side before moving away.

Jared rolls down his window as Chester approaches his door.

"Hey, bro." Chester gives me a fleeting glance.

"What's going on?"

Jared nods before hitting Chester's outstretched hands—first a slap, then a back slap, then bumping fists. "Nothing much. What are you doing here?"

This time, Chester looks at me while raising his head. "What's up?"

My mind falters. *What's up?* My mouth is dry as I force myself not to get up and run. I just nod back.

"I was looking for you." Chester grins at Jared.

Is Jared in some kind of trouble? I crumble internally.

"You could have called me." Jared's fingers dance across the doorframe as he speaks.

"I did, brother. I got no answer," Chester says, his glance flickering to me again.

Another car pulls into the parking lot, and I can't make out the driver. Only their profile as the daylight is starting to fade.

Unbuckling my belt slowly, I try to be quiet so I don't draw attention to myself until I'm ready to leave. "I'd better go." I finally look at Jared to find him studying me.

"I'll drop you home."

Chester is taking us in, and shivers snake across my skin. I rub the back of my neck. "I'm good." I need to leave.

My heart palpitates.

"Go get your bag. I said I'll drop you home." Jared leans forward, his hands clasped together, his gaze intense.

"Jay, my car is right there. There is no need." He's being overbearing right now, and with Chester watching me too, I just want to get away from them.

"I'll wait here until you're in your car."

I glare at Jared. "What, you think someone might kidnap me?" I snap at how ridiculous he's being.

His lips twitch, but they don't form into a full smile. He brushes dark locks off his forehead.

"Nice seeing you, Layla." Chester's voice has my shoulders curling in, and I don't look back as I make my way to my car.

My nerves are shot, and I have no idea how I feel about everything that just transpired. From being dumped in the lake, to his crude words about fucking me, all the way to that kiss.

When we were younger, Jared held my hand as we walked to the shops or to go to his hangout spot with the guys. I never thought anything of his nearness to me, but now that we're older, it feels so much different. The moment I slide into the car, I scoop out my phone and see four missed calls from Evelyn. I don't look over to where Jared's car had been parked. My pulse spikes as I imagine him walking toward me, ready to force me back into his car. I hit the locks on the doors.

This is Jared, I remind myself. So why am I having such a hard time with my feelings toward him? My mind seems to race at a million miles an hour. How can anyone evoke so many different emotions in someone?

The ding of my phone niggles at my nerves. I click the yellow open icon, and my body stills. It's a text from Jared.

Why are you sitting in your car?

I glance around me. He's leaning against his car with his hands deep in his pockets. His eyes clash with mine, and I shiver. The chill has nothing to do with the weather. He doesn't move a muscle.

My fingers move quickly over my phone. **I'm thinking** I type quickly before looking at him in the rearview mirror. He has his phone out and is typing.

About what? His response is one I expect. My answer and decision are already made. I was weak then, but I am strong now.

You. I watch Jared as I hit send. His brows drag down, and he glances up at me from under thick, dark lashes. Stuffing his phone into his pocket, he pushes off the hood of his car and starts walking toward mine.

I peel my hands off the steering wheel and unlock the passenger door to let him in.

The smell of his cologne immediately fills the small space. He shifts, taking his phone out and setting the slick black device on the dash before twisting his body so he can face me.

"Talk to me."

I chew my lip, trying to think of the best way to phrase this.

"Don't think. You always overthink everything. Just talk." The command from Jared startles me. I can't read any expression on his face, but I'm familiar with his tone. He's worried.

"You haven't said anything about Nelson." It's my turn to be perturbed. I wasn't exactly sure where that came from, but that's what pops out of my mouth.

Jared glances away, his hand going to his phone. He picks it up and taps the device on his knee as he speaks. "What's there to say? He's dead."

My shoulders tense. This isn't the Jared I remember. Jared, who stood up to the bullies and the monsters. Jared, who took on the world with his ten-year-old fists. Jared, who protected all of us, including Nelson.

I swallow the emotion that swells inside me. "You could say how you feel about it, maybe."

He works his jaw, his focus out the window. "How do you feel about it, Layla?" he asks while glancing at me.

"Upset, of course."

Jared's gaze is hooded, and I'm not sure what he's thinking. A knock on the window drags a startled cry from me. He rolls down the window to Chester.

"Didn't mean to frighten you," Chester says, his words heavy with so much more. Jared continues to tap his phone on his knee.

"That's okay," I manage to get out between dry lips.

"Just give me a minute," Jared says, and Chester nods at him before standing up and out of my view.

"No problem, bro," Chester responds as Jared rolls up the window.

My brows rise as Jared turns to me. I have so many questions to ask him, especially about Chester. But now isn't the time.

Rubbing his hands on his jeans before scratching his jaw, he faces me once again. "When can I meet Evelyn and Carl?"

Coldness seeps into my skin before a blast of heat burns my blood. I look away this time, my hands going to the steering wheel. "I... I don't know." I glance at him.

He sits stiffly. Can he hear the rest of that statement? The part where I haven't told them about finding him. Also, if this were Jared, I would have him at our dinner table, but Jay? That's the part I'm not sure about.

Jared scratches his jaw again, where a shadow of new growth is forming. I didn't notice it before. "I've got to go. But I'll text later."

I'm nodding when the smell of his cologne intensifies as he leans in and kisses me softly on the cheek. Our gazes collide when he leans away, but neither of us says anything.

"I've got to go," he repeats.

"Yeah," I say as he climbs out of my car. Once the door closes, my whole body sags.

***

After pulling into the drive, I sit in my car for a few moments. I'm not sure what's eating at me more—the fact that I lied to Evelyn and Carl about Jared, or that I haven't told Jared the truth about not telling them about him. Or maybe the fact that Jared pushed me into a lake. Or that he has looked at me with hate more times than I can count.

Carl comes out of the house as I close the car door. I clutch my bag tightly.

"Is everything okay?" I ask as Carl nears.

He smiles faintly. "Yeah, I just have to go to work. Are you okay?"

My pulse picks up. "Yeah, just tired."

Carl doesn't say anything, but his eyes narrow slightly. "Evelyn is inside if you need to talk." He squeezes my shoulder while his thick brows rise. "But work can wait if you need me?"

His words cause a heaviness in my chest. Lying to them is wrong. They've taken me into their home and have always maintained an open relationship with me. I've never been dishonest with them before.

"No. Thanks, Carl. Honestly, nothing's wrong. I'm just tired." After another squeeze of my shoulder and a promise that I can call him if I change my mind, I go inside with my head hanging. I feel like such a terrible person. After dumping my bag in the hall, I enter the kitchen, having decided to tell Evelyn the truth. She has her back to me as she shuffles potatoes on the baking tray. The smell would typically cause my mouth to water, but not now. The warmth of the kitchen has me stripping off Jared's jacket. I pause as I place it on the back of the chair. I'd forgotten about his clothes. Evelyn glances over at me quickly while pushing the tray back into the oven.

"Oh, you're just in time. It's nearly ready," Evelyn says while closing the door. Her long silver sweater and tan leggings fit her perfectly. She really is a beautiful-looking woman. Pushing her glasses up into her hair, she fully faces me. Her brows pull down, and she gives me nearly the identical look that Carl gave me.

"Is there something bothering you?" She picks up a cloth while moving around the island to sit beside me. I join my hands together and rest them on the table to stop myself from fidgeting. The need to touch my face or neck has me considering sitting on my hands. The heat coming from the oven is starting to make the room uncomfortable. Evelyn glances at my hands. Immediately, I loosen my grip.

"Is that a man's T-shirt you're wearing?" More worry worms its way into Evelyn's eyes.

"I found Jared." It comes out in one rushed breath.

Evelyn sits back slightly in her chair. Others might not have noticed it—the movement is that slight. But I've spent a lot of time being counseled by Evelyn, and this tells me she's shocked but is processing the knowledge. When I spoke about Bert and all he made me suffer, she would listen and talk me through my feelings. Most of the time, it frustrated the crap out of me. I just wanted to tell my story, not zone in on feelings. In my head, I thought Evelyn was stupid. How could she not know I was angry and hurt?

But as I put my emotions under the microscope, I began to see something different. My feelings of anger were directed at myself for allowing Bert to catch me off guard. Or for not speaking up when he asked a question. That's when I started paying closer attention to my emotions. When I could tell Evelyn what I was feeling, she would always tap her notepad or folder with two fingers. I didn't think she knew what she was doing at the time. It was her 'tell' that let me know she was proud. At times when I spoke of Ronnie, Evelyn would sit back ever so slightly. She would listen, and it would take her a few moments to respond. She was gathering her thoughts, just like she is now.

"You must have been relieved."

That isn't the response I expected. I nod. "I was shocked." I let out a small breath along with a shaky smile, allowing myself to really feel the happiness of finding Jared alive.

Evelyn smiles faintly. "I can only imagine. You must have been overwhelmed."

"I'm still processing it," I tell Evelyn.

Tapping the table with two fingers briefly, she smiles. "I'm happy for you, Layla."

I loosen the grip on my hands, and a smile takes over my face. "Thanks, Evelyn. I... He's... different now. But still the same. You know?" I chew my lip, hoping what I'm saying makes sense. How could it? She didn't know him then. She doesn't even know him now.

"It's been seven years. That's a long time. I'm sure he's feeling the same about you as you are about him."

My face burns. I don't think Evelyn would be happy to know how Jared feels about me now. I'm honestly not sure what Jared feels when he sees me. A reminder of a past he'd rather forget?

Evelyn wipes the table with the cloth; I can tell she's choosing her next words carefully.

"I'm happy you found him, but Jared is from your past. One that gave you a lot of heartache. I just worry that his reappearing will bring your past back up. You've come such a long way, Layla. I would hate to think anything would set you back."

I react like a goldfish: my mouth repeatedly opens and closes. I have so much I want to say to that. Evelyn's hands cover mine now.

"I'm underestimating you. I know what he meant to you. How he basically kept you alive. I'm not going to lie. I worry about you." Evelyn brushes my hair back from my forehead—a motherly gesture that always causes a pang in my chest, though I've never told her that. She pauses, looking me in the eye, a smile on her face. "I will always worry about you."

"Thank you," I say, feeling lighter, but so tired. A final pat to my hand and Evelyn gets up.

"I better take out the potatoes and chicken, or we won't have anything to eat."

I watch Evelyn move around the kitchen. She isn't moving as freely as she usually does, but I don't expect her to take this news with smiles and hugs. I knew it would be a struggle for all of us. My phone dings, and I slip the device out of my bag.

You will have lunch with me tomorrow.

My pulse starts to pick up as I stare at the message. Time passes, though I'm not sure how long. I just now notice the piping hot plate of food in front of me and that Evelyn sits across from me.

"Is it Kieran?" The hope in her voice shatters my guilt-free ride. I lied about Kieran too. Something says I shouldn't tell her yet. Telling her about Jared is enough; I'll deal with Kieran another time.

"It's Jared." It feels nice to be honest again. Lying is way too much work.

Evelyn leans back in her chair slightly. I don't rush her but let her fight whatever internal debate she's clearly having. The pause feels like it goes on forever.

"You never told me where you found him." If my guilt-free ride shattered earlier, it's squashed into oblivion now.

Don't lie, Layla. Just tell the truth and face the consequences.

"Kingscourt College. He goes there also." I chew my lip.

Please don't ask for a timeline.

I don't want to let Evelyn down. She's been so good to me. I pray for this one small detail to be overlooked, and guess what?

It is.

CHAPTER FIFTEEN

LAYLA

I LIE IN BED that night, staring at the ceiling. Carl comes home from work, and I wring my hands as I listen to his and Evelyn's hushed voices. Carl's is raised slightly, but I still can't understand what he's saying. A part of me wants to leave my cozy double bed and try to listen in on their conversation, but the sensible and tired part of me keeps me in bed. Their discussion lulls for a while, and I start to drift off. The ping of my phone has me pushing the lavender duvet off me as I reach for it on the side table.

Don't make me come looking for you.

That one sentence from Jared plays havoc with my emotions. I want to pause them and place them under the microscope like Evelyn had taught me, but I'm drained. Instead, I text back quickly, not doubting his threat.

I'll have lunch with you tomorrow. I hit send before I can think any more about him. I don't even get the phone put back down when it pings again.

That was a given. See you tomorrow, Layla.

I stare at his message. Footsteps on the stairs have me putting the phone down and pulling the duvet up to my neck. I don't want to have a conversation with Carl about Jared. My door opens slightly, and I release the death grip I have on the quilt. I can picture Carl raised up on his toes, trying to see me under the mountains of blankets. My breathing sounds so heavy and fast, and I try to even it out.

"Night, Layla." Carl's words have me crashing and burning.

"Night, Carl," I whisper back, unable to keep up the pretense. As he turns on my bedroom light, the harsh brightness burns my eyes, and I close them tightly.

"I thought you were asleep."

Okay, so we're doing this now. "Not yet." I sit up and rub my eyes.

The heaviness of his gaze and the dark circles indicate just how tired he is. "So you found Jared?"

I nod, stopping myself from clutching the blanket.

"When can we meet him?"

That, I didn't expect. "Meet him?" I say back, not sure how I feel about this.

"Yes. As in, he comes over for dinner, and we all chat." Carl smiles now while squeezing my knee through the quilt.

"Yeah, we can do that. I'll ask him."

Carl jerks his head while standing. "Great." He seems really happy. When he flips off my light, I flop back down into my pillows.

"Good night, Layla," Carl says before closing the door.

"Night, Carl," I respond, even as my mind reels. They want to meet Jared. They don't want to meet Jay, but Jared. I need him to be Jared when he comes here. Jared *is* Jay. He's just different. I toss and turn until I try to settle my mind with memories.

The grass brushes my shoulders. The daisies give life to the greenery spring-ing up and overtaking an area. Walking with my arms stretched out, I let my fingers thread through the grass. The earth dips beneath me when we're close to our destination.

"Why did she have to come? She always slows us down."

I roll my eyes at Ray's stupid words. Jared always takes me with him, even though the other boys complain. He's bigger and stronger than they are, so I'm allowed to come.

"Shut it unless you want me to knock out your teeth," Jared threatens. Nelson and Rocky snigger. The grass falls away, and a barbed-wire fence with a forest beyond comes into view. The forest is our destination. It's where we spend most of our days playing warfare. I don't do much; I stay by the tree and attend to any wounds that the boys get.

"You could make him hold the wire for ten seconds," Nelson says, his grin huge across his face. He's originally from Kenya. His dark skin is something I haven't seen much of, so he always fascinates me.

"Twenty seconds," Rocky says, and Ray holds his hands up, taking a step away from the boys.

"I said I was sorry." I usually don't feel sorry for Ray. He's always moaning about me coming along, but the boys teasing him isn't nice. And we all know the fence is electrified to keep the cattle in the field that we stand in now.

"You sound like a bunch of girls." I step out of the grass, and all heads turn my way. Jared is holding a stick as tall as himself. A grin spreads across his face at my words.

"Layla's right. You do sound like a bunch of girls," Jared declares.

Nelson tuts while he moves closer to the fence that's now within reaching distance. "I'll touch the fence."

"No, you won't." Ray smirks now, the brazenness returning to his stance. His short beige cut-offs showcase his stick-thin legs, which are coated in bruises. I've heard that Mrs. April is mean with her wooden spoon.

"Yes, I will." Nelson doesn't sound so sure anymore. I can see sweat starting to appear on his forehead.

"Oh, for Pete's sake. Jared, tell them to stop." Someone is going to get hurt. Everyone listens to Jared, so he should stop this. His grin grows as he leans with both hands on his stick.

"I'm not their daddy, and if they want to touch the fence, I can't stop them."

I narrow my eyes at Jared, and he laughs, the sound echoing across the fence and into the forest.

Now all I want is for someone to touch the fence so we can stop standing around like a bunch of ninnies.

"I knew you didn't have the stomach," Ray says, as he starts to walk away from us, and I'm glad to follow. I haven't taken a step when Nelson grabs the fence. I scream as his body shakes violently. Ray and Rocky race to him, but no one touches him as he continues to be electrified. Jared drops to the ground as we all stand stunned, watching Nelson.

Will he die?

One thing I've learned is to not touch someone in this situation, because the electricity will pass into your own body and the pain is worse. Jared unlaces his shoes and stands with them on his hands. He's reaching out toward Nelson when Nelson stops shaking, and an odd sound comes from him. I'm ready to puke.

Laughter? Nelson is laughing wildly as he turns to us. "I got you all." I slowly sink into the grass. He was only pretending.

"I knew that," Ray says, but everyone looks a little pale. Jared drops his shoes and punches Nelson in the arm, cutting off his laughter.

"That wasn't funny." Now he points at me. "You scared Layla half to death."

I want to protest and state that everyone was pretty scared, but I know it's pointless. They would all deny it. I stay seated as everyone looks around, pretending to scout for... what? Cows? Jared laces up his battered shoes close to me. The strain on his laces makes me believe they'll snap at any moment. But they don't. Jared glances at me through his long, thick hair.

"You okay?" He reties his hair while waiting for me to answer.

I nod and stand, smoothing down my yellow butterfly dress. It's my favorite. Jared said it's the same color as my hair. The dress is bright yellow, nothing close to my hair, but I thanked him and agreed.

"We're moving out." Jared's command has us all falling in line behind him. I'm directly behind him; he wouldn't have it any other way. No matter where we are, he's always protecting me.

Behind me, Nelson still mocks Ray and Rocky about believing his little trick. "Even Jared knew it was a joke."

I roll my eyes at Jared's back. Jared's their leader, so obviously, he knows when they're joking. The bleeping has me glancing down at my cracked watch that's never worked. I stop walking, bringing the watch closer to my ear. The beeping grows louder. Looking up, Jared is still walking.

"Layla." I squint and see brown eyes, caramel skin, and a recognizable female voice.

"Layla," Evelyn says louder while turning off my alarm.

"I'm up," I say groggily, pushing the blankets back and letting my feet touch the wooden floor. The smell of the forest still lingers in the air. That felt so real. I haven't thought about that day in such a long time. I don't have to ask why I'm dredging up old memories. I know why. Between Nelson's death and Jared's reappearance, old memories are bound to resurface. Even the good ones. That was a good day, even if I didn't know it at the time.

Light streams in as Evelyn pulls back the curtains. "Carl told me he spoke to you last night." I don't have to see Evelyn to know she's smiling; her voice carries the happiness around my room.

"Yeah, he wants to meet Jared," I say, still shaking off the memory of my dream. Evelyn appears in front of me, holding my washing to her chest. "Are you okay, sweetheart?" Her brows pull down with concern.

My toes wiggle against the wooden floor as I shake off the final threads of the memory. "Yeah, just weird dreams. I'm excited and nervous for you guys to meet him."

Evelyn smiles, the crinkles growing around her dark eyes. "Don't be nervous. We promise not to embarrass you."

"I'm not worried about you, Evelyn," I say, smiling.

A small laugh erupts from Evelyn's mouth. "I'll keep Carl in order. Don't worry. Now, come eat breakfast so you're not late for class."

Class. I almost forgot. Evelyn leaves, and I get dressed in a red shirt and black trousers. After braiding my blonde hair over one shoulder, I wash and make my way downstairs. Evelyn has my breakfast ready. I grab a slice of toast off the table while picking up my bag, keys, and Jared's jacket.

"Are you not sitting?" Evelyn's disapproval of eating on the go fills her words.

I kiss her quickly on the cheek. "I'm late, so just this once." I smile while she wipes crumbs off her cheek from where I kissed her.

She calls goodbye as I leave for class.

***

I end up making it just in time. Ashley is waiting for me near the main doors. The moment her gaze settles on me, she unfolds her arms and walks across the hallway to meet me.

"Are you okay? I heard that Jay dragged you into his car. I mean, Sam said he was terrifying." Ashley's head jerks as she speaks.

"I'm okay." I shrug.

. "It's fine. He just wanted to talk," I say.

Ashley looks concerned, and the more I look at her, I notice the dark circles that pull the normal brightness from her eyes. She grips a ballpoint pen and clicks the top down. The click seems loud between us, and she does it again.

"We had some unfinished business to discuss. I'm fine," I reassure her and hate how she still looks at me. "Is everything okay with you, Ashley?" I focus on her thumb that keeps pushing down on the pen top before glancing up at her briefly.

She gives me a tired smile while tilting her head to the side. "Nicco was up a lot last night. He was sleeping when I left this morning. I wanted to climb into his crib and cuddle up beside him."

A small laugh bursts from me, picturing her with her son. "Do you have a picture of him?"

Ashley's eyes light up as she bounces before shifting her notepads to one arm so she can pull her phone out of her pocket. Her fingers move across the screen, and she turns the phone to me. She slides a small image of the cutest baby I've ever seen up on the screen. My heart melts.

"Oh, Ashley, he's so adorable. I want to hug him," I tell her.

Her smile widens. "I know. He brings me so much joy."

He's a miniature version of her. With big brown eyes and a wide smile, his face looks so animated. The little red pajamas cover his tiny but pudgy body.

"But he also wants a lot of attention—sometimes too much." Her smile grows tired as she takes her phone back and pushes it into her pocket.

"If you're ever looking for a babysitter, I'm available." My cheeks heat as I say it. It's stupid; she doesn't know me, and she would hardly trust me with her little baby. "I mean, if you're stuck. Don't feel obliged." I shrug, making a mess of the conversation.

Ashley lowers her gaze. Oh god, she doesn't know how to say no. Heat starts to flow all over my face now.

"That would be great," Ashley says.

My eyes widen with surprise.

"How about tonight?" Ashley is squinting briefly. "Only if that suits. I hate to take you up on your offer so suddenly, but I actually would love a night out, and it so happens I was invited to a party."

"Yes, perfect."

"I'll give you my address later. Is eight okay?" she asks.

"Yep. That's great." I swallow now, a little nervous as I head to class. I've babysat kids before, but it's been a while. A long while.

I settle into my seat and sigh. I don't want the class to end, as it's closing in on lunchtime. I haven't seen Jared, but his promise that we were having lunch together makes my stomach squirm way too much and for lots of different reasons.

***

When I leave class, a shadow looms beside me. I know it's him. I don't even need to look to know.

It's Jared.

The smell of his cologne circles me and crushes my chest until I stop walking. He does too, and I take my first look at him.

My nerves jump and flail. All I see is Jay, who's god-like and angry and waiting for me to say something. I try to find Jared in his eyes so I can calm my frazzled heart.

"Do you remember the electric fence?" My words aren't what I wanted to say, but I don't stop the flow of babble. "The day Nelson pretended to be electrified?"

Jared folds his large arms across his chest. The gray sweater stretches with the movement. The shadow of anger grows, and I can't hold his stare. "What about it?"

I swallow a lump. "Did you really know he was joking?" Why did this matter to me?

Jared unfolds his arms. His gaze dances across my face, and each touch latches on to some fragile part of my being and gives it comfort. "No."

Surprise lifts my lips. "Really?" My question comes out in half a laugh.

One dimple appears on Jared's cheek. "He scared me that day." Jared takes a step closer.

I swallow and focus on his dimple. I want to touch it.

"But I was the leader, so I couldn't show fear. I had to know everything."

"You hid it well." I speak to his chest as the air grows heavy between us.

"You hide things well too."

The wrath in his gaze has me stumbling back into the wall; the sounds of the hallway and people come crashing back. Everyone who passes us stares openly.

Jared steps back, his features becoming indifferent. "It's time for lunch, so I'm here to join you."

One full hour with Jared. I have no idea how I'm going to survive this.

CHAPTER SIXTEEN

JARED

SHE'S NERVOUS. HER GAZE keeps darting around as we walk to my car.

"I have class after lunch, so I can't go anywhere with you," she states as we pass the picnic bench that she sat on with Lucas.

I haven't seen him at school today and wonder if she warned him. My hands ball into fists in my jacket pockets, and I remove them. The action has Layla looking up at me. The red shirt she wears hugs her small waist. Red is the best color on her. I don't reply as I click the car open.

She doesn't look happy as she climbs in. "I have your jacket in my car."

I close the door and love how close we are. I turn to Layla, gripping the steering wheel with one hand. She fidgets with her hands in her lap. "You can keep it."

Her lips appear swollen, and I love when she bites on the lower one. She shakes her head and faces the window, her profile toward me. Her swanlike neck would fit in one of my hands. I can imagine bending it to my will, bending her, fucking her. My fingers twitch like a pencil might materialize between them. I want to draw her right now.

"Evelyn and Carl want to meet you." She continues facing the window.

Her blouse gaps slightly from the side, and I can see the top swell of her breast. How the fuck does her skin look so good? I still have the top she left in the trunk of my car. She isn't getting it back. It now resides in my bedside table.

"Do they?" I ask offhandedly.

She frowns as she faces me. "You want to meet them?" It's half a question, half a statement.

"So you told them about me?"

Her chest rises. I've hit a nerve with Layla. "They know everything about you."

I sneer. "I fucking doubt that."

Her frown deepens. "I spoke about you. You know, when Evelyn first found me." She picks at her nails as she speaks. "I mean..." Her face scrunches up. "You were gone, and I never knew..." Her eyes water, and all I want to do is drag her into my arms and hold her against my chest until the air stops filtering into her lungs.

"Never knew what?"

Her gaze dances around the car before landing back on me. "What happened to you."

"How would you, Layla?" I shift so I'm closer to her. She doesn't move. "You left and never returned." My mouth dries up as memories from that day start to seep into my system. It takes away any warmth and leaves bitterness behind.

"How could I come back?" Her breathing grows heavy. "I barely made it out alive."

The silence grows restless and I give in. "What time shall I come by your house?"

"You're not." She nods several times like she's made a decision. "I can't be around you when you're like this. I've tried. But..." She shakes her head several times. "I just can't."

Laughter licks my lips. "Well, I'm sorry to bust your fucking bubble, but you will be around me."

"Jared... Jay..." she tries, but I cut off the pleading in her voice as I move closer. "What are you doing?" Her gaze flickers to my lips.

"You want me to kiss you?" I tease.

She huffs, but I see the want in her eyes. "No," she lies.

I want a kiss, but I'm looking at my Layla, and when I'm this close to her, it's hard to believe that she's deceiving me. I reach out and she flinches. "I'd never hurt you."

She swallows. "I know, Jared." She deliberately drags out my name.

I nod. "What time should I come by your house?" I ask, softer this time.

"I'll find out what day suits them." She doesn't sound so sure.

"Don't keep me waiting."

"I'll send you the address." She tries to reach for her phone but stops when I touch her cheek, which is hot under my fingertips.

"I already know where you live. Let's get a coffee."

"I'm not leaving the school grounds."

"Neither am I." I grin and lean away from her, hating the loss immediately. I get out of the car, and Layla follows as we make our way back to the school.

"How do you know where I live?" she asks.

I spot the girl who she called Ashley lingering along the wall. She gawks at us, but Layla seems oblivious to everyone, even me. Her head is down as she walks, and I want to reach out and take her hand. She should walk with her head held high. She's worth a thousand Ashleys. I bury my hands in my jacket pockets as we walk toward the school. I open the door and let Layla go in first. "I know lots of things."

She doesn't step through immediately. "Like my phone number."

I grin. "Like your phone number."

She huffs and steps inside the school. Her nose scrunches up, and I want to kiss it, but everyone is fucking watching us—until they meet my eye and look away. Alex isn't here today, and it's working to my advantage. I can walk freely with Layla without any consequences for one day.

Layla waits outside the cafeteria. I have to issue a warning to her not to leave. When I return with two coffees, she's still standing where I left her.

I hand her a coffee, and she takes it with a ghost of a smile on her lips. We walk and it's not aimless. I'm leading her toward the library, where we won't have everyone watching us. Once again, I notice how oblivious she is to all the stares and hushed voices. She sips the coffee while peeking up at me like I might not notice.

It's cute.

I open the library door, and she steps inside. I have to stop right behind her as she pauses. As I dip my head, I inhale the scent of her hair. "What's wrong?" I whisper into her ear. Her head tilts toward my voice.

"The library?"

"It's nice and quiet." I step around her and start to walk toward the back. She's looking around her as we walk. This time she's aware of her surroundings, but luckily, only a handful of students are here. The deeper we go, the slower her footfalls become.

I spin and walk slowly backward. "I'm not going to murder you." I open my arms as far as the bookshelves on either side of me will allow.

Her mouth twitches before forming a smile that stalls my steps, and I'm moving back toward her, allowing my fingers to trail along the spine of the books. "I mean, in a library. It's too cliché."

She nods before taking a sip of her coffee. "A lake would be more appropriate." She slips under my arm, and I'm following her with a stupid fucking grin on my face.

"I wouldn't have let you drown," I counteract.

She fires a glare across her shoulder.

"I like when you're mad. I've never seen this side of you." I'm tempted to reach her and spin her around.

She tucks her hair behind her ear and sips from her coffee.

"Tell me about Evelyn and Carl."

We walk past more bookshelves as we near the back of the room.

"They're amazing." Her smile cracks the last of my anger. "I have a curfew." She's still beaming. "They're delighted when I break it." A soft laugh tumbles from her mouth. "They just want me to be happy, Jared." She stops walking and faces me. She picks idly at the lid of her coffee. "I want them to be happy too."

"Why wouldn't they be happy?" I place my cup on the edge of one of the shelves. A row of tax books is there to rest my hand against.

"They love me."

I love you.

"I can't have them upset," she finishes.

I push away from the shelf and step closer. The bookshelves don't allow her to go anywhere. "You think I'd upset them?"

Her mouth moves, but no words come out as my gaze glides to her lips. "Yes," she whispers.

"Why's that?" I touch her neck, and her eyes flutter closed at the contact.

"Jared." My name sounds like a plea.

I put pressure on her neck, and her eyes snap open. "Why's that?" I repeat.

She shuffles back, but there's nowhere to go. "They're very protective."

My gut twists. I let my fingers trail down her neck. "I'm very protective too. Or have you forgotten?" I whisper into her ear.

"I'd never forget you." Her voice shakes.

My cock hardens. Words I've always wanted to hear just spilled from her mouth. A mouth I capture with my own. Her warm, moist lips have my control slipping further, and when Layla kisses me back, every ounce of hate or anger I've been holding on to vanishes, and all I want is her. All I truly want is her.

I tilt her head so I have more access to her pretty lips. My tongue sinks into her mouth, and I taste coffee and lust on her tongue. I push my body against her, and she groans. Her face fills both my hands as I grip her, wanting to control each movement so I have complete access to her mouth. I want to savor every single second with Layla.

"Jared." Her voice is breathless as I give her lips a break and kiss her jawline.

"When I fuck you, it's going to be painfully slow."

Her hands reach up and grip my arms as I continue to hold her face. Her pulse pounds along her neck, and I press a kiss to her frantic heartbeat.

"I've waited too long." I look her in the eyes. "I want to explore every part of you. My mouth will touch every single inch of your skin."

She inhales sharply, and if I don't step away now, I'm not going to be able to stop myself.

I don't step away. "I want to taste you, Layla."

Her eyes widen, yet she doesn't run. She's staring up at me, and I've never wanted to defile someone so much. "Would you like that?"

"Ms. Masters, Mr. McGivney. Fornicating in the library is against school policy."

The brightness seeps from Layla's eyes, and fear takes over.

I'm spinning, blocking her from Coach. I want to plow his fucking face in for frightening her.

I grin and nod. "Teachers fucking students is definitely against school policy, too."

His face reddens with a temper as he steps toward me. "How dare you."

I meet his steps. "Lucy—is that your latest victim? You sound like a right pedophile to me."

His mouth opens, and a vein bulges along his neck.

"Is that why you're creeping around the library? Watching young girls? Your wife would be appalled."

He grits his teeth, but I know when I have someone by the balls. "Maybe I should tell her."

"Jared." Layla's voice is low, but I curse her internally for calling me by that name.

Coach doesn't even seem to notice; he appears ready to throw up. He just better not fucking do it near me. "Now listen, you fucking donkey. You breathe one word, and I'll let everyone know what a creep you are."

He doesn't say anything but scrambles away.

"Jesus, Jared."

I reach back for Layla's hand to give her comfort as I make sure Coach is gone, but her fingers are yanked from my hand, making me face her.

"You can't..." She shakes her head. "You can't talk to a teacher like that." She frowns. "Or me." Her words are an afterthought. "I'm going to be late."

She's ready to dart past me, but I stop her. My hand circles her wrist. "Monday, we're having lunch together again." My gut tightens.

Layla doesn't rush off. "Fine, I'll be there."

"Okay." I release her, not happy that a whole weekend separates us.

She's still staring up at me.

"Go before you're late."

She nods and quickly leaves. I watch her until she disappears around the bookshelves and out of sight. It causes such instant emptiness that it shocks me into moving.

Like I could even run away from the void.

CHAPTER SEVENTEEN

LAYLA

I'M IN A DAZE as I leave the library. Everything in me burns. The cold air outside doesn't do much to cool me down. I should be in class, but after that kiss... My tongue flicks out, and I lick my lips. As I make my way to my car, I tug my bag up on my shoulder. I need to text Jared and tell him he can't meet Evelyn or Carl. I can't do this. I need time to think. His words about kissing every inch of my skin have me walking faster. I hate how badly I want him.

I get into my car and don't look around as I leave the parking lot. I blare a classical music station to get my mind off Jared, but forgetting him is like forgetting to breathe. My mind would burn as violently as my lungs would, and it would fill with Jared just as my lungs would fill themselves with air.

My breath grows frantic, and I have no idea what's happening to me. My vision dims, and I pull in off the road.

"Let it out." I speak out loud to give myself permission to cry. No tears come, and my laughter is angry and bitter. I lean against the headrest and take in my surroundings. A small grocery store is what I've pulled up outside of. I didn't eat lunch with Jared. I'm not hungry, but I know I should eat something. Since my body wouldn't allow me to cry, I grip my bag and make my way into the grocery store.

The overhead music is soft, and the air conditioner is on full blast. My light blouse doesn't take the bite out of the air that brushes my skin, but I welcome the cold as it steals some of the heat.

I'm roaming aimlessly down the aisle when someone walks toward me a little too closely. I look up, and the moment I see Kieran, he smiles. He steps into my personal space and gives me one of those half hugs with one arm. It's seriously awkward on my part. He doesn't seem to notice.

His blond hair is pushed back out of his face. The Aran beige sweater looks way too heavy for the warm weather we're having today. Along with dark brown trousers and heavy boots, he looks ready for a fishing boat.

"Fancy meeting you here." He speaks with laughter, his eyes baby blue and bright. I feel like I'm caught up in a whirlwind, or maybe it's like I've just walked out of one. A tornado would be more fitting.

"Yeah."

He nudges my arm. "Still the talker, I see."

I smile at his stupid words and grin. "Yeah, a real chatterbox."

Surprise lights up his face, and he laughs. "So, how have you been? Any more parties?" He folds his arms and dips his head, waiting for my answer. I would have stuffed my hands into my pockets if I had any. Instead, I let them hang on either side of me so I'm aware of them. I shrug. "Yeah, great. Just school, no more parties. I'm actually babysitting tonight." *God, why did I tell him that?* He's a stranger, after all.

He nods. "Let me check my calendar." Kieran pauses while staring briefly at the ceiling, confusing me until he looks back at me with a smile. "Nope, it's all clear. I can babysit with you."

Heat blazes across my face. "Kieran, I'm not trying to be rude, but I wasn't inviting you."

He clutches his chest. "What a way to shoot a guy down."

I'm shaking my head like a crazy person. "No, no. It's just I can't invite you to someone else's house." Mortification is burning a permanent red mark into my skin.

"So you would go on a date with me?"

This conversation has taken a nosedive. Now I'm stuttering. "Hmm... I... I..."

"It's cool. Maybe another time," Kieran says, not looking at all fazed by my response.

I nod my head, and he nudges my arm again.

"Great seeing you, Layla." He steps around me and moves toward the fridge.

"Yeah, you too, Kieran."

What a strange day. I leave the shop, not buying anything, and climb into my car. I start the engine right away. Before backing up and leaving, I glance in my rearview mirror to make sure no cars are coming.

My phone rings, and I put it on speakerphone without looking at the caller ID.

"Hello."

"Hi, sweetheart. Just calling to let you know I won't be home. I got called into the hospital, and Carl has to work late again." Evelyn's words have me sinking back into the seat.

"I'm actually babysitting for someone," I say, hoping she doesn't ask where. Ashley sent me her address, and the area doesn't have the best rep. I don't want to worry Evelyn.

"Oh. For who?" Her voice raises a few bars. I have a social life all of a sudden. It surprises me too.

"Ashley, a friend from school." I flip the turn signal to make a left onto the road.

Evelyn seems happy that I'm getting out more and ends the conversation with "Okay, well, I'm headed out the door. But I'll call you later."

I say my goodbyes and hang up.

***

When I get home, Evelyn is gone. There's a buzz in my head while I shower. So much stuff flows around, and it's hard to concentrate on just one thing. I keep wanting to check my phone, keep waiting for Jared to text. I miss him. I think I'm starting to become immune to the chaos he causes to my emotions.

What is wrong with me?

I spend the time grabbing food and flicking through the TV channels before I have to leave for Ashley's.

The area in which Ashley lives is one you wouldn't walk through at night. I've never been there, but I have heard about it. But people can be vicious with words, and rumors are rumors for a reason. Yeah, maybe it isn't as bad as I think.

My black leggings still have that soft, fluffy feeling that I know will soon be gone. But right now, they make me feel warm and cozy. Throwing on an oversized army green sweater and slipping into my white tennis shoes, I run my fingers through my hair. I'm kind of lucky like that; my fingers are as effective as a brush.

On the way to Ashley's, my mind runs rampant with awful scenarios. The tang of blood makes me stop chewing my lip. Scenarios like being held at gunpoint to being beaten by some drug addict. I take a left; two large arched red brick walls sit on either side of me as I pass through the large black gates.

The entrance is very grand, but that's where the curb appeal stops. Rows and rows of trailers line the large site. Small patches of grass cut off by small fences or random items cut up the yard space. An old brown sofa with one missing cushion sits on the sidewalk. The grime and holes tell the story of its abandonment. I pull up to the trailer that has "7" on a small wooden sign out front. Turning off the car, I get out my phone and ring Ashley. Drumming my fingers on the steering wheel, I watch the trailer for any sign of movement as I wait for Ashley to answer. The phone rings out and goes straight to voicemail.

She said number seven. I could just take a chance and knock on the door. It's nearly dark, and no lamps light up the site, only small pockets of light from some of the other trailers' windows, just not Ashley's.

I squeal when my phone rings, and a shaky laugh leaves my mouth as I look at the caller ID.

"Hi, Ashley. I'm not sure if I'm in the right place, but I'm parked at the front of site number seven," I say while my heart calms down.

"Give me one second." I can hear the coos of a baby. "Oh, I see you."

The phone clicks off, and the door opens, letting light pour out. Ashley waves at me as she stands on the step with Nicco on her hip. Jumping out of the car, I throw my phone in my bag and lock the car doors as I head up to meet Ashley on the step. Ashley has the door open and wears a warm smile as she lets me in.

"You are a godsend," she tells me, but my attention is on Nicco.

Cute isn't the word. He's even more adorable in person than in his photos. Little hands reach out for me, and I look at Ashley first for permission. She hands over Nicco, and I wait for him to cry, but he doesn't. His large brown eyes examine my face while his chubby little fingers touch everything his eyes take in.

"You guys are bonding well. So, I'm going to get ready." Ashley smiles at me and closes the front door.

"No problem. Nicco and I will just hang out here." I speak in baby talk.

Ashley laughs. "You're a natural," she says while leaving the room.

I love children. They just carry such innocence and honesty that most adults don't. They are simple, and once you feed them and play with them, all's right with the world.

As Nicco plays with my hair, making cooing noises, I sit down on the sizable beige sofa that rests under the window. All the curtains are open, making me feel exposed. The trailer is a lot larger than I previously thought. This room serves as a kitchen and den area, with everything that a regular house would have. An arch leads into a hallway that Ashley went down. The TV now catches Nicco's attention, so I turn it up. A large bear roams through a real forest and Nicco laughs. His little white onesie leaves his chubby legs bare. I turn up the TV so we can hear what the bear is saying.

When Ashley comes back out, I'm shocked. "Wow, you look stunning."

She smiles, showcasing her snow-white teeth. With a killer skin-tight white dress and red heels, she looks ready for the catwalk. She's beautiful every day at college, but tonight, she'll turn a lot of heads. She doesn't look like a woman who's had a baby.

I get the rundown of what Nicco needs: just one more bottle before bed, which will be in twenty minutes. There's Coke and chocolate in the fridge, and she shows me where Nicco's bedroom is, along with the bathroom. The trailer is nice; it's clear Ashley really takes pride in her home.

"I'm nervous. I've only ever left him once."

I can understand that. "Go and enjoy yourself. If anything happens, I promise I'll call you," I say.

She gives Nicco several kisses before getting her bag and coat. "Seriously, Layla, you are a godsend," she tells me before leaving. I lock the door and wait until I feel she's out of sight before closing all the curtains.

"That's better, isn't it?" I ask Nicco, and he smiles.

Nicco goes down with no problem, and I get myself a Coke from the fridge. It's only nine thirty, and I don't expect Ashley back anytime soon, so the knock on the trailer door sends my heart skyrocketing.

I sit still, clutching the remote, listening. But it's all gone silent. Whoever it was has left. The knock on the glass behind me has me jumping up. I clamp my hand over my mouth to contain the squeal that wants to emerge. I don't want to wake Nicco. But the person outside is now back at the front door calling Ashley's name, and he isn't going away. That gives me a little relief, knowing it isn't a burglar or anything. I answer the door.

I nearly fall back as Chester pushes his way in. He's down the hall before I can even get my bearings together.

He bursts back into the room. "Where is she?"

His anger and hostility have me frozen. I'm shaking my head, trying to say she isn't here, but the words get lodged in my throat.

"I know you can speak. Your mouth sure moves fast when you're talking to Jay." He licks his lips with a sneer on his face, but his tone is still angry, hostile.

He isn't violent like you, I want to say. But as he takes a step toward me, I back up, not able to say a word.

"Listen, bitch, tell me where she is." His raised voice ricochets around the space, which feels tiny now. Nicco's cry unfreezes me, and I dart around Chester, only to have him pull me back. His touch ignites an old fear. It's like Bert is looking down at me, and I can feel my lip tremble as my body locks up. I'm looking at him, but I can't see properly. The insistent cry of Nicco once again has me moving, and I pull my arm out of Chester's hold.

"Nicco's crying," I say with a heavy tongue. I have trouble forcing the words out. My speaking seems to make Chester realize how threatening he is, and he takes a step back and lets me get to Nicco. My breaths become raspy as I rock Nicco, and the tremble in my hands grows worse. The need to cry is choking me.

What am I going to do? First, I need to calm down.

My breathing settles, and soon Nicco is asleep on my chest. I put him back in the crib, and I want nothing more than to stay there and hide until

Ashley comes home. Maybe five or ten minutes have passed, but it feels like forever. Chester is silent in the den. I can only wish that means he's left. With Bert, me staying silent or hiding got me the worst beatings. It was always easier to face him. But I never could. Looking down at Nicco, I swallow the tears of self-pity. I don't want to bring Chester in here, on top of an innocent child. Jared spent his whole life protecting me. To step out of this room will be huge for me, but I will for the baby.

I'm not like Jared; my steps are unsure and clumsy. Trying to push my fear away, I tell myself this isn't Bert. This is just a boy with anger issues who is looking for a girl. My heart jumps when the couch comes into view. Chester sits on it, his elbows resting on his knees while he stares at me.

"Now tell me where she is." His words are calm and low, but they still hold a threat.

Sweat makes the base of my neck itchy, but I don't dare scratch the skin. I move as slowly as possible. It's an old trick, one that seemed to infuriate Bert, like it's annoying Chester right now.

"Fuck's sake. I swear, I don't know what the fuck Jay sees in you." He stands, and I stop moving.

Layla, speak, and this will end, I tell myself. But words once again fail me, and dread curls its cruel hands around my throat.

CHAPTER EIGHTEEN

LAYLA

U SE YOUR WORDS.

"She went out and asked me to mind Nicco." There. That wasn't so hard. I would have been pleased with myself, but Chester doesn't seem happy with my answer.

"I can see she's not here. Out where?" His clenched fists have me taking a step back. My back hits the wall. "I don't know," I answer honestly and praise myself once again for speaking.

"Dumbass white bitch."

I pick a spot on the floor as he walks to the fridge, helping himself to a drink. Tears burn my eyes. Tears that I refuse to let fall.

"You really are stupid."

I glance up at Chester as he gulps down the full Coke before burping loudly. My hands shake as I roll them into fists. Heat travels up my neck until it scorches my cheeks. "I think you should leave." God, I wish my voice sounded stronger. It's as weak as a newborn kitten.

He laughs at me before taking a step closer. "Don't think. Just get on the phone and call Ashley."

I don't hesitate. I want out of this situation. I can't even stay unscratched for a day. The old fear is there in full force like I'm ten again.

I keep one eye on Chester as he walks around the trailer. Ashley answers. Loud music pumps behind her.

"Ashley, this is Layla. Chester's here," I say.

"What?" She sounds like she's moving; the background noise becomes more distant. The phone is swiped from my hand as Chester starts to shout down the phone.

"Where the fuck are you? Whoring around?" He sneers. "No, I won't. He's my son."

Chester is Nicco's dad? Oh, the poor kid.

I move away from him and find myself at the door. My bag sits on the sideboard with my keys in it.

"You left our son with this stupid bitch."

I freeze once again at the hateful words.

"I'll call her what I want. Get home, now." He throws my phone at me. I don't catch it; instead, it hits the ground and separates into three parts. "You can leave."

My heart rate seems to slow, and my feet feel like lead. "No." I want nothing more than to leave, but what if he gets mad and hurts Nicco? I would never forgive myself.

He snorts before sitting back on the couch and flicking through the TV stations. Meanwhile, I stand rigidly at the door, just listening for Ashley. The beat of my heart is all I can hear. I try to calm myself and stop the onslaught of thoughts. I focus on picking up my phone and putting it back together as quietly as possible. But Chester glances at me every few moments.

My phone isn't broken and switches on straight away. Six missed calls from Ashley. I don't call her back for fear of provoking Chester. It doesn't take much to set him off. The silence in the room makes me aware that the TV has been silenced. I glance up slowly, and Chester stares back at me. The anger he displayed earlier is gone.

"So how do you know Jay?"

Really? He wants to chat after all that? But if he's calm until Ashley gets here, that's all that matters.

"We grew up together," I manage to say, with only a slight tremor in my voice.

He sits back, scratching his face with the remote, which I will never touch again. "Yeah, he mentioned that, but not much more."

He's waiting for me to expand on the matter, but I'm not going to. I don't want to tell him anything about me, most certainly not about my past. The fact that Jared even mentioned me to Chester makes me think they were close in some way. I want to answer just to keep things flowing, but my tongue grows heavy in my mouth, so I just nod.

He snorts and sits back, flicking through the stations but not turning up the volume.

"Jared's doing well here, you know." The look he gives me causes a shiver to chase up the back of my legs. He waves his hand in my direction. "We don't need white girls comin' in, stirring up shit."

I swallow the lump that's forming in my throat as I glance at the distorted glass on the front door. I'm just waiting for the light of a car to reflect off it, or a shadow to appear.

Come on, Ashley.

I back further into the wall as Chester gets up, yanking up his jeans as he walks toward me.

"Why you actin' like a little mouse?"

I almost can't hear his words over the roar of blood in my ears.

This isn't happening.

Chester is in front of me, one arm leaning against the wall only a few inches from my head. "I don't like you." His eyes roam my face, and I hold my breath until black spots appear in front of my eyes. The noise of keys in the door has me almost falling to the ground in relief. Ashley bursts in, along with the smell of alcohol and perfume.

"What are you..." Her glance jumps from Chester to me. "Are you okay?" Her hand goes to her hip as her head swings back to Chester. "Did you touch her?"

I blink as all the sound comes rushing back to me.

Chester looks me up and down like I am nothing, and the tips of my ears burn.

Tutting, he doesn't answer Ashley.

I move, grabbing my bag off the counter. "I'll leave you to it." I can't bear being in the room with him for one more moment. I'm out the door, not stopping as Ashley follows me. The night carries with it a soft spray of rain. The type that soaks you without you knowing.

"Layla, wait."

I don't stop but get my keys out of my bag. It gives Ashley the chance to catch up with me.

"What did he do?" It's the fear in her voice that makes me pause. Turning to her, I have so much I want to say. Like how did she, for one second, allow him near her? She seems so nice and put together.

"He didn't touch me, if that's what you're asking," I tell her. Her white dress is getting wet now, making it partially see-through. "Will you be okay with him?" I have to ask because as much as I want to run, looking at Ashley in her see-through dress, I'm not thrilled with the idea of her being alone with him.

"I can handle Chester." She takes a deep breath. "I'm sorry about this," she says.

"I'd better go." I open the car door and jump in, yet I don't leave until Ashley is back in her trailer.

The whole drive home, I tell myself it's okay to cry, but no tears come.

***

I wake to my alarm ringing and a headache. Flailing my hand toward the screeching device, hoping to hit it and turn the bloody thing off, doesn't help; the alarm clock continues to ring. That's when I realize the sound isn't coming from my alarm, but my phone. Wiping the sleep out of my eyes, I answer it.

"You're a hard woman to track down."

I sit up straight in the bed, wide awake. "Jared. Hi."

My stomach quivers.

"I texted you last night, and when I got no reply, I started to worry."

"Sorry, I had an early night." I take the phone away from my face to see I have several messages.

"Yeah, I was chatting with Kieran, and he told me you were babysitting for Ashley."

I freeze at that, the whole night slowly trickling back in like a broken tap.

"You there?" Jared asks, and I try to shake off the night before.

"Yeah, sorry. I didn't know you knew Kieran."

"I didn't know you did."

That's fair enough. But I don't want to get into this conversation. "So... is everything okay?" I ask, pushing off the duvet.

"There's a party tonight. Do you want to go?" Jared sounds unsure. I don't understand why.

"I'm not really into parties," I say, getting out of bed and pulling back the curtains. The sun beams in through the window, and I pull them closed. I need to get some painkillers.

"It's not really a request."

"Then why ask?" I need the painkillers a little more now that I've been standing.

"I'm trying to be polite."

"If I say no?"

"What do you think?"

Is that anger I hear in his voice?

"Great. I have to go, Jared." I hang up and go downstairs. I check out the house to discover I'm home alone. That often happens if Evelyn gets called into the hospital late. She'll stay the night with the child who'd been brought in.

She'd done that with me when I was taken to the hospital. I didn't speak to her then. I can still remember when she walked into the room.

I haven't spoken one word in nine days. I've had so many people arrive and try to make me open up, only to realize I'm not talking. They always leave, but today is different.

A woman with soft brown eyes enters. She doesn't acknowledge me but merely sits down on a chair, takes out a magazine, and starts reading. I lie patiently for fifteen minutes as she flicks through her glossy magazine. Finally, she looks at me with a smile. When I glance away, she starts rummaging in her bag. Curiosity gets the better of me, and I watch as she takes out a pack of Oreos. She stuffs one into her mouth and then eats two more before offering me one. I don't know why, but I take it. As I pray she'll offer me another one, she eats the rest of the pack and crumbles up the package. I feel disappointed. To my surprise, she gets up and stuffs the magazine into her bag and leaves my room. I'm floored. I reach for the buzzer, tempted to call the nurse and tell her that someone just hung out in my room, read a magazine, ate all the Oreos, and left. The door opens and a nurse comes in. I drop the buzzer and remain quiet as they change my drip and refill my water. Instead, I stare at the ceiling, wondering where Jared is and what will happen to us.

The next day, the same woman who ate the Oreos arrives to my room with a breakfast roll that makes my mouth water. The hospital food is bland, and I push each meal away. She starts to eat it. I'm not sure what is going on. Then she pauses and takes a second roll wrapped in foil from her backpack and hands it to me. I take the roll, and as I munch on it, I discover food is my weakness. When my belly is full of real food, I lie back.

"Thank you." My voice sounds strange after not using it for such a long time.

"You're welcome. I'm Evelyn."

She reaches out her hand, and I take it. "Layla."

She smiles, the corners of her eyes crinkling.

"I'm a counselor." That surprises me. I wasn't sure what she was going to say, but she doesn't look like a counselor. All the rest of them have been persistent and just snotty. Like they feel like they have to fix something because it's broken and check it off their lists.

With Evelyn, there's a kindness that makes me want to talk to her and tell her everything I've suffered.

"Is there anything I can do for you?" Evelyn tidies up the papers from our rolls as she speaks.

"Yes, there is."

She stops what she's doing and turns to me. Her face looks serious as she waits.

"Jared... Jared was in the house with me. I want to know if he's safe."

She nods. "Do you know his last name?"

I look away. "No. None of us do. It's just Jared."

She pauses, and I wonder if she's going to say no. "Okay. I'll try to find out." Her words give me hope and have me sitting up a bit straighter.

"When?" I don't want to be pushy, but I need to know he's safe.

"I'll go now." She speaks with a softness that matches her kind smile.

"Thank you, Evelyn."

Her smile widens. "You're welcome, Layla."

I get the bottle of aspirin out of the medicine cabinet and take two with a large glass of water before going back to bed. But of course, I can't sleep.

Bzzz. Another text message.

I'm sorry about last night.

It's from Ashley. I chew on my lip, thinking about what to write back. It isn't her fault Chester showed up, but I still hate that she didn't tell me he's Nicco's father. Would I have babysat if I had known?

I groan before texting her back.

It's cool. It's not your fault. Hope you and Nicco are okay.

I look at the other messages; all three are from Jared.

Where are you?

Answer me now.

You're babysitting? You should have told me. At least I know you're safe.

Safe. I was the furthest thing from safe last night.

I lie in bed for a while. My mind keeps wandering to Jared. No matter how much I try to pull my thoughts away from him, I can't. He's safe. I smile, really letting that fact sink in. He isn't just safe; he's in my life. He has a father and friends. The smile slips when I think of Alex. Will she be there tonight? Jared said she isn't his girlfriend, but I wonder if she knows that.

Should I go? I grab my phone off my nightstand and open up the last message from Jared, staring at it longer than is normal. I close the phone before flopping back on the bed.

"Everything alright?"

I bounce back up as quickly as I had flopped down. "I didn't know you were home." I clutch my heart as Carl opens my curtains with amusement on his face.

"Came home last night. I found a note from Evelyn saying you were babysitting." Carl faces me now.

"Yeah, for a girl from school." I sound calm; I'm not on the inside—my heart pounds.

"Did you have fun?" he asks, stepping away from me.

"Oh yeah, loads," I say.

He smiles again as I turn to face him. He stands at the door, one hand on the frame.

"Who called you this morning?"

Heat scorches my cheeks. He was listening. I go over the conversation in my head. Nothing bad was said, so why the hell am I burning up?

"It was Jared. He was inviting me to a party."

Carl seems stiff; his hand tightens on the door. "That was nice of him." I can hear the forced calm that he puts into his voice.

"Yeah, it was." I start to make my bed just to give myself something to do and hope that it ends this conversation. As I move around to the opposite side, I notice Carl is still watching me and has some internal battle going on behind his eyes.

"You should go."

I still at his words, then slowly turn toward him. "You think?" I ask, narrowing my eyes slightly, wondering where he's going with this.

He gives a quick laugh. "Yes, I do. And don't look so suspicious. You deserve it."

My cheeks heat, and I nod. "Thanks, Carl," I say. His words mean so much to me. He nods back before gently tapping the door and leaving.

I get dressed in my gardening clothes. It's something I love to do. My army green long-sleeved top fits me snugly, and I drag my overalls over my legs before getting into my old, tattered tennis shoes.

After piling my hair on top of my head, I grab a granola bar, my knee pads, and the key to the shed.

A gentle breeze caresses my skin as I step outside into the heat. It's going to be a hot day. For February in Ireland, that's unusual, so I intend to soak up the pleasant weather. I eat the granola bar as I drop my knee pads beside the line of shrubs I've been working on. Carl and Evelyn are so great at letting me dig up and plant their yard. They told me that it saved them from hiring a landscaper. Their compliment meant a lot to me.

I think back to when I first started gardening. I wasn't good at anything, really, or at least I didn't think so. One day, I decided to tackle the overgrown and unloved yard, and they seemed genuinely amazed at how much I had done. It was my way of giving something back to them.

After removing rocks and mowing the lawn, I had a far better idea of what area I had to work with. I spent a few days drawing out a plan of what I was going to do. Carl and Evelyn said I should plant some shrubs along the paved path that curved through the yard. I had never planted a flower in my life, so that had been a first. The idea of giving life to something made me excited.

I know that sounds silly, but I spent so much of my life watching things being caged and suppressed, that watching plants grow and blossom gave me hope.

The yard is square; there's a large brick wall six feet high in the rear with wooden fencing on either side, and it's clean and easy to work on.

Carl had to help me create the concrete circle I wanted. In the middle of the yard, he cut out a circle of sod, and he poured the circle for me. He did a great job. Him being an engineer helped with the measurements. Along the left side of the developing garden, we framed up flower beds with railroad ties that we repurposed from the local train tracks that were being rebuilt. Once stained and set, they looked great. I painted the back wall white and stained the fence with the same brown as the ties. Now I'm starting to plant.

I grab my gloves and trowel and pick up the lavender plants that I'm going to place in the center of the concrete area. The smell of the small green plants is intoxicating, and I inhale the scent. They're still young, but when they grow, they will bloom with lavender-colored flowers. The images on the plant markers that came with them look great.

How many people my age find peace in gardening? Morgan's idea of peace is shopping or going to parties. To me, that's torture. My back is to the sliding door as I plant; the swish sound of it opening has me sitting back on my heels while wiping off the sweat that's gathered on my forehead. Wearing heavy overalls in the heat we're experiencing is crazy, but I feel comfortable, and they are my gardening clothes. I shield my eyes as I turn to Carl. I hope he likes what I've done.

I look in the general direction of the door and blink, not sure if what I'm seeing is a mirage. Brown eyes, banked by broad cheekbones and a mouth that is partially open, watch me.

Jared.

CHAPTER NINETEEN

JARED 24 HOURS BEFORE

I LEAVE THE LIBRARY with a raging hard-on. My mind jumps to Alex. She would blow me if I found her. My cock starts to die instantly at the thought of anyone other than Layla touching me. I've entered the main hall when my attention is snagged on Layla as she races out the front door of the college.

"Hi, Jay," some guy, who I think is Jack, calls across the hall. I ignore him and all the other greetings.

Layla said she was going to class. My feet tear up the floor as I follow her. My phone rings as I burst out of the front doors. She's speed walking to her car as I answer the phone without looking at the caller ID. I don't dare take my gaze off Layla as she gets into her car.

"Jay, how are you?"

Rex's voice steals my focus. "Is everything okay?" I ask. Rex isn't someone who rings randomly, and the thoughts of anything happening to him has me covering my other ear so I'm blocking out all sounds around me.

"Yeah, I just need to swap your training around. Could you come in tomorrow instead of today?"

I look back up as Layla drives out the school gates.

Fuck.

I start walking to my car. "Yeah, that's no problem, Rex."

"Good man. I have a new member I couldn't say no to."

I get into the car and turn on the ignition. "Who?" I ask.

"Warren O'Reagan."

That makes me pause. "I know him."

Rex is silent, and I can just imagine what he's thinking. "Jay, he isn't someone you should be around."

"He goes to my college, and I actually like him. But I don't get involved in his family life."

Rex snorts. "That's why I couldn't turn him down. I don't want to make an enemy of the O'Reagans."

"They're good to have on your side."

I grin as Rex snorts again. "Time will tell."

"Speaking of time, is three good tomorrow?"

"Sure. I'll see you then."

I hang up and leave the school grounds. Layla is long gone, and I have no idea which way she went. Ringing her phone is futile. I drive straight and get lucky as I see her pulling out of a grocery store. What makes me pull in is the guy who's standing outside with his hand still raised in the air as he stares after Layla's car.

My blood roars in my veins, and I pull up, ripping up gravel and missing Kieran by millimeters. He's the guy from Chester's house, the one who inquired about Layla. I roll down the window and smile like I didn't just nearly run him over.

"What's up, Kieran?"

"Apart from you nearly killing me, I'm good." He shifts his grocery bag into his other hand.

"Sorry, I didn't see you."

Like fuck you didn't see me shines in Kieran's eyes, but he's wise enough not to voice it. Chester must have educated him about who I am after I left the party the other night.

I look in the direction Layla's car disappeared down and now regret my decision to stop. "You know Layla?" I ask.

Kieran smiles, and I want to wipe the look off his face. "Yeah, she's cool. A little quiet, but pretty cool."

I force a smile. "Yeah, I was trying to get in touch with her."

"I don't have her number, but she's babysitting tonight. That's all she told me."

Babysitting?

"For who?"

Kieran laughs. "What are you, the Gardaí?"

I don't react.

Kieran's smile melts off his face. "She didn't say who."

I rev the car and nearly crush his toes as I tear after Layla, but I have no idea where she went.

Where are you? I send the text as I drive aimlessly. I'm tempted to go back and kill Kieran. I need a release, and Rex canceling my session today really hits home.

I continue to drive and fire another text to Layla.

Answer me.

Ringing her again doesn't get me answers. Does she really think she can ignore me? I drive to her house, and some part of me relaxes when I see her car in her driveway. I'm still pissed she's ignoring me.

I check the time. My father is returning home from London, and he wants a word. I have a fair idea it will be about Layla. She isn't going anywhere for now. I take one final look at her house before I drive home.

***

"Welcome home, Master Jay." William is waiting for me in the hallway. I've never given much thought to him, but I pause.

"Do you live here?"

"Pardon, Master Jay?"

"Do you have a family, William?"

He seems flustered but answers me. "Yes, Master Jay. I have two daughters and a son. They are grown up now."

"Do you see them much?"

William appears even more uncomfortable. "Sometimes, Master Jay."

I nod, realizing I'm fucking useless at small talk and have no idea why I care about William all of a sudden. "Is my father here?"

William's features settle with contentment now that we're no longer discussing him. "He's in his study waiting for you, Master Jay."

I check my phone to see if Layla has returned my calls or messages, but she hasn't. Placing my phone on silent, I enter the study. My father is on a ladder pulling a book from a top shelf. I could knock the ladder over. I'm sure the fall would snap his neck. I'm picturing him lying on the ground, his head at an odd angle, blood pooling around the crown of his head, seeping across the wooden floor, reflecting the bookshelves in a distorted image.

My father glances at me and starts to climb down, hugging a book like it's treasure. "You brought her into my home."

I don't have to ask who he's referring to. I know who. Our home has cameras in every corner. I never expected Layla to go undetected. "I was under the impression that this was my home too."

My father walks to his desk, not showing any emotion until he drops the book heavily on his desk. The noise bounces around the large space. My father's lips rise slightly, and it's not a smile—more of a grimace. "I remember when I found you after years of searching."

Everything in me grows rigid. My father never speaks about what happened in his life before he found me.

"Bringing you into my home." He steeples his fingers against the book cover. "Helping you become the son I lost."

"Lost." I repeat the odd word and take a step toward my father. "I was in the foster system. Something I've often wondered about."

My father stands up straight. "You never asked."

"You never spoke of it, so I assumed it was off-limits."

"Nothing in this world is off-limits to us." *Except Layla.* My father's smile is foreign to me. "Your mother put you there. I already told you that."

That still hurts like fuck, but I bury the pain quickly. "You never told me why."

He shrugs. "I don't know."

"Where is she now?" I ask. I hate her.

"I don't know."

It's my turn to sneer. "You don't know much."

My father's features grow tense before he waves a hand dismissively in the air, the large silver watch that he always wears on his wrist catching the light. "Evelyn Masters tracked you down two years ago. I warned her to stay away, but she didn't listen."

Evelyn. Layla's adoptive mother. It takes me a moment to process what my father is saying. "You knew where Layla was two years ago?" My accusatory voice drips with venom that turns my tongue heavy.

"Layla has known where you were for two years," my father reinforces. "Now she is here for your wealth."

My father's greedy fingers open the book in front of him, like he has made his point and I should leave.

"She can have every single fucking penny."

His head snaps up. His brows drag down. "What did you say?"

"You heard me. She can have it all."

"Have you lost your mind?"

"No." I grin. "You knew where she was, and you didn't tell me."

My father tuts like I'm being an errant child. "If I had informed you, you would have set off and made a fool of yourself. Since she already knew you were here, she clearly didn't care."

He's fucking lying. Layla didn't know. Layla cares. I can tell when she lies, and that day at the gym—seeing me shook her to the core.

"That was my decision to make."

"Women make men weak." My father's voice rises, and he steps away from his desk.

"This isn't about me. It's about you. Are you still bitter that Maura left you?" Saying my mother's name pierces my heart, but it drags more anger from my father.

"You will mind your tongue."

"Will I now?" I give a smug smirk, feeling giddy from standing up to him.

He stares at me before his anger settles, and he starts to think. "Very well, Jay." He walks away, plotting his next move.

"She's off-limits," I say to his back.

He doesn't respond.

"Layla is not to be touched." I continue walking to his desk and stop when he unbuttons his suit jacket and sits back down while looking up at me.

"Your mother hid you from me. Hid you in the foster system so I wouldn't find you."

His confession floors me, but I still cling to my conviction that he is not to touch Layla. "Layla is a good person," I start.

His fist hits his desk heavily. "Listen to me, boy. Everything that happened to you was inflicted by your mother's actions. And now, Layla is causing a rift between us. Look at yourself." My father rises.

I try to control the darkness that swirls inside me. My mother hid me from my father.

"Why?" The question doesn't rattle him.

"Why what?" He sits back down.

"Why did Maura hide me from you?"

My father shrugs. "I don't know."

More lies.

I can't look away from him as he pretends I don't exist. Calling him out on his lies will get me nowhere. The information he just gave me is the most I've gotten in years. "I'll be the son you need me to be," I say.

My father nods, and his shoulders relax. He's happy with my response.

"As long as Layla remains safe."

His jaw tightens as his eyes flash with fury. "If you want to be a fool for that girl, then be a fool." I'm waiting for more, but my father bends his head, picks up a pen, and starts writing in the open journal in front of him. "You can leave, Jay."

Disappointment isn't something I've heard in his voice, and I've never given it much thought, but I want to erase the tone from his mouth and never hear it again. I'm staring at the crown of his head, waiting for him to look back up, but after a few minutes, when he continues to ignore me, I leave his study.

William is outside the door when I exit my father's den. "Master Jay, Miss Alexandra is waiting for you in your quarters."

I nod at William, unable to say anything, and make my way upstairs. I haven't cleared the last step before she harasses me.

"I didn't take you for someone who was weak, Jay." Her smile stretches her ruby red lips across straight white teeth.

"I'm not in the fucking mood, Alex," I warn, and her smile dims but doesn't disappear completely.

"I can see that. Mark is having a party tomorrow night on his private beach. So I'll need you to pick me up at eight."

I pull off my jacket and throw it on the chair. William has a fire lit, and I'm drawn to the heat, or maybe it's the distance from Alex.

I thought she would start about me leaving school with Layla and how I nearly ran over her, but she doesn't say a word about it. She missed school on Friday too. I wonder what she's plotting.

"Jay, we have to be there. It's important to Mark." Alex has moved beside me.

I glance at her. "I'll be there."

She smiles victoriously. "Good."

"But you will have to find a way there yourself. I won't be picking you up." I move away from the fire.

"Why is that?"

I face Alex. "Because I'm taking someone else."

She doesn't react straight away. "I don't think I need to ask who."

"Then don't."

She moves closer. Her hand reaches out and touches the belt of my trousers. "You seem tense. Let me fix that for you."

I brush her hand away. "I'm not tense."

She exhales. "Tell me what you want. Sex?" Alex tugs at her top, and I don't stop her. The red material floats to the ground. "Let's have sex if it takes the scowl off your face." She reaches back and unclips her bra. It joins her top on the floor, releasing her artificial breasts. When she reaches for my trousers, I stop her by gripping her wrists. She looks me dead in the eye, not fazed that she's topless.

"I want you to leave." I release her wrists and step around her.

She moves, and I hear the ruffle of the material. When I turn back, she's pulling her top back on. "Your father said you haven't been the same, and he's right." She lets her hand flitter in the air from the top of my head to my feet. "This... this isn't what I signed up for."

Does she think I'm insulted? "Then leave." I don't like that Alex and my father were talking about me.

Irritation tightens her features, but she smiles and takes a step toward me. "Fine. I get it. You have a thing for Layla. Right now, she's a new, shiny toy. So fuck her and get it out of your system, and when you are ready"—Alex reaches up and touches my chest—"we can get back to being grown-ups."

"Is that what you call this?" I ask, and once again, I have to remove her hands from me. "Us being grown-ups?"

Alex exhales loudly again. "After you grow a pair of balls and sleep with Frankenstein, come back to me."

I'm moving quicker than my brain can register. Alex screams as my hand tightens around her throat. "You fucking listen to me. You go near Layla, and I'll tell everyone about the whore you are."

Alex's face grows red, and I remove my hand.

The grin twists my lips. "I've cameras in this room with footage of you on your knees. I'll let everyone watch."

She rubs her throat.

"Get the fuck out of my house." I don't wait to see if she leaves, but I walk away from her. All I can think about is Layla. The day she left our foster home, she broke me. Since she came back into my life, she's destroyed what's left of me, and once again, I like the feeling of chaos.

***

I wake up to a text from Chester.

The package has arrived.

My clock reads three in the morning. Flicking on the light, I run my hands down my face while climbing out of the bed. Grabbing my jeans, I slip into them before picking up my jumper. I'm quiet leaving the house. I can't say the same for my BMW, but this meeting is too important to miss. This is what it's being all boiling down to. This one meeting would change everything. I will finally have the justice I seek.

Woodview Estate is in darkness as I drive slowly up to Chester's house. The curtains shift and light filters out before it gets swallowed up behind the heavy curtains. Killing the engine, I get out of the car and slide my phone into my pocket. The front door opens and Chester pops his head out.

Scratch marks down his face have me raising a brow as I move past him and into the house. The click of the front door closing has me glancing at him over my shoulder.

"What happened to your face?" I ask as he circles around me and pushes the sitting-room door open. We're the only people here. Every other time I've come to Chester's home, his crew has been hanging out here. Music plays quietly from a stereo close to the door. The bass sends a current around the room.

He sits down on the couch, and his bare feet shift back and forth as he rolls a cigarette. "That bitch, Ashley"—he licks the roll-up—"had a stranger babysitting my fucking kid." He places the cigarette in his mouth and lights it. "Fucking idiot," he mutters under his breath.

I sit down on the chair.

"No offense, bro," he offers up.

I relax my fingers and rub my palms along my jeans. "Why would I be offended? Do I look offended?" I smirk.

He shrugs and sinks back into the couch. "I know you have a thing for Layla, but she doesn't know my kid from Adam."

He has my full and undivided attention. I sit forward, resting my elbows on my knees. So that's who Layla was babysitting for. What fuck was she thinking?

"Ashley got you good." I take a quick look around the room. I don't see any gun or weapon near Chester.

"Fucking bitch." He takes another drag of his cigarette.

"Are we alone? I don't want anyone knowing my business." I don't want any witnesses.

He sits up, and his feet tap along the floor. "Nah, just me and you, bro. You want the goods?" His lip rises on one side.

I stare at him. We're alone. There's no one here to stop me. Should I ask for the gun first or hurt him first?

He gets up while crushing the cigarette in the large crystal bowl. "I'll be a minute." His smirk has me tightening my jaw.

"Did you frighten her?" I ask.

He stops walking and rubs his chin. He stutters a laugh. "She scares easily."

I get up. "Did you frighten her?" I'm no longer smirking. I'm trying to control the pure and undiluted anger that filters through my veins.

Chester licks his lips and shuffles from foot to foot. "I said the bitch scares easily."

My forehead connects with the bridge of his nose. The break is instant, along with the flow of blood. He grips his nose, and that gives me the perfect opening. My fists connect in rapid succession into his ribs, driving him back. Left, right, left, right. I dance the motherfucking dance, and he reels back onto the couch. He's howling. I turn up the music. The beat is fuel to the flames that are consuming me. I let it all go as I stand over Chester. He protests, but it doesn't last long as my fist connects with his face. My knuckles burn, but I don't slow. I make each hit count. He never gets one in, and the song finishes. Another one starts before I stop.

I'm breathing heavy. Blood coats the couch behind Chester's head. I can't make out his features as I gasp for air and my sanity. I think he might be dead.

I felt possessed. His hand twitches. One eye opens.

"You ever look at Layla again, and I'll come back and finish the job," I promise before leaving to wash his blood off me.

CHAPTER TWENTY

LAYLA (PRESENT)

I SWALLOW AS MY thoughts take a dive in a direction they have no right to go. His lips look... kissable.

How inappropriate.

"You're a sight, Layla." Jared's words carry a heaviness that has me swallowing. I brush some falling strands away from my face and get ready to get up.

"Don't. Stay where you are." Jared is with me in six large strides before kneeling. His red T-shirt clings to every defined crevice of his body. I swallow again, focusing on his jeans.

What's wrong with me?

He's watching me.

"What are you doing here?" I finally ask. I glance at the door again, only to find Carl observing us. He gives me a quick wave, which I return before he closes the door.

Carl doesn't look angry. After all, he said he wanted to meet Jared, and he did encourage me to go to the party. But I'm not sure what I saw on Carl's face. A part of me is happy that Evelyn isn't here. This feels like too much.

"He's a really nice man," Jared says. His brows furrow as he reaches for me. I freeze when he moves a piece of hair from my cheek before placing the lock behind my ear. The small bit of contact causes my breath to hitch.

"Yeah, he's the best," I manage to say. "Jared, what are you doing here?"

"I heard about what happened with Chester." Jared's gaze is heavy as he searches my face.

That's why he's here. Why am I disappointed? I'm not sure. I dig the trowel into the clay beside my thigh. "Yeah. Look, it's fine."

His tanned hand grabs my free hand, and even though it's gloved, I can sense his touch. His stare is unrelenting, and my breath stalls briefly.

"It's not fine. He will never speak to you like that again." My throat burns, and I drop my gaze, only for him to pull me toward him. I reach out, gripping his forearm to stop myself from falling completely into him. His grin has my heart stuttering in my ribcage.

His head dips, and a vise tightens around my chest. His grin grows, and his brown eyes are now flecked with gold. It's like he knows the effect he's having on me. My lips part as my heart accelerates into top gear.

Oh God, he's going to kiss me.

I need to stop this. When his forehead touches mine, the intensity I see in his gaze shocks me, and his grin is no longer in sight.

"He's an asshole."

My brain seems to short-circuit. *What? He's talking about Chester again?*

I lean back. "He's scary," I finally say, removing my gloves from my overheated hands.

"Did he touch you?"

The stare with which he pins me holds anger that has me immediately shaking my head.

"No, he didn't." I know I will never put myself in that predicament again. I wipe my forehead with the sleeve of my top. It feels like the temperature has jumped up several degrees.

He nods now, but no warmth has reentered his eyes. "It won't ever happen again."

"It's fine. How did you know about Chester, anyway?" I ask.

"He brought it up in conversation." Jared's jaw hardens.

"I'd like to know how that conversation went." I can't see Chester giving up the information, and right now, looking at Jared, I wonder if Chester is still breathing.

I've never seen such wrath in someone's eyes.

"You don't," Jared fires back.

Do I really care about Chester?

We sit in silence, and his gaze shifts to my plants. One of his brows rise in surprise. "So, you garden? And very well, I might add."

The change of topic has me sitting back. "Yep." I grin. "I try," I add.

Jared's head cocks to the side as a smile tugs at his lips. "You never could take a compliment." He examines the rest of the garden. There really isn't much to see. "Anything you touch blossoms. It always has." His tone drifts off as if he didn't mean to speak out loud.

"Thank you." My words are only a whisper, but he hears me as he looks at me with hooded eyes. Everything about him is so familiar, yet so new.

"You should really put down some membrane under the plants," he says, jutting his chin out toward the large, empty flower bed.

"Yeah, I will be. Since when do you garden?"

His smile turns into a full-blown one that has my heart skipping. "I have many talents, Layla." His double meaning has the tips of my ears turning red. His laugh at seeing me burn up nearly undoes me. I am so grateful when Carl arrives.

"Plants look great," Carl tells me with a soft smile on his face. Stuffing my hands into my pockets, I have to stop myself from bouncing up and down on the heels of my tattered shoes.

"I've four more to plant, and then I'm going to put wild indigo between every second one. They'll work very well together."

I can picture the garden when it's in full bloom; the off-white and lavender colors will blend beautifully against the gray slabs.

"May I help you?" Jared's question has me quickly looking at Carl, who's staring off into the distance.

"It's okay. I'm sure you have more important things to do," I answer him. Jared's mouth twitches like he's holding in laughter.

"Did you teach her how to garden, Mr. Masters?" Jared looks so confident with one hand tucked into his jeans pockets as he stands beside Carl. They're nearly the same height.

I have so many questions for Jared. First of all, *Mr. Masters*? How does he know their second names? And also, how does he know where I live? I narrow my eyes at him with suspicion.

Carl laughs, holding up his hands. "I wish I could take the award for that. But it's all on Layla."

"Not really. I wouldn't be able to do this if it weren't for you guys giving me free rein of your garden. Plus, you're paying for it."

The corner of Jared's lip lifts. "It looks like they made the right investment."

I blush at the compliment.

"It's a bargain, and we're grateful." Carl moves to me, kissing me on the forehead. The affection surprises me. "Okay, I'll let you kids get back to it."

Surprise fills me for the second time as Carl shakes Jared's hand before leaving. "Thank you for taking care of her, and I'm glad to have met you."

Jared's gaze flickers to mine before returning to Carl. "You're welcome, and thank you for taking care of her for me."

My breath catches at his words. Carl puts his second hand over Jared's, sandwiching it between his. I can't see Carl's face, but Jared's flashes with emotion. Carl gives their joined hands a final soft tap before turning to me.

I want to tell him how grateful I am for how he's treating Jared, how much it means to me. I hope he sees the gratitude in my eyes as he leaves.

I blink when the sliding door closes, only to find that Jared is watching me. I rock on my heels. "What?" I ask, wondering why he's looking at me like it's the first time he's seeing me.

His eyelashes flutter, and he's Jay again.

"So, what time will I pick you up tonight?" he asks.

I sit back down and pick up my gloves. I don't put them on, just hold them, and Jared sits down beside me, his shoulder flush with mine. We both face out toward my empty flower bed. He bumps into my shoulders.

"I've nothing to wear." Yeah, that sounded as lame as it did in my head.

"Wear whatever you want."

I glance at him sideways. "Fine, I'll wear my overalls."

His lip twitches. "That's fine by me. You look cute in your overalls."

I laugh at him. "Yeah. People will be dropping at my feet," I say, sliding on the gloves.

Jared's gaze drifts to me. He's focused, serious. "You're right. You can't wear your overalls." He grins now, not able to remain serious. "So, what time?"

My senses are committing to memory all these wonderful things about Jared: his smell, his smile, how his eyes light up, how he feels so right beside me. My pulse jumps along my neck as I focus on his lips. When I return his gaze, his pupils are dilated.

"I'm not sure."

My words have him blinking, and when he looks at me again, his eyes have returned to normal, and he stands up. "Great. I'll pick you up at eight. Wear something casual."

That's abrupt. I start to rise.

"Stay. I'll let myself out. Finish your planting." His face has softened again, and I find myself smiling at him.

"Okay, see you later." I watch him leave, spending a bit too much time watching his backside. I sigh and scold myself.

I stay out in the sun until I have all my plants in the ground. I need a shower, as I can feel the sweat dripping down my back. At the sound of the sliding door, I turn, expecting Carl, but it's Evelyn.

"How's my girl?" she asks. Her smiling face is like a hug. She spends most of her time happy. She's human, so she has her moments, but overall, she's a very happy person.

"I got the centerpiece finished." I stand up so I can admire my work as Evelyn joins me.

"Looks great. I hear you had quite the day." I glance at her to gauge her reaction, and her huge smile has me relaxing.

"Carl told you, then," I say, folding my arms.

"Yes, he did. He said Jared is very handsome."

Heat races across my face. I tilt my head slightly with a shrug. "I suppose." Handsome is an understatement.

"You suppose?" she says. I can hear the laughter in her voice.

"Yes, I suppose," I repeat and pick up my tools. "He has lots of admirers." I'm referring to Alex, who already staked her claim on him.

"And you have Kieran. That doesn't stop anyone from saying a person is attractive."

I cringe at Kieran's name. Ugh. I should have never lied. That's something I will have to come clean about, and sooner rather than later. But I'm not ready for that conversation.

"Yeah, I know. So how was work?" I ask, and I'm grateful when Evelyn allows me to change the conversation. I know we'll get back to Jared, and I'm okay with that, but right now, my body is filled with nerves as I think about the party tonight. Evelyn tells me about her day as we leave the heat of the garden behind us. We make our way inside the house, and the cold air hits me immediately.

"How are you feeling about everything?" Evelyn asks with her back to me. She turns and leans against the island. "I mean, is your sleep affected again?"

"No." I frown. "I toss and turn, but no night terrors."

Another gift of many that my upbringing gave me.

"I'm so happy to hear it." The smile that Evelyn wears is tight. The crinkles grow around her eyes.

"It was hard on you and Carl." The need to apologize has me brushing off imaginary clay from my overalls.

"Parenting *is* hard."

My eyes sting at her words. She says things so easily, like I've always belonged here. The truth is, my own parents didn't want me, so I was placed in the foster system, only to meet the worst side of life first. Jared, he was the light. The light in a world plunged and soaked in darkness and hate.

No wonder I ended up with night terrors. The small space I found myself in would grow tighter in my dreams. My hysteria couldn't be tamed.

Waking someone from a night terror is dangerous. I remember that when I would wake up covered in sweat, Evelyn would be awash with tears. The distress on Carl's face used to twist my heart, and each time, I feared they would send me back.

"Thank you for always being there, Evelyn. You and Carl."

Evelyn walks around the island, and I'm encased in one of her hugs. "Always, sweetheart." A kiss is pressed to my forehead, and I smile up at her when she releases me.

"I better wash up. I stink."

"I agree." Evelyn laughs as she steps away.

***

The spray of the warm water hits my back as I press my palms against the tiles of the shower wall. My mind throws me back into a haunting memory, and my heart starts racing. I squeeze my eyes shut, and when I open them, I'm staring at the white tiles. I focus on my fingers, spreading them out. I lift the pinky up before pushing off the wall and leaning back into the water.

Closing my eyes, I see him—smiling at me, his dimples on full display. His large, tanned hands appear so much bigger, and I run my hands across my abdomen, pretending they are Jared's. Flutters start low in my belly, and they spread fast and hard, leaving a throbbing between my legs. His kiss flares to life, and I lick my lips as if I can almost taste him on my tongue. My hand dips lower, and my teeth sink into my lip. I imagine Jared's fingers dipping inside me. I burn as I drag my fingers to my clitoris and rub it in a circular motion. The thoughts of Jared naked inside me rocks my body, and with very little effort, I release in the shower. I'm panting and a little stunned as my body jerks with pleasure.

I've come before, but it never felt like this. I've never had the reality of Jared all grown up, with his wicked words and deadly ways. I've never even tried to picture him as a man.

I stay under the water, and it feels like something inside me is changing, and I have no idea what it means. But a new want is rising inside me. I want Jared. That thought terrifies me.

CHAPTER TWENTY-ONE

JARED

I HAVE A SOUR taste in my mouth as I get into my car. I don't turn the ignition but look back at Layla's home. I don't know what I was expecting when I knocked on the front door, but it wasn't Carl, a man who truly loves Layla. He was genuinely happy to meet me. I came with the intention of confronting Layla for not answering her phone and warning her never to do that again. But as I stepped over the threshold, my intentions changed. Their home is modest, but it's a real home. I can picture Layla laughing here, eating, sleeping. I want to see her comfortable with her surroundings, and that's exactly what I found outside.

To see her kneeling, planting flowers, did something to me. Her eyes widened when she saw me, and I soaked up her surprise and stayed in for a while before finally sitting down beside her. With my shoulder so close to hers and the sun beating down on us, I found an odd peace that I've never felt. Each time she looked at me, I knew my father's words last night were lies. She didn't have it in her to deceive me. Layla is too good of a person. Too good for me. I should let her go. I should have listened to my father three years ago and allowed the idea of Jared and Layla to die. Everything she touches blossoms. Maybe deep down, I want her to do the same to me. I'm disturbed by that thought and leave abruptly, not wanting to dig any deeper. I have a plan, and Layla being here is making me question my plan to kill Bert. Before, I had nothing to lose. Now, I have everything to lose.

I turn on the car, knowing that letting her go isn't an option anymore. I drive straight to the gym. I'm thirty minutes early, but I don't think Rex will mind. Slipping my phone into my pocket, I get out of the car. Before entering the gym, I check my phone one more time. Rex isn't a fan of technology. No phones while training is another one of his policies. I have several missed calls from Alex. No messages. I place the phone on vibrate and grab my gym bag from the trunk of the car before going into the gym.

The smell is familiar, and it gives my mind instant permission to allow my body to relax. My brain seems to switch gears, and all that exists is here and now. Rex is in his office. The glass wall allows me to see him. He looks up from a stack of dockets, and I wave before pointing to the changing rooms. He salutes me with two fingers.

The locker room has recently been washed down. Rex doesn't have a cleaner, and he's too much of a perfectionist to hire one. So, I know this is his handiwork. I change into shorts and a T-shirt and return to the gym floor. He's no longer in the office but waiting for me by the main ring. I take his outstretched hand, and he half hugs me.

"Let's work on defense today." He speaks while releasing me and picks up the pads that are positioned on the edge of the ring. I pull on my boxing gloves and don't lace them up, as I won't be swinging any punches today. We enter the ring. We don't talk, and I'm in the zone, stopping every hit. I strike back a few times, only to have Rex reprimand me.

I grin. "It's automatic. I can't help it."

He's not amused. "You have to control your reaction. You know that. Shit like that makes fighters lose a fight. You have to keep your head in the match."

I slow down and drop my hands. Sweat soaks my body. We might not be full-on fighting, but we've been dancing around the ring. "I don't want to do any more tournaments." I know my winning fights gives Rex a large sum of money, but they just don't give me the same kick they once did. "I'll continue training and make sure my father gives a generous donation."

Rex waves me off. "I don't want your money, Jay. Your skill isn't something money can buy." Rex pulls off the pads from his hands. "What's brought this on? You have plagued me for tournaments for months, so why stop now?"

I have no idea why. *Layla.*

"My father wants me to take a more serious role in the family business."

Rex nods before running his hands through his hair. "I knew that would happen. I just hoped we had more time."

The gym door opens, and Warren O'Reagan steps in with a cigarette dangling between his lips. I'm waiting for Rex to have a fucking fit, but he doesn't say anything about the cigarette. Anyone else, he would have by the balls.

"We have assigned times here, Warren." Rex stretches the ropes and gets out of the ring.

I lean against the rope. "What's up?" I ask Warren.

"Jay," he greets. "I just need to blow off steam," Warren tells Rex. He isn't fazed as Rex continues toward him.

"Warren, I'm happy to have you here, but I don't operate like this. It's a one-on-one basis during training hours."

Warren looks at me. "I'm sure Jay doesn't mind."

This all feels like a déjà vu. I did this to Rex only recently with Lenny. I step out of the ring, wanting to make amends and not make this any harder on Rex.

"I do mind," I say to Warren. "I need all the help I can get from Rex. Hope that's okay."

Warren snorts before holding up both hands. "Okay."

"I'm not going to have to start ducking and diving from snipers, am I?" Rex is half teasing.

Warren takes the cigarette from behind his lips. "Nah, not really my style. I'll ring ahead next time." It's funny to see the level of respect in Warren's eyes toward Rex. I can't imagine Warren hears the word "no" very often. Warren gives a final salute while his cigarette ashes float to the ground. Rex and I watch him go, and I'm sure Rex is itching to clean up the ashes.

"You really think he'd hire a sniper?" I ask.

"He's an O'Reagan," Rex fires back before turning to me.

I know they're powerful, but to think they have that kind of power makes me pause. Having a friend who knows a sniper isn't something that comes around every day.

"I don't want you to give up on boxing, Jay. Just think about it." Rex gets back into the ring.

"I will," I offer before we start back into our training. My mind is made up about the competitions, but I don't want to end my time with Rex. I'll find a way to keep money coming to him. After all, in a few months, I'll inherit everything. I've never allowed myself to fully accept that I will have riches beyond anything I can imagine.

If Rex doesn't expect my money, then maybe I can help him find someone to fill my place. Maybe Warren might be the answer to that. Then again, I can't imagine him having any discipline. Time will tell.

The two hours fly by, and it's close to five when we stop. I'm soaked in sweat and take the bottle of water that Rex tosses to me.

"I have an old student returning. He's a cage fighter. I want you to come by one of these days and meet him." Rex isn't giving up.

"What's his name?" I ask.

"Max. He's a beast. Think Conan the Barbarian."

I drink half the bottle of water down. "You think I'd take him?"

Rex grins. "We'll see. I might let you spar with him."

I finish the water and hit the showers. When I'm redressed and leaving, Rex is back in the office, going through the stack of paperwork in front of him. Guilt causes a thickness in my throat. Me not fighting professionally will cost him, and I don't want to see him go into a bad financial situation. Maybe I can do a few more fights until he finds someone else. I wave to Rex as I leave the gym.

Throwing my bag into the trunk, I check my phone. I have two more missed calls from Alex. Worry worms its way through my system. She isn't normally persistent, but I've never turned her down before. I've never spoken to her badly either, and I've most certainly never put my hands on her. I push the phone into my pocket and get into the car.

When I get home, William has food ready for me. He follows our schedules closely, and at times like these, I'm grateful for that.

I take the sandwich and bottle of water upstairs with me. My hands are itchy as I hold the bottle of water under my arm and balance the sandwich in my other hand. I pull the key from around my neck and open the door, and the room bursts into light as I flick the switch. I make sure to lock the door behind me before I leave my water and food on the workstation.

I pick up one half of the sandwich and start to eat as I stare at Layla's face. I need to draw her in the garden. I need to capture that moment of her profile. Not seeing her fully didn't stop the contentment from showing on her face. I finish my food as I walk around the room, taking in all the pictures of Layla. She's so full of expression—each picture tells a story. In the one I stand before, her bottom lip is slightly pulled down, her eyes wide, and her hair rests on her shoulder.

She's staring at me with that look of hope and disbelief on her face. I continue to move along the images, and when I finish my food, I start to sketch. My hands take over as they move fluidly across the blank page. After an hour, Layla starts to take form on the paper. My phone buzzing in my pocket keeps distracting me. I check it, and it's Alex again.

It's also six thirty. Time is slipping away. I leave the room and lock the door behind me, then call Alex back as I place the key around my neck.

"I need you." She's been crying.

"What's wrong?" I'm moving faster. My mind jumps to the worst possible scenarios. Like she's being robbed, someone died, or someone really hurt her.

"Can you come over to my house?" Her voice doesn't hold fear, and I slow my footfalls.

I need to change for the party. "Can't you just tell me what's wrong?"

"Not on the phone, Jay." She snivels, but I can picture her rolling her eyes.

"I'll be there in twenty minutes." I hang up and get into a clean pair of jeans and a white shirt, then I pull a navy sweater over it.

***

Alex's home is a mirror image of ours, only hers is painted the ugliest peach, and the garden is filled with artificial plants. It looks flawless, but the smell is wrong. It's fake, like most of the people in her home.

I park outside the front door and not in the garage, as her parents insists everyone must do. I don't plan on staying long. The front door is unlocked, and I enter the foyer. I don't call out as I'm greeted by a member of the staff. She's a short, heavy woman who holds her hands in front of her. She's new, but Alex's family goes through staff members on a regular basis. I've stopped memorizing names at this stage.

"Mr. McGivney. This way, please."

I follow her to a sitting room that has the curtains drawn, and Alex is sitting on the couch looking the picture of an upset rich white woman. She has a crumbled-up tissue in her hand, her eyes are watery, and her lips are painted a stark red. Even in her distress, she still managed to put on lipstick. The room is lit by several lamps; the overhead chandelier hangs in darkness.

"What is it?" I'm irritated that I even have to be here. I check my phone. It's seven o'clock. I've one more hour before I need to pick up Layla.

She pats the seat beside her on the large gold couch. I'm ready to snap at her, but she blinks, and tears fall. I'm not a completely heartless bastard. I walk stiffly to the couch and stuff my phone into my pocket before I sit down. "What is it?" I ask again.

"My parents are getting divorced. I have no one else I can talk to about it." She gives a shrug of her shoulder that's bare; her white top has fallen down, revealing most of her left shoulder. Alex won't tell anyone about this. They'll keep it hidden. Appearances mean everything to them.

"I'm sorry, Alex." I have no idea what she wants me to say.

"I mean, I could expect my father to leave, but not the other way around." Alex blinks, and more tears fall. "My mother doesn't even want me. She didn't fight for me to live with her."

I feel the weight of her words and a sense of expectation that I need to tell Alex that her mother does want her. But maybe she doesn't—just like mine never wanted me.

"I'm sure your mother loves you. Would you want to live with her? What if she moves far away? What about your friends?"

Alex hiccups, and more tears fall. "I suppose they wouldn't be able to cope without me. But she should have at least asked me, Jay. Everyone thinks I'm some unfeeling and insensitive girl, when I'm just scared."

I've never seen or heard Alex so vulnerable, and it twists at my gut. "Look at me," I tell her. She does, and I feel like shit for my threat to her yesterday.

"I was an asshole yesterday. I shouldn't have spoken to you like that. But no one thinks you're unfeeling. Look at you." I reach out and touch a tear to make my point before dropping my hand.

"I wasn't fair either," Alex says. She doesn't look away from me as she dabs her eyes with the tissue. "You're forgiven." She smiles widely.

I'm aware of the time ticking away. "You'll be okay, Alex."

Her eyes fill up again, and she moves closer. "Can I have a hug?"

I hug her, and she buries her head in my neck. She doesn't smell like Layla. After a few moments, I break the hug. "I'd better go." I stand.

She's scrambling off the couch. "Could you give me a lift to the party?"

"You still want to go?" She doesn't look like she's in any state to go to a party.

"I won't let this drag me down." She forces a smile. She bounced back fucking quickly. My sympathy starts to dwindle.

"I'm sorry. I'm taking Layla."

Her mouth twists. "I don't mind. I'll sit in the back."

She's desperate. Alex not being the center of attention is something I've never seen her accept.

"Alex, don't," I warn as she makes her way to me. I can already see it in her eyes before she reaches up and places her hands on my chest.

"We are so good together."

I remove her hands. "I'm sorry," I say again. "I have to go."

"I'll find a way for myself, then." Anger fills her words.

I'm ready to leave, but I look back at her. "We *are* friends, right?"

She holds her head high and nods. "Yes." Her reply is filled with venom.

I've never thought about Alex in any way, really. She was always just there, and we played our roles that we knew we were expected to play.

"You're better than this," I tell her before I leave.

I hope she will see her worth and stop dancing to her father's tune.

I know I'm not playing this game anymore.

I know what I want.

That's Layla.

CHAPTER TWENTY-TWO

LAYLA

EIGHT O'CLOCK ARRIVES, AND the doorbell rings. My hand flutters to my white sleeveless shirt before grazing my knees. The rough material of the denim shorts scrapes the tips of my fingers. The see-through shirt material is light, and the cami underneath doesn't stop the cold air from touching my skin. Despite that, my temperature rises dramatically as the doorbell rings for the second time. My white tennis shoes sound loud as I walk down the hall. Taking one last look at myself in the hall mirror, I brush my hair back over my shoulder. My minimal makeup will work to my advantage as the night wears on, but seeing myself, I feel maybe I've made a mistake and should have applied a bit more.

The girl who stares back at me has large blue eyes that look wide with fear. Pulling my bottom lip between my teeth, I look away. It doesn't matter how I look; Jared is my friend—I grew up with him—and I need to remember that.

Within seconds of opening the door, I lose sight of Jared just being a friend. He's facing the road, his hands deep in his pockets. I'm snagged on the heavy black tattoo that encircles his wrist. I want to get a better look at it, but he turns, and his eyes flash before roaming across me from head to toe. I hold on to the door like it's a lifeline. His navy sweater fits him perfectly. As my eyes move higher, his Adam's apple bobbles, and I pass his plush lips before settling on the deep pools of his chocolate brown eyes. I pull my lip in between my teeth again. Jared's gaze flickers to my mouth. I release my lip immediately.

He stares at me, and I can't hold his gaze. I wonder what he sees when he looks at me like that. Am I dressed okay?

"You ready?" he asks. His brows furrow, and he turns slightly away from me. His change confuses me. Maybe it's the way I'm acting. I'm looking way too deeply into everything between us.

"Just let me grab my bag," I say as he steps off the porch.

"I'll be in the car."

I close the door and try to calm my erratic heartbeat. A squeal tears from my throat. "Oh, I didn't hear you."

"Just came to see if you were leaving. I wanted to say goodbye, and I hope you enjoy your night," Evelyn says, mirth in her voice, and she smiles. She hugs me, and I return the gesture. Her arms are so warm. She always runs a little hotter than most people. Carl often teases her, saying he should run a few pipes off her in the winter to heat the house.

When she releases me, I smile up at her. "Yeah, I just need to get my clutch." I pause before entering the kitchen to get it. "Evelyn, do I look alright?" I hold out the white shirt while chewing on the inside of my cheeks.

"You're beautiful, Layla. You're beautiful no matter what you wear, but tonight you look even more so."

Evelyn's words stay with me as I leave the house. Jared is in the driver's seat, his hands clutching the steering wheel as he faces forward, working a muscle in his jaw. I move around the car and open the door. Immediately, he releases the steering wheel and gazes at me. His jaw eases.

"I thought you changed your mind," he says as his lip twitches. His joking mannerism has me relaxing as I close the door.

"I was thinking about it, but the only way out is through the front door. So..." I clip my seat belt and glance at Jared.

His eyes light up with surprise, and his mouth pulls on one side. "Yeah, you wouldn't get away from me that easily."

I smile at his words. They make me happy, really happy. "I don't know, Jared. I think I could give you the slip." The deep laugh that erupts from his mouth as he pulls the car away from the sidewalk sends a shiver down my spine.

"We'll see," he says as his gaze bounces between me and the road.

After dropping my bag on the floor, I lay my hands on my lap. "So, where are we going?" I ask. It's something I've wondered all day since he left the garden.

He grins, and I'm grateful that he has to focus on the road. I use this moment to take in his profile. His jaw that twitches. I quickly look away, wondering if he's aware of me watching him.

"We're nearly there," he says after a moment.

I nod, but he doesn't see the action. "Okay."

"Don't be nervous, Layla." That surprises me. What makes him think I'm nervous? Then when I really think about it, I am nervous, but not about where we're going. No, it's how I'm feeling about him. "I won't let anything happen to you." When he says this, I have to look out the window. He still sees me as a victim.

"Yeah, I know," I tell my reflection. The night sky is a blank canvas waiting for the stars to appear. We pull off the main road and drive down a side road that's lit the whole way by small twinkle lights. They hang from every tree, and at the sight of them, I sit up and pay more attention to my surroundings.

A man in an illuminated jacket directs us to a temporary parking lot that's been set up on a beach.

"A beach," I say, staring out the window. Jared turns off the car, and my heart leaps as he takes my hand in his.

"Do you still trust me?" he asks, his eyes filled with raw emotion that causes my breath to hitch. I nod, and a slow grin spreads across his face.

"Let's go." He's out of the car and at my side in a moment. I pick up my bag as he opens the door for me. One hand is outstretched, and I reach out. My fingers look so small in his hand. He tightens his grip, and I'm not sure what to do. I keep waiting for him to let me go, but he still holds my hand as we walk down to the beach, our fingers entwined. Jared tugs on me, and I look up at him. His brows rise, and he has a silly smile on his face. This part of the beach is empty. A few people walk toward the larger gathering further down.

"Come on." Jared tugs me again, and he runs. We continue toward the water. We kick up the sand behind our heels. His large hand holding mine, the wind whipping past us, and the taste of salt on my lips is a moment of moments—one I will never forget.

When Jared releases my hand, I feel the loss immediately until I realize what he's doing. I copy him, tugging off my tennis shoes. I strip off my long blouse and dump my bag onto the sand. Jared has rolled his jeans up to his knees. I take his outstretched hand without hesitation this time, and we grin at each other before running into the water. This is us—we were thick as thieves as kids. Where he went, I went.

The cold spray hits me so hard that I'm laughing and screaming and running back to my pile of clothes. Large, strong arms wrap around my waist and lift me up into the air. The excess water that drips off me is freezing. I squeal as Jared pulls me back into the water.

"It's too cold!" I scream, and he dips my toes into the water. My mind goes to the lake, and the excitement leaves me. Then the heat of his chest against my back makes the whole thing feel different. He drops me lower until the water nearly touches my knees. I'm standing as the waves crash against my leg.

That's when I spot a star, the first one to show up on the blank canvas. Jared's arms hang close to my hips. I try to ignore the heaviness of them. Pointing to the star, I tilt my head back to look at Jared. "Make a wish," I say, and his nostrils flare as a tightness enters his jaw. My stomach hollows, and his hand touches my cheek—his brows furrow.

"I wish…" He pauses, and my heart drums.

"What are you doing?"

The warmth is gone. I only feel the cold, salty night water that laps against the back of my legs as I turn, along with Jared, to see someone standing near our pile of clothes.

"We'd better get back," Jared says, not looking at me. I'm surprised to find Kieran standing on the shore. His white shirt is light, nearly like mine, only his has sleeves. The shirt fits snugly against a surprisingly toned body.

"You're trouble, Layla," Kieran teases the moment I step out of the water. Jared tugs on his socks and shoes, not even waiting for his feet to dry.

"Yeah, a real troublemaker," I say, pulling on my shirt. Kieran laughs. Jared glances up at me. I can't get a read on him. He appears almost confused.

"I'm taking notes. Layla likes babysitting and water. You'll be a cheap date. I just need to find a baby."

I snort at Kieran. "I'm crossing babysitting off my list," I say.

He grins. "Amending notes. Only water on a first date."

Now I look away.

"She can't swim." Jared finally speaks, his words clipped. "Let's go, Layla."

Kieran looks between Jared and me, and I give him a tight smile. Jared picks up my shoes and bag, and I reach to take them from him, but he pulls back. I notice a red mark on the collar of his white shirt. I want to ask him where the lipstick came from, but he's looking away.

"I'll carry them." It isn't a statement, but a demand. Jared waits until I walk before falling in behind me. Kieran shadows me, taking each step with me.

"So, about that date," Kieran says, and I glance at him. He's attractive, with blue eyes and a cheeky smile. But I haven't forgotten how he was with Morgan the night of Chester's party.

"I don't really date," I say with a shrug. I can feel the full weight of Jared's stare on my back. This is like having a conversation with my dad behind me.

Kieran glances back at Jared, his brows pulling together before he turns to me, a smile replacing his frown. "Me neither. Hate dating."

I laugh at Kieran. He's persistent; I will give him that.

Up ahead, the party is starting to take shape. This isn't a regular beach party—a bar, DJ station, and even a dance floor have been erected. Most people wear white. Fire pits are spaced out and placed sporadically. The light from the fires doubles the shadows of all the people who stand close.

I notice some people sit on blankets. I'm about to mention not having a blanket but stiffen as Alex bounds toward us looking like one of those women from a Bond movie. Her gold bikini top is generously filled, water still clings to sun-kissed skin, and a flat stomach disappears under a long skirt that seems to flow across the sand. Her hair is wet and swept back. Drops of water hit me as she passes by. She stops at Jared, stretches on the tip of her toes, and kisses him softly on the cheek.

"Thank you for today." She sounds sincere.

I look away as my stomach falls like a rock. It's worse than the coldness of the water.

"No problem." Jared sounds stiff.

Alex giggles. "Oh, I got some lipstick on your shirt earlier."

Earlier? He was with her before he came to get me? My mind conjures up descriptive images of what they were doing.

I notice Kieran watching me, and I hope my emotions don't show. "I have a blanket if you need somewhere to sit," he says.

Yes is the right answer here. I need to leave Jared and Alex alone. But some part of me clings to Jared like a child to a parent's legs.

"It's fine. She can hang out with us," Alex says. She stares at him, blinking in rapid succession, but Jared is focused on Kieran so intently that I wonder what's keeping Kieran here. *Yeah, that isn't going to happen.*

"No, I don't want to intrude," I say.

Alex looks relieved.

"You're not. I'm the one who brought you." Jared finally looks at me, and I'm surprised that he can't feel the furious and beautiful female at his side. What is he doing? He clearly spent time with her before picking me up. The lipstick on his collar can't hide that fact. I have to stop this. He's trying to keep his promise that nothing will happen to me. His bringing me here is out of pity. But I'm not a victim anymore, and I actually, surprisingly, trust Kieran. He isn't a bad guy. Taking matters into my own hands, I gently take my shoes and bag out of Jared's hand. He resists at first but finally lets them go.

"I'll sit with Kieran. It's not fair leaving him alone." I turn to Kieran.

He gives me an easy smile. "Yep. If I'm alone, I may be attacked."

"Well, you kids have fun," Alex sings and reaches for Jared.

When Jared turns his gaze on me, I'm stunned to see so much anger in his eyes. "You aren't sitting with him." Jared's jaw is clenched, and this situation just went from uncomfortable to awkward.

My mind races, trying to make sense of his actions. One minute we're going to a party. The next, Alex, who really seems like his girlfriend, is here marking her territory. Now he wants me to join them—and something clicks. An unnatural stillness fills me, and I paste on a smile.

"I'll join you," I tell Jared, as if not joining him is an option.

I turn to Kieran, wanting to apologize, but he holds up both hands. "I'll leave you to it, but my offer still stands," he says, walking away.

I give him a soft smile before turning back to Jared. But It's Alex who I focus on, and the phrase 'if looks could kill' springs to mind. Yep, she hates me. But she has no need to. What clicked with me only a few moments ago is that Jared sees me as the young girl he spent his childhood protecting. For that, I will be eternally grateful. But I'm not a victim anymore, and after tonight, I'll have a chat with him and let him know he's off the hook. I don't need protection. The thought of losing him for a second time halts the air in my lungs.

Breathe. Just Breathe.

CHAPTER TWENTY-THREE

LAYLA

"L EAD THE WAY," I say before glancing up at Jared. A muscle tics in his jaw as his eyes cloud with sadness, which makes no sense.

I would have asked him what was wrong, but Alex tugs at his arm, getting his attention. "Come on. Mark's waiting for us," she says.

As I walk behind the happy couple, I glance over at Kieran, who's observing me. He gives me a wave, and I wish I were sitting with him. The idea of Alex and I in such close proximity is making my belly ache. But these are the people that Jared loves. Nothing is going to happen at a crowded party, and so far, Alex has been sociable. I need to be happy for Jared.

The fire pit that we stop at has several students I recognize from Kingscourt College. Alex accepts a kiss on both cheeks from the man she acknowledges as Mark. Mark's gaze finds mine, and he inspects me like I'm a fly he wants to squash. I'm sure Alex shared some delightful details about me. I think he was in gym class on my first day. Now that I really think about it, I'm sure he was there.

I glance around and focus on the friendly smile of Sam, Ashley's brother, who's at a fire pit across from us. I recognize the other boy who stands with him from my first day of class, but I can't remember his name.

"Layla, isn't it?" Sam asks as he makes his way over to me. His green eyes twinkle with alcohol. The smell of his breath brushes my face as he speaks.

I can feel the heat of Jared on my left-hand side, and I know Mark is only inches behind me, along with Alex.

"Yeah. Sam, right?" I say.

His face opens up into a huge smile. "I knew I made an impression."

I nod before glancing over at Jared. He folds his arms across his chest, and my gaze snags on the band of ink tattooed on his wrist. Mark speaks to him, but Jared doesn't even look like he's present. He turns in my direction.

I swallow under the intensity. I want to ask so many questions. I've never felt so conflicted before. The pull that I feel toward him is clearly one-sided, but I still want to talk to him. I still want to relearn everything about Jared. I wonder what his life is like.

"Do you drink?" I ask, focusing on my words and not my emotions. Jared's lips part. Surprise flickers in his chocolate eyes.

"Yeah, I do."

He pauses before stepping closer to me. The world around us gets swallowed up, and it's just Jared and I.

"Are you going to tell me what you drink? Or do I have to guess?" I ask.

He smiles, dimples appearing, pushing my mind down the wrong path again.

Just friends. Just friends.

"Guess."

"He looks like a brandy kind of drinker to me," Sam says. That's when I notice everyone is listening to us. But I remind myself that we're two friends having a chat.

"Nah, I think Scotch," the other guy says. He has the same smiling green eyes as Sam. They are definitely related. They high-five.

"I wasn't asking either of you morons," Jared says.

"A beer?" I ask to erase the tension.

Jared's eyes light up, and his smile widens. "Nope."

I don't look at Alex or Mark, but their silence tells me they're listening.

Alex lets out a heavy sigh, one that can't be ignored by anyone. "He likes vodka and 7UP," she tells me with narrowed eyes before focusing on Jared. "That wasn't so hard, was it?" Her angry words are delivered with a shake of her head.

Heat filters across my face.

"You're being fucking rude." Jared's response is delivered with his own anger, and I want to dig a hole in the sand and disappear.

"No, Jared, you are. And after everything I told you." Alex's eyes fill with tears, and she takes a step away from Jared.

I have no idea what to make out of what's happening. My heart gives a heavy thud, and she runs off.

"You should make sure she's okay," Mark encourages Jared.

"I'll be back in a minute." Jared leaves, and it shouldn't hurt this much.

"She's very protective." Sam speaks beside me, giving me a kind smile.

"Well, when people stomp on your territory..."

My body freezes at Mark's words.

"Layla isn't stomping on anyone's territory," Sam says over his shoulder.

"I'm just saying. And who invited you to my party?"

Sam shifts uncomfortably. "You invited the whole college."

Mark looks Sam up and down with a sneer. "Oh, I forgot. Some of you are here on scholarships."

A group of girls approaches the fire pit and starts hugging and kissing Mark. He gets saturated with their affection and attention. They all walk away from the fire pit, leaving me with Sam and his friend. I'm wedged between the two.

"What a fucking dick," Sam growls after Mark and his friends. Mark can't hear him at this distance, but I nod my head in agreement. I want to look in the direction that Jared went, but I don't. He needs his time with Alex.

"So, how's my sister treating you?" Sam asks. His eyes sparkle. The darkness that clouded them only moments ago is erased.

"Yeah, she's great. Ashley's been really good to me," I answer honestly. Sam's friend leaves and heads in the direction of the bar; my assumption is to get another drink, leaving me alone with Sam. I just pray Sam doesn't leave. It'll look like I scared everyone off. Actually, I kind of have.

"Do you work?" I ask, wanting to keep him engaged in conversation.

"Nah, it's hard to get a job when you're living on my side of town." His words have lost the joking tone. He has been jovial since I arrived.

My gaze takes him in. He has on tracksuit bottoms and well-kept but worn shoes. The T-shirt he wears is clean but has that worn look to it. His friend arrives back carrying two red plastic cups. One, he hands to me. I take the cup and thank him. It will give my hands something to do. Sam returns to his joking way with his friend, who I find out is named Nathan. I relax, just listening to their banter back and forth. My eyes occasionally meet Kieran's from his own fire pit. He isn't alone anymore.

A dark-haired girl stands with him. He speaks easily to her, but she isn't leaning in toward him or doing anything romantic. They look comfortable with each other. My throat is dry, and I take a deep drink. The liquid soothes my throat immediately. I take another sip, liking how it's making me forget my problems and relaxing my body. When my cup is empty, I leave Nathan and Sam and go in search of the supply of alcohol. The bar is mostly empty. A girl with pink pigtails takes my outstretched red cup and fills it up. She looks like she's drinking more than she's giving out. Watching over the partygoers, I drink this cup slowly. My spine straightens as Mark materializes beside me.

"You're still here enjoying my alcohol?" he questions. He appears half-drunk, but awareness is still there.

"Yes, it's a great party," I say and feel a little surprised at my bravery. He smirks but with no humor. Mark's gaze takes me in from my bare feet all the way back up to my eyes before he walks away. I shiver.

I gulp down my drink and turn to the girl with pink hair. She seems even more drunk, if that's possible. I get half a cup this time as she sloshes the rest over her hand. As I glance around at everyone talking and laughing, I've never felt so alone. It's the worst kind of loneliness to be surrounded by other human beings, surrounded by noise, yet feel so insignificant. Even Nathan and Sam laugh about something I can't hear from this distance.

I look at the cup and make a decision. "Why not?" I speak my thoughts aloud and gulp the rest of the drink as I watch Kieran make out with the girl that I had assessed as a non-romantic friend. Yep, I have a great love radar. Just like I had with Jared, who enters the circle of light.

My stomach tilts when I see him across the beach. The light flickers across his face. He's looking for someone. Maybe Alex has returned too. I take another drink, only to find my cup empty again. Turning around to get a refill, I find no one is there to serve me. I reach across, turning the tap that's attached to a keg before filling up my cup.

"Hey."

I continue filling up my cup without looking at Kieran. "Hi." My greeting sounds sharp, electing a laugh from Kieran. I turn to him with narrowed eyes. "Why are you laughing at me?" I question him while taking another drink. Some reasonable part of me is saying I need to stop drinking and go home, but this angry part of me is growing and expanding, taking over every space inside my very drunk brain.

"Let's take a walk." Kieran takes my arm with a warm smile still on his face. He reaches for the cup, but I pull it out of his reach. "You've had enough."

My cheeks heat because I know he's right, but I drink nearly half the cup before handing it over. Then we head out across the beach.

The sand feels nice between my toes. The breeze tousles my hair. I glance down at our joined hands and focus on what I feel. Funnily enough, I don't mind his hand in mine; it doesn't cause the turmoil that Jared's does. I don't want to think about Jared like that. It just isn't right.

"Where's the girl you were kissing?" I ask.

Kieran kicks up the sand as we walk, and I notice he isn't wearing shoes either. "Not sure. Maybe she's off kissing some other guy." He glances at me.

The light of the fire pits is no longer our guide as we stroll down the coast. The moon, which is bright and high in the sky, shows us the way.

"Did you kiss any guys?" Kieran asks.

I burst out laughing. The sad reality is that I might have kissed guys before, but that's as far as it went. "No. I didn't get many offers."

He looks back at the sand, a smile still on his face. "I mean, I can change that."

I stop walking. "What are you going to do? Kiss me like you did the other girl?" I ask bravely. The drink is giving me a backbone.

"No. Never." Kieran lets my hand go and folds his across his chest. He wears the most serious look I have ever seen on him.

"So now you won't kiss me?" I continue on my very bold streak.

"I only kiss strangers. If I like someone, I'll take the time to get to know them."

I'm smiling, and Kieran smiles, too, while retaking my hand.

"You like me?" I ask, based on his logic of not kissing me.

He gives a short laugh. "I've asked you out several times. I thought that would let you know I like you."

"I just thought you were messing around." We've stopped walking again; I'm not sure why. But the moon seems to shine on Kieran like a spotlight.

His eyes roam my face as he speaks. "I was serious. Still am."

I feel grateful for his affection toward me, and I find myself taking a step closer.

"If I like someone, I kiss them," I say.

I watch as his lips part while his eyes flick to mine as I wet them.

I make a move, something I've never done in my life. The sad reality of my non-existent romantic life doesn't go beyond a kiss. My lips meet his soft ones. They feel warm against mine. My brain tries to make a comparison to Jared's. There is none. I hate that I'm even thinking about Jared. My tongue flicks out, and Kieran moans, pulling me closer to him. One moment I'm wrapped in his warmth, trying to push thoughts of Jared away, and the next, we're struck by someone. I open my eyes as Kieran is dragged and dumped into the water. The drink slowly fades as I race into the waves.

"Kieran!" Water splashes against my ankles as Kieran sits up, wiping water off his face. Jared stands over him. I can't see Jared's face, but I can tell he's breathing heavily from the movement of his shoulders, and before I can move another inch, he's reaching for Kieran again, and I'm running.

CHAPTER TWENTY-FOUR

JARED (BEFORE)

"**I**'LL BE BACK IN a minute," I bite out, and I don't look back at Layla.

I search for Alex, but the drama queen has disappeared. I stop by the bar, and I'm ready to order a vodka and 7UP, but I think of Alex telling Layla that's what I drink, and I hate it.

"A beer." The red cup is filled from a keg. I expect the beer to be flat, but it tastes nice. I turn and keep scanning for Alex. I'll give her five more minutes, and then I'm going back to Layla. I finish the beer and see Alex with a group of girls who are squealing as they race into the water. They all huddle together as one of them snaps a photo.

Alex is smiling and laughing, her lips pursed for the photo. I'm wasting my time.

"Jay." The guy's accent has me turning away from the sea and toward the two guys who stand near the edge of the beach. Some underbrush has broken through the sand and taken over a small patch. I don't step closer to them. The tattoos that snake along their necks, and the small ones on their faces, mark them as part of Chester's gang. I knew he would send his men. I just didn't think it would be in such a public place.

"That's me," I answer while keeping a relaxed pose as I scan them for weapons. I don't see any, but that doesn't relax me.

"You've been issued your warning." He juts out his chin before taking a long pull of his cigarette.

"A warning for what?" I ask, dread tightening itself across my chest.

"You ever hear the term 'If you cut off a snake's head, eight more will appear'?" He doesn't wait for me to answer. Instead, he flicks his cigarette onto the sand; the amber burns brightly. "We're like that. You hurt one of us, and you have to deal with eight more."

I shift my stance, ready to fight. I grin. "You want to hobble home to Chester and join him with his recovery?"

My bravado is smashed as he grins back, like he knows something I don't. He holds up his fingers and makes the motion of cocking a gun.

"You fucked with the wrong people, bro."

I grin. "I ain't your bro."

The other guy, who has remained silent, slaps the fucker who still holds his hands up. He jerks out his chin. "Let's split."

He nods and drops his hand, but not before grinning at me. "Eight snakes," he says before leaving the beach, and it feels worse than anything. I need to watch my back. I don't regret beating the shit out of Chester. I made sure he'll never speak to Layla again. The delight I felt at breaking his bones was worth it. He isn't going to shoot me, but I'm sure I'll be jumped at some stage. I just need to make sure it's not when Layla is with me. I need to go to Chester again and issue him one of my warnings.

Hurting Chester has already cost me everything. The gun he was meant to supply me with won't be happening now. Killing Bert has been my focus for my months, my way out of this torture.

But I'll find another way.

I return to the bar with worry worming its way through my body. I don't want any repercussions for Layla. I can't let that happen. What if they hurt her? I'm turning away from the bar and making my way back to the fire pit where I left her. My fear almost consumes me when I return to find her gone.

Alex smiles at me sweetly. Water still drips off her body. She drinks through a straw while smiling.

"Where is she?" I ask and take a step toward Alex.

Her smile falters, but there's a level of satisfaction in her eyes that alarms me. "She went off with Kieran."

Before I can ask where, Alex points down the beach. I don't say a word as I take off after Layla. Please, God, tell me she's safe. If anything happens to her... I slam into a group of people, knocking them to the ground. Their shouts don't slow me down, and I race past the party, and the sounds fade away. I start to imagine what could be happening to Layla. What I don't expect is to find her kissing Kieran.

I don't slow down as I plow into him and drag him to the water, where I intend to drown him for touching what's mine. A thirst for blood drives my fist into his face, and I don't think anything could stop me, not even Layla's screams, as I plunge Kieran's head underwater and refuse to let him up. Madness drives me further as I watch him fight for air that I deprive him of.

He will never touch what's mine again.

CHAPTER TWENTY-FIVE

LAYLA

"**S**TAY AWAY FROM HER, or I will fucking kill you," Jared threatens.

Kieran's complexion loses all color. My heart thumps heavily in my chest as Jared's fist connects with Kieran's face. Kieran howls in pain, but his screams are cut off as Jared pushes him under the water. I've nearly reached them, and I keep thinking that Jared will let Kieran go, but he pushes his hands lower into the water, sending Kieran deeper.

"Let him go!" I push Jared with as much strength as I can muster, but he doesn't stop. "Jared!"

He looks at me, and it's like he doesn't see me. Cruelty darkens his eyes as Kieran swings blindly, struggling for air.

He's going to kill him.

My hands connect with Jared's side, but they make no impact. "Let him go! You're going to kill him!" I scream my fear, and Jared releases Kieran, who bursts through the surface, gasping for air while trying to get away from Jared. I reach for Kieran, but he moves away from me. He doesn't stop until he reaches the shore, where he falls to his knees.

I can't even look at Jared as I race toward Kieran. "Are you okay?"

He's still gasping for air, and when he looks up at me with angry eyes, I step back. "He tried to fucking drown me."

"Don't speak to her like that." Jared drags Kieran off the ground.

Fear drives my next words. "You're just like Bert."

It's like a blow, and Jared releases Kieran. This time, Kieran doesn't wait around. He takes off down the beach.

I've never seen Jared like this. I've never seen him so violent.

Jared is huffing, but he doesn't move. I want to take my words back because he's not a monster like Bert.

"You can't just do that," I protest.

"He was taking advantage of you." His eyes harden as he glances in the direction that Kieran ran off in.

"*I* kissed *him*, Jared," I whisper, not sure why I'm whispering.

Jared doesn't say anything for a moment; he just glares at me, burning away the last of the alcohol from my system.

"I can smell the alcohol on you. You're not thinking clearly." Jared takes my arm and leads me toward the party.

"I'm not a ten-year-old victim anymore." I pull my arm out of his hand angrily, and his eyes soften a fraction. "You keep looking at me like I'm a little girl." He seems to think I need to be saved.

He shakes his head while exhaling air from his body. "I definitely know you're not a little girl, Layla." The way his eyes roam my body as he speaks has sparks coming to life inside me.

"You need to stop putting yourself in bad situations."

Those sparks die a painful death. My eyes and throat burn. "Like what I did when I was twelve?"

Jared runs his hand along his jaw. "That's not what I meant." The silence stretches out.

"I didn't mean that about Bert."

Jared doesn't answer.

I fold my arms across my chest and glance down the path that Kieran took. "He's the first normal thing that's happened to me," I say, and as the words leave my mouth, I realize how accurate they are. He liked me. That was it. So simple.

Jared's shoulders are tense. His whole body looks like it's carved from stone. His eyes are a black abyss in which I think I might drown, so I look away.

"I'm taking you home. And don't argue with me." He reaches for me once again, but I pull away. "Layla." His warning has me moving.

"No. You don't get to tell me what to do, Jared. I mean…" The air grows heavy, and I wrap my arms around my waist. "I don't understand. You have Alex." I sound pathetic. "And that's fine," I add the lie.

Jared steps closer to me. "I don't want Alex."

I want to ask him what he wants, but a fear I've become accustomed to buries that question.

"I'll go home. But I wanted to go home, anyway." I turn away from him and start to walk back toward the lights of the party. Neither of us speaks. Jared stops by the fire pit and picks up my bag and shoes. Alex and Mark give me death stares. They don't ask Jared any questions. I use the moment to look around for Kieran, but he isn't at the fire drying off like he said he would be. I really messed up.

"Ready?" Jared asks.

I start walking—that's my answer to Jared. I take my bag from him as we reach his car. I wait for him to unlock the doors, but when the locks don't click, I look up at him to find him watching me.

"Even at twelve, you were never a victim. I have never met anyone as strong as you."

My eyes burn at his words. I never felt strong. I always hated myself for being so weak. My gaze flickers over the roof of the car to Jared, who places both his hands on top. I again notice the band on his wrist. His eyes burn with a conviction of his words.

"How can you say that? You had to save me every time." Jared blurs as my eyes fill up. Memories of Bert slapping me, closing his fist to me, kicking me, choking me, even spitting on me, come crashing back like a wave, and my body starts to shake.

I tuck my hands behind my back so Jared won't see the shakes that have taken over. "What's the tattoo for?" I ask to try to take the spotlight off me, but my voice trembles, and a tear escapes the tight prison I kept it in, trickling down my face.

Jared shakes his head as he moves around the car. His warmth envelops me, and I sink into his comfort, feeling like a coward once again. I always seem to need him. I think I'm starting to crave him.

Maybe I always have.

"Nothing will hurt you again." His hand moves through my hair so gently that I sense the touch down to my core.

"I'm sorry," I say, feeling embarrassed. I want to be strong. I need to be strong. But this isn't being strong. I swallow my emotions and move reluctantly away from Jared. His hands tighten on my forearm, keeping me from getting too far. I don't struggle or try to get away. Being here with him feels so right.

"I want you to listen to me." His head dips so I'm eye level with him. "Don't ever apologize."

I glance away, feeling my face burn.

"Layla." This time, the warning is different from only a few moments ago on the beach. It's strong, yet gentle. "You hear me?" Jared's eyes gleam like he's fighting back the tears, and that makes me pause.

"Yeah, I do. Are you okay?" I ask, and it breaks the spell. His violence toward Kieran scared me, and the look in his eyes now sends shivers skittering across my flesh.

He releases me and looks away briefly. When his gaze returns to me, his stare is empty, and I wonder if I imagined it only moments ago.

"Come on, let me take you home." He unlocks the car, but I stand there and watch him open his door. Our eyes collide once again over the roof.

"Get in, Layla," he says before disappearing into the vehicle. I get in but can't help that something niggles at me. For a moment, he looked so broken, and it's a look I used to see him wear when he thought no one was watching. But he was only a kid then. I never really questioned it, but seeing that look of pure devastation in his eyes makes my stomach tighten. I can't take my eyes off him as he reverses out of the spot, his arm behind my headrest as he looks out the back window.

"Why are you staring at me?" he asks, still reversing.

"I'm not sure. You just looked so sad a moment ago." Sad isn't the correct word. Brown eyes focus on me as his hand shifts the stick into gear.

"I hate to see you upset." Even as he says it, his voice holds a note of something else.

A lie?

"Why do I feel like there's something you aren't telling me?" I ask, and he zones in on the road with a laugh that doesn't sound real. It comes out more bitter than anything.

"Like what?" he asks as he puts his foot down way too quickly, jerking me forward. His arm shoots out to keep me from hitting the dash. "Put on your seat belt." He speaks through gritted teeth. He's like four seasons at once tonight. I can't figure him out. The snap of my seat belt has him pulling his arm away from me.

"Like how you're all emotional tonight." Emotional isn't the right word, but I don't know how to explain this.

"Yeah well, Layla, I just had a fistfight with someone..."

I sink back into the chair, my adrenaline crashing.

A fistfight? To me, it looked like Jared really wasn't going to let Kieran up. Another shiver assaults me at the thought. Maybe I saw it wrong. Maybe it was a fistfight. I forgot he knew Kieran. Are they close friends? My actions may have caused a rift.

"I'm sorry," I whisper.

His jaw twitches before he speaks. "It doesn't matter," he says, and I beg to differ, but I decide to leave it alone. Guilt eats away at me. I caused this. As I look out the window, I notice most of the houses are dark. Only one or two have lights on behind curtains. It takes us another five minutes of torturous silence before Jared pulls up to my house. The porch light is on. Bless Carl's and Evelyn's hearts.

My shoes sit on the floor of the car, and I unclip the belt while pulling them on. Sitting back, I grab my bag while reaching for the door.

"I never liked Kieran anyway, but he knew you had a drink in you."

I sit back and look at Jared, my mouth slightly ajar. His words are reflecting my thoughts, but I just nod, and Jared lets out a heavy breath.

"I don't want you thinking it's your fault." His hands clutch the steering wheel tightly. My suspicions are rising. "Same with Alex. That's not your fault either."

"Okay... Is someone going to say it's my fault?" I question slowly. Jared's gaze flickers to mine before he observes me. I want to squirm in my seat despite the heaviness of his stare.

"Yes. Alex will blame you, but it's bullshit."

Oh God, did she notice how I looked at him?

"Bullshit. You're not to blame," Jared tries to reassure me. But of course, he sees me as a friend and thinks that's how I see him. But Alex can see the truth.

"What did she say?" I whisper, not wanting to know but needing to.

"Stupid stuff that makes no sense." He shakes his head and releases the steering wheel. "Look, I'm exhausted. We can talk more tomorrow."

I swallow the fear that's clawing its way up my throat. Did I cause this? Is Jared too embarrassed to tell me what Alex said? I nod and open the door, one foot on the road, when Jared's hand circles my wrist. The heat of his hand warms the coldest parts inside me, and my eyes burn. I squeeze them before looking at him with a forced smile.

"We'll talk tomorrow," I say.

He studies me, his gaze making a pathway along my face.

"Good night." Two words, but it makes my stomach fill with lead.

"Night, Jared." He doesn't release my wrist, and I'm facing him again.

"I got the tattoo three years ago."

I glance down at his fingers that still encircle my wrist. Reaching out, I push the sleeve of his sweater up, and there it is, a dark ink band on his wrist.

"What happened three years ago?" I ask, looking at the smaller details on the band. It appears to be Celtic knots.

"I lost someone."

I look back up at Jared. "I didn't know. I'm so sorry." Shivers race up and down my arms.

"It's my handcuffs." His smile twists my gut painfully. He releases my wrist. "That's what it felt like. I was a prisoner in my own life."

My heart thumps heavier as he runs his fingers along his wrist, along the band of ink. "A reminder that this life would be torture without..."

I have no idea who this person was, but jealousy rears its ugly head, and I want nothing more than to find out who caused him such pain.

"Was it sudden?"

Jared's focus returns to mine. The haunted look leaves his eyes, and he sits back. "No."

I don't want to pry, but I can't help all the questions that flood my mind. "Was it family?" I ask.

His smile is bitter. "Yes, and No."

His mother? Ashley said his mother might be dead.

It's clear he doesn't want to talk about this, and I'm not ready to leave him. I search my mind for something to say. "I've always wanted to get a tattoo."

Jared's eyes widen with surprise, and both brows rise. "Layla with a tattoo," he teases. "What would you get a tattoo of?"

I shrug. "I'm not sure." An image of Tinnies springs to mind—happier times—and I use that humor to hopefully lighten this moment with Jared.

"Maybe a heart over my right breast."

Jared's laughter has me joining in. "Like Tinnies," he says.

My laughter starts, and it shakes my belly as I think of her. She was a large blonde Dublin woman with a heart tattoo on her right breast. She always pushed our faces into that breast while hugging us.

"Her boobs were so big." I nearly can't breathe with the laughter.

"She got off on it." Jared joins in, and when our laughter slows down, I realize how nice this is— laughing over the fun times. There was no harm in Tinnies.

"What was her real name?" I ask.

"Not a clue." Jared sighs like he's content, and I wonder how long it's been since he's laughed. I think of the look in his eyes earlier, and it dries up all my humor.

"You know, I'm here if you need to talk."

"Yeah, I know." Jared reaches across and touches my cheek tenderly. "Now go to bed before I change my mind."

I want him to. "What will happen if you change your mind?"

He releases my face. "Don't, Layla."

I want to poke at him, but instead, I lose any semblance of bravery and exit his car.

CHAPTER TWENTY-SIX

LAYLA

I WAKE UP SUNDAY morning to a message from Jared.

I'm sorry for being a dick last night. I was out of order. Can I make it up to you?

I smile at his words. Even after so much time away from each other and after his argument with Alex, he's still here for me. Thinking of him not dating Alex gives me way more joy than it should. I'm still unsettled with his violence toward Kieran. I have no idea how he is. Maybe it was just a fistfight between two guys. I had a lot of drink, so I may have judged the situation wrong.

Sure, what do you want to do? I type back quickly and leave the phone on the bedside table as I enter the bedroom and wash my face and brush my teeth. I hear movement downstairs, and I can smell breakfast. The crispy bacon has my stomach grumbling—the scent is divine. I leave my bedroom and make my way to the kitchen.

Evelyn is waiting in the kitchen with a plate of toast on the table. I go straight for the coffee, my head complaining about all the alcohol I drank last night. Evelyn doesn't say anything until I sit down. Instead, she butters a slice of toast and cuts it into triangles, then piles bacon on my plate before passing it over to me.

"I know we haven't put down any ground rules, but I think we should."

A flush creeps across my cheeks.

Evelyn immediately waves her hand at me. "I'm not reprimanding you, sweetheart. It's just that I worry."

I take a bite out of my toast to give myself something to do. "No, I get it."

Carl arrives in the kitchen then, with a gray suit on, his face freshly shaven. He's leaving on another business trip. He kisses me on the head before moving quickly through the kitchen, gathering up his travel mug, keys, and phone.

"Fun night?" he asks while looking for something else—most likely his wallet, which he always leaves in the woven basket on the hall table.

"Yeah," I answer as Evelyn watches me. A soft smile tugs at her lips.

"It's in the basket in the hall," I tell Carl.

He finally looks up at me, his eyes lighting up. "You're right." He gives me another kiss on the head before kissing Evelyn softly on the cheek. "I'll see you girls tomorrow night," he says before leaving.

I chew on the toast as Evelyn drinks her coffee. "I think we should limit ourselves to three drinks."

I nod immediately. I'm not one for drinking anyway, so I won't be repeating last night again.

"How do you know I had more than three?" I ask.

Evelyn grins. "Have you looked in the mirror? And I was your age once."

I haven't looked in the mirror, but I obviously look terrible. I'm about to comment on the age thing, but the doorbell rings. Evelyn gets up to answer the door, and I wonder what Carl has forgotten this time. He's always leaving something behind. I break up the bacon and put it on my toast.

I can hear the front door close. "What did he forget?" I call. I look toward the door, and there's Jared, looking so out of place in my home. He towers in the doorframe.

"Jared! What... Why are you here?" I ask.

Evelyn steps up behind him. She tilts her head so I can see her and widens her eyes. Humiliation stains my cheeks as Jared steps into the modest kitchen. He sits down beside Evelyn's chair.

"Don't be so rude. He's obviously here to see you," Evelyn tells me.

My humiliation triples.

Before I can reply, Evelyn speaks to Jared. "Tea or Coffee?"

Jared watches Evelyn, and there's something in his gaze that I can't decipher. It's not like the way he looked at Carl. With Carl, I saw respect; I saw a relaxed Jared. Right now, he seems guarded.

"Tea, please. Thank you, Mrs. Masters."

Evelyn's about to pour his tea, but she pauses with a smile on her face. "Call me Evelyn. Otherwise, you will make me feel like an old woman."

"Thank you, Evelyn." Jared's voice is smooth.

He glances at me, and his lip quirks up. A dimple erupts on his cheek, causing my heart to falter.

"Every time you see me, you make me feel so unwanted." His teasing tone has a chuckle coming from Evelyn. I'm trying to take in that Jared is sitting beside me in my kitchen as Evelyn makes him tea. Then I remember I'm in my bedclothes, and after Evelyn's statement, I more than likely look like someone who has a hangover.

"You keep arriving unannounced," I say in my defense.

"You never answer your phone."

I narrow my eyes on him. He has a point. I left my phone upstairs, but his arriving unannounced still rattles me.

"Here, sweetie," Evelyn says as she places the mug in front of Jared. Evelyn sits down with a raised eyebrow at me. I know that look she's giving me. It's to mind my p's and q's.

"So..." I say to Jared, whose eyes light up gleefully at my discomfort.

"So..." he says before taking a sip of the tea, dragging out my torture. "I'm here to take you out."

My face heats. Thankfully, Jared focuses on Evelyn. It gives me a second to try to gather myself. Instead, my eyes roam over him. His gray T-shirt fits him snugly. Tanned arms rest on the table. The tattoo sends the small hairs on the back of my neck to rise. He lost someone three years ago. Maybe one day he'll trust me enough to share more with me. My gaze follows the curve of his neck and across his sharp cheekbones.

"This tea is great. Thank you," he tells Evelyn, making me look up to find her watching me. She glances back to Jared.

"You're welcome. So where are you thinking of going?" The question isn't asked with the recent joking nature that she's taken since Jared arrived. She sounds like a mother. What has changed?

Is it because she caught me looking at him?

"To my house," he says before looking at me. "I thought you might like if I showed you around our gardens."

My heart swells in my chest. When I glance at Evelyn, she's hiding a smile behind her mug.

"Yeah, sounds great. I'd love to see your gardens," I tell Jared, and he lets out a little breath like I might have said no to him. I'm beginning to learn that saying no to Jared isn't exactly an option.

"Whenever you're ready."

I wonder if today is because of last night. Does he feel guilty about Kieran? He's here because he cares about me. Because I'm his friend. Right now, I want to hug him. Jared tips his head to the side. "You okay?"

I've been staring at him for far too long. My gaze snaps to Evelyn, and I get up to try to hide my embarrassment. Yeah, she's amused by it.

"Yep. I'll go get ready." I don't look at either of them as I leave the room.

***

The blue sundress makes my already large blue eyes pop. It's my favorite—the one I keep for special occasions. But I rarely get to wear the dress. I only wore it one time, when Evelyn's sister's son was being deployed, and we had to attend the 'final meal.' That's what Carl called it once we got out of the house. I hid the grin, but his wink told me he saw my smirk. It was the most depressing meal I've ever attended, and I had so many shitty dinners with Bert and Ronnie that I didn't think anything could be worse. I was wrong.

Evelyn's sister, Rose, looked nearly identical to Evelyn and spent the meal sobbing onto her fork, which she would fill with food, push into her mouth, and then cry on. The fork would remain locked between her lips. It wasn't until her husband comforted her that she removed the fork and chewed her food slowly and loudly. The son—I can't even remember his name; Scott I think—ate his food mechanically, and every once in a while, he would glance over at us and apologize before patting his mother's hand.

My fingers run down the buttons on the full length of the dress. Giving myself one final look in the mirror, I flip my hair back over my shoulders.

As I approach the kitchen, I can hear Evelyn's and Jared's voices. They chat easily; the topic is the weather. Once I open the door, my stomach flips as Jared turns toward me. A slow smile spreads across his face, and his dimples appear. I stop at the door, trying to calm myself.

"You should maybe grab a jacket." Evelyn's voice pulls my attention from Jared to her. Her eyes say so much more, like: *maybe grab some common sense while you're at it.* I get my jacket and bag off the hook in the hall as I talk to myself. "I need to pull myself together." When I return, I'm more composed and smile at Evelyn. "I shouldn't be too late," I tell her.

"Have a good day." Evelyn gets up.

"I've got it from here," Jared says while taking my elbow. Something in the way he speaks to Evelyn leaves me uneasy as he escorts me out of the house.

"Was there a problem while I was getting dressed?" I ask as Jared opens my car door.

"No problems. Why?" He grips the door, and I'm not ready to get in.

"If there were, you would tell me, right?"

"There is no problem, Layla. Get in the car." He says the last part with a slight grin.

I slide into the car, and he closes my door. Jared gets in, and I'm consumed with his scent.

"So what do you think?" I ask as Jared starts the car, and we take off. It's warm, and I roll down my window.

The slight breeze that floats in cools me down nicely.

"I have AC," Jared says with a smile in his voice.

"I know. I like the natural air."

"I think you look beautiful."

My heart pitter-patters at his words.

"I can't stop thinking about fucking you," he continues.

The saliva in my mouth feels heavy, and I swallow it with a bit of trouble before coughing. Why would he say something like that? Did I hear him wrong?

"You keep saying that."

He looks at me, his eyes dark. "Because it's true." His gaze roams down my body.

He confuses me. My mind goes to a place where Jared's hands are on me, and the hairs rise on my arms.

"How?" I whisper.

"How would I fuck you?" Jared doesn't hold back.

I realize I'm not ready for this conversation. "When I asked you what you thought, I was referring to Evelyn. What did you think of her?" I hope moving to safer ground will cool me down. I push the window down a bit more and have to grab my hair as it whips around my face.

The natural air stops, and a blast from the AC has me releasing my hair as Jared rolls up my window.

"Talking about Evelyn in the same conversation about me fucking you seems a tad bit inappropriate." He smirks at me. "Don't you think?"

I try to open my window again, but it's locked. "That's not fair," I say to the window.

"You can't run, Layla, or hide."

I look back at Jared. He's enjoying this too much.

My heart races. "I've never been with anyone." My face blazes as the car swerves slightly before Jared gets it back on the road.

The blood roars in my ears. I shouldn't have told him that, because it looks like I'm thinking about sleeping with him. Which I am.

"Like *dated* someone?" Jared's mouth is slightly ajar; his brows drag down. He keeps looking at me.

"Focus on the road!" I bark, and he switches his attention from me to the road.

"Layla, answer me."

"No, Jared, not like dated!" I don't know why I'm shouting.

He keeps looking at me like I've just materialized out of thin air. He refocuses on the road, and when he looks back at me, I see the truth settle in his mind. "You're a virgin?"

I hate that word. "Yes."

I don't want to look at him. I'm sure he won't want to touch me now. That thought is crippling.

"That's perfect."

My gaze snaps up to him.

"You're perfect." He's speaking to the road, but he finally looks at me. "It will make each second even more enjoyable."

I swallow at his words, and the funny thing is, they excite me. Jared doesn't ask why I'm a virgin. He doesn't seem to think I'm broken or that

I must have some damage on my body. He knows every part of me. I find myself reaching for my scarred leg.

"You're fucking perfect." His words are harsh. "Every single part of you." He reaches toward me and touches my face.

I could get used to his words. I nod. A sense of being overwhelmed at his compliments flood my body.

He releases my face, and we stop outside his house. The thought of being alone with him is frightening but exciting too. I keep stealing glances at his profile as the gates open, and he resumes driving up to his home.

"So, what did you think of Evelyn?" I ask, trying once again to move our conversation to more comfortable grounds.

"She treats you well?" he asks.

It's not the response I want. But I answer his question. "Yes."

"You love her?" He shifts the car into drive and pulls into a garage.

"Yes, I do," I answer easily.

"She loves you too?" Jared looks at me after killing the engine.

I find myself smiling. "Very much."

"Then I like her," he answers.

His gaze burns deeper than anything I've ever felt before. It sends electricity racing through my body. "A virgin."

"You make it sound like I'm going to be a sacrifice," I try to tease.

Jared leans closer. "I mean, ropes and candles do sound nice."

My face blazes. I'm not naïve, but the thoughts of Jared like that make me see him differently.

Jared smiles. "Don't look so terrified."

"You're joking." I let out a heavy breath and try to calm down.

"No."

I'm waiting for him to laugh, and when he doesn't, I have no idea what to say.

Jared gets out of the car. "Let me show you the gardens."

Right now, I don't care about the gardens. I get out of the car and follow him out of the garage.

Ropes and candles.

"I'm just showing you the gardens. You look ready to run." Jared's teasing tone surprises me, and when he reaches back, I zero in on the ink on his wrist before taking his hand, and my soul sighs.

It's like I'm finally where I belong.

CHAPTER TWENTY-SEVEN

JARED

SHE'S A VIRGIN. THE more I get to know Layla, the harder I fall for her. She couldn't get any more perfect. She's mine and no one else's. She will be willing to learn with no preconceived notions. My fingers tighten possessively around hers.

"You own all of this?" Layla asks, looking around. I've never given much notice to the gardens, but Layla makes me see the vast space differently.

"Yes." Privileged. That's what I would have said when I stood on the other side of money. This is a life of privilege. Funny how it's never felt that way. I've always felt like I don't belong in this world. I belong with Layla. I'm tempted to tighten my hold on her, but her hand is fragile in mine.

"It's beautiful. It makes my garden look pitiful." She's half laughing, but I don't like when she belittles herself. I don't like it one fucking bit.

"Landscapers did this. It's not a labor of love like your garden. I'd prefer to sit in yours with you than here."

Her laughter dies, and she smiles at me. "Well, here we are. Alone." Her cheeks heat.

"Yes, we are." I stop and pull her closer. I still hold her hand in mine as she looks up into my eyes. Her lips are the most perfect shade of pink I've ever seen. Her blue eyes swim with a want that I'll gladly satisfy.

I press my lips against hers. The warm and moist feel has my cock growing instantly. Releasing her hand, I grip her face to drag her closer. Her lips move under mine, and I smile into the kiss. She's a quick learner. The memory of her kissing Kieran has me pressing harder on her lips, trying to erase the image. My tongue darts out and quickly fills her mouth. I release some saliva onto her tongue and break the kiss, wanting to leave my mark in her mouth. I feel satisfied when she swallows. She looks uncertain, and I don't give her time to think about what I just did. Gripping her hand, I keep us moving until the orchard starts to take shape. I had William set up a table and chairs in the middle of the orchard. Food covers the top.

"Wow." Layla takes it all in, and I watch her. She's so fucking perfect. The thought of grabbing her and fucking her on the table has me releasing her hand.

"Are you hungry?" I ask as I step over and pull out a chair for her.

"You didn't have to do this, Jared. It's too much."

I pick up a plate and stack it with a little of everything. William didn't hold back. "I didn't. William did."

I pass the plate of salad, cucumber sandwiches, and a selection of cheeses to Layla. Opening a bottle of red wine, I pour her a glass before filling one for myself. My chair is positioned at the opposite end of the table. I take a gulp of wine while picking up my chair and bringing it closer so I'm seated right beside Layla. She glances at me from the corner of her eye. Once I'm seated, our thighs brush the other's.

"Are you not eating?" Layla asks.

I pick up a sandwich and take a bite. "Satisfied?" I ask.

She picks up her own sandwich and nibbles on it. I love how her mouth moves around the food. I finish mine and sit back, just taking her in. It's like magic that she's here drinking wine with me.

"I never thought I would find you," I admit.

I like watching her reaction to everything I say. She's so filled with expression. She tilts her head, her drink halfway to her mouth. She's breathing a little heavier. "I never thought I'd find you, either."

I glance down at the glass that I hold, seeing the inked band on my wrist that still feels relevant, even though I found her. "I got this tattoo because of you."

Her eyes widen, and she places her glass on the table. "I don't understand. You said you lost someone three years ago. We've been separated for seven."

"You've been keeping count," I joke, but the humor doesn't drop. "Three years ago, I came to the conclusion that I wouldn't find you." Half-truth. Three years ago, my father told me to bury the notion of Layla and Jared. Three years ago, I became a prisoner in my own story.

Layla reaches out, and her fingers trace the band on my wrist. "I don't think a day has passed that I didn't think about you. The first few months"—she shakes her head—"nothing made sense. I kept thinking something inside me had finally broken, but I couldn't explain it. I've never felt whole, Jared." She blinks and tears fall.

Her words hit me so fucking hard.

"But I do now." She's smiling through her tears.

I tilt my chair further so I can reach her and pull her closer. I lean my forehead against hers. I wish I could tell her the same, but sometimes I still feel so dead inside. I know why. My gut clenches, and I refuse to acknowledge every emotion that slams into me, demanding my attention.

I half stand. My mouth finds Layla's, and when she moans, I pull her out of the chair without breaking the kiss. My cock grows hard, and this emotion I allow to fill me up feels like lust, but so much more. It consumes me. I run my hand across the table. Plates of food clatter to the ground and smash, but I don't give a fuck as I grip Layla by the waist and lift her up onto the table. I drag her to the edge, and her breath halts as I push my erection close to her opening.

I want to be patient, but there's a roaring demand in my mind that I take what is rightfully mine. My kiss grows savage. My fingers work on the buttons of her dress. Her small hands push against my shoulders, and somehow, she manages to pull her mouth away from mine.

"Jared, wait." She's panicked and breathless.

I don't move away as I fight for control, but I stop and allow her a moment to breathe. My gaze meets hers. "We're outside in the open. Someone could see."

"No one is here." It's a lie. The staff is here, but I don't care if they see. I've never wanted anyone so badly. I slowly hike her dress up past her knees, dragging my hands along her warm flesh. I pause and allow her a moment to stop me. I don't break eye contact as I continue to push the dress past her thighs. I release it and let my fingers trail across her flesh.

She tries to pull away when I touch her scar, but I don't let her out of my hold as I continue up her legs. Her fingers dig deeper into my shoulders. Her gaze clouds as I make my way to her panties. Gripping either side, I shift them, and Layla lifts her bottom so I can drag them down her legs. My erection strains painfully against my jeans as I pull her white thong down. Once it slips over her feet, I take the fabric and push it into my pocket. She watches me and doesn't move as I press my hands against her thighs. Her breath hitches as I drag her closer.

"I want to taste you," I say.

She nods.

Bringing her to the edge of the table, I bend down and press a kiss to the inside of her thigh as I part her legs. She exhales loudly at the contact. She smells perfect; her arousal and natural scent are heavy between her legs.

My mouth finds her pussy. I suck her clitoris and let it go abruptly. Her hands sink into my hair, and she hisses in shock. I don't give her a moment to recover before running my tongue along her clitoris and down to her opening. She's wet, and my cock throbs painfully. I want to bury myself inside her sweet pussy. My tongue sinks deep, and I taste her. I swallow her juices before releasing my saliva across her clitoris, making my mark again.

Her fingers tighten on my hair as I press a kiss to the inside of her thigh before looking up at her. Her hands slip to my shoulders, and she appears disoriented and breathless—a perfect combination.

I slowly pull her dress back into place. Her mouth opens and closes, and her brows drag down.

"I just wanted a taste." I lean in and press my lips against hers. "You taste fucking perfect."

The agony in her eyes for more makes every passing second a pure pleasure. I'm the only one who can take that agony away. I'm not ready to do that just yet.

"Let me show you the rest of the garden." I grip her waist and lift her easily off the table. Once she's standing, she glances around her like she has no idea what's going on. The table is a mess, the ground coated in broken plates.

"We should tidy up." She's already flushed, but her face grows redder. I take her hand, making her look at me, and pull her away from the mess. "That's why I have staff."

She looks back at the broken plates, but she has no choice but to go with me. I reach into my pocket and touch her panties, making sure they're safe.

"I need my underwear back." Layla's gaze snags on my pocket, and I grin.

"I'm not done with you yet," I say.

Pleasure dilates her eyes, and I stop and kiss her again. I don't make the kiss long—just long enough to keep her blood heated.

I continue through the garden, identifying the different areas. I don't think Layla takes in a word, and I'd laugh, only my cock hasn't softened. It's like a lump of steel in my jeans. We reach the destination I had in mind. A small courtyard hidden behind the gardens comes into view. Its open walls and huge roof keep the cushion furnishings dry. The area is surrounded by large palm trees and an array of potted plants. It's the most secluded area in the garden.

We walk through the rows of vegetables, and Layla looks around like she's interested, but my erection keeps dragging her gaze to my jeans.

I stop walking as we approach the courtyard and spin her so she's facing me. Her breathing grows frantic with anticipation, and it's fucking delicious. I reach out and unbutton her dress further. Her breasts fill her white bra, and I push aside the material, exposing her breasts. She reaches up to cover herself, but I stop her.

"I want to taste you," I say and hold eye contact.

She nods.

I bend my head and suck on her rock-hard nipple. My trousers grow damp with precum. Moving my mouth to the other side, I suck on her nipple before grazing the sensitive skin. She hisses in pleasure. My own composure is slipping as I slide my hand up her leg. Layla's pussy is wet, and my fingers easily slip inside her. She gasps.

Releasing her nipple, I look up at her, wanting to see her face as I push two fingers inside her tight pussy. Layla's eyes are closed as she moans. Her hands tighten on my shoulders, and I wonder if she's going to come. Removing my fingers has her eyes snapping open, and I see the delicious torture there.

I wrap my fingers around hers. "Let me show you the courtyard," I say, and Layla stumbles as I tug her. When I glance her way, I can see the annoyance and frustration hardening her features. Yet, she won't voice what she wants.

"Is there something wrong?" I ask.

"Nope," she bites out, and I grin.

"If something is bothering you, just tell me." I step up onto the wooden platform that has a tiled roof. The L-shaped couch will really let me spread Layla out, but I want her to be comfortable enough to ask for it.

"Nothing." She exhales. "It's beautiful here."

I release her hand and remove her panties from my pocket.

Her cheeks flame.

"I'll give you a choice. You can take your panties back and put them on, or I can put them in my pocket and finish what I started." There really isn't a choice. I am going to taste her ecstasy on my tongue either way.

She reaches for her panties, but her hand drops away. Her pulse flickers in her neck. "I want you," she whispers.

I stuff the panties back into my pocket and erase the distance between us. I reach for her dress and unbutton it further until I can push it down her shoulders.

She's looking around us.

"No one can see," I whisper as I brush a kiss to her earlobe before pushing the dress down until it pools around her feet. I get a glimpse of her pussy, and my cock throbs. I lean in and steal a kiss while I unclip her bra. The straps slide easily down her arms, and I capture a nipple in between my thumb and forefinger. Her head rolls back as she moans.

Watching her is a new kind of pain that I know I could become addicted to. I continue to play with her nipple before pressing a kiss to the pulse on her neck. Her earlobe is warm in my mouth as I suck the soft flesh before I pinch her nipple. Her groan has me guiding her back to the couch. I don't have to tell her. She sits at the edge of the L, and she lies back.

My balls are heavy, and the torture of spreading her legs and not sinking my cock inside her has me groaning. Wetness gleams off her inner thigh, and when she sits up, she looks delirious.

I don't keep her waiting any longer before I dip my head and bury my face in between her legs.

"Oh my God." Her words and groans have me sinking my tongue inside her. Her hands are heavy on my head as she shifts, and when she puts pressure on me, I'm good with burying myself deeper in between her legs. I lick her clitoris and suck it until she's squirming under me. Her pants grow frantic, and I consider stopping so I can watch this all play out. I must have paused.

"Please, don't stop." She's breathless, and her plea is music to my ears.

I reach up and dip two fingers inside her as I race my tongue up and down her clitoris.

"Oh God. Oh God." Her pleasure heightens, and I move my fingers quicker inside her. Her pussy is tight, and I'm tempted to add a third finger, but she starts to tremble as I lick her faster. She comes hard on my tongue, and I swallow as much as I can as I remove my fingers and lap up every single drop of Layla.

CHAPTER TWENTY-EIGHT

JARED

She's been quiet ever since I made her come. I want to do it all over again. She's walking aimlessly around the courtyard. It's clear she's frazzled. I enjoy sitting on the couch and watching her. She repeatedly glances toward me and pauses before she starts walking again.

I'm entertained, but my cock is painfully hard. I sit forward, placing my elbows on my knees. "Has anyone made you come like that?" I ask.

Her cheeks heat. My suspicions are confirmed. Her experience is far more limited than most nineteen-year-old girls.

"It's okay. It just means you have a lot more to experience." I push off the couch. Her hands instantly go behind her back, like she's forcing herself to stay still as I walk toward her.

"I need my panties back."

I reach her and mirror her stance, placing my hands behind my back. I do it to stop myself from taking her as I truly wish to. "I'm afraid that isn't possible."

She tilts her head, but I notice the smile in her eyes. "Jared."

My name sounds perfect on her lips. "Layla." I draw out her name.

Her lip twitches.

Standing this close to her is torture. "Let me finish your tour of the garden. I think you may have been distracted earlier."

Her cheeks are pink, but I love the smile that grows on her face. I keep to my promise and show her the gardens that are set on twenty-two acres. Layla is more relaxed, and she takes in most of what I'm saying. Every once in a while, her gaze slips to my pocket, and I can tell she's thinking about her panties, which she isn't getting back.

We ended up back near the area where we had food and my first taste of her pussy. Everything has been cleared away, and I proceed to the house. It's been a while since we barely ate, and I'm sure William will have food ready for us.

Opening the front door for the first time, I feel relaxed. I disabled the camera system in the house. My father isn't here, and I want complete privacy with Layla.

She's quiet as we climb the stairs, and I want to know what's going on in her pretty head. She's looking around her, taking in all the pictures.

"Is that your father?" she asks as we continue to climb the stairs.

I don't have to look at which one she's referring to. His picture can't be missed by the sheer size of the photo that takes up residence on a large portion of the wall. "Yes."

"You don't talk about him."

I glance back and stop midstep.

Layla's eyes widen, and I see a flash of fear. I take her hand in mine and continue up the stairs. "What do you want to know?"

Her shoulders relax. "Do you have a good relationship with him?"

No.

"He's never hurt me." Physically. "He gives me everything I need," I answer honestly. I wouldn't have the life I have without him. He pulled me from the gutter. Yet there's an emptiness in this life that can't seem to be filled. I thought finding Layla would fill the void, but I don't feel whole.

"Emotionally?" Layla's question is low.

We reach the third floor, and I release her hand. Food is waiting for us in the living area. William has left two hotplates filled with food. I hold out my arm for Layla to go first. She steps up to the small table. I love the smell that emanates from her hair as I stand behind her.

"Are you hungry?"

She glances at me over her shoulder. "Yes."

I grin and pull out her chair. "You have worked up an appetite."

I love watching her get embarrassed. It's refreshing. I sit across from her and lift the lid off the plate. Steam and the aroma from the steak satisfy me.

Layla lifts her lid and smiles. "Wow, this looks amazing."

She starts to eat, and I watch her for a few moments until she notices and stops. "You never answered my question about your father."

I know.

I cut up a piece of steak. "No, not emotionally. He's a man." I grin and chew.

Layla's brows drag down. "Who do you talk to?"

"I'm okay, Layla." I want to erase the worry from her features.

She eats a few more bites of steak before she asks her next question. "What about your mother?"

These questions were to be expected. They shouldn't feel so hard. "Her name is Maura. She left when I was young." I hope my quick answer has Layla leaving it alone. I could ask her about sneaky Evelyn, who knew about me all along. I don't. I don't because Layla loves her, and she doesn't need another person to fucking disappoint her. And it doesn't matter anyway. She has me now, and she doesn't need Evelyn or Carl.

Layla thankfully directs the conversation to happier times. I'm laughing as we relive sledding down the hill at the back of our estate. We would steal empty coal bags, get inside them, and slide down the snow-covered hill at record speeds. The climb back up was just as fun, and when we got back to

Bert and Ronnie's, we would be red from the cold, but inside, we would be warm from fun and laughter.

Time slips away, and I love this part—how easy it is with Layla. She's so animated when she speaks, and when she laughs, I want to smile.

"I'd better go soon." Layla sounds apologetic.

I check my phone. "It's only eight." What's the rush?

She shrugs. "I have a curfew at eleven."

I get out of my seat. "Curfew? You're nineteen." I reach for Layla and hold out my hand. She hesitates but takes my hand and stands up.

"I know, but they're protective."

A little too fucking much.

"I'll have you home by ten thirty." I cross my heart.

Layla laughs. "Why don't I believe you?"

I lean in, and her smile vanishes. I press my lips against hers. "I can call Evelyn and let her know you're spending the night."

Layla freezes. Desire darkens her blue eyes. She shakes her head. "I'd better stick to the curfew."

"I can't tempt you?" I press another kiss to her lips. This time, I'll let her go home, but it won't be for long. Soon, she'll be right beside me.

"Can I use your bathroom before I go?"

I reluctantly release her. "There's one in my bedroom."

She raises a brow.

I cross my heart again. "There is a bathroom in my bedroom."

She pivots toward my room but glances at me.

"You want me to show you?"

"I remember where your room is."

She leaves, and once she's gone, I take her panties out of my pocket. Holding them up to my nose, I inhale before stuffing them back into my pocket. I adjust my hard cock, which is bulges against my jeans.

The lights go out in the room. Evening light streams in front of the windows, casting shadows. I step out of the living room, and the hallway is also in darkness.

"Layla," I call and take a step toward my room.

The cock of a gun has me freezing. I turn slowly.

"You shouldn't have put your hands on me." Chester stands in the stream of light. His face is virtually unrecognizable from the beating I gave him. His left arm is in a sling, but he holds the gun steady in his right.

"What are you going to do? Shoot me?" I sneer.

He doesn't answer, and fear coils in my gut. "You think you can get away with it?" I ask him. "That no one saw you come in? My home has cameras everywhere."

"The cameras are off, Jared. Thanks to you."

How could he know that? My mind goes frantic. I hear the creak behind me, and Chester's head rises in that direction.

"My staff would have seen you." I step to the right, and his focus returns to me. He holds the gun higher.

"This is the gun you wanted me to get you. The serial number is erased. It's untraceable. Just like you wanted."

"Jared." Layla's voice is so close. A shiver steals the last of my warmth. The gun is no longer pointed at me. I turn as Layla frowns and steps closer.

"Go back!" I bark.

She looks at Chester with narrowed eyes, like she can't make him out. From her point of view, she wouldn't be able to.

"The lights went out." She's beside me now, and I grab her wrist, stopping her from going any further. She inhales sharply.

"The little bitch." Chester sounds gleeful. I'm ready to pull Layla behind me.

The explosion of the gun rips through the space, and warm blood coats my face.

Save Me

Broken Peple Duet Part Two

CHAPTER ONE

JARED

*B*LOOD.

I'm staring down at the stark red liquid flowing across the white tiles. I can't look away as the warm liquid pools around my bare feet. I'm tempted to step back, but I'm captivated as it makes a path around me. It's like water. I see my reflection in the blood. The light is dim in my parents' bathroom, but I can still make out my face. A vibration races across the liquid, and my image wavers. My eyes travel a little further ahead. His chunky silver watch catches the light, and before I can raise my gaze any higher, the world turns dark. The image before me disappears, and I am airborne as my mother lifts me from the tiled floor of the bathroom. The scent of her Eternity perfume surrounds me. My feet are still warm. I want to tell her about the red liquid that I stepped in.

"Keep your eyes closed, Jared." Her voice is a whisper as she sits me on a soft bed. She leaves me, and I do as she says. I keep my eyes closed. Behind my lids, the red liquid keeps repeating in my mind. A warm cloth touches my feet, and I want to look, but once again, I obey her.

"You're a good boy." My mother's voice wobbles. "You're my good boy." Her hands shake as she tugs on a pair of socks over my damp feet. When she pushes on my shoes, I peek at her with one eye. She's still in her pajamas, and so am I

I want to ask her what's happening. "Why are you sad?"

Tears stream down her face. She tilts her head and touches my face. For a moment, through the upset and confusion, it's just us. I know how much she loves me. She knows how much I love her.

Voices from the hall have her gaze shifting, but not before her eyes fill with dread.

Something in me feels unsettled. I want my dad.

My mother rises and blocks me as the bedroom door opens.

"Master Jay." A hand touches my shoulder. I'm snapped back to the present and look down at Layla. I'm on the ground, and she's in my arms. My fingers are coated in her blood. Her face is ghastly white.

"The ambulance is on its way, Master Jay."

I can't speak. I can't separate the memory from what's happening in front of me. I press down on the wound on Layla's shoulder, which oozes too much blood. The blood continues to pool around us, and my mind keeps jumping to my parents' bathroom. I have no idea where that came from. How old was I? Five or six? I've often tried to remember what my mother looked like, but nothing has ever been as clear as that memory. I have photos, but that's all they are. Photos of a woman they say was my mother.

I take one hand off Layla's wound as I reach for her neck. "Layla." Her name comes out a pained growl. I search with my other hand for a pulse. It's there, but the beat is slow and slight. I hear heavy footsteps on the stairs like I did when I was a child. The footsteps were loud outside my parents' bedroom door that night. I lose my focus and blink as paramedics and the Gardaí reach us on the landing. It's now I notice that the lights are back on in the hallway. I look to where Chester once stood, like I expect him to be there smiling. But the space is empty.

Too many people flood around us, and I'm moved aside as they lift Layla onto a stretcher. I'm staring at the blood that stains my hands. It seems to have flowed into every groove and crescent, tainting me.

"Master Jay." William stands over me, and two Gardaí wait by his side.

I stop staring at my hands and get off the floor.

"You want to tell us what happened?" the first Gardaí asks, and they all seem to lean in. Others move around the space. Are they searching for a weapon? Do they think I did it?

I look at William and wonder how much he saw, what he knows. Did he see where Chester went after he shot Layla?

I tighten my jaw as I glare back at the Gardaí. They're fucking laughable. Justice will never be served at their hands. How many nights did I pick up the phone, dial 999, and start to report what was happening, only to have them ask for my name and address? Stupid stuff. *Where are you? How old are you? Are you alone?* Instead of listening to me.

"A man broke into my home and shot my girlfriend. Who I need to be with." I step aside and no one stops me as I race down the stairs. The lights from the ambulance illuminate the foyer with blue and red strobes. I'm too late. They're pulling away and taking Layla with them.

"Jay, what happened?" My father drops his suitcase and jacket on the floor and moves swiftly toward me. Fear twists his features as he grips my shoulders and looks me over.

"It's Layla. She was shot." My words are painful. "I need to be with her." I'm ready to step away from my father's grip when he tightens his hold on me.

"You need to take a moment."

I'm shaking my head. "You never liked her."

My father waves his hands in the air before placing them back on my shoulders. "Son, I would never wish this on anyone. If you are worried, I'm worried." His fingers sink a little deeper into my arms. "You don't want to go to the hospital covered in blood."

I frown, but as I look down at my shirt and jeans, I see I'm covered in Layla's blood. There's so much fucking blood.

I can't lose her.

My father must see the alarm that consumes me. "Trust me, go change. I'll get you a brandy and then take you there myself."

I'm turning back to the stairs. "I don't want a brandy. Have the car ready." I race up the stairs. It's like a fucking TV crime scene.

By the time I get changed and return to the landing, a forensics team has arrived. William meets my gaze and nods. "I'll stay here, Master Jay."

"Thanks." I keep going so the Gardaí can't stop me. My father stays true to his word and is in the car waiting for me.

Once he starts driving, he leans over and pops open the glove compartment. The brown liquid swishes in the brandy bottle. He doesn't say anything, but I take it out and uncap the lid. I don't ask why he has a bottle of brandy in his car. I take a few swallows before putting the lid back on.

"Why don't you tell me what happened, son?" His calming tone settles the frazzled panic inside me.

"We were talking. Layla was getting ready to go home." I glance at my father. "I need to tell Evelyn and Carl."

"They already know."

I want to ask how, when, and who told them, but it doesn't matter. "She went to the bathroom, and the lights went out. I went into the hall to see what was happening, and a man was there."

I uncap the bottle again and take a drink, knowing if I stay on this path, there is no coming off it. I had a chance to tell my father and report Chester to the Gardaí.

But it didn't feel like enough. Not after what he's done.

"He was looking for the safe. I told him I didn't have money."

My father meets my gaze. I can't decipher what I see, but the look disappears, and he nods. "You should have given him the money, Jay. Jesus, son, you could have died."

"I didn't think he was going to shoot me."

He tightens his hold on the steering wheel, and I keep watching him as I speak. "He raised the gun and got ready to take his shot. I was going to tell him where the safe was when Layla appeared. She stepped in front of me and..."

My father grips my arm. "We will get him," he reassures me.

I don't want them to get him. I'll do it myself.

We arrive at the hospital, and he parks the car while I go to the main reception area. The receptionist takes far too long to find out where Layla is, and my agitation is at its max. She's aware of my anger as I tower over her; her gaze keeps diverting to me, and her eyes widen.

"Got her." There's relief in her voice, but I don't feel it.

My father arrives at my side when we're motioned toward a waiting room. The minute I step in, I want to leave. Evelyn stands up from a row of blue plastic chairs, and she has a look of hate directed at us. Carl reaches out and takes her arm. He knows, I know, everyone in this room knows, that she blames me. It's written all over her fucking face.

She pulls away from Carl, and I don't react as I allow her hand to connect with my face.

"Why couldn't you just leave her alone?" Her hysterical words don't affect me, and when she reaches up to hit me again, I grip her arm.

"You brought her here, remember, Evelyn?"

"Get your hands off my wife." Carl stands tall beside her.

I don't like being told what to do. I don't release her.

"I think everyone needs to calm down." My father steps up beside me, and only then do I release Evelyn's arm. She's still staring at me like I'm Satan. "It was a robbery. This is no one's fault."

Evelyn finally looks away from me to my father, with the same level of hate in her eyes. She turns to Carl and starts to cry. "My beautiful daughter."

Carl consoles her. I try to give her a moment, but I want to know what's happening. They won't tell me anything, as I'm not blood related, though I'm more to Layla than these two combined.

"What did the doctor say?" I ask Carl.

Evelyn spins. "That our daughter was shot."

I step away from her. This is pointless. I turn to my father.

"I'll find out." He keeps his voice low as he leaves to get me answers. Money will make the doctors talk. I don't want to be left with Evelyn and Carl, but for Layla, I'll show some respect.

"If you need anything, just ask," I say.

"I don't want anything from you," Evelyn bites.

My frayed patience snaps. I face her fully. "You knew where I was, so let's not act innocent."

Evelyn's face fills with color.

"You wouldn't want Layla to know that you kept us apart all these years, would you?"

Carl steps closer to me. "Are you threatening my wife?"

I ignore him and try to reason with Evelyn. "I love her. I would never hurt Layla." I leave them with my parting words and wait in the hallway for my father to return.

Noise filters in from all angles, but it's a lonely fucking place. Very lonely, when my mind keeps replaying the scene in the bathroom. I'm trying to analyze everything about the memory I had earlier. Was it a memory? I have no idea where it came from, but it felt so real. I can remember the smell, sharp like iron, almost cold to my lungs.

I can almost taste my mother's smell in my mouth. I slide down the wall and place my head in my hands, hoping to erase some of the confusion. The watch I remember seeing on the lifeless wrist was my father's, which he still wears. Had he fallen? Was it some sort of accident? Did Layla's blood trigger the memory?

Layla.

When the gun went off and her blood hit my face, the world went blank. My mind, for a split second, fired too much at me, and I couldn't react to anything. I wanted to kill Chester. Take the gun from his fingers and make him eat the fucking bullets. I wanted to make sure Layla was okay. I wanted to close my eyes and pretend it wasn't happening. Instead, I sank to the ground with her, and my mind went somewhere else.

"Jay."

I rise quickly as my father returns. My heart hasn't slowed down, and it threatens to pound out of my chest. I'm shaking my head. She can't be dead, yet my father is wearing a look that terrifies me. The door behind me opens, and Evelyn comes out, pauses, and is ready to go back in.

"She's in an induced coma," he tells the room.

"What?" Evelyn's cry matches my internal fear. Carl arrives out of the waiting room. "How do you know that? Where is the doctor?"

My father keeps his composure as he delivers the news to me like we're alone. "Her blood loss was too severe, so they need to stabilize her in order to keep her alive."

Evelyn's cries drown out everything else, and I want to tell her to shut the fuck up.

"I want to see her," I say to my father. He doesn't answer, but he leaves, making my request a reality.

Evelyn's wails are enough to drive me from the hallway, but I stay where I am and try to find some sympathy for them. They've raised Layla and kept her safe. I owe them that much.

Clearly, they love her.

"She's strong. She'll make it," I try to reassure them.

It stops Evelyn from crying. She runs a hand across her face and tries to compose herself. "She's the strongest child I've ever known." Evelyn smiles through her pain, and I see the love there for Layla.

I nod.

"Did you see who did this?" Carl asks.

"It was dark. He cut off the electricity." I shake my head. "I wish I knew."

Evelyn steps away and returns to the waiting room. Carl doesn't follow her like I thought he would. Instead, he stays.

"It's not your fault, Jared. Evelyn doesn't blame you."

"She does."

Carl half smiles. "She does. But she's upset. She'll calm down."

There's an awkward silence, and Carl leaves me alone. I wait another twenty minutes. I'm close to searching the hospital for Layla's room when my father returns.

He glances over my shoulder as if looking to make sure I'm alone.

"They're in the waiting room," I say and nod my head in the direction Evelyn and Carl went.

He nods, and I see something close to pride shine in his eyes. "You can see her."

CHAPTER TWO

LAYLA

I'M SWIMMING IN A sea of darkness. At times, I hear voices before I get swallowed up and the voices dim.

"You know, when you first came home, you never slept in your bed. You would mess the quilt up and make it look like you did…"

A soft laugh that I recognize soothes me.

"I used to go into your room in the middle of the night, and you would be bundled up on the floor under the bed with one of Carl's sweaters. And in the morning, you would be back in your own bed, the sweater nowhere in sight."

Silence stretches, and the murky water swallows me again. The woman's voice doesn't stop, and when I break the surface of pain and mist, she's still there, still talking.

"I never really liked him, to be honest." She pauses. "The flowers he keeps sending are divine." Another pause. Her voice grows muffled as I sink, but I want to stay with Evelyn. I want to know who she's talking about. Who is sending me flowers, and why?

"It's been days, and he hasn't left. I think he's sleeping in the room next to yours. He takes up most of the visiting times." I hear the fondness in Evelyn's voice even as she tries to hide it.

"He doesn't say much." She grows distant, and heat behind me has me turning in my dark pool. A red hot wave moves too quickly, bringing with it pain that has me screaming.

"Get a doctor! Help!" Evelyn's screams follow me until I'm pulled deep under the water. Long seconds pass, and it feels as though I've been submerged there before I break the surface.

Only this time, I return to silence. No one is speaking, but there's movement. His smell triggers an image of Jared's handsome face, and with it comes a want. A yearning that aches. I want to see him. I want to kiss him.

Jared.

I float and he never speaks, but he stays for a while. I want him to talk, but he doesn't.

"I think the whole school is out in the waiting room."

I perk up at Evelyn's voice. *Where is Jared?*

"I met Ashley. I can see why you like her. She's such a sweetheart, and Nicco." I can hear the smile in Evelyn's voice.

Her hand touches mine and pulls me higher out of the water. "I prayed for a child and God gave me you. I'm praying to Him again to give me back my baby." A kiss is pressed against my cheek, and moisture seeps down my face. "Come back to your mother."

Mother.

Her tears pull me higher, and I want to return to Evelyn, my mother. I want to comfort her and tell her it will be okay, but I'm sinking again.

Then the dark water consumes me.

***

Why is someone shining a light in my face? I raise my arm, which is as heavy as lead, managing to get my hand close to my eyes. The light dims, but something pulls on my arm.

"Careful. You'll pull out your needle."

My eyes flitter open at Jared's voice, only to slam closed again. The light is too bright. "The light," I croak.

My words send a whoosh of Jared's breath across my face.

"They said you might not be able to talk," he says, his voice growing more distant as he moves away. A rattle of metal ceases, along with the bright light. I blink. My vision isn't clear.

Jared returns to my side, and it takes me a few more attempts to focus as he slowly comes into view. He's growing a beard. He appears older. He doesn't touch me.

"Why wouldn't I be able..." I stop to moisten my lips. Jared picks up a drink and brings it to my mouth. I take a small swallow. Once I'm done, I try to piece together what's happening. "Where am I?"

My body aches, especially my shoulder.

"You're in the hospital." Jared places the drink back on the bedside table. He stays standing, and there's something standoffish about him.

I'm trying to jog my memory, but I can't seem to recall what happened. I squeeze my eyes tight as it slowly trickles back in. I was at Jared's house. We took a walk in the garden.

"You were shot."

I try to sit up, but the pain keeps me lying down. "Shot?"

"You lost so much blood, Layla. They had to put you into an induced coma."

Coma?

"For how long?" How much time has passed?

"Ten days."

The door rattles, and someone knocks on the top glass portion. I can't see who it is, as the blind has been drawn.

"Do you remember anything?" Jared doesn't even look at the door. He's speaking like no one has knocked.

I try to think of Jared's house. All I remember is having a picnic. Our time in the garden. Moving inside his house, and the lights going out. "It's fuzzy."

The banging on the door grows more insistent.

"There was a robbery at my house. The gunman fired, and you stepped in front of me." Jared speaks in a monotone voice.

He's watching me, waiting for my response. The knocking stops.

"I was shot," I repeat. My fingers glide along the bandage. "I don't remember."

Dark circles under Jared's eyes have me wanting to ask if he's okay. I swallow the dryness in my throat. The knocking returns, and Jared leaves my bedside. He pulls his navy jacket off the back of a chair. I watch as he crosses the room, opens the door, and lets the doctor and two nurses in. He doesn't stop as they question why the door was locked.

The room is a fluster of activity as I'm checked, poked at, and asked too many questions. My mind is snagged on Jared. There's something he isn't telling me.

A squeal from Evelyn has me finally letting go of Jared for now. She makes her way to my bedside, and the doctor stands aside to let her close to me. She hugs me gently, and her cries are pressed into my neck.

"You're awake!"

Carl walks to the opposite side of the bed and takes my hand.

"I'm sorry I scared you."

Evelyn breaks the hug. "How are you feeling?"

Before I can answer, Evelyn turns to the doctor. "How is she? Is there any damage? She seems fine." Evelyn reaches down and grabs my other hand as she fires questions at the doctor.

The doctor smiles kindly and holds up a hand. The nurses check stats, but their smiles are there too.

"We can't say for certain, but so far, it's looking really good." For the first time, the doctor looks at me. "You are a very lucky girl. I'm confident you'll make a full recovery."

I nod and force a smile, like this isn't weird. What happened to me? I wish I could remember.

"When can she go home?" Evelyn releases my crushed fingers, and I find myself looking up at Carl. His gaze is filled with tears, and he squeezes my hand softly.

"We need to keep her here for a few days for observation. If everything is clear, she can go home then."

Evelyn looks at me with a huge smile. "Thank God."

The doctor and nurses leave. Evelyn doesn't ask me questions about what happened. She keeps fussing with the blankets and pillows. Food arrives, and I eat a little under Evelyn's supervision. Carl sits down, and after an hour or so, he puts on the TV. He doesn't watch what plays out on the screen. He's too busy watching me like I might disappear.

They keep looking at me like it's a miracle I'm here. Maybe it is.

The day dwindles on, and I keep falling in and out of sleep. Each time I open my eyes, Evelyn is hovering over me. It takes Carl pulling her away for food to get her out of the room. I feel terrible, but when they leave, I sit up with relief. The distance gives me a moment to try to figure out what's happening.

I touch my bandaged shoulder, and pain ignites quickly. The memory of a bang of a gun has me snapping my eyes shut. Someone shot me.

A shiver assaults me. The door opens, and once again, I get a wash of relief that it isn't Carl and Evelyn. The doctor enters with a soft smile that lights up his eyes, which are framed with black glasses.

"How are you feeling?"

"Confused. Tired. Sore."

He nods at each word. "That's normal. Have you had any memory loss?"

"Yes. I don't remember what happened."

He nods again and moves closer to my bed. "That's normal as well. In most cases, memories return. And it's looking good, Layla."

"Thank you."

"The Gardaí are here to ask a few questions. If you don't feel up to talking, I can send them away."

It doesn't matter. "I don't remember what happened."

"I'll tell them to come back another day." The doctor smiles again before leaving the room.

I drift into a light sleep. At some point, Evelyn and Carl return, and their whispered words float around me.

"Jared, she's awake. She came out of the coma, and they don't think there are any long-term injuries." Evelyn's voice carries a note of hostility.

I open my eyes slightly. Jared closes the door. He's freshly shaven, and my stomach quivers at the sight of him in the room. His black clothing and hooded gaze make him appear dangerous.

"That is great news," Jared responds.

He doesn't tell them he was here when I woke up. Jared looks right at me, and I open my eyes fully. I want to ask where he was. Why did he leave, and why is he acting so off? I don't ask any questions.

He greets Carl, and the room grows silent.

"Are you okay?" I ask Jared as I try to sit up.

Carl and Evelyn move at the same time to help me sit up.

"I'm fine," I reassure them, but Carl lifts me while Evelyn stacks my pillows behind my back. They're both so careful with me.

Jared has his back to me. He's staring out the window. The blinds are no longer pulled, and the moon hangs low in the darkened sky.

"Do you want a drink?" Evelyn asks, already holding the glass.

I shake my head.

"Why don't we get a coffee?" Carl suggests.

"I don't want a coffee," Evelyn fires back.

Carl clears his throat, and he and Evelyn have a silent conversation with their eyes.

"Coffee sounds lovely," Evelyn says stiffly. "Jared, will you stay with Layla?"

Jared looks away from the window. "Of course. Take all the time you want."

Evelyn and Carl leave, and once the door closes, I'm expecting Jared to speak. He doesn't. He puts his hands in the pockets of his dark jeans.

"You don't have to stay, if you don't want to." My voice holds the note of bitterness I feel at his distance.

"I want to." Jared takes his hands out of his pockets and pulls up a chair beside the bed. He's not close enough for me to reach him.

"The Gardaí came to question me."

Jared finally looks at me. "What did you say?"

"What aren't you telling me?" I try to sit up higher, but the burn in my shoulder stops me. I hiss.

"Be careful. You'll hurt yourself." Jared moves, and his scent circles me as he helps me. His large hands grip my waist, the heat searing my skin. I lean forward, wanting to make him look at me, and when he glances down, my heart beats faster in my chest.

"I remember the lights going out," I whisper. I lick my lips. Jared doesn't move. His hands dig a little more into my hips, and I like how close he is. I feel safe. I feel secure. "That's it. Then the noise of the gun being fired."

Jared's eyes flutter closed before he releases me. "They're looking for the suspect." He sits back down, and I miss him already. I place my hands in my lap.

"I want you to stay with me." His request surprises me. He looks like he'd rather never see me again. Talk about mixed signals.

"Why?"

"To keep you safe."

"Didn't the shooting happen at your house?"

He works a muscle in his jaw. "I have added extra security."

As much as I would love the idea of being with Jared every second of the day, it isn't logical. "That robber isn't going to come after me, Jared."

"I still want you to stay with me."

He leans a little closer. The movement is subtle, but I sense him all the way down to my toes.

"No."

"It's not a request, Layla."

"Evelyn and Carl would never allow it. You're being paranoid. Like you said, it was a robbery," I reinforce.

"Evelyn and Carl won't be a problem." He sounds so sure, and I don't like it.

"They won't allow it, and they won't be bullied, Jared." My voice hitches as my heart pounds in my chest.

Jared inhales heavily. "Don't work yourself up," he grits between his teeth. Like this is my fault.

"Then stop being overbearing."

His grin is quick and unexpected. All the worry erodes away, one layer at a time.

"Overbearing?" His voice is light for the first time since I woke up, and I take full advantage of it.

"Yes, overbearing." I relax a little into the pillows. "Can we not fight? I just woke up from a coma," I remind him.

Brown eyes flash with guilt, and that wasn't my intention. I just want him to relax. Jared nods. "A truce for now."

I don't like the 'for now' part, but I take it.

"Tell me what I missed." I snuggle in deeper into the pillows and relish in Jared's deep voice as he tells me about all the visitors I've had.

I smile on and off before drifting into another peaceful sleep. When I wake, I'm alone and the room is in partial darkness. Images flicker across the television screen. I look to where Jared was seated and disappointment twists my stomach. That is, until I look beyond the chair and see a figure asleep on the couch.

"Jared." I say his name softly.

His reaction is immediate. He's standing and looking around him, his face tense.

"Jared."

His gaze lands on me, but he's still tense.

"You fell asleep."

He moves toward my bed. "How are you feeling?" he asks while running his hand across his face.

"I'm okay."

"You'd say that even if you weren't." His words aren't accompanied by a smile. He's still tense, even as he drags the chair closer to my bed. He's just sat down when a knock sounds at the door.

Jared gets up and answers it. I don't want anyone else to come into the room. Jared bends down and picks something up off the ground.

"Who is it?" I ask.

He glances at me over his shoulder while trying to hide what he's holding in his hand. A black wreath.

I'm about to ask who died, but he's racing from the room like a man possessed.

CHAPTER THREE

JARED

I'M STARING AT THE wreath in my hands. A small note has been attached.

RIP Layla.

I pull off the note before racing from the room. The hallways are pretty much empty. Three people approach, and one by one, I stop them.

I block the pathway of the first man. He tries to step around me, but I don't allow the movement as I pull down his collar, checking his neck for tattoos.

"What are you doing? Get off me!" The man fixes his shirt back in place after I release him.

I keep walking until I reach the reception desk.

"Who was just at Layla Masters's door?"

The receptionist frowns, and I slam the wreath on the counter.

She jumps slightly, her hand fluttering to her chest. "I didn't see anyone."

I spot three cameras. "I want to see the footage."

"I'm sorry, but I can't authorize that."

"Who can?"

She picks up the phone while I survey the area.

***

The videotapes show a man with a blue cap pulled low over his eyes. He drops the wreath, knocks on Layla's door, and takes off. There's no way of identifying who he is. The Gardaí take the wreath. I wish I had thought about my actions before the receptionist alerted them.

"It could be a prank," one of the Gardaí tells Evelyn, who's beside herself. "A jealous kid at school." I leave her and Carl in the hallway and spend my time helping Layla get everything packed up. Today she's going home. I'm beyond pissed that she isn't coming with me.

"You really should stay with me," I try again.

She's dressed in jeans and a T-shirt, her arm in a sling. She smiles at me and takes a tentative step forward. She taps her chin as if in thought, and I wait patiently, hoping she says yes. One word, and I'd have her out of here in seconds and secure in my home.

"No."

Disappointment turns to annoyance, which I try to hide. She brushes a lock of hair over her shoulder, and color blossoms on her cheeks. She's self-conscious as I watch her. I clear the distance between us and love when she looks up at me with her lips parted and eyes wide.

"You aren't making this easy." I reach out and touch her face.

"You wouldn't want me in your home. I snore."

I hold her face in my hands. "I said my home. I never mentioned my bed."

Her face burns red, and my cock gets hard.

"I snore loudly," she continues. "The sound travels through walls."

I love how flustered she is. "You don't snore. In fact, you barely move." How many nights have I watched her sleep here in the hospital?

She frowns. "How would you know that?"

"I know a lot about you, Layla." I dip my head to capture her mouth, when the door opens. I don't release her face. She's mine and I won't be rushed. I'd kiss her, only she's trying to look at the door. I slowly take my hands off her face, but I don't move away.

"Are you ready, sweetheart?" Evelyn asks, and Carl steps into the room. He picks up Layla's bags. I don't like this one bit, her staying with them. But I have several men stationed around her house. I won't rest until I find Chester and put a bullet into his head.

"I'll drive Layla to the house," I say.

"There's no need. Carl has the car ready." Evelyn smiles sweetly at me.

"I insist."

Her smile falters as her eyes narrow.

"That would be great, Jared," Carl, ever the diplomat, intervenes.

I hold out my hand for Layla. She flashes a glance at Evelyn before taking it.

"We'll be right behind you." Evelyn sings her reassurance, but I think it's more for me not to veer off with Layla.

As we leave the hospital, I keep checking all around us. My own security is positioned around the area. When they see me, they leave their stations and get into their vehicles. Layla slides into the passenger side of the car, and once I'm in, she struggles with buckling her belt.

I take my time reaching across her and clipping the belt closed.

"You seem tense," she tells me.

I sit back. "You do that to me." I grin.

Her cheeks heat. "Jared, be straight with me. Is this about the wreath? Because the Gardaí said it was most likely a prank."

I relax my shoulders. "Yeah, it's been on my mind." I start the car and pull out of the parking space. The Jeep with my security inside follows close behind me.

"I mean, it wasn't funny, but don't let it get to you."

I nod. "Okay."

"Why don't I believe you?"

I glance at Layla. She's observing me, her pouty mouth begging to be kissed. "I want to kiss you."

"You can't start saying that just because you want to change the topic."

"It's the truth."

She shifts, but I see a ghost of a smile.

"Do you not believe me?" I ask and slow down, pulling into a rest stop off the road. The Jeep pulls in behind us, but Layla doesn't seem to notice. She's too focused on me.

"What are you doing?"

Her breaths come out fast. I unbuckle my belt and move closer to her. Taking her face in my hands, I glance at her lips before I press mine against hers. She melts into me, and I hungrily take what is mine. Her mouth is warm and soft, and I run my tongue along her lips before breaking the kiss.

"I want you to stay with me," I try again.

Her laughter washes across my face. "You aren't going to give up?"

I run my thumbs across her cheeks. "Never."

She smiles, but it dwindles away. "I can't, Jared."

"For now," I answer. I'm patient.

After releasing her face, I pull us out of the parking space and get back on the road. I have to talk myself out of driving to my house and just forcing her inside. It takes a lot of restraint to take her home. Evelyn is standing beside the front door. Jesus fucking Christ, she's starting to wear on me.

"Will you come in?" Layla sounds unsure.

"No."

The disappointment flashes in her blue eyes.

I unbuckle my seat belt and reach across before unbuckling her too. "But I'll come by later."

She smiles. "That would be great."

"You can show me your bedroom."

Her face lights up like I knew it would, and I steal a quick kiss.

Her gaze darts to the house, where I know Evelyn is watching, before returning to me. "I doubt that."

I grin before releasing her from my stare. I slide out of the car and walk around to the passenger side door and open it for her. Evelyn makes her way toward my car.

"I got it," I tell her.

She reaches in to help Layla.

"I said I got it." I take Layla's arm and help her out. I let my fingers trail down her skin, and I'm tempted to push her back into the car.

"Welcome home, sweetheart." Evelyn leans in, and Layla breaks away from me and accepts the hug from Evelyn.

I close the passenger door. "I'll be back later," I say.

"No need. You've done enough."

I smile at Evelyn's condescending tone. "I insist."

Layla gives me a small wave as I get back into my car. I don't want to leave her, but once she's inside, I pull away from her house. The Jeep follows me closely, while my other security salutes me as I drive past their parked car and make my way home.

***

I arrive home, and the moment I open the door, Alex smiles at me. "What do you want?" I ask her.

"I wanted to make sure you were okay. You weren't answering my calls."

I don't go upstairs. I haven't since Layla was shot. "I'm fine." I make my way to my new quarters.

Alex follows me. "How is Layla?"

I stop walking and turn on her. "You don't give two fucks about Layla. Let's not pretend."

Alex tries to look shocked, but when I don't give her a reaction, she drops the act.

"I care about you." She folds her arms across her chest. The red V-neck jumper reveals just how large her breasts are, which I know is intentional. "You care about Layla. So I care."

I resume walking. "She's out of the hospital."

Alex's heels click noisily on the marble floor as she follows closely behind. "I'm so happy to hear it."

I snort at her lie. My bedroom is in darkness. I open the large, heavy green drapes.

"Look, I just want to support you, Jared. Like you did for me."

I haven't seen Alex since Mark's party. I don't want to have this conversation with her, so I pick the easy way to end it. "Thanks. But I'm good."

She's picking up my clothes off the floor, and God love her as she attempts to fold them. They end up being rolled into balls.

"You are folding creases in my clothes."

Her mouth forms a thin line. "Fuck's sake, Jay. I'm trying to help."

She's likely never folded a piece of laundry in her life, and I know her intentions are good. I run my hands down my face and sit on the edge of my bed. A part of me wants to let out all the fear that I'm drowning in.

"I'm tired."

Alex still holds one of my shirts as she sits down beside me on the bed. "You haven't been home. Were you staying at the hospital?"

"Yes."

"Your dad is worried." Alex rests a manicured hand on my thigh.

I remove it and get up off the bed. "I'm home now."

Alex wears a look of hurt before she recovers and stands up too. "Good. It will be great to get back to normal. Especially with the school dance coming up."

"I have to be somewhere soon. So..."

Alex forces a smile. She's really trying. "I'll come by later."

I'm ready to tell her I won't be here. "Great."

Her smile picks up. "See you then."

No, you won't.

She leaves me, and I ring my PI to see if there's any news on Chester. None. He hasn't been seen since the shooting.

"Call me if you hear anything," I say.

"I will."

I hang up and leave my room while I text Warren.

Are you around? I was thinking of catching up.

I send the text and make my way to the kitchen. Muffled voices have me stalling before I enter. My father and the head Gardaí are in the kitchen.

"Son, I didn't know you were up." My father walks toward me, directing me to the man beside him. "This is Inspector Reilly. He's been assigned to the robbery case."

Inspector Reilly places his coffee on the table before reaching out his hand. "Pleasure, Jay."

I shake his hand. He's freshly shaven, with two knicks along his jawline.

"I'm just going over the case notes, trying to figure out the entry point."

I release his hand, and my father sits down, but I don't join them. My phone dings and I take it out. Warren has agreed to meet me. *At least something is going right.*

"I have no idea. I didn't even hear him come up the stairs," I offer up.

Inspector Reilly helps himself to another biscuit. His gut begs him not to, but he shoves it into his mouth. I meet my father's gaze and wonder if he handpicked Inspector Gadget here.

"The good news is that we have word out to all art buyers about your stolen pictures."

Stolen pictures. This is news to me.

"Good," my father interjects. "They are highly valuable."

What is he doing?

Inspector Reilly opens a brown folder on the table. Crumbs fall onto the page, and he wipes them away. His nails are bitten down to stubs. I have zero confidence in his ability to do his job. He's sloppy. That has to be the reason he's here investigating a false robbery.

"Is William available? I just want to run through the details with him one more time. Make sure we haven't missed anything."

"Unfortunately, he is not. But I have spoken to William, and I can answer any questions." Father takes a drink of coffee.

The Inspector tuts. "It needs to be him."

"I am at your disposal, Inspector Reilly." My father smiles, and I want to know what the fuck he's doing.

"It's only between us." He smiles, and I want this cowboy out of my home.

"After the gun fired..." My father glances at me like mentioning a gun will set me off. I fold my arms across my chest, and when I don't flip out, he continues. "William went to go upstairs when he heard a noise down the hall. He arrived to find two pictures missing, and a man dressed in black slipping out the window."

"Once we find one of them, we'll get the other." The inspector closes his file and stands. "Thanks for the coffee. I better get to work."

"Yeah, you better," I say.

His smile falters as he looks at me.

"My son is eager to find the people who nearly killed him." My father is trying to cover up my hostility.

I stay in the kitchen as he escorts Inspector Reilly out. I don't give him a second when he steps back in.

"What are you doing? He isn't a real inspector."

My father isn't fazed. "He's investigating a robbery. You said there was a robbery."

I grit my teeth. "You didn't have to stage one."

His features twist with anger. "That's exactly what I had to do. But when you decide to tell me the truth, we can end this ruse."

"You dragged William into this?" I'm shaking my head.

"You left me no choice, son. A robber that takes nothing?" He raises a brow. "Even Inspector Reilly would figure that one out."

I refold my arms across my chest. "What exactly have you figured out?"

"This wasn't about you. It was about her. She dragged you into this mess," he says.

"I can't even mention her name without you getting defensive," he adds. "I bet he was a jealous ex of hers. God only knows what kind of people she hangs out with."

I take a step toward my father, and surprise lights up his eyes. I tell myself not to do something I might regret. "The gun was pointed at me. The bullet was meant for me, not her. No one knew she was here. So you're wrong."

My father doesn't look convinced. "Then tell me, son. Tell me what's going on." He closes the space between us. "Let me help you."

He wouldn't be able to do any more than I could with finding Chester, and I wouldn't implicate him in this. The fact that he and William staged a robbery is enough.

I have a meeting with Warren, and I hope it will put an end to Chester for good.

CHAPTER FOUR

LAYLA

I'M COUNTING DOWN THE hours until Jared arrives. In the meantime, Evelyn doesn't leave my side. Flowers arrive from Jared, and Evelyn's tight smile tells me she isn't happy. Her behavior toward Jared feels heavy on my heart. Two of the most important people in my life don't seem to like each o t h - er.

Their animosity is becoming tiresome.

The television is on, but I don't believe that either of us is watching. "I want you to get along with Jared," I say while muting the volume.

"I do."

I don't respond.

Evelyn shifts on the large armchair, keeping her legs together, and veers toward me. "It's hard, Layla. He's a lot."

I nod. "I know. He's a lot in a good way."

She doesn't answer immediately. "He watches you so much." She frowns. "It's unsettling."

"Jared can be intense. But when you get to know him, you'll really like him."

Evelyn gets off the chair and joins me on the couch. "I don't doubt that, sweetheart. It's not about how he is with me. It's..." She's careful with her words. "It's how he is with you." She pauses again. "How you both are around each other."

I have no idea what she means. Evelyn takes my hands. "When you're with each other, it's like nothing else exists."

Embarrassment fills me right up to my bursting point. She's right. But that isn't a bad thing. "We haven't seen each other in such a long time. I think we just got caught up." I do my best to try to explain it.

"It's heavier than that."

I take my hands out of Evelyn's, not sure what she's implying.

"It's unhealthy," she finally says with a nod, like she's found the perfect word for what she's trying to explain.

My heart crashes, and pain uncurls its tight fist in my chest. I'm about to wrap my arms around my waist, but the sling restricts the movement. I can't keep looking at Evelyn.

"I'm sorry, sweetheart. I don't want to upset you. That's not my intention."

I can see the internal battle in her eyes.

"It's hard to explain, but I know what Jared and I have isn't unhealthy." When I say the words, I hate the fluttering that starts in my stomach.

Is it unhealthy? The way he beat Kieran nearly to death over a kiss, or the way he wants me to live with him? No, we know each other on a level that most don't. No one will ever understand what we have between us.

"Okay. I'm sorry." Evelyn pats my leg as the doorbell rings. The transformation is so obvious as she rises to open the door. She's shaking off our conversation with each step. Yet each step she takes away from me makes me feel sick.

Jared and I aren't unhealthy, I say again in my head. We saw the worst of each other. He saw me when I was vulnerable and broken. When everything was taken from me and I felt so destroyed, Jared would be there to piece me back together. That's not unhealthy, that's love.

So why do I feel sick at Evelyn's words?

"I'd love to know what you're thinking."

Jared fills the doorway. How can he continue to get better looking? Yet, he does.

"I'm thinking about you."

He steps into the room, and his grin makes my own lips rise. "I'm glad to hear it."

"It could be a terrible thought." I'm trying to fight the smile that wants to take over. He sits on the couch, leaving only a foot between us. A foot is too much.

"At least you're thinking about me."

I laugh. "How could I not?"

Jared takes my hand, and the look in his gaze makes me feel exposed. Like he can see past the smiles and laughter. Like he can see the agony that twists me up sometimes.

"What are we?" I ask.

"Jared and Layla," he says simply.

It's not the answer I want. Maybe he sees the disappointment on my face before I dip my head.

His fingers touch my chin, making me look at him. "We can be whatever you want us to be."

His finger taps my jaw as he waits for an answer. I notice Evelyn standing in the doorway and immediately take Jared's hand off my face. He doesn't react. I'm sure he's aware we aren't alone, but he pretends like it's still just us as Evelyn enters the room and sits down. Is this what she meant about Jared?

"Evelyn is making a stew for dinner. She's the best cook," I find myself saying.

Jared's eyes sparkle with amusement, but that smile doesn't grace his lips as he turns to Evelyn. "I can't wait."

She forces her lips to rise. "Great. We're very grateful to you, Jared, for staying with Layla at the hospital."

Jared stiffens beside me. "I wouldn't have it any other way."

"I know this isn't the best time, but I've spoken with Carl and we're covering the hospital bills."

Jared waves her off. "That's not necessary."

"We are her parents."

My face blazes. Talking about money makes me uncomfortable. Maybe growing up with nothing does that to a person.

"I'm grateful you would offer, Evelyn," he continues, "but it's already being taken care of."

"You had no right." Evelyn stands, and I'm shocked at the level of anger in her stance. She's not an angry person.

"You didn't have to do that, Jared," I agree with Evelyn. He shouldn't have paid my hospital bills. "It's not your responsibility." It isn't Evelyn's and Carl's either. I need to get a part-time job when I heal and pay Jared back.

"Or yours," I say to Evelyn before she can gloat.

"Yes, it is Layla." Evelyn's eyes widen.

"I'll get a job," I start.

Both Jared and Evelyn say, "No" in unison.

I get up off the couch. "At least you both agree on something."

"Where are you going?" Evelyn asks as I move past her.

"To the bathroom. Is that okay?" I hate biting at her, but she's not making this easy. I spend a little longer in the bathroom than necessary. A soft knock has me glaring at the door. I haven't locked it, and the handle rattles before the door opens.

I'm sitting on the edge of the bathtub. He leans against the frame and tilts his head to the side. "I had a chat with Evelyn."

I'm ready to tell him to get out.

His smirk makes me stop. "We've agreed to do better."

Surprise flitters through me, but I don't say anything.

Jared pushes off the doorframe. "I apologize for overstepping."

I nod. "Good."

"I also apologized for snapping." Evelyn's voice comes from behind the door.

I get up from the tub. "I don't want my favorite people in the world fighting," I say.

Jared doesn't smile but nods. Evelyn appears, and Jared steps aside so she can see in.

"We won't. Let's eat." Evelyn smiles, and I leave the bathroom with her.

We eat dinner, the conversation flowing steadily. Evelyn and Jared are still uptight with each other, but I don't expect things to change quickly. The fact they've acknowledged the hostility between them makes me happy.

After food, I'm hoping to have some time with Jared, but that doesn't look like it's in the cards.

"I'm going to have to cut this short," he tells me. "My father needs my help with some business jargon."

Evelyn looks way too happy. "That's a shame." She picks up his plate and takes them to get washed.

Jared smirks at her. "I know you'll miss me, Evelyn." He's teasing, and that makes me happy.

Evelyn seems surprised as she returns to get my plate. She raises a brow. "Drive safely," she tells him as she returns to the plates.

I get up to walk Jared out, but he holds up his hand. "Stay. I'll call you later." He walks around to me, and he's so confident as he bends down and takes my face in his hand. "Try to rest," he says before pressing a featherlight kiss to my lips.

I bob my head as he releases my face and leaves. I sit as Evelyn washes the plates. The noise is soothing, and all of a sudden, I do feel tired.

I get up from the table. "I think I'll go lie down."

"Do you need a hand getting upstairs?" Evelyn asks from the sink.

"No, thanks. I'm fine."

"Okay, sweetheart. Sleep well."

"Thanks." It's awkward with one arm, but I manage to drag the curtains closed, not before I spot a car outside the house. A man sits in the driver's side, his head bent as he looks at something in his lap. Fear has me watching him, but I dismiss my paranoia as an effect of Jared. He's so cagey, and I think it's rubbing off on me.

I lie on the top of the duvet. I didn't think I would really fall asleep, but I do.

Everything in the bathroom drips with gold. The chandelier is a ridiculous size. Each small teardrop crystal sparkles, and the reflection dances along the cream tiles. I step up to the double sinks. I press my index finger to one of the gold taps, and when I remove my hand, my imprint is left. As I move to grab some tissue to clean off my fingerprint, the lights go out. The room is pitch black, and I feel my way along the wall to the door.

I enter the hallway that has some light. I pause when I hear voices.

I can't make out the words or who Jared is speaking to. I walk in the direction of their voices.

"Jared." He has his back to me, and when he turns, the light from the window catches his features.

"Go back," he snarls.

Trepidation drips slowly down my spine as I look past Jared and to the other person, who I can't fully make out.

"The lights went out," I say when I reach Jared, wondering what's going on. I get a clearer view of the man in front of me. Jared's hand clamps down on my wrist. The impact startles me.

"The little bitch," Chester says, and that's when I follow his raised hand to the gun he's pointing at me. I'm ready to run when the world is ripped apart, and all I feel is pain.

Sweat coats me, and my shoulder throbs with a new kind of pain. It's like the wound is remembering again. My heart won't slow, and I sit up on the edge of the bed.

Chester shot me.

Chester was in Jared's home.

Chester shot me.

My heart palpitates as my brain decides to keep playing the last few seconds on a loop. I'm standing, trying to make the memory stop. Nothing makes sense.

Why did Jared lie? They'd been talking before I arrived...

My brain feels fuzzy. I shiver as the sweat dries on my skin. Reaching out, I pick up my phone. I've been sleeping for a few hours, and Jared has sent a few messages. I open his first message.

How are you?

His second message.

I hope your silence means you are sleeping

His third message has me sitting up.

I'll be back shortly.

I respond quickly.

I fell asleep. Can you leave coming over for tonight? I'm very tired.

I need time to figure out why Jared would lie. Why he lied to me, to his father, to Evelyn and Carl, and to the Gardaí. Was the wreath from Chester? Is that why Jared wanted me to stay with him? Disappointment continues to grow until it's all consuming.

My phone flashes with Jared's name. I hit the red button, cutting him off. Getting up, I enter the bathroom. Washing my face is a task with one arm, but I manage to freshen up. When I return, I have three missed calls from him.

I don't know what prompts me, but I make my way to the window. The car that was parked there before I went to sleep is still there.

Jared's name flashes up on my screen again. I swipe 'answer.'

"Why are you ignoring my calls?"

"Why is there a car parked outside my house?" I ask while clutching the curtain.

"What kind of car?" Jared is driving.

"Is this you, Jared?" I want him to say no. I want to be wrong about everything. But my doubt continues to grow.

"What kind of car?" He's angry.

"A black Audi."

He lets out a whoosh of air. "I'm on my way."

"I already told you not tonight. I'm tired." Guilt churns in my stomach, which makes no sense. I have every right to be mad at him.

"I won't keep you up." My guilt dissolves quickly at how easily he ignores my requests.

"I remember, Jared," I finally say and release the curtain. "I remember what happened."

He hasn't spoken, but he's still there. I can hear the hum of his car and the sound of his breathing.

"I remember being in your house."

"I'm on my way," Jared repeats.

"Am I a target?" I ask as fear clutches my throat. "Is that what the wreath was about?" All my fears come gushing out. "Will he come back and finish me off? That's why you're being so protective."

"Layla. I'm nearly there. Just stay calm. Where are you in your house?"

I wipe falling tears. "What does it matter?"

"Just tell me."

"I'm in my bedroom."

"Describe it to me."

I want to hang up on Jared, but another part of me doesn't want to be alone. "I have a double bed. The quilt has a purple flower pattern. I have a bedside table on either side. Jared, why did you hide this?"

"Do you remember the song about the fish?"

My eyes burn because I remember every single detail about myself and Jared. Every memory with him stands out, and Evelyn's words repeat in my head. *It's unhealthy.*

"Do you think we're unhealthy?" I ask, closing my eyes. Tears trickle down my face. Confusion with everything has me wanting to run.

"I think you're perfect."

I open my eyes at his words. He isn't driving anymore. I walk back to the window and pull open the curtains. His car is parked behind the Audi. He knocks on the window, and he says a few words to the man in the car before turning to the house. Our gazes clash.

Worry tightens his eyes, but he tries to cover it up with a smile as he holds up his pinky finger. "Remember the fish bit off this wee finger." He wiggles it like a worm, I can't see the action clearly from here, but from memory, I know what he is doing. This used to make me laugh, but I don't feel like laughing right now.

"I'll let you in." I hang up and make my way down the stairs, quickly hoping Evelyn doesn't hear us. I don't say anything as I open the front door. I place my finger over my lips so he's quiet as he follows me up the stairs. We need somewhere private to speak.

Once Jared is in my bedroom, I close the door and turn to him.

"I want an explanation now." My undamaged hand goes to my hip. Jared appears larger than life as he takes up all the space and air in my room. I try not to think of the fact that he's in my bedroom.

He nods. "Okay."

CHAPTER FIVE

JARED

"WHAT DO YOU REMEMBER?" I don't want to say more than I have to as I sit down on her bed.

Layla's hand leaves her hip, and she marches over to me. "No. That's not how this is going to work. Tell me why Chester shot me!" she whisper-shouts, and I reach out to touch her, but she moves aside, out of my reach.

"He was there for me. The bullet was meant for me." The truth stings worse when I say the words out loud. Layla getting shot was my fault.

Layla jolts back until she leans against the wall. Her lip wobbles, and she nibbles the pink flesh. "Jesus Christ, Jared. Why? Why would he want to kill you?"

"We had a fight, and it was retaliation."

She's shaking her head. "A fight? About what? Did you threaten him? His family? People fight all the time. I mean, I don't understand why you didn't tell the Gardaí that it was Chester. Now he's still running around out there with a gun." Layla's voice is tinged with hysteria.

I get up from the bed and advance toward her. She holds up her hand for me to stop, but I ignore her and gently pull her into my arms.

"The fight isn't important, Layla. I didn't think this would happen." I press a kiss to the crown of her head and she shoves me away.

"It doesn't make sense. Why are you hiding this?"

"Because I went to Chester to buy a gun. So if he's arrested and starts talking, I don't think it will work out well for me."

Layla blinks in rapid succession. "A gun?"

"Yes." I hadn't intended to share that fact with her.

"For what? Or should I say, who?" Her complexion pales, and when she makes her way to the bed and sits down, I don't stop her.

I'm close to the wall, and I stay put as I face her. "That doesn't matter."

She's shaking her head. "Please stop saying it doesn't matter. Just fucking tell me."

I shouldn't tell her. No good can come from sharing the truth. Yet, I find myself opening my mouth and letting it out. "For Bert."

Layla presses her hand to her lips, and a loud sob erupts. "Oh, Jared."

She stays like that for a while, and I have no idea how to comfort her.

"You got a gun to kill Bert?" she asks.

I nod in acknowledgment.

She cries again. "You were going to take a life?"

My fury spikes. "Fuck's sake, Layla. It's not a life. He doesn't *deserve* to live."

She's shaking her head. "You were going to take a life, Jared."

I'm kneeling in front of her. "Keep your voice down."

I reach up and brush her face, attempting to erase her falling tears, but she jerks out of my grasp. The look of revulsion I see in her stunning gaze forces me to stand.

"You need to pack a few belongings. I can't protect you here."

She sniffles. "What? You want to take me to your home, where I got shot?"

I grind my teeth. "It's the safest place right now. I have plenty of security."

"I already said no."

"This time, I'm not asking."

She stands up. I've pushed too hard, but I'm sick of playing nice with Layla. It's been too long of her staying here and me having to deal with fucking Evelyn.

Layla clears the space between us, and her hand smacks into the center of my chest. The impact is minimal. "No. You can't boss me around."

"You're still a target."

"I'm not going." She hits me again, a bit harder this time.

"Evelyn and Carl will be targets too."

Her lips part, and indecision filters slowly into her features. "Don't try to manipulate me."

"I'm telling you the facts. If you come with me, I'll send word out so Chester knows not to target your home. I'll leave some security here."

Layla turns away from me. "Get the word out? Are you part of his gang?" She waves off the question. "Just say I'm living with you. Won't that be enough?"

"No, it's not enough. Someone might see you here." I'm clutching at fucking paper straws that have spent too much time in water, but she doesn't know that. Having her with me is all I want.

Her gaze wavers, and she's about to respond when the door opens.

Evelyn appears. "I'd like the door kept open."

I can't even glance at her. Layla is nineteen, not nine. But out of respect for Layla, I say nothing about Evelyn's intrusion.

"Yeah. No problem," Layla says.

Evelyn steps into the room. "Are you okay?" she asks Layla.

Layla looks at me before forcing a smile onto her face. "Yeah, yeah. Just talking."

Evelyn taps her foot on the floor several times. "I'm only downstairs." Her tone is sharp.

What the fuck did she think I was doing? I finally glance in the direction of Evelyn and find her watching me.

"Okay," Layla says and Evelyn leaves.

"What the hell do I tell them?" Layla whispers.

"I can do it," I offer. I won't be gentle either. My intentions coming over here were to carry her down the stairs and into my car.

Layla glares at me. "Wouldn't you love that?"

I'd smile at how beautiful she looks when she's pissed, but this isn't the time.

"Why don't we tell them the truth?" Layla tries to negotiate.

"What will they do, Layla? They'll go to the Gardaí, and I might find myself in a lot of trouble."

She rubs her face. "How long will I have to leave?"

"Not long," I reply.

"Chester isn't just going to go away, Jared." Layla intakes a large gulp of air. "What do you intend to do? Shoot him too?" Layla's eyes widen. "Oh my God. When did this become okay?" She's hyperventilating.

I go to her and take her face. "Take a deep breath."

She's trying to push me away. I've given in to her tantrums before, but this time, I keep my hold on her face and speak with more force. "Take a deep breath, Layla."

She does.

"No one is going to die."

"You swear?" Her sharp intakes and loud exhales are what I concentrate on.

"If Chester were shot, they would blame me. I'm not stupid. As much as I want him dead, I won't be shooting anyone."

Layla's eyes water. "Promise me, Jared." Her lip drags down.

I lean my forehead against hers. "I promise." I press a kiss to her lips. "Pack a few things. We can always come back for more."

"What do I say to Carl and Evelyn?" Panic widens her eyes.

"I can tell them. In a nice way," I suggest, and I would be nice for Layla, seeing she's in such a state.

She shakes her head. "I'll do it."

Her body deflates, and her shoulders drop.

I release her.

"This is for their protection," she says, as if trying to reinforce that lie.

I incline my head. "Theirs and yours." I don't give two fucks about them, but Layla does.

"I want you to wait in the car."

I take a step toward her. "No."

"Jared. Just give me a minute. Please."

I want to warn her not to keep me waiting, but the pleading in her voice has me clenching my jaw.

"I'll be in the car." I press a kiss to her forehead before leaving. Evelyn is at the bottom of the stairs.

"You're leaving?" she asks.

I smile. "Yes, I am."

That leaves her unsettled, and she marches up the stairs.

Outside, I get into my car. I have two missed calls from Alex.

I'm busy, I text her and look back at Layla's house.

I can't imagine the conversation is going well with Evelyn. It takes a lot of restraint not to get out of the car and rush into the house to get Layla.

Thirty painful minutes pass before Layla leaves the house with a small backpack. She won't meet my gaze as she climbs into the passenger side. The door closes, and with shaky hands, she struggles to put on her belt.

"Let me help you." I reach across to grab the belt.

"I got it."

I ignore her.

"Jared, stop." Her gaze meets mine, and she's beyond pissed.

"I'm trying to keep you safe."

She clips her belt into place. "You know when people say take off the band-aid quickly? That it's less painful?" She looks up at me. "It's not. I think I broke her heart."

Layla looks out the window, and after a few moments, she speaks quietly. "Just go."

Evelyn will recover, and Layla will be safe. That's all that matters to me. "I'll leave two of my men here to keep Evelyn and Carl safe," I offer up as I pull onto the road.

"Thank you."

"You're welcome." The drive to my home is silent, but the quiet is not uncomfortable. With Layla at my side, silence isn't a void I want to fill. I could sit with her like this forever.

The gates to my home open, and I drive up to the house. I'm sure my father is going to be ecstatic when he sees Layla.

"You will be safe here," I say when I unclip my belt.

Layla doesn't respond. She's working on her own seat belt and struggles to get the door open. By the time I get around to her side, she's still trying to get out. I could stand here to prove a point that she needs help. I open the door and pick her bag up off the floor while offering her my hand. She has to take it. She's still pissed, and it's not a look I've seen on Layla before.

"I'll show you to your room." I close the car door and Layla follows me into the house. She pauses at the stairs, and a new kind of fear enters her features.

"I won't let anything happen."

She resumes walking, and that fucking bothers me. She doesn't think I can keep her safe. I've always kept her safe.

"You would have been upset if I shot Bert?" I ask.

Layla stops walking and turns to me. "Of course." She frowns while wrapping one arm around her waist. "It's murder, Jared."

It would be justice. I don't voice my true motivation.

"If you had," she continued, "you would have gone to jail."

I nod. I knew that, and I had been fully prepared to do the time. I would have tried to stay out of jail, but it was a gamble I was willing to take if it meant bringing him to his fucking knees.

Layla unwraps her arm from her waist, and she's in front of me like a spitfire. Her hand hits my chest heavily. "What about me? You would have just left me? How could I have coped with that?"

Her breathing is growing harsh again, and she's struggling to keep focus. Her gaze darts everywhere as tears leave her eyes. "How could you give up your life? Have we not given enough of our time?"

She's in my arms, and her tears grow heavier, her sobs louder. This is where I'm meant to be. Right here protecting Layla.

"Everything is okay." I press a kiss to the crown of her head.

"No, Jared. It's not." She tries to wriggle from my hold.

I let her.

She wipes her eyes. "This is just all too much."

She'll get used to her life here. I continue walking, and she follows as I take her to the room I had prepared for her two weeks ago. The moment she ended up in the hospital, I knew I had to bring her here.

I open the door and let her step into her new room. I don't really intend to leave her in here for long. She'll be in my bed soon, but I have to show patience. She walks around the large space.

"Do you like it?" I ask.

She runs her hand along the white duvet. "It's lovely." Her voice is heavy.

I look back down the hall and notice William waiting for me. I place Layla's bag on the floor. "I'll let you get settled."

She doesn't look at me, but I see the nod of her head.

William waits as I close Layla's door, then he hands me a slip of paper. I want to tell him to just say what my father sent him to say, but I open the note instead. I'm surprised to see I have a visitor in the library. I look up at William, but he doesn't meet my eye, and he's getting ready to walk away.

"Who is it?"

He swallows. "Your mother, Master Jay."

CHAPTER SIX

LAYLA

I FOLD MY HANDS in front of me, trying to find meaning in all of this. Jared's plan to kill Bert has dread chasing me. I look over my shoulder, expecting to see something large and dark looming. Instead, the bedroom door opens and three women file in.

They wear the same uniforms—navy trousers, a white shirt, and a navy jacket. The ladies have their hair pinned back so severely that it stretches the smiles on their faces.

"Miss Masters, we are here to serve." The taller of the three steps forward, and her lips curl back over her teeth. Thoughts of a horse spring to mind. It's not a fair analysis of her looks, but I can't stop the comparison.

"Serve me?" I'd laugh, only the dread I've been sensing hasn't left. My confusion keeps deepening.

"Yes..." She glances over her shoulder while sweeping her hand toward the other two ladies. "We are here for you."

Servants. I have servants.

"There's no need. I'm sure you have other things to do."

The lady's smile falters, and she clears her throat. "Please. Master Jay has assigned us to help you."

There's an awkward silence as they wait for me to say something. I've never had anyone serve me before. I need to talk to Jared about this. We weren't brought up with silver spoons in our mouths. More like cheap plastic ones.

Each lady waits expectantly. Maybe having them here will be a welcome distraction until I tell Jared how ridiculous all this is.

"Maybe we can start with your names."

"I'm Kerry." Kerry continues to smile, and I try to shake off the horse comparison, but it's impossible. Her smile is so wide that I can see her gums. Her black bangs are thick and rest just above her brows. The rest of her hair is pinned back neatly.

The second lady steps forward. Her brown hair is in a tight bun, and she has red, rosy cheeks. "I'm Andrea."

"And I'm Amanda." She's the smallest of the three, and the youngest. All her features are pixielike, but from the sharpness of her brown eyes, I don't think her size would have anyone underestimating her.

"I'm Layla." I look at each lady. They don't tell me they already know this, which I'm sure they do, but I want to even the playing field.

"I've never had anyone take care of me before." The awkwardness returns, but Kerry gives a little clap of her hands.

"Let us take the lead, then."

My shoulders relax. "Thank you, Kerry."

The activity around the room is instant. Kerry gives instructions, and the ladies move. Amanda makes her way to the bathroom, while Andrea lights the fire. Kerry has picked up my bag, but I immediately reach for my only possession.

"I can do that."

She has so much gum on display. "Not at all. Allow me."

I don't want to be rude. "No, please." I hold out my hand, and she passes me the bag.

"I'll get some food," Kerry says.

I'm not hungry, but I don't stop her as she leaves the room. I sink onto the bed with the bag in my hand. I pull down the zipper and reach in, taking out Carl's sweater. This is the sweater I keep hidden from Carl and Evelyn. For so many nights, it gave me comfort as fear tried to keep me awake. I raise the garment to my nose and inhale the smell that still lingers in the fibers. The crackle of the fire has me opening my eyes.

Andrea has her back to me. The distant rumble of the bath filling has me getting up off the bed and walking over to the large antique chest of drawers. I don't bother with the top drawers but bend down and struggle to open the bottom one with one hand. I finally manage, and it's there I put Carl's sweater for safekeeping. I push the drawer back in with my foot, but I don't step away from the dresser as the conversation with Evelyn I had plays out in my mind.

"You're leaving?"

"Only for a few nights, Evelyn." I try to downplay the hurt that's blatant on her face.

"Is this because of me and Jared?"

"No. I just want to spend some time with him." I cling to the strap of my bag.

"I don't think this is a good idea, Layla." Evelyn's fretting. That's something I've never seen her do.

My lip trembles, and I bite the meaty flesh. "I need you to trust me."

Evelyn steps closer. "I do trust you. I just don't think going back to Jared's home is wise. I don't understand the sudden shift in your decision."

No words will make this right, I know that. The fact is, I have to leave. I need to keep Carl and Evelyn safe.

"I need space from you, Evelyn. I need time with Jared without you hovering over me." I can't stay any longer as I watch the woman who gave me a home crumble in front of me.

I turn away from her but pause at the kitchen door. "I love you, Evelyn. I'll call every day."

"I love you too."

I can't look back. The pain in her words propels my steps out the door.

"Miss Masters, your bath is ready."

I stiffen as Amanda appears beside me. I exhale loudly, trying to relax as I shake off the memory of Evelyn.

"I'll need you to help me with my clothes." I don't exactly want help, but I'm exhausted, and removing everything with one arm is something I don't look forward to doing.

Amanda helps me, being careful with my arm. Once I'm down to my underwear, I make my way into the bathroom alone. The steam has fogged up the mirror, like it knows I don't want to see my face. Guilt is choking me, and I don't need to see it in my gaze.

My underpants slide down easily, and I kick them off. Removing my bra with one hand is a problem, but one I manage to resolve. Once naked, I step into the bath. The heat encases me as I sink right under the water. I'm trying to outrun my thoughts, but they haunt me like a ghost, and I break the surface of the water. Raising both hands, my shoulder burns, and I reduce my movements but move my fingers around, allowing my hands to filter through all the bubbles.

Sounds come from my bedroom. The ladies are still there, waiting to serve me. I don't think I could ever get used to having people waiting on me hand and foot. I don't stay too long in the bath because I don't find the freedom I'm seeking from my thoughts.

A soft knock on the door has me calling out. "Yes."

"May I come in?" I think it's Amanda.

I glance down at my body, which is hidden under all the bubbles. "Yes."

It is Amanda who enters, with a white bathrobe and some towels. "For when you're ready to get out."

I sit up slightly. "I'm ready now." She places the towels on the vanity table and steps closer with the bathrobe, opening it.

She already helped me get undressed, so what does it matter if she offers me a little more help. I stand up quickly and get out of the bath. The robe is placed on my back, and I slip my arms into the sleeves before bringing the gown together with the large belt. When I turn, Amanda hands me a towel for my hair.

"Thank you."

"You are very welcome." She makes herself busy getting out a hair dryer as she uses it to dry the steam off the vanity mirror.

"It's okay." I don't need the mirror cleared. I don't want to see myself.

Amanda turns off the hair dryer before pulling out the small stool. "I'll do your hair."

I sit down. Amanda works on my hair, and I shift in the seat, wanting to get up. Darkness keeps creeping in, and if I move, I might be able to outrun the dread that won't leave me alone.

My hair is only half-done when I stand. "It's fine. I like it to dry naturally." The bathroom is too warm, and I don't wait for Amanda to reply before entering my bedroom. Fresh clothes are laid out on my bed; clothes I didn't bring. A pair of gray high-waisted trousers with wide legs are the first thing I reach for. The woolen material and the cut of them tell a story of their worth. The cream cashmere V-neck sweater is soft under my fingertips. The rattle of a tray has me looking at Kerry as she sets the silver set down on the table nestled close to the window.

"Some tea and sandwiches." She glances at me with a smile before taking everything off the tray and placing it neatly on the table.

Amanda arrives out of the bathroom. "Shall I help you dress?"

I want to say no, but her help will make the process quicker. I give her a nod of my head.

Andrea moves across the room and into the bathroom. Kerry leaves with an empty tray, and it's just me and Amanda.

"Have you worked for Jared long?" I ask. She frowns and I correct myself. "Jay."

"No. We were only recently hired by Master Jay."

I'm nearly dressed, and as perfect as this outfit feels, it also causes me concern. He had time to get these clothes, the right sizes, and have them placed in this room. Now, I have staff that he just all of a sudden hired?

"When did Jay hire you?" I ask.

Amanda looks over at the table where Kerry had been, and I wonder if she's searching for approval to speak. When she realizes it's just the two of us, she answers. "Two weeks ago."

My stomach tightens. "Thank you, Amanda."

Amanda helps me put my sling back on before gathering up the bathrobe. I sit at the small table, and it's not until I start to eat that I realize I'm pretty hungry.

Andrea finishes cleaning the bathroom, and Kerry returns. "Thank you, all. But I'm fine now."

Without question, Andrea and Amanda leave my bedroom, but Kerry lingers.

"Our sole purpose is to serve you, so one of us will be outside your door if you need."

My God, this is ridiculous. I really need to find Jared and speak to him about this.

"Thank you, Kerry."

Kerry leaves, and I push my food aside. I sit a few minutes, until the crackle of the fire drives me out of the chair. I grab a pair of white tennis shoes that take me a few minutes to get into before leaving the room. True to her word, Kerry is standing outside my room. She glances at me.

"I'm just taking a walk," I say, hoping she won't follow me. She doesn't.

The foyer is enormous, and I don't think I could ever not be amazed at the sheer size and décor of this mansion. The stairs come into view, and I pause. Jared's quarters are up here, and I'm sure that's exactly where I will find him. He placed me on the ground floor, so I didn't have to remember…

Each step I take is heavy. I'm tempted to turn around and wait in my room for Jared to come to me, but I keep pushing up the stairs. I don't want to be alone. I don't want to stand still. I don't want to feel this fear I can't shake off.

I reach the third floor, and the air is heavy. I'm not supposed to be up here. That's the feeling that tightens every bone in my body as I move mechanically across the landing. I stop at where I stood the night of the shooting. There isn't a blemish on the oak wooden floor. The smell of fresh paint and polish covers up the blood and fear of what took place.

"The little bitch." Chester's words send a shiver along my spine. I dip my head into my chest on reflex as I glance at the window where he stood. Light flitters across the floor, blinding the darkness of the moment.

I close my eyes and let the warmth of the sun caress me, but everything in me screams. I open my eyes as my vision wavers, and I want to cave in and curl up right here on the floor. There's something building inside me as I turn away from the window and the heat of the sun, stepping deeper into the space. I pause at Jared's bedroom door before entering; he isn't here. The bathroom I used the night of the shooting makes me pause as well. It's like standing on the edge of a platform, and there's a speeding train making its way toward me. I have no control as my foot lifts, and I step into the bathroom.

I run my tongue along my teeth as everything blurs. My strength evaporates as the burn in my shoulder erupts. Jared is safety. That's all I've ever known. I'm here in his home, and I've never felt so lost, so unsafe, so confused. I leave the bathroom, and I'm ready to give up my search when a door at the end of the hall catches my attention. I saw Jared look at it before while touching the key that hung around his neck.

Each step I take toward the door has my pain falling off me like a second skin. I can almost imagine the anguish sliding off me and leaving a trail behind. *Curiosity Killed the Cat.* Those words ring in my mind as I reach for the door and turn the handle.

CHAPTER SEVEN

JARED

I ENTER ONE OF the many sitting rooms. I refer to this room as the waiting room, because this is where most visitors are taken.

I try not to react as the woman who claims to be my mother stands. I don't like how I recognize myself in her dark eyes. The bow of her lips is a replica of mine. She's tall, especially for a woman. Her slight build doesn't make her look timid or tame. She holds herself with a fierceness that reminds me of a lioness.

"What do you want?" I ask.

She bristles. Her reaction is instant. "That's how you greet your mother?" Hurt flows quietly under her words; I can detect the pain.

"You claim to be my mother," I answer. It's obvious that she's my mother from her features alone, but I also remember her. She's older, but she is my mother.

She nods solemnly. "It's been a long time."

Did she expect me to feel sorry for her? She gave up on me.

"What do you want?" I ask again. I wave her off and close the door heavily behind me as I step deeper into the room. "Does Father know you're here?"

It would undo him, and I can't allow that. No matter how angry I am with him, he found me and gave me my life back. She, on the other hand, destroyed my life.

My mother's eyes widen, and panic has her gaze darting around the room. "No. I only wanted to speak to you."

I grin. "Are you sure I shouldn't get him? Let this be a family reunion." My grin melts off my face.

Her frantic eyes settle on me, and she wrings her hands in front of her. "I was trying to protect you."

I can't give her a second look as hatred burns through my veins, destroying the last of my control.

"Trying to protect me by taking me away from my father? By placing me in the home with those fucking monsters?" I'm in front of her. "Do you have any idea what they did to me?" I want to kill her.

My mother startles, her brows dragging down. "Monsters? What happened? Jared?" She reaches for me.

I step away and pull my control back, building the walls that will keep me sane and safe. "Why are you here, and why now?" I appreciate how controlled my voice is, and with that knowledge, I grow calmer.

"I put you in the foster system to protect you. I didn't think anything would happen. Did someone hurt you?" She reaches out to me again but wisely stops and places her hands behind her back. She gathers some of her emotions.

"This is your last chance, Maura. I've been here for seven years, so why are you here now?"

"Seven years?" She seems to stumble before seeking out the chair behind her. "He's had you here for seven years?" Her emotions level, and I think she's going to throw up. "I saw an article about a shooting in the house. When your name was mentioned, I realized he had found you." Her focus bounces around the room before she looks at me. "I was only trying to protect you."

I smirk, and I hope she feels the coldness down to her soul. "Well, you didn't."

Her throat bobbles as she swallows and nods. "All he wants is your money." Tears fall from her brown eyes. "He will do anything to have your money."

The door to the waiting room opens, and my father steps in. I'm walking toward him. I don't want him to have to deal with her. "I'll get rid of her," I tell him.

He closes the door like I haven't spoken. "Maura, I was wondering when you would make your reappearance."

There's no devastation in his voice. If anything, he sounds gleeful. When I look back at Maura, she's standing. Her chest rises and falls rapidly, and she reminds me of a drowning man. I'm okay watching her drown. In fact, I hope she does.

"Seven years, you've had my son." Each word is low, but it drives her feet toward him. I step in her way, blocking her. She halts and frowns.

"You have no idea what he's capable of." She's pointing around me, but my father's hand on my shoulder has me stepping aside.

"I think you should leave, Maura. You are upsetting Jay."

I don't have time to react as she slams her open palm across my father's face. "You changed my son's name." She's screaming, and I've fucking had enough. I grab her hand before she hits him again.

"Get out of our home. Neither of us ever wants to see you again."

My father backs me up. "You heard Jay. Leave."

I release my mother.

The door to the waiting room opens, and two security guards step into the room. I look at my father. I don't think that's necessary, but I don't stop them as they step toward my mother, who is growing frantic.

She's shaking her head as they take an arm each. "Jared, listen to me. He only wants the money."

I don't respond as they drag her from the room.

"He killed my husband." Her accusation is the last thing I hear as she's dragged from the room.

"How did she get in?" I ask.

"That is a question I'm asking myself." My father steps up to me and places a hand on my shoulder. "Are you okay, son?"

I nod. "She doesn't think you're her husband," I say. She's lost her mind. That fact should sadden me, but it doesn't.

"I'll make sure she never gets in here again," my father promises as he goes to leave the room. Instead, he turns to me.

"Are you okay?"

"Yes." I want to ask why I wouldn't be. She means nothing to me. But, the more I want to elaborate, the more silent I become.

My father takes my silence to mean I don't care. "I wanted to speak about our houseguest."

I tighten my fists, ready to defend Layla.

My father raises a hand, the large silver watch catching the light. It's the same watch from my memory. He drops his hand, and the watch disappears. "I understand that she's important to you, so I want to meet her."

"No," I say immediately. I won't let anyone hurt her.

"Jay, I just thought the three of us having dinner together would be nice. I want her to like me." His voice holds a note of vulnerability. A note I've never heard before.

I still don't want him near her.

"You have my word," he continues. "I will keep the conversation to civil matters."

I'm still not convinced.

My father stands straighter. "The weather and school."

"No mention of the shooting or her foster parents or how we grew up." I take a step closer to my father. "I won't allow one word to hurt her."

He nods. "I'm starting to understand that, son." He reaches out and squeezes my shoulder before leaving.

I go in search of Layla. She's not in her room. Kerry is outside her door and points at the stairs. "She took a walk, Master Jay."

I'm taking the steps two at a time. What is she thinking going up here?

I reach the third floor, and she's nowhere in sight. "Layla?" I call.

"Here."

I stop walking and return to the living space. She rises from the couch.

"What are you doing up here?" I ask.

"When Chester shot me, I don't remember what happened after he fired the gun." She sits up further, her blonde hair spilling over her shoulder. The *V* of her cream sweater shows off her generous cleavage. When I had selected the top, I knew it would be perfect on her.

"William rang an ambulance." I don't step into the living space.

"It's funny. I could have died, and everything, every single moment, would have ceased to exist for me. But for you, it would have gone on."

I scratch my forehead. Her thoughts are morbid. "Come back downstairs."

"Did you cry?" She gets up from the couch.

"No," I answer honestly.

Is that disappointment I see in her eyes? I grin. "Would you have wanted me to cry?"

She steps around the couch and walks over to me. She shrugs and lets out a half-hearted laugh. "I don't know."

"I mean, I'm sure I can cry if it makes you feel better." I narrow my eyes.

She laughs. "I was just curious."

I reach out my hand, and she takes it. "My father wants to officially meet you. We're going to have a meal together tonight."

She's looking up into my eyes with the fear of God in hers, and I pull her a little closer. "I swear to you, he only wants to meet you."

She swallows and nods. "Yeah, I can't wait."

I'm not sure if she's telling the truth, but I accept her words as truthful. I just want us back downstairs. We leave the living room, and Layla stops, looking behind her.

"The room at the end of the hall. What's in it?"

My gut twists. "Why?"

She shrugs as she glances up at me. "I was exploring, and it's the only locked door on this floor."

What would she think if she knew? I'm staring back at the door along with her. My gut twists again.

"It was once a servant's room. Now..." I meet Layla's gaze. "It's storage."

"Okay." She accepts my word. "Speaking of servants, I don't need any."

I take her hand in mine and start pulling her back down the stairs.

"That's no problem."

She narrows her eyes. "That easy?"

I grin. "I will dress you and undress you. You can't manage with one arm."

Her face burns, and I stop us at the top of the landing. "It's up to you, Layla. Either they serve you, or I do."

She's struggling with her answer, and it delights me. Will she pick me?

"Fine. Kerry and the girls stay."

I continue our descent down the stairs. "Good. I want you to be happy here." *Happy with me.*

Layla can't hold my stare. "I am," she lies. I accept her lie, as one day I know she will be happy with me.

"I took the liberty of buying you some dresses. I think the red one will be stunning on you tonight."

Layla doesn't speak until we reach the foyer. "It almost seems you've been planning this for a while."

"I have been." I have no need to lie. "Ever since you got injured, I've wanted you here with me, where I can keep you safe."

Layla reaches up and touches my face. "You don't have to keep protecting me." Pain radiates from her eyes.

I capture her hand in mine again. "I will always protect you, Layla."

No matter the cost.

CHAPTER EIGHT

LAYLA

"COME ON." JARED APPEARS relaxed as he takes my hand in his. His smile showcases his dimples, and I can't stop the smile that grows on my own face.

My nerves seem to be jumping all over the place. Meeting Jared's father for the first time is daunting and yet exciting. Jared's dimples disappear, and he squeezes my hand as we walk through the foyer. I feel overdressed as the red material swishes a fraction of an inch above the marble floor. My hair is loose, and Amanda worked so carefully on my hair and makeup that when I looked in the mirror, I was surprised by what I saw. I've opted to leave my sling off so as not to ruin the stunning dress. I'm careful with the placement of my arm and keep it stiff along my side. Jared stops walking, and I'm surprised when he releases my hand and faces me.

"If for any reason you feel uncomfortable, just let me know."

His words make me unsure. A nerve tics in Jared's jaw.

"Why would I feel uncomfortable?" I ask.

I don't get an answer.

"Exactly, Layla" Jared's father appears in the hallway, and he's a formidable force. "That's the same question I would ask, too."

I don't expect his next action as he reaches me and carefully pulls me into a hug that drags a small, short squeal from me. My hands hang at my sides until the shock passes, and I hug him back. He smells of cologne and carries the coolness of fresh air; the cologne tickles my nose.

"So glad to have you in our home," he says, not letting me go as he holds me at arm's length.

"Alright, Father." Jared speaks from behind me.

Jared's father releases me, and I quickly glance at Jared and raise both brows. He had no need to worry. Straight away, his father is being nice. "Great to meet you too, Mr. McGivney."

"Athar. You can only call me Athar. Mr. McGivney makes me feel old."

I nod that I will as he steps aside to let both Jared and I walk in front of him. Surprise flitters through me as Jared takes my hand, and my head twists up to him. He isn't looking at me; instead, he is leading me down the hall and into the dining room.

The room is large, but I expected nothing less. The chaos of paintings, flowers, and furniture isn't what I expected, though, and it's the first room that seems like it's being used.

Both men allow me to take in the room. One side has photographs, and I take my hand out of Jared's and walk toward the large gilt edge frame. I want to know everything about him, and I focus on the images that hang on the walls. Jared steps up beside me, and even though the room is vast, it feels so small with him at my side. Emotionally, I can't concentrate, so focusing on the images gives me a moment before Jared's body heat burns my back. He reaches over my shoulder as he points at the picture I'm looking at. It's Jared holding a mic. The assembly in front of him holds hundreds of people, and they're caught up in whatever Jared is saying. The photo is black and white, and he looks breathtaking.

"A speech I had to make on responsibility."

I look over my shoulder at Jared and stare at his chest before slowly meeting his dark eyes. "Responsibility?" It sounds like a silly question.

"Yes, Layla. Don't seem so surprised." The laughter in Jared's voice has my lips rising. "Maybe one day you might address the school, too."

I blink a few times at his sentence. That sounds like a nightmare. I don't get to voice the horror I feel, but from the dimples that appear on Jared's cheeks, I see he already knows. A servant arrives, carrying a tray with steaming plates of food.

Athar is already seated at the head of the table, and Jared and I join him. I'm to Athar's left, and Jared is to his right. Sitting down, I exhale and then breathe in the scent of food that is lowered in front of me from a second servant. A third servant places Jared's food in front of him, and when I meet his gaze, he grins.

I can't stop staring at the fish that looks undercooked on my plate. A few leaves and shavings of vegetables are all that decorate the fish.

Jared laughs. "That's squid, in case you're wondering."

I pick up my knife and fork and have to really work on cutting off a piece. Stuffing it into my mouth, I give Jared a quick smile. "It's nice."

Chewing the fish takes a while. Surprisingly, the small shavings of vegetables are divine. We chat as we eat. Athar sticks close to the topics of school, the weather, and shockingly, gardening. Jared has shared that knowledge with him. He doesn't mention the foster home we grew up in or anything about the shooting that took place in his home. It makes the avoided topic hang heavy in the air.

The plates are removed and our drinks are replenished. Athar sits back in his chair.

I'm waiting for the conversation to move to what everyone is thinking, but it doesn't go there. Instead, Athar stands.

"I think I'll take my leave."

"It was lovely meeting you, Athar."

"You too, Layla." Athar smiles before giving Jared a nod of his head.

I take a peek at Jared, and he doesn't seem surprised at all by this. In fact, I'd say he appears relieved.

"Next time, I will cook for you," Jared says once his father has left.

"The fish was lovely," I lie. He laughs as I sink into the chair. "That sounds nice, you cooking," I add.

Jared rises. "You might regret saying that."

I doubt I will.

"Come on," he says, holding out his hand for me to take.

I take it and don't ask where we're going as he leads me out of the room. The staircase comes into view, but he doesn't veer over to it. Instead, Jared takes me down the hallway where my room is. My pulse spikes as he stops at the door beside mine. I'm surprised to see Kerry still stationed outside my room. I swallow words as Jared tugs on my hand.

"This is my room."

His room.

Jared keeps his fingers threaded through mine as we enter.

Jared's room is tidy, but that doesn't surprise me. It always was. A large queen-size bed is situated on a huge black shaggy rug. The moss green bedding drapes on either side of the bed. The furniture is antique, like the rest of the house. The wardrobe, nightstand, and dresser all match. Once again, I can't stop the thought that it's so far away from how we grew up.

Jared releases my hand and walks over to his bed. He sits down and observes me as I check out his room. My heels click on the dark wooden floor. The blank walls are freshly painted in a soft gray. Jared was always a fan of movie posters, and now I wonder what had happened to them. Did they remind him of before, or had he just outgrown that time of his life? It's moments like these that I realize we lost so much time with each other.

Casting my gaze back to Jared, my stomach flips. The way he's looking at me has me fidgeting with my hand. Jared gets up and goes to his wardrobe before returning with something grey. My heart leaps with recognition, and he pats the bed beside him.

Oh my God.

I gather the red material of my dress as I walk on shaky legs over to Jared. I sit down slowly, never taking my eyes off the sweater. My vision blurs a little, and I look up at him. "You kept it."

"It's all I had of you." His voice deepens. I reach for the sweater, and without hesitation, he gives it to me. "Jared." My vision blurs again, and his face quivers.

"It's our past, and I won't ever let it go."

I stare at the sweater. No, it's so much more. It scared away the monsters at nighttime. It smells like Jared. Not thinking, I do something I've done a million times. I bring the sweater to my nose and choke on a laugh that escapes me as I inhale the same smell.

Jared.

This is why I grabbed one of Carl's sweaters when they took me in. I had tried to replace Jared's sweater, but nothing and no one would ever replace him. My chest is caving in as I look up at him.

Looking straight ahead, he lets out a breath before getting up again and going to the dresser. His hands seem rigid as he takes something from the top drawer and comes back to me. As he walks a few paces, he doesn't look in my direction. He seems tense and nervous as he hands me a small piece of paper.

He doesn't sit beside me as I glance down at the paper and turn it over. My heart stalls in my chest. I see a girl looking back at me, one I used to know. It's all too much. Slowly, I lift my gaze, and our eyes meet.

"It's the last day I saw you."

My chest squeezes, and I nod as I continue to crumble.

Jared kneels in front of me and extracts the drawing from my hands. He places it on the bed to my left before taking my fingers. My heart triples in speed.

"But now," he says, "this is our future."

A weakness enters my body, and I think this is it; he's going to say he loves me. I don't move or breathe, and a slow grin spreads across Jared's face.

"Breathe, Layla." He says the words softly, and I exhale. His grin widens. "Good girl."

After a moment, Jared's grin disappears. "The day at Mark's beach party... Remember you asked me to make a wish? Did you make a wish?"

I swallow and look down at our joined hands. "Hmm..." I pretend like I have to think about the answer.

Gazing up at him, I feel a bit tongue-tied with the intensity that burns in his brown eyes. The way his head is tilted and how his gaze takes in every inch of my face makes me feel like I'm a treasured painting or someone he's put up on a pedestal for him to gaze at. My pulse spikes, and I sense the fluttering in my neck.

"I wished that your wish would come true," I answer honestly.

His brows rise in surprise, and his dimples appear as he barks out a short laugh. The sound is deep and causes butterflies to erupt in my belly.

"What did you wish for, a million dollars or something like that?" I tease, knowing it wouldn't be money. A hyperawareness of my hand in his hits me as he grows serious.

"A kiss," he says, and I find myself wetting my lips at his words.

"A kiss?" I repeat. Like he hasn't kissed me before? The fact he wished for it makes something about this moment different. "From me?"

"Yes, a kiss," he confirms.

My heart pounds as Jared moves closer. I'm breathing heavily through my nose.

"Are you going to make my wish come true?" The cheeky grin that accompanies his words has me biting my lip. I'd give him so much more than a kiss. I'd give him every single piece of me. Every secret, every wish, every dream, my heart; I'd give him everything. I'd give him all of me.

Jared presses up on his knees, and he lets my fingers go so he can take my face in his large hands. My knees are weak. There's a look in his gaze that I recognize. My hand goes to his shoulder, and before he can kiss me, my truth spills out.

"I love you."

CHAPTER NINE

LAYLA

MY HEART BEATS WILDLY. Blood rushes and roars in my ears as he stares up at me.

He reaches up and touches my cheek. I lean into his touch like it can heal all the broken parts of me, and he stretches a little more. Brown orbs fill my vision before Jared closes his eyes just as our lips touch. His lips are soft and gentle. He applies more pressure, and my hand flutters to his chest. My veins burn, and my body throbs in a way I didn't know was possible. When my lips part slightly under his, electricity flows through me as the tip of his tongue enters my mouth. I inhale sharply at the sensation, giving him more room to deepen the kiss. Our tongues touch, and I tighten my grip on his shirt, pulling him closer.

He's perfect. A part of me thinks I might be dreaming. My brain is screaming for oxygen; it's the only reason I break the kiss. A slight tremor has entered my hands as I cling to Jared. When he opens his eyes and looks at me, a prickly sensation crawls all over me. The fine hairs stand to attention.

"When I was ten, I had this feeling when I looked at you. It was a feeling I didn't understand at the time. I thought it was that I needed to protect you." Jared's fingers trace the outline of my mouth as he speaks. "As I turned twelve, I thought the feeling was because I fancied you. It wasn't until I saw you again that I knew what that feeling was—what it is."

I can't breathe; my heart is going to come out of my chest.

"I love you, Layla. I always have." His forehead touches mine. "Always will," he whispers. I blink, and tears make a pathway down my face. His thumb is there, wiping them away. "Don't cry. Why are you crying?"

I duck my head down, and he follows me, not allowing me to hide. I'm nodding as tears drip off my chin.

I don't want to hide from him. I'm just overwhelmed. I raise my head, and he follows.

"You..." I swallow my emotions as salty liquid finds its way into my mouth. "You were like a superhero to me. During the day, you were there. You always seemed to tower over everything. You cast shadows. You hid me, protected me, and at night, you were there too. Just in a different way. You scared off the monsters. Now in this life, you're fighting for me. Loving me."

I reach up and let my fingers trace his lips, just like he did with me. I'm finding it so hard to tell him what I want to say. "Love just doesn't seem to cover all that I feel. You are everything to me."

Jared has grown still as I speak, and then his mouth finds mine again. The kiss isn't gentle; it's urgent and filled with not just love but loss and tears.

When we break the kiss, Jared rises. With one hand on my chest, he pushes me back onto the bed. The ceiling seems so far away as I stare up at the golden coven. The pattern of small, intricate flowers takes shape the longer I look. My attention is stolen as Jared grabs the material of my dress and slowly slides it up my legs. As he bunches the material, I suck in my stomach and try to drag my legs closer together. Large, warm hands push my legs apart, and I attempt to sit up to see Jared.

"Stay where you are."

I get a glimpse of him before he disappears between my legs. I gasp at the initial contact. His tongue runs along the line of my underpants. Teeth graze my flesh, and I clench my legs around his head. His hands push my thighs back, and he drags down my underpants.

The air is cold against my core as he moves away. I'm aching for him, and when he returns, he doesn't move slowly but plunges his tongue inside me. I want to see him, and I try to look up, but his hand pushes me back down before he reappears. His face is wet. He crawls on top of me, and the air halts in my chest. His tongue flicks out and races across his lips. When he descends over me, he pauses, and I'm aware of how careful he is being with my shoulder.

"I want to try something with you," he says softly.

My heart skips a beat.

He leans down and kisses me. I can taste myself on his lips. His tongue sinks into my mouth, and all I taste is my excitement for him. He breaks the kiss and climbs off me. The bulge in his jeans has a sympathetic agony speeding through me. I want him back. Jared walks to his dresser and opens the second drawer. I can't see what he's doing, but now I wonder if he's getting protection. Am I ready to go the whole way? I love him, yet the thought has my shoulders stiffening. Jared pivots back toward me with a scrap of material in his hand.

His eyes are light and hold a smile at my confusion as he comes back to the bed. He slowly sits me up.

"Trust me," he says before holding up the blindfold that he ties around my head. The room is blackened, and he carefully lies me back on the bed.

My gaze dances behind the blindfold, searching for what will happen next. He's back in between my legs, and before I can react, his tongue runs along my clitoris.

Oh, God.

Jared's fingers run along my legs until they touch my ankles, which he brings up. I feel more exposed. He groans. "So fucking perfect." His words end when he dips his head back down between my legs. I reach down, not sure if I want more or if I want him to stop. But my body arches high, deciding for me.

His tongue leaves my core, and one hand leaves my ankle. The anticipation has me arching a little higher before his fingers dip inside me.

I groan. As his mouth joins his fingers, a current pulses along my flesh. The static races across my chest, pebbling my nipples in his wake, and I feel the pinch along my lips as I bite down while his fingers move faster and harder. Desperation for more has me gripping his head and forcing him deeper. He adds another finger before the rhythm increases, and I release his head. My shoulder burns, and my core throbs painfully. Jared continues to stimulate my pussy, and when he stops, I'm up quickly. Too quickly. I get lightheaded, and I'm reaching for the blindfold, only to be stopped.

"Trust me," he says again.

My heart races, and everything inside me is screaming for release. With his fingers around my wrist, he trails my hand down his chest. The further we go down, the more my excitement builds. I swallow as my fingers graze the large lump in his jeans. He groans, his breath brushing my face, and I want to see him.

I reach for the button of his jeans, feeling brave, but I can't manage it with one hand. Jared's fingers work the button before I hear the zipper. I swallow again, and my heart thumps away in my chest. The material is pushed down, and when I reach out, I touch his large and very erect cock. His groan, this time, sends my head into a spin. I have no idea what I'm doing, but I wrap my fingers around him anyway.

"I want to see you." I release his cock to reach for the blindfold, but he stops me again.

"Leave the blindfold on." He retakes my hand and wraps it around his cock. He moves our hands up and down slowly. His cock bulges, the wetness between my legs continuing to grow with each stroke I give him.

"That's it, baby," Jared croons, and he bends slightly so he can reach me. His hand trails back up under my dress, and I obediently spread my legs with a yearning as he sinks his fingers inside me. His movements are as quick as our hands over his cock. His fingers tighten on mine painfully, but I don't complain as the rhythm grows faster. My body seems locked in a cycle of rapture that I don't want to escape.

My breaths grow faster, and I push myself down on Jared's fingers as we both pump at his cock.

"Oh, fuck!" His groans have my pleasure heightening even further, and I'm moving swiftly over his fingers. His fingers tighten further on mine, cutting off my circulation as he pumps furiously. His groans are cut off, and warm liquid pours over our hands. The sticky substance drips onto my leg, and Jared's fingers loosen over mine as his strokes reduce in speed. The final splash of his cum falls on my leg, and his fingers inside me continue pumping. As he completely takes his hand off mine, I release his cock.

"Lie back." He sounds breathless, but I obey. My body pulsates as Jared runs his tongue along my clit. I'm already so close, and I bring my fingers to my mouth and taste his salty cum. I know I'm close.

I stick my finger into my mouth, wanting to taste Jared again, and it's what breaks my hold. I quiver as I come. I try to pull my legs together as my core vibrates, but Jared is still licking and fucking me with his fingers. He slows with each wave of pleasure that runs through me until they stop. I'm breathless, and my eyes dance frantically behind the blindfold.

"I'll be back in a minute." Jared's words have me nodding. The bed dips as he leaves, and I lie still, trying to allow my heart to find its normal rhythm that it's not quite ready to return to.

A warm washcloth is pressed in between my legs, and when Jared is finished, he runs the cloth along my leg, cleaning up his cum. He takes my hand and cleans it also before he helps me up. My dress is fixed, but I'm aware my panties aren't put back into place.

The bed dips again, and then Jared walks away. I reach up to remove the blindfold, but I can't get it open with one hand.

"Let me." Jared's cologne circles me as he leans in and removes the blindfold.

"You are so beautiful." His words have my heart stalling. I slowly open my eyes. He's so close that if I lean in even slightly, I could kiss him. So I do.

A knock on his door has him stepping away. He grins, and his dimples are on full display as he answers the door.

Words are spoken low, and when Jared turns to me, he's holding two large dessert glasses filled with ice cream.

"Dessert is ready."

I shift to the edge of the bed. "Dessert?" I ask. But I'm wondering when he ordered it.

His cheeky grin accompanies his next words. "I mean, I already had dessert, so this is seconds."

I want to tease too as I slide off the bed. "You are very greedy."

"Greedy?" he questions just before placing a kiss on the tip of my nose. My brain is scrambled from everything that is happening.

We sit down at a small table that mirrors the one in my room. It's nestled between the large open windows. I'm floating and can't stop smiling at Jared. I can still taste salt on my lips, and when I lick them, my cheeks heat. I like the taste of Jared.

"There's a party Friday night. Will you come with me?"

I'm sitting sideways, watching Jared eat his ice cream. I openly ogle him. I don't know why, but he looks different.

He takes the final few scoops out of his dessert, and I assume he's focused on eating and not aware of me. I'm wrong. "Why are you staring at me? I'm not complaining, just curious," he asks.

"It's just nice to watch you without worrying about you noticing," I answer honestly, even as heat rises in my cheeks.

"You used to watch me?" he sounds amused. He glances at me, his grin so self-assured.

I roll my eyes. "Sometimes. But don't let it go to your head," I tease.

"Too late. It's gone to my head."

I laugh.

"So, will you come with me?"

My first reaction is that I need to ask Carl and Evelyn, but that's not necessary. "Yeah, of course."

"As my girlfriend."

My heart leaps at his words and deep voice. He looks at me with uncertainty, as if I might say no. I know that no isn't an option. But right now, I don't want it to be an option.

"Yes. Yes, of course."

"Great." The smile that accompanies his words tells me he's very happy about my acceptance.

I have a boyfriend. And not just any boyfriend, but Jared.

***

It's been two days since I told Jared I love him and he said it back. Since then, we've spent every second together. But behind all the smiles and laughs, along with our roaming hands, I can't stop thinking about Evelyn and Carl. So today, I'm going home to visit. Jared isn't exactly happy about it, but I didn't think he would be.

When I arrive home, the moment is tense. I'm alone, as I asked Jared to give me some space.

I took another huge bite of stir-fry after announcing I was dating Jared and going to a party with him. It lodges itself in my throat, and it takes half a glass of water just to wash it down. Evelyn sets her knife and fork on the plate while joining her hands together, her elbows resting on the table.

"You're dating Jared?" she questions with her head tilted.

I quickly glance at Carl, who isn't eating either. I nod. "Yeah, I am."

Carl clears his throat. "Since when?" No one sounds happy.

"A few days." They glance at each other, and straight away, I think I should have kept that small bit of information to myself.

"A few days?" Evelyn's ordinarily level voice is high pitched.

I swallow. "Yeah."

Evelyn picks up her knife and fork and starts back into her dinner. Carl and I watch her. I think that this can't be it, no more questions. She's cutting into her meat like it's livestock, not a soft piece of chicken. Carl covers her hand with his, stopping her, and they have a conversation with their eyes, which is something I've seen them do before. A part of me wants to leave, but I wait until Evelyn looks up at me.

"This party. Where is it?"

"It's at one of Jared's friends' houses."

Evelyn doesn't look sure, and my stomach plummets. I want her to be happy for me so badly. "Morgan is coming with me," I blurt out.

"Morgan's nice," Carl says while nodding, as if he's trying to convince himself of that fact.

Silence from Evelyn. I squirm in my seat as she watches me.

"This is your first boyfriend." Her tone has softened, but my face burns at her statement. She isn't going to do this in front of Carl. I want to crawl under the table, and by the looks of it, so does Carl.

"As long as your mother is happy, you have my blessing. You're a good kid." Carl's words run deep into me, seeping into my soul. I don't think he understands the impact his words have. Evelyn's eyes glisten, and I can see she knows what his words mean to me.

"You're growing up too fast," Evelyn finally says. Her words are low, but she's smiling. This is a moment I didn't think would ever happen to me. Where parents would use a line like, *You're growing up too fast.* I dreamt about it, fantasized about it, and now it's real.

"So, is Morgan picking you up?" Carl has started to eat again, which is a good sign.

"Actually, I'm picking her up," I say, and I pray that when I text her and tell her that she isn't just going to a party but going with me, that she'll agree to it. Carl and Evelyn exchange more looks.

"Okay," Evelyn says.

We eat in silence. Evelyn keeps stealing glances at me, and I know she has so many questions. I hate that she appears older. Have I done that to her?

"He's really good to me," I confess, and both Evelyn and Carl stop eating. "He treats me like a queen," I admit as my eyes burn.

"I've never wanted anything so badly." I'm trying to make them understand. "I love both of you so much."

"That's what scares me, Layla." Evelyn gets up, and my heart deflates as I think she's going to leave, but she stops at my chair and pulls me into a hug. She's still so careful with my shoulder.

"I'm trying so hard," she whispers into my ear. For now, that will have to be enough.

When Evelyn releases me, she sends Carl and me into the sitting room as she gets dessert. I tell Carl about Jared's father and how nice he is. The conversation flows as Evelyn returns with pavlova and strawberries. My favorite.

I take out my phone as we all eat and watch TV. I need to text Morgan and keep Evelyn and Carl happy. It's a small question, but my nerves fly through me as I text her.

Party Friday night. Will you come with me?

I don't have to wait long for Morgan to respond.

Yeah, cool. What time?

Relief swims through my veins, and I sag briefly. My fingers move over the keys.

Can I borrow a dress?

I have nothing to wear. My wardrobe at Jared's is filled with gowns, and I need something more casual, but I also want to make an effort. And since I'm going as Jared's girlfriend, I want to look good. My phone buzzes in my hand. Morgan's name flashes up on the screen. I answer the call.

"What have you done with Layla?" she asks, suspicion in her voice.

"I just want to look nice," I tell her. Evelyn and Carl glance my way. "It's Morgan," I say, covering the microphone.

"It will take some work. But..." The insult isn't lost on me, but I'm on a high and nothing is going to take me down.

"Morgan," I warn and am surprised at the small chuckle that resonates through the phone line.

"We can get dressed together." Her words sound nervous. Getting ready with Morgan isn't exactly something I want to do. "Or not," she says, her voice snappy.

"No. We can do that. Friday night around eight?"

"Great, I'll see you then."

Great.

I hang up. "Is it okay if I get ready here Friday night?" I ask.

Evelyn wrestles with a smile. "Of course."

CHAPTER TEN

JARED

IT'S OUR FIRST DAY back on campus, and everything about this moment feels right. Layla, in a pair of black skinny jeans, is slowly killing me.

"If you aren't ready, we can stay at home." I reach for her leg and give it a squeeze.

She grins. "We need to get back to school." She has more use of her arm, but her movements are slow as she unclips her belt. I lean in and steal a kiss. Her gaze darts to me. Her smile widens and my cock grows hard.

"I'm not sure I can get used to this," Layla says, ducking her head.

"Used to what?" I try to catch her gaze.

"Us."

I tip her chin up. "It's always been 'us.' It's never been any other way, even when we were apart."

Layla's attention leaves me. I follow her stare to see my friends watching my car. *Friends.* I use that word so fucking loosely. I'm already about to pound anyone who even looks funny at Layla. I see Warren, and I want to have a word with him.

"Are you sure about this?" I ask Layla again.

"Yes." She reaches for the door handle while gripping her bag in her other hand, and I watch her slide off the passenger seat, enjoying the view of her perfect ass.

I rearrange my erection before getting out of the vehicle. My friends move closer. Mark is the first to reach me, and he smiles while giving me a fist bump.

"Great to have our leader back." He grins.

Alex, Abby, and Caroline make their way to Layla, and they gush compliments over her outfit. Layla's eyebrows rise, and she searches for me. When our gazes clash, I walk to her and entwine our fingers together. The girls stop cackling, but Alex, always the professional, carries on the discussion a few seconds later, chattering like this isn't odd. Warren flicks a half-smoked cigarette on the ground and leans against his own car. The red BMW has been upgraded with all the specs. I want to talk to him but remember that I'm here with Layla. I jut out my chin in greeting, and he pushes off his car. He walks over and fist-bumps me.

"Thought you'd fucked off." He grins while taking a pack of cigarettes out of his pocket and lighting one up.

"Well..." he greets Layla.

"Hi." Her voice is small.

"This is Warren," I say.

Warren grins before blowing smoke into the air.

"I'm Layla." Layla takes her hand out of mine and holds it out to Warren, who takes it with a grin on his face.

"You new here?" he asks while releasing her hand.

Alex and her sidekicks talk fashion, but I can sense Alex's attention on us. Mark steps up beside Warren.

"Yeah, I transferred halfway through the year," Layla tells him.

"You like it?" Warren asks while blowing smoke in Mark's direction.

Mark coughs, and I swear Warren grins.

Layla glances up at me before she answers. "Yeah. It's a nice school."

I spot Ashley and Lucas in the distance. I harden my stare, and they scurry the fuck off. I don't want them near Layla. I retake her hand.

"Rex was wondering about you," Warren says.

"Are you still training with him?" I'm surprised Warren has stuck it out for so long.

"Yeah, he busts my balls. But it keeps my uncle happy."

I want to ask which uncle in particular. His uncles are notorious in this area. I've never met them in person, but if the opportunity arose, I'd snap it up.

Mark points at Warren. "Didn't one of your uncles own this place?" Mark asks, and Alex and her friends stop talking. What the fuck is wrong with Mark?

Warren drops his cigarette and crushes it under his boot. He glares up at Mark, and I don't want any shit to go down.

"They still do." Warren grins.

That's news to me. I don't comment, but it's something I'll ask my dad about. Maybe he's in partnership with them. It doesn't seem likely, but honestly, I don't care.

"I better get to class," Layla says softly.

I squeeze Layla's fingers, and the group breaks up as I walk with her to class.

I spot Ashley to my right and tighten my hold on Layla.

"You don't have to walk me to class," she says.

I grin. "I want to walk my girlfriend to class."

She can't hide her smile, even as she ducks her head into her chest. I don't think she notices Ashley as we pass her. I give her a look that tells her to stay the fuck away. I don't want her anywhere near Layla. I part with Layla at her classroom door. She fidgets with her hands as everyone watches us, and I know she doesn't like the attention. I've never thought anything of always being watched, until now. I want time with Layla. Being at home was perfect. Here, reality has come crashing back.

"I'll be here when class is over," I promise as she enters her business class.

I return outside in search of Warren, but he's not there. Taking out my phone, I ring him and the sound of a cell phone comes from around the corner. I walk along the wall, the ringing growing louder, and when I'm nearly to the sound, I hang up. I find Warren, but he's not alone. A girl is on her knees giving him a blow job.

He notices me and holds up his index finger. The brunette doesn't stop, and I walk back around the side of the building. A few people pass me, and I grin when I hear their surprise. I bet Warren hasn't even stopped. It takes another five minutes before he appears. The brunette runs off into the building, looking very happy with herself while she wipes her mouth with the back of her hand.

"I needed that," Warren says as he lights up a cigarette.

"Do you have any news for me?" I ask, leaning against the wall.

Warren pockets his lighter and runs his hand through his hair. "Yeah, I got that sorted for you."

I push off the wall. "Are you serious?" I ask. I want him to be serious. He looks serious.

"He wants fifty grand."

I nod. Money is no problem. Warren reaches into his pocket and passes me a scrap of paper. "That's the account number." I take it and open the paper.

Warren's watching me. "You know there's no going back after doing this." His eyes are haunted, and I wonder about Warren's life with the O'Reagans. Has he ever taken a life? And if so, did he get his hands dirty or pay someone else to pull the trigger?

"Good," I answer. "The money will be wired today."

"Did you find your man?" Warren asks.

"Not yet. But I will." My PI still hasn't found Chester. The fucker is hiding, but he'll have to come out, eventually. I promised Layla I wouldn't shoot Chester, but that doesn't stop me from hiring someone else to kill him for me.

"I'd better get to class." I fist-bump Warren before walking away. I have no intentions of going to class. Instead, I take a detour to the dean's office. His door is open, and I knock once before entering.

"Welcome back, Mr. McGivney." He doesn't seem overly pleased to see me, but I don't give two fucks.

I close the door behind me and walk deeper into the office. I don't take a seat but stuff my hands into my pockets. "Lucas and Sam Garcia need to be removed from the school."

The dean exhales and leans back in his chair, pressing the end of his pen to his chin. "And why would that happen?"

I want to say because I fucking said so. "Because Sam is dealing drugs out of his car," I lie.

He was hanging with Chester the night Layla was at Chester's home, and so was Sam.

"That's a matter for the Gardaí." The dean sits forward, placing his pen on the table.

"If you bring the Gardaí here, I'm sure they'll find a few cars with gear in them." He knows this, so I'm not sure why he's stalling.

"And the reason that Lucas should be removed?" He waits.

"He's been harassing some of the female students." I picture him stalking Layla. The dean doesn't answer, and I remove my hands from my pockets. "I want their scholarships revoked," I say clearly. I'd pull Ashley's too, but I don't want to upset Layla.

"If I were to leave here"—the dean steeples his fingers into the desk—"and check Sam Garcia's car, I would find drugs?"

I sneer. "No. But if that's what you want, I can make it happen."

He finally understands what I'm saying.

"I want it done today." I leave on that note and burn through the rest of the time allotted for class by ringing my PI. Still no news on Chester. I check in with all my security. Once again, there has been nothing unusual. That doesn't sit well with me.

Lunchtime comes around, and I wait outside Layla's class. She smiles when she sees me, and I eagerly take her hand as Ashley waves at her.

"See you later, Ashley," Layla says.

"You know she used to date Chester," I tell her.

Layla's body grows rigid, and I hate doing this to her, but she needs to keep away from Ashley. I have no idea what the girl is capable of or what she might do for Chester. She could lure Layla away from the safety of the school.

"Yes, I know she dated Chester. That doesn't make her a bad person," Layla defends straight away. "Stupid, yes. But not bad."

I pull her closer to the wall, and we stop walking. "Just hear me out. He might use her to get to you."

She's shaking her head. "She wouldn't do that."

I lean in closer. "How well do you know her? *Really* know her, Layla?"

Doubt clouds Layla's gaze, and she chews on her lip. I quickly press a kiss to her mouth. "I don't want you to worry, but I also want you to be aware. Okay?"

She nods.

I feel far more assured as I take Layla into the full cafeteria so everyone can see we're together. I don't want any other guy so much as looking at her with interest. This makes it clear. She's mine.

CHAPTER ELEVEN

LAYLA

WILD THOUGHTS SPIN IN my mind as I enter the cafeteria with Jared. He has no idea how magnetic he is. He's a force that draws everyone's attention. Their gazes hover over me with curiosity, but it's Jared that holds their interest. I glance up at him. He's nodding greetings at people, and he walks with such confidence. I could never possess that type of surety. Even as a kid, he was charismatic. It's not something anyone is taught; they're just born with it.

His fingers tighten on mine, and I take comfort in his touch. Alex and her two friends move ahead of us and grab the one table in the center of the cafeteria that's remained empty. Every other table is taken, and as we join them, I wonder if it's held for them.

Alex smiles, and I'm waiting for her to turn on me. It's such a negative thought, and I try to brush it away. Mark sits across from us, and two other guys join in.

"This is Simon and Gary," Jared says while releasing my hand. I fold both on my lap.

"What's up?" Simon asks. His long hair is swept back over one shoulder. He's built like a quarterback. Gary jerks his chin out at me.

"Hi." I feel so self-conscious, like the girl who shouldn't be sitting with the cool kids.

"I'll be right back." Jared gets up, but before he leaves, he presses a kiss to the top of my head.

I freeze under the affection and how everyone watches. Once he's gone, I'm waiting for the wolves to circle.

"So, the girls and I are going to go shopping after school to get a dress for the party. Do you want to come?" Alex asks.

I'm stumped at being invited. "I have loads of dresses," I say.

"Yeah, but it's an excuse to get a new one," Caroline says sweetly.

Alex smiles. "What she said."

I'm not buying that Alex likes me for one second. Jared reappears carrying a tray of food. I glance over at the very long line that he's privileged enough to skip. He sits down. A sandwich and tea are placed in front of me. He reaches into his pocket and extracts a red apple that he hands to me before taking a bread roll and his own tea off the tray.

"Thanks."

"So, what do you think?" Alex asks.

I blink a few times, feeling overwhelmed with all this.

"About what?" Jared asks, and he sounds defensive.

"The girls and I are going dress shopping for the party, and we invited Layla to join us."

I take a quick peek at Jared, wondering if he wants me to go. These are his friends, and they're making an effort.

"I'd love to," I answer.

Caroline claps, and Abby forces a smile. She's the only one who isn't pretending this is normal, and I like her for that.

"Great. We can go in my car after school," Alex says.

I nod before I back out and open the packaging from around my sandwich. It's hard to eat knowing everyone is watching us, and by the time we leave the cafeteria, I'm exhausted. Jared takes my hand again, and we walk ahead of the rest of his friends.

"How do you do this all the time?" I ask out of the corner of my mouth as Jared continues to nod and greet all the passing students. "How can you know everyone?" I add.

"I don't know everyone. They just know who I am."

I glance up at Jared. "Don't you ever get tired?" I couldn't do this daily. I mean, this was one day in the life of Jared, and I'm ready for bed.

"I don't ever think about it."

We stop at my classroom door. "How do you know what class I have?" I'm suspicious, but Jared seems to know everything.

"I may have broken into the dean's office and copied your schedule."

"Jared." *Jesus, if he got caught...*

He laughs. "I checked your schedule this morning before we left."

"Oh." Of course he did. It was in my backpack.

"I won't see you after class since you're going shopping with Alex and the girls?" It's more of a question than a statement. Jared pulls me in close to the wall to let several students pass. They gawk, and I try not to let their stares bother me.

"She's making an effort. So I should too."

Jared tilts up my chin. "You don't have to, Layla."

"I want to." I do. I want to try for him.

He plants a soft kiss on my lips. Even though it's soft, I feel it all the way down to my toes.

"I'll see you later, then."

The room's full, and I take the only vacant seat. Even though Jared is no longer with me, everyone still stares. All of a sudden, I'm visible to these people. Only a few days ago, I was a nobody.

Class ends, and with it comes the end of the day. Alex, Abby, and Caroline are waiting for me outside the building. Jared is there too, and I hate how my body sighs at the sight of him. He said he wouldn't be here. My body leans toward him, like he can take away the uncertainty I'm harboring about going shopping.

Caroline wears a look of pure joy. "This is going to be such fun."

Jared steps closer to me, and I take his outstretched hand as he pulls me into his body. "I can take you if you want," he offers with a slight raise of a brow.

I bite my lip. How I would love that. "No. Like Caroline said, it will be fun."

Jared fights a grin, but a dimple makes an appearance. I'm tempted to touch the indent.

"We aren't going to eat her." Alex tries to sound playful, but irritation circles her words.

Jared presses a kiss to my lips. It's light and featherlike, but it doesn't stop the kiss from sneaking past my defenses.

I inhale all of him as he releases me.

Jared addresses the three ladies who he holds in rapt attention. "She better come back to me in one piece."

"Don't worry, she will." Caroline smiles sweetly.

It's too sweet.

I release Jared's hand.

Alex rolls her eyes. "We'll have her back in better condition than we got her in." Alex exhales before her lips curl back, displaying snow-white teeth.

Stepping away from Jared and the trio isn't a smooth transition, but I'm proud when I don't look back as we walk to Alex's car.

Alex drives, and I get to ride shotgun.

"So, Layla, do you have any color in mind?" Caroline pipes up from the back seat. I open my mouth to answer but don't get to as she continues to ask questions, not leaving room for me to actually answer her. "I think red would suit you. Or maybe blue. Like your eyes." My seat is jerked back as she grips the headrest to pull herself forward. Her face is near mine. "You have such pretty eyes."

I take a peek at Alex. She appears relaxed, but it's the permanent smile on her face that's concerning. She reminds me of a Stepford wife.

"Thank you," I answer Caroline and try not to fidget.

"Anytime." Caroline sits back. The click of her belt is deafening in the quiet car.

We drive in silence to the mall. I'm regretting my decision to come with them, but I remind myself that I am doing this for Jared. These are his friends, and I need to make an effort.

"I appreciate you asking me to come along," I tell the girls.

"Absolutely," Alex says.

"What are friends for?" Caroline grips my seat again, and I can see that becoming annoying pretty quickly. Abby is the only one who isn't over the top.

The mall is thronged, and I'm already uncomfortable. We have to swivel around shoppers, and staying together isn't easy, which delights me. That is, until Caroline finds me and takes my hand in hers.

"We don't want you disappearing." The lazy smile lifts her pink-painted lips.

"I won't." My words are lost as she pulls me through the crowd while she sings pretty apologies to make people move out of her way.

We take a quick right and step into a shop that has barely no shoppers and lots of space. I can already tell this is going to be expensive. I have my purse with me, but my budget won't stretch as far as the price tags.

Caroline still holds my hand, and I wiggle my fingers out of her grasp. I don't make eye contact but walk away and hope I can get lost in the spaced-out racks. What a waste of floor space.

"Since it's just you and me, I think we need to cut the crap." Alex speaks while shifting a dress shirt aside. She takes out a pinstripe skirt and holds it up before putting it back on the rack. "I'm doing this for Jared. Not you." She continues to move clothes around, wearing her Stepford-wife smile.

I move to the rack beside her and do the exact thing, mimicking her motions. "Funny, I'm doing this for Jared as well."

Our gazes clash, and all I see is hate burning away in hers.

I don't hate Alex. I'm weary of her.

She reaches into the rack, and without looking, pulls out a green dress. "You should try this on."

She keeps it held out, and when I take it, she walks off.

God, I was a fool to come here with them.

A squeal erupts as I spin to come face-to-face with Caroline.

"Oh my God, I didn't mean to scare you. She's being super mean." Caroline twirls a lock of brown hair around her finger. She leans in. "I like you."

I have no idea if she means that or if this is all part of her and Alex's grand plan.

"Thanks." I sound unsure.

Caroline doesn't seem to notice. She releases her lock of hair and spins on the tip of her toes. "Let's find you a dress and blow Jared's socks off."

Her humor steals a smile from me.

I end up in the fitting room with six dresses. Caroline picked three of them, I picked one, and two are from Alex. The girls hover in the fitting room as I strip out of my clothes. I start with Caroline's dress, a blue one. She was right, it compliments my eyes. Confidence has me pulling back the curtain. Alex and Caroline straighten up. Abby remains in a slumped position like she'd rather be watching paint dry.

"Wow! Jared's socks will be officially blown," Caroline declares.

She's so unaffected by the narrowed gaze Abby makes in her direction or how Alex's smile widens, making her face appear ready to crack.

I lose some of my enthusiasm and try on four more dresses, including the one I selected.

They don't get much of a reaction from Caroline as she declares that the first blue dress is the one.

I'm avoiding trying on the one that Alex chose. It's to the floor, frumpy, and just has no shape. The color—I'm tempted to say it's mud brown—is ugly. But I still put it on and step out of the fitting room.

Caroline's gaze widens in horror, but Alex rises from her seat and clicks her fingers. Abby sits up, and I'm concerned with her sudden rise from her slumber.

"I love it," Abby deadpans.

I pretend I buy her lie.

"What she said. It's perfect." Alex claps her hands happily, and if I didn't know her, I'd think she was genuinely happy for me.

"I'm not sure." I turn and pretend to take a second look in the mirror. I could take a hundred looks, and the dress would still be ugly.

"I mean, it's cute." Caroline's words are pained before they lower. "I did love the blue one."

"Don't be so cruel, Caroline. She can't wear the blue one," Alex snaps.

"Why not?" Caroline sounds confused, and so am I.

I face the trio. Is this a case where she's wearing blue so nobody else can wear blue?

"You know why. Layla doesn't want to show off her grotesque leg." Alex flings a glance at me real quick. "No offense." She turns back to Caroline, a smirk crawling on her lips. "I doubt that would blow his socks off. More like having him keep them on."

Pain starts in the center of my chest and spreads at an alarming pace. Heat races up my throat, and I hate the look Abby wears.

Pity.

She's pitying the girl with the deformed leg. I want to crawl back into the fitting room but find myself robotically moving while Alex declares we've found the winning dress.

CHAPTER TWELVE

LAYLA

LAST NIGHT AFTER COMING back from shopping with the girls, I went straight to my room with a headache. Amanda, Andrea, and Kerry parked themselves outside my room, and once I mentioned a headache, I was shuffled into bed with two painkillers and a damp cloth across my eyes.

I appreciated their attention, as it kept Jared away for a while. He wasn't happy and had entered even as Kerry insisted I needed my rest.

"Is everything okay?" he asked.

I pressed the cloth against my eyes. "A headache. I suffer with them sometimes." It was easier to lie with the cotton cloth covering most of my face.

"Are you sure? What about dress shopping?" He shifted beside my bed.

"I got a dress."

He was silent, and I just wanted him to leave.

"Okay, I'll let you rest," he said after a moment.

I didn't move the cloth until the bedroom door closed, and I stayed hidden in my room like a coward for the night.

***

The scent of peanut butter in Jared's car has me raising a brow at him. His laugh pulls a silly grin onto my face, and yesterday's ordeal seems unworthy of the attention I gave it last night.

"I made sandwiches," he confesses before starting the car and pulling out of the garage. I'm shaking my head while grinning, but my heart is all over the place.

"You made peanut butter sandwiches," I say, and when Jared glances at me this time, he isn't smiling, and my chest squeezes. Is he remembering back to Lucas giving me one? Funny how that led to my first kiss with Jared and him nearly drowning me.

"I made them just in case you were hungry." He focuses on the road. He says it so offhandedly, as if we aren't going to pass several restaurants or stores. He made them because it's something else we share.

He still amazes me. I glance out the window before looking back at him. An overwhelming feeling to reach out and touch his hand has me stuffing mine between my legs. My knees bobble, and I look out the window. I hate how many emotions swirl uncontrollably inside me.

I focus on all the houses we pass, trying to force my body to relax. I close my eyes and try not to think of each time we shared a peanut butter sandwich. I glance over at him, realizing I've been holding my breath while fighting tears.

"You don't have to eat it if you don't want to." He says this after a moment, and I wonder if his mind has gone where mine has.

I'm making this seem like I'm ungrateful, when really, the stupid sandwich is making my heart hammer. "No. I want it," I say.

His dimples appear before he speaks. "I knew you couldn't resist a peanut butter sandwich. If I ever wanted to kidnap you, all I would have to do is leave a trail of them from your door all the way to my car," he teases.

"You wouldn't need to do that. I'd come without the sandwiches."

Our gazes connect, and I see a look on Jared's face that I recognize. Happiness.

Jared pulls over after only an hour of driving. We're in a parking lot overlooking the beach. It's a strip of the beach I've been to before. He reaches into the back seat, the scent of his aftershave feeding my hungry lungs. He's so close that I have to look out the window before I do something crazy, like sniff him. How many times has he openly inhaled me? Did he ever have the same tornado of emotions spinning out of control like I do?

Once he sits back, he opens the bag and takes out the sandwich and a bottle of water. Handing me one, he smiles. I unwrap the foil, thinking about how he took the time to make this sandwich, wrap it for me, and put it in the bag. A lump forms in my throat.

"Thank you."

"What's wrong?" His own sandwich sits in his hand, the bottle of water between his legs.

"Nothing's wrong, it's just so nice."

Relief sweeps over Jared's face. As an afterthought, he smirks and takes a bite of his sandwich. "I'm a nice guy," he says. The cockiness in his voice has me snorting a laugh.

I open my sandwich, telling myself to stop being sentimental. Taking a bite, I sink back into my seat, exaggerating how tasty it is. I ignore the thump of my heart as Jared laughs.

"That's it. I'm keeping a stash of them in my car. Every time you get in, you're eating one."

"I won't argue." I take another bite before looking out at the beach. Not many are around, but you can already tell that today will be unseasonably hot. It's hard to believe that only a few weeks ago we were at another beach.

For the first time, I think of Kieran. Taking a drink, I wash down the sandwich and the guilt I still feel about that day. The image of Jared's violence flashes in my mind, and I take a peek at him. He seems content as he eats his sandwich. There's an uncomfortable feeling in the pit of my stomach when I think of his rage, how far gone he looked that day.

I resume trying to eat but glance at him sideways. He's looking out at the beach, chewing the last of his sandwich. His hands rest on his lap; he appears relaxed. His black T-shirt clings to him, and my gaze trails down to the necklace that disappears under the T-shirt. I know a key hangs on the end, another mystery about Jared I don't understand.

"So, how are you?" I ask and am surprised by how much his body tenses. His jaw grows tight. Is he thinking about the night at the beach too?

He crumbles up the foil, his focus on the shiny material like it holds all the answers. "I'm good. Why do you ask?"

He sounds so defensive. *Is he mad at me?*

"I'm sorry." I look up at Jared, and he's watching me, brows furrowed like he's confused. "About everything," I add. "I just..."

The waves break against the shoreline, and I focus on them. "So much has happened since I came here and"—I shrug—"I feel responsible." He crinkles the foil again, and without thought, I take it from his hand.

"I mean, I didn't force Chester to shoot me, but yeah, other stuff." This is coming out all wrong.

"Like what?" Jared reaches out and takes his foil back. He keeps clenching the ball in his fist.

"I'm thinking of Kieran," I spit out.

His lips drag down as he jerks his head. "Kieran?"

God, he sounds pissed. His gaze darkens, and he's waiting for me to explain myself.

"You were so angry," I whisper.

"You kissed him, Layla. I was homicidal."

"That's what every girl wants to hear," I say without thinking.

His grin makes no sense. "I was jealous. So we took a few swings at each other. Boys fight. You have nothing to feel guilty about. Kieran and I are cool now. In fact, he apologized." Hearing his words helps the guilt I felt sprout wings and fly away.

"So yeah," he murmurs before glancing away. "All's good."

I take the foil out of his hand, and his brows rise. I have no idea why I keep taking it back. Maybe so I can be closer to him. This time, when Jared takes the foil out of my hand, our fingers brush slightly. The contact causes my pulse to skip. I shift back at the unexpected feeling that takes over all my senses. Jared doesn't seem to notice my reaction as he stuffs the foil into the brown paper bag.

As he puts on his seat belt, I focus on putting on mine and dispel the want to have him right here and now. "Well, if you ever want to talk, you know I'm here." This time, he observes me slowly. The shift of his gaze over my face has me forcing myself to stay still.

"I know you are. Thanks." His long, tanned fingers entwine with mine, and I focus on our hands. This isn't the first time he's done this, so I don't know why it feels more intimate. Maybe it's my thoughts, the two of us alone in his car overlooking the beach. Or maybe it's how his eyes seem more golden than I've ever seen them before. The dimples are out now in full force, and my lips twitch before turning into a smile.

"I'm here for you, too," Jared says, still looking at me and smiling.

"I know." A man passes in front of the car and catches my attention briefly. It isn't the man, but the huge St. Bernard he has with him. As I watch them pass, I don't say anything, just smile. When I was little, I always said that when I grew up, I would have one.

"Still want one?" Jared asks the question, along with a slight squeeze of our still joined hands.

Glancing from the dog and back to Jared, I'm not completely surprised that he remembered.

"Yeah, I still want one. I just have more sense now to know it might not be viable." I stare at our joined hands. The contrast of my pale skin to his tanned fascinates me.

"You do know they slobber everywhere, right?"

My gaze flickers up to Jared's, and I smile. "Yes, I do. Do you know that—"

"They can die of a broken heart," Jared finishes my sentence. The amusement in his eyes has my cheeks turning pink.

"Well, did you know the St. Bernard got its name from a snowy pass in the Alps? That type of dog was used to rescue stranded travelers in snowstorms in the Great St. Bernard Pass between Italy and Switzerland and earned its name that way." More amusement flashes across Jared's face, this time with a raised eyebrow.

"You're full of facts, Layla Jordan."

The world around me grows fuzzy. It's been such a long time since I heard my old surname. Although I'm elated Jared remembers, it also reminds me of my life with Bert and Ronnie. Avoiding Jared's gaze, I remove my hand from his. My palms grow damp with sweat, and I don't want him to notice.

After a couple of silent moments, Jared asks quietly, "Have I upset you?"

"No, it just surprised me a little. I haven't heard that name in so long." I speak while staring out the window. The sky has grown overcast, promising a downpour of rain. That's Ireland for you. One minute the sun is splitting the stones, and the next it's a washout.

"Layla, I'm sorry. I didn't think."

When I feel more in control, I glance at Jared. His expression is unreadable as he leans against the steering wheel. His head rests on his arms, and his eyes have darkened.

"Don't be. I need to learn to control my reaction," I say. As I speak, my brows drag together. Can I ever control my reaction to a past that terrifies me? The sound of a seat belt unbuckling has me turning to Jared. He's so close, our noses nearly touch. My heart pounds like I've run up and down the beach that sprawls out in front of us.

"I..." I'm not sure what I even want to say. He's there. His gaze roams my face, and he wears such a serious look. I swallow.

"If you feel sad, be sad. If you feel happy, be happy. If you want to scream, then do it." Jared's voice grows with each word, and I smile at how passionate he sounds. But he doesn't mirror my smile. Instead, his warm hands grip my face until I think my heart will explode right there and then.

"Stop apologizing for how you feel. This"—his eyes travel across my face—"is perfect and I love how real and honest you always are. So don't try to hide anything."

The heat of his hands on my face has to be the cause of the sudden increase in temperature. The air feels hot as Jared continues to invade my space. I'm breathing heavily through my nose, and all I can do is nod as I inhale the scent that is uniquely his, along with his cologne and warm breath. Jared bites down on his lower lip, the movement capturing my attention.

The sensation starts to build, as it had earlier. A voice in the back of my head tells me this isn't good at all. I need distance, but I can't seem to move. I do, however, break eye contact, and that has Jared releasing me. He sits back in his seat, and I try to settle my heart down. Rain pelts against the windshield. The beach has disappeared now. Only colors are visible with the onslaught of rain.

I swallow, realizing I need to say something. I can't let this get awkward.

"That gray wool sweater that you loved... I used to steal it at night." The confession is abrupt, and I want to sink into the seat.

What is wrong with me?

"When you came to my room each night, I would pretend to be asleep so you could take it," Jared says.

I look at him. He isn't looking at me but out the window. Sadness shadows him, and my throat burns. He knew and had let me take it. It was his favorite sweater.

"I used to smell it at night, so it was like you were there with me." My eyes burn.

"I would have stayed with you, Layla. Why didn't you just ask?" His raised voice carries a harsh tone and causes my wet eyes to dry up.

"I was a child, Jared. Why are you so angry?"

"Because... I just... I would have stayed with you." His own eyes glaze as he grits his teeth.

"You were like my big brother. I didn't think you would."

Jared looks away, his grip tightening on the steering wheel until his knuckles turn white. "What were you afraid of?" His question is asked of the beach, then his gaze flickers across to me. I can see his pulse pound in his neck.

"I was afraid..." I say, trying to think back to what scared me so much. The dark? The teddies were old and too high on the shelf for me to remove. I always thought they were looking at me.

"Of what?" Once again, Jared's whispering, his whole body tight with tension.

"The dark, Jared. Wasn't there anything you were afraid of?" I ask, and it's like a hand reaches in and pushes him against the seat. The movement startles me.

"No, what could I have been afraid of? The dark? I'm not a girl." The quick words and forced smile have me sitting up even straighter.

His body relaxes now as he cracks his knuckles. It's the first time I've seen him do it since I've met him again. He's forcing himself to relax. I've seen him do it before, but as a child, I didn't understand it.

"Jared."

At his name, he finally looks at me. "I just wish you had told me. I would have scared away the dark." He smiles, and I push away my uncertainty.

"Your sweater did the trick. We didn't need you."

His laugh at my words and the dimples that appear relax me further.

"We?" he questions.

"Yeah, me and your sweater. It was more like a teddy. So I named him."

"You named my sweater?"

My face heats up, but I don't care. I'm just so happy that he's happy again. That darkness has left his eyes. Now they shine, the gold flecks lightening up.

"Mr. Grey."

His laughter has me joining him. I don't know if it's been the heaviness of before, but we end up laughing loudly. When we settle down, I feel better. Lighter.

"I'm glad Mr. Grey kept you safe at night," he says.

"Yeah, he did." I think how safe I felt with Jared's smell and the warmth of Mr. Grey. I was untouchable. It was my safe place.

"I hope you and Mr. Grey didn't get up to anything else."

I narrow my eyes at Jared. His grin stretches across his handsome face.

"I was ten!" I exclaim.

Jared chuckles again while buckling up his belt. "We better get moving." When the wipers come on, the view of the beach is beautiful. The rain still falls. The sky is purple and blue against the water. I keep watching the waves crash as Jared starts the car, and we make our way to the garden show.

CHAPTER THIRTEEN

LAYLA

Hundreds of people mill about the indoor garden center. I take one final look down at my dress. It's a bit crumpled from the car ride, but with the heat in the building, the creases are sure to fall out. Jared's fingers twine with mine.

"You look perfect. Come on." A small tug and an encouraging smile from him have me moving.

The hanging baskets that conceal the ceiling above us give the first section a magical and even secretive feel. The exhibition is broken up into different segments. Right now we're in the flower section. Ceramic flower pots and seller stands create a zig-zag path that is overcrowded. I can hear water in the distance. The heat from all the people so close has me moving faster toward the sound, but at a snail's pace. We end up being stopped at the cactus section. The baby ones that are no bigger than my thumb are so cute.

"They're adorable," I say.

Jared snorts, causing the woman in the oversized white hat to look back at him. Her jacket and tailored pants must have been sweltering. I'm glad about my choice of dress.

Jared stands up on the tip of his toes to see what the holdup is.

"Anything?" I ask. He shakes his head. "I can't see what's causing the jam. Only more people and plants."

I grin. "How odd. People and plants at a garden exhibition." Jared narrows his eyes but smirks.

"Yeah, as odd as that thing." We're already standing pretty close to each other, so when he reaches behind me, his chest brushes against my shoulder. The contact has my pulse spiking. It takes me a moment after he leans back to focus on what he holds. The baby cactus.

"It's not odd. I think it's cute," I say.

"We'll see how cute it is when you touch it," he says.

The woman once again turns, looking at the cactus, then from me to Jared.

"Do you want to touch it?" he asks, and she swings back around. His hand curves slightly around the cactus. I don't think he knows what he's doing. He's protecting it.

"Ouch."

I grin as he quickly opens his hand.

"You find that funny?"

"It's so tiny, and you're so..."

His grin rises quick and fast. "So..." he encourages, and my mind goes back to his room, and with it the memory of my hand wrapped around his cock. My heart pitter-patters, but I can't stop wanting him to touch me.

"Big," I say the word out loud. The woman who is clearly listening to our conversation stiffens.

The crowd moves, and Jared puts the cactus back on the stand, leaning in again. My heart picks up, but it doesn't go into a frenzy. My body's enjoying the contact with him way too much. When he leans back, he pauses, his gaze flickering over my face. Amusement shines in his eyes like he knows what he's doing to me.

"I want to be with you." My breath catches in my chest after I say the words.

He doesn't have to ask in what way. My nipples press against my dress and feel heavy in my bra. The thoughts of having Jared inside me are all-consuming, and I haven't stopped thinking about having him fully.

A girl brushes against me as people are trying to get past us. I take the lead and tug Jared's hand so we continue to walk. I want him to say something, but he isn't giving anything away, and I wonder if I even said the words out loud.

I focus on my surroundings again. I have no knowledge of ninety-five percent of the plants, but Jared compliments my knowledge of flowers continuously throughout our day. Of the mere five percent that I have some knowledge of, I've gathered from books, Google, and going to our local Garden center. Tom, a horticulturist who works at our local garden center, also has a garden show on my favorite radio station. It's always fun to listen to and is very knowledgeable. I usually listen to Tom every Saturday morning at nine thirty, but I haven't in a while.

We finally come across the waterfall that has been erected in the center of the exhibition. The bottom is full of loose coins. An elderly couple sits eating ice cream opposite us. I lick my lips, my mouth dry from the heat of the day. But we haven't come across a stand that sells water.

"Open your hand."

My attention snaps to Jared. I do slowly, not trusting the grin on his face. "Do you need me to close my eyes?" I ask.

"No." He places some coins in my hands. "Go make some wishes. I'll be back in a moment."

I force a smile and a quick nod as I walk to the waterfall. I swallow another lump in my throat. Every time I'm around him, he either makes me want to burst into tears or touch him in some way.

Every Saturday when we were kids, we would go into town with his friends. He always took me along, even when they protested.

At the Kid's Center, there was a maze of mirrors, and right in the middle was a wishing well. We never had much, but Jared always managed to get a coin for me. Every time we went, I would spend what felt like hours in the maze. I never gave up until I found the wishing well. Once I was there, I made the same wish every time.

I look down at the coins in my hand. I always wished that someone would come and take Jared and me away from Bert and Ronnie. That we would grow up together and be happy.

"I've upset you again."

I squeal, not expecting Jared to be there.

He sits down beside me.

"No, I was only thinking about the wish I always made when we were kids," I say.

He raises an eyebrow. "You made the same wish every time?"

I nod. "Yeah."

"Was it to have your wicked way with me?" Jared grins before reaching over and closing my hand around the coins. The heat of his fingers sears me. "I mean, I can make that wish come true." Jared takes his hand off me but still wears the cheeky smile.

I open my hand and look down at my palm. "I wished that someone would take us away, and we could grow up together and be happy."

There is a long pause, and around us, the sounds press in.

"Well, we found each other, and we are happy." He leans away so he can look at me. "I know I'm happy now that I've found you."

"I'm happy I found you too, Jared."

His warmth and smell surround me as he pulls me into his chest. I don't want to cry. So I focus on the rapid beat of his heart. It pounds heavily against his solid chest.

"I was lost without you." His words and the gentle stroke of his hand down my back have my nerve endings on fire. What is happening to me? These feelings that rush through my body make me feel like breathing him in is the only right thing to do. Like he's my oxygen, my life support, and if I lose him again, I won't survive. I move out of his arms with reluctance, but I need to answer him.

"Me, too."

He visibly takes in a deep breath, his hands on my arms. I'm not sure if he's aware of his movements. He rubs his hands up and down my arms, causing a frenzy inside me. My thoughts veer off the PG-13 road again, and I know I need to stop them, for a million reasons. One reason is that we're in a very public place, and we've already drawn attention from passersby and the elderly couple.

"Let's make a wish together," I tell Jared. It takes him a moment to respond. He blinks several times, like he's just waking up.

"I mean, don't waste a wish on wanting to have your way with me. I surrender." Jared holds up his arms.

I shake my head and grin, pushing the coin into his palm. He takes it and drops his hands.

"Should we tell each other?" he asks.

I roll my eyes. "No, then the wishes won't come true."

"I know. I'm just teasing." The corner of his mouth quirks up, and he winks.

My stomach tightens, and I focus on the water in front of me. I'm not sure what to wish for. Glancing at Jared, I notice he has his eyes closed and the most serious expression on his face. He flips the coin in and doesn't look away until the water swallows it up.

I wish that Jared's wish comes true. I toss in my own coin, and when I glance up, Jared stands with his hand outstretched.

"Let's get some ice cream."

I take Jared's hand. This time, when his fingers entwine with mine, it doesn't completely scramble my brain. It still sends my pulse racing, but it's my body's reaction to Jared. I'm starting to associate it with elevated heart rate, and my thoughts scattering whenever I am near him.

We are finally close to the ice cream stand that has been specially set up for the exhibit. Jared once again recites the same order we often got. Two scoops of chocolate ice cream with tons of chocolate syrup. It simply would not do to just get one. When he passes me mine, I immediately start eating. We walk through a calmer area of the center. This area is mostly seeds; there aren't many potted plants to see. A few garden sheds fill the floor space, and there are also kiosks with leaflets. It makes me think of my garden at home. Maybe a new shed would look nice. I know if I suggested it to Carl and Evelyn, they would buy it without hesitation. But that doesn't seem fair. I should finish the planting and maybe give the shed a fresh coat of paint. Thinking of the garden has my thoughts turning to Evelyn and Carl. How nice it was the last day I was there with them.

"So, it's been over a week?" I take a large bite of the chocolate flake. Jared is eating the cone, his ice cream gone.

"I was wondering if there's any news about..." The person who shall not be named. I don't want to say Chester's name out loud, and thankfully, I don't have to.

"Are you in a rush to leave me?" Jared tries for a light tone, but he doesn't succeed.

"No, of course not. I just also don't like the idea of him walking around."

Jared doesn't answer, and I hate the stiffness of his shoulders, so I make conversation. "Tell me about something that makes you happy." I start eating the second scoop, not sure how much more I can eat. I hope my change in conversation helps relax Jared.

"Boxing. My trainer, Rex, is really supportive. He's the one who encouraged me to compete. I spent so much time training when I first arrived here. It was an outlet I needed at the time."

That makes sense to me, with how buff Jared is.

"I'm really glad you found boxing." I glance at Jared while taking a lick of my ice cream.

"I'm really glad you're enjoying that ice cream." Jared grins.

"Yeah, it's pretty good," I answer, taking one more lick, but I'm searching for a trash can. I can't eat much more.

A green bin with the letters TRASH engraved in gold gives me a moment to allow my stomach to settle. As I pass, I throw in the ice cream.

"Too much?" Jared asks while his eyes dart to the bin, eyebrows drawn down.

"Yeah. My eyes are bigger than my belly," I tell him.

His mouth curves into a smile. "In your case, it is true. You have big eyes."

People often comment on it when they meet me for the first time—either how white blonde my hair is or how big my eyes are. When Bert or his friends mentioned my eyes or hair, it was said with malice, like I was a freak, so I'm still struggling with the idea that people are complimenting me. It's too engraved in me from my childhood.

"Well... you have dimples," I fire back at Jared to take my mind off things that terrify me.

His dimples are on full display as he laughs gently. "I'm complimenting you, Layla. On your eyes."

"And I'm complimenting you on your dimples," I say, feeling confused.

His hand finds mine as we walk, and he twines our fingers together.

"You sound defensive," Jared says, bringing my attention back to his face.

"Sorry, I'm bad at taking compliments," I admit. We have reached the back wall of the garden display and start to make our way back.

"Well, we have to fix that," he replies. "Every day, I'm going to send you a compliment, and soon, you'll accept them."

I swat at his arm, and his eyes flash with amusement. "Don't start texting me stuff," I say, shaking my head, but deep down, excitement bubbles inside me.

The crowded area we first walked into appears quicker than I expect. Knowing that the day is almost over has me feeling disappointed. I've been enjoying myself. We check out some plants that are two years old; their colors are refreshing. I lose Jared at one stage, spending too long looking at a row of pink clematis vines that have been hung from a massive wall. The display is magical. Other plants sit on the base of the stands. The smell of lavender and cape jasmine fills the air.

After I walk through the area and out into the ornamental section, I can still smell the lavender and Jasmine. It's there that I find Jared sitting on a bench, and I steal the moment to study him. His long legs stretch out in front of him and cross at the ankles. He's watching a stream of people move past him. His large tanned arms are folded, showing off his muscular biceps. I bite my lip as I allow myself to take in his strong jawline, perfect lips, and straight nose. His hands tighten around a bag that's tucked under his arm, almost hidden.

"Excuse me." A woman speaks as she slips by me. Now I wonder how many people saw me blatantly staring at Jared. I'm nearly beside him when his gaze travels across me, leaving a path of heat in its wake.

"I'm not sure where I lost you," I say, just trying to keep the heat at bay. Jared is observing me, his eyes darker. I sit down beside him; it's easier than facing him right now. My emotions are running high.

"Thanks for today."

"It's not over yet." Jared smirks at me now.

He stands, his hand stretched out before me.

"What are we doing next?"

"I was thinking of going back home, and you can try on that dress you got."

"The one that Alex picked out for me?" The one I most certainly won't be wearing. "I'm sure she'd love the thought of me modeling it for you." It's a slip of the tongue, which causes Jared to stop walking. The skin around his mouth tightens. He faces me, and my mouth grows dry. His eyes flash with anger.

"I'm sorry. It was a joke." I quickly try to retract my sarcastic statement, but as Jared shakes his head, I know it's too late. I grow concerned and try to pull my hand out of Jared's, but he won't let mine go. My eyes flicker from his tight grip to his fiery eyes. The world shrinks to just him. Everything around us disappears, even the noise. A tremble enters my lip, and I bite down to stop it.

Rocks fill my stomach, and a haze starts to close in around me.

"Jared." One word and it sounds breathless, terrified. It's mine, and I look away from him, waiting for everything to crash down around him. How many times have I been there at the end of someone's wrath?

Countless.

But never Jared's. Never.

I can't bear the silence. Why isn't he saying anything? This is torture.

"Jared," I say again.

"I'll kill her." Jared's eyes flicker around the crowd that has snapped back into focus. His flaring nostrils and tight fists aren't lost on me. I feel a moment of happiness that his anger isn't directed toward me, but it's short lived.

"No. No, I don't think she meant it. You know, she wasn't thinking about my leg." When I speak, Jared's eyes snap to me, and the anger makes me flinch.

"Don't lie to me. What happened?" The tightness around his eyes and jaw has me considering precisely what to say.

"Nothing. Jesus, it's me. I'm just taking everything too personally."

Jared's face reddens. "What happened?" He speaks through clenched teeth. I don't get to answer as Jared starts walking quickly with his long legs, dragging me along with him. I'm half jogging. I should have kept my mouth closed.

CHAPTER FOURTEEN

JARED

I KNOW THAT LOOK. She's trying to backpedal. I'll fucking kill Alex. I can imagine what they did to Layla, and to hear the pain in her words has me marching to my car from the exhibition center. I release Layla's hand and open the door for her. Once she's in her seat, I close it too hard and the car shakes.

I'm trying to calm down, so I don't get into the car immediately. Instead, I stand outside my door. I don't want her to see me this volatile. She's already half-afraid. I can tell by the way she spoke of Kieran. I never want Layla to be afraid of me. I've done so much bad shit, but I always put her first. Never me.

I take a few more calming breaths before I slide into the driver's seat. My temper hasn't disappeared, and I squeeze the steering wheel. I try to relax my clenched jaw. "You should have told me."

She won't answer as she puts on her seat belt and stares out the window.

I start the car and drive home.

"What are you going to do?" She wedges her hands in between her legs.

I loosen my hold on the steering wheel, and color comes back into my knuckles. "Have a word." The words grind through my teeth.

Layla shifts in her seat. "Just don't fall out over it. She's your friend. I'm sure she didn't mean any offense."

I work a muscle in my jaw. Why is she always so eager to push people's behavior aside?

"Promise me, Jared, that you won't fall out with her."

"Yeah." It wasn't the most convincing promise, but right now it's the best I can do.

"I don't like this at all." She rotates so she's facing me.

"Tough, Layla." I slow down as we approach my home.

"Jared, you've already fallen out with Kieran. Now Alex?"

The gates take longer than usual to open, or maybe it just feels that way.

"Jared." Layla sounds exasperated.

I unbuckle my belt and look at her. "Kieran kissed you. If I could do it all again, I would have kept him under the water." I shift gears and drive up to the house. The garage doors open.

"You don't mean that," Layla whispers.

"I have a boxing session with Rex. Will you be okay here with Kerry and the girls?"

Layla doesn't move. "You know how I feel about unresolved problems. We always sort our differences out before going to bed. No matter how bad things get between us, we sort it out and never let it carry into the next day."

I run my fingers along my lip before speaking. "I suppose, in a way, we weren't like regular kids. Layla, I'm not just going to let this go with Alex."

"Fine." Layla reaches for the door but doesn't get out. "Jared, please."

I sit back in the seat before tilting my head toward her. "We're good, Layla. I promise."

"You promise me you'll remain friends with Alex," Layla pleads.

I look away from her. That should be an answer enough.

"Oh my God, Jared. It's not a big deal."

"Why are you so hell-bent on me being friends with her?" If she had a male friend, I'd lose it completely. Why is she so okay with me being friends with Alex?

"Because she's your friend, and I don't want to be the cause of you falling out. I feel enough has happened since we found each other."

I face her. "None of that is your fault. We can brush things under the carpet all we want. You can stay quiet to keep the peace with Alex, but inside"—I tap her head—"you will have no peace. So I'm just going to have a chat with her."

Layla stretches out her fingers, and her shoulders roll. "Okay."

Relief immediately floods me. She's starting to see that people can't hurt her and get away with it.

"Thank you." She leans in and kisses me softly on the cheek. She quickly pulls away, turns, and gets out of the car. "Thanks again for today," she says, not looking at me. She's out of the garage and disappearing into the house.

Once Layla is out of sight, I allow all the rage to flood back in. A tornado tears through my system, and I'm reversing out of the garage.

***

I pull up at Alex's front door, which is ajar. Noise coming from the state-of-the-art kitchen has me making my way down the hall.

"Mrs. Davis, you are a sight." I pick up a red apple from the oversized fruit bowl.

Mrs. Davis pushes the glasses from her nose, and they dangle from a crystal chain on her chest. She swats my compliment away while wearing a smile. After moving aside her magazine, she walks around the island to me. I accept a kiss on each cheek.

"Jay, you get better looking every day. I can't wait for you to marry my daughter."

I smile while raising both eyebrows. Like fuck I would ever marry Alex. "Speaking of your daughter, is she here?" I glance around the kitchen.

"I'm afraid not." Mrs. Davis releases me from the brief hug.

Perfect.

I take a bite of the apple, then offer my condolences. "I'm sorry about you and Mr. Davis."

Mrs. Davis half smiles. "Whatever do you mean?"

"Alex was very upset about the divorce. It was a real shock to her."

Her laugh is forced. "Divorce? No one is getting divorced. What did Alex say?"

Alex was lying. I'm not surprised. It's just like her to use any tactic possible to get me alone.

"I must have misheard her," I answer, taking another bite of my apple.

Mrs. Davis grips the crystal chain around her neck. "I doubt that. She must be looking for more attention." Miss Davis forgets herself for a moment. Her speaking so freely isn't something I've heard her do before.

When I chomp on the apple, she forces another smile, like she remembers I'm here.

Her phone rings, and she raises a hand while looking at her screen.

"I have to take this."

"No problem."

She answers the call.

With her back to me, I don't linger but make my way to the stairs.

When I reach Alex's room, I've finished my apple and throw the core in her empty velvet wastebasket. Alex's room is the opposite of the house she lives in. Here, she favors the color black. Black bedding, a black leather headboard. The canvas painting behind her bed is all different shades of black. It's angry and interesting. When I asked her about it, she shrugged and said she just wanted a painting.

A wooden ladder to the left takes me to the loft above her bedroom. It looks right down on her bed. Up here is where we often studied—or pretended to anyway. A large white desk, which I'm sure her mother selected, is bare. The only thing that decorates the space is a black lamp.

I open the first drawer to find scraps of paper. I have no idea what I'm looking for. Maybe some dirt on Alex so I can humiliate her like she did Layla. There's nothing here; only a few notes from William about times for her to be at the house. Three of them are clipped together. One was from when we went to a charity event, and one was a request from my father after the shooting. Funny how he dates them all. The third is from the fifteenth of January. I'm not sure what that was for. That was before Layla arrived, and I'm sure I had a competition that day and was gone for the entire weekend.

I leave the loft and do a quick check of her underwear drawer, but there's nothing but her panties and a purple vibrator. When I return downstairs, Mrs. Davis is still talking on the phone. The sound of her raised voice carries into the hallway, and I don't return to the kitchen but leave their home.

So, Alex was lying about her parents' divorce. I didn't think I could really do anything with that information, only call her out on her lie.

I go straight to the gym. The urge to drive home and check on Layla nearly has me turning the car around.

I arrive at the gym and get my pre-packed gym bag out of the trunk. Like always, the gym is empty, and Rex is in his office. I knock on the glass, and he raises his head. I open the door, but I don't enter.

"When I fought in that competition in Inishmore, was that in January?" I ask.

Rex squeezes the bridge of his nose before folding his arms across his chest. "I think so. Why?"

"No reason. Just curious." I tap the doorframe.

"Are you thinking of fighting again?" Hope fills his voice.

I hate to be the one to kill that notion. "I'm still thinking about it," I lie before leaving his office and getting ready to practice.

Rex is waiting for me by the ring when I come out onto the gym floor. I crack my neck from side to side.

Rex is quiet as he wraps my hands. I zone in on the beat of the music that pumps out from the overhead speakers.

"That fight down in Inishmore was in January." Rex tugs on my gloves. "It was the weekend of the fifteenth. I looked it up for you."

"Thanks." Why did my father request to see Alex that day? To talk about me, no doubt.

I'm ready to get into the ring when Rex grips both of my gloved hands, stopping me from walking away.

I knew something was bothering him with his silence, and now I'm about to find out. "You're a good kid, Jay. I don't want to see you getting hurt." He releases my hands.

"Why would I get hurt?" I smash my gloved hands together and smirk, trying to lighten the mood. "I mean, I can take care of myself, thanks to you."

"Warren O'Reagan is bad news."

I exhale and stop smirking. "Not this again." I climb into the ring, and Rex takes a moment before he joins me with the boxing pads in his hands.

"Yes, this again. That kid..."

I strike hard, but Rex holds still.

"He's angry, and angry people..."

I strike harder, and Rex moves back slightly.

"Are dangerous people." Rex drops his hands.

I nearly hit him but pull back at the last second. "What the fuck, Rex? I nearly hit you!"

Rex isn't fazed at all and takes a step closer to me. "I'm trying to look out for you."

"I don't need anyone looking out for me." I've spent my whole life taking care of myself. I don't need someone else.

Rex holds up his padded hands. "Fine, Jay. If you ever need me, I'm here."

Fuck's sake, why did he have to get like this? "I know," I tell him. I take a swing for the pad, and Rex says no more about Warren.

I'm soaked by the time we finish training, and some of my anger toward Alex is gone. Rex unwraps my hands, and I hit the shower.

He's back in the office when I leave. I salute him, and he responds with a jerk of his head. I leave the gym. The light outside is bright. Removing my phone, I think of ringing home to check on Layla, but I pause.

Words are displayed across my car windshield. I glance around the area, but the only vehicle that's here is Rex's pickup truck. The closer I get, the tighter my fists grow.

"RIP" is sprayed in thick black letters.

I drop my gym bag, unzip it, and grab my workout top while dialing home.

William answers on the first ring as I run my top along the glass.

"Is Layla there?"

I scrub harder, but the letters won't come off. I turn as Rex comes out the main door. He must have seen me on CCTV.

"Yes, Master Jay. She's in her quarters with Kerry."

"Go check, William," I say as I drop my top back into my gym bag.

Rex stands beside me, and his jaw twitches as he reads the letters on my windshield.

"One moment, Master Jay."

I look around the area and walk toward the bushes. Some rocks are placed throughout the undergrowth. I hoist the largest one.

"What are you doing?" Rex asks as I come back to the car with the rock.

"Yes, Master Jay. Layla is in her quarters. I'm looking at her right now. Shall I put her on…"

I hang up and push the phone into my pocket before launching the rock at my windshield. The impact is instant, and the glass splinters and cracks, the center caving in on itself.

"Are you going to explain to me why you did that?" Rex folds his arms across his chest.

"It's a warning." I pick up my gym bag.

"I can see that, Jay." Rex's voice carries a note of irritation.

I face him while slinging my bag over my shoulder. "Can you give me a lift home?"

He keeps his arms folded.

"I'll tell you everything on the way."

That has him unfolding his arms. "Let me grab my keys."

I wait outside as he heads back into the building.

I ring the breakdown service to pick up the car and fix the windshield. I leave the keys on the front tire. I'm finished with the call when Rex returns with his car.

I throw my bag in his open trunk before climbing in.

"My girlfriend, Layla, was shot."

"When? Why didn't you say anything?"

Is that hurt I see in his gaze? "I don't talk about her," I admit. Layla isn't something I've discussed before, so it's like all I know is to keep everything about her to myself.

"Is she okay?" Rex's voice lowers.

"Yeah, but the guy who shot her"—I point over at my car—"isn't finished yet."

Rex follows my stare to my car. "Can I ask why someone wants to kill your girlfriend?"

No.

"Retaliation toward me."

"You've been mixing with some bad people, Jay." Rex leans on the steering wheel. This is a lot for him to take in.

"This has got nothing to do with Warren." I defend him straight away, seeing where this conversation is going.

Rex nods before starting the Jeep. "So why did I just watch you smash your windshield?"

"I don't want Layla upset," I admit. "She ended up in a coma and had some memory loss, but recently she remembers who shot her."

"But you knew him? So the Gardaí can deal with this."

I take out my phone and check the time. It's nearly six in the evening. "At the time, she didn't remember," I repeat.

Rex gives a laugh. "I see, and you were hoping it would remain that way."

I glance at him.

"What did you do, Jay?"

"I beat up their gang leader."

Rex shakes his head. "Never use your skills like that." Disappointment is heavy in his words.

"Yeah, I fucked up. Take a left here," I instruct, realizing that Rex doesn't know where I live, and we're out of the main part of the town.

"I'll go to the Gardaí."

"Good."

Silence follows, and the only words exchanged are me giving instructions to Rex.

We pull up at the gates. "I'll walk from here." I don't need my father to see Rex. I'm sure that would set him off.

I get out, and Rex rolls down the window. "If you need me, Jay, you know where I am."

I look away before getting my bag out of the trunk. "Thanks for the lift," I call over my shoulder before ringing the gates, and they open.

I had no luck finding Chester, so I think going public will flush him out. I want him dead.

William materializes in the hallway. "Good evening, Master Jay. Your food is in your room, and Miss Masters is in her quarters."

"Thank you, William," I say while handing him my gym bag. I don't make my way to my room. Instead, I go to the security hut that's stationed in the back of the property. It's not somewhere I've been before, and when I open the door, the two men who are having a chat stand up. The first nearly sloshes his tea across his knee as he rises, dropping a chocolate digestive onto his desk. He fixes his tie. "Master Jay."

"How far back do we keep footage?" I ask.

It takes him a moment to recover. "A full year."

I have no idea why we would. "Can you get me the tapes for the fifteenth of January?"

He swings into action. The other guy stands close to the door.

"Take a break," I tell him and he leaves, closing the door behind us.

There must be twelve televisions in the room—a bit overkill if you ask me. "This is a lot of surveillance," I say, looking around the room.

"Your father wanted the best, Master Jay."

I lean in behind the security guard. He glances at me but gets back to work.

"Well, I'd say you did a piss-poor job. People seem to be able to waltz in and out of here. Like the day of the shooting."

He tries to turn his chair, but I grip the back of it. "Do your job."

He goes back to looking through records. "The day of the shooting, someone had cut the cameras, Master Jay."

His snooty tone has me grinning at the back of his head. That one mistake cost me dearly. "Did you not look into the fault?" I ask. I had cut the power from the main board, but they must have known that.

"We were told it was better to turn a blind eye."

I don't have to ask who said it. My father. So he'd known Layla was here that night, even before the shooting. "By who?" I still need it clarified.

"Your father, Master Jay."

"What about my mother? How did she get in so easily?" I stare at the screen as he continues to search.

"I can look into it for you."

"You do that." I lean in closer as he opens a file.

"Here we are."

"Take a break," I say, and he gets out of his chair right before I slide into it.

I stay with the camera on the front door and fast forward it throughout the day. It takes a few more minutes before Alex arrives. I sit closer to the screen to see where she reappears. In the hallway downstairs. She reappears in my father's study. Alex walks along the bookshelves, and he appears. There's no audio, so I have no idea what's being said. A very pointless search.

I'm ready to turn it off when Alex leans into my father and kisses him. *What the fuck?*

I must be mistaken. Any uncertainty I have vanishes as she slowly drops to her knees and starts to give my father a blow job.

CHAPTER FIFTEEN

LAYLA

AFTER TAKING A BATH and changing into another dress, this one baby pink, I sit down for my food at the table that's nestled between the windows. Kerry hasn't left my bedroom, and Amanda arrives back in. Amanda tidies the area while Kerry brushes my hair. I'm glad I don't have to wear my sling anymore. I can move my arm more, but brushing my hair won't   be easy.

It's been hours since Jared dropped me off, and when he enters my room, there's a clear shift in the air.

He juts his chin toward me and lowers his eyebrows. "You okay?"

The sandwich I've been eating feels lodged in my throat. "What's wrong?" I get up, and Kerry steps away from me.

Jared holds up his hands. "Nothing."

Everything.

"Can you give us the room?" Jared addresses Kerry and Amanda.

"Yes, Master Jay." Kerry holds out her arm toward Amanda to hurry her up. Amanda places the clothes she was holding onto the bed, and within seconds, the bedroom door closes, and it's just Jared and me. I get up as Jared steps closer to me, and the way he's looking at me makes me unbalanced.

"I love you, Layla." Jared touches my face.

"I know. I love you too." Fear finds its way into my words. "What's going on?"

Jared touches his lips against mine before releasing me. "We need to go to the Gardaí about Chester. He left another message, and I'm realizing he won't be going away."

My legs should buckle; my body should sag. I should be overwhelmed with relief, but I'm not. Instead, I have this feeling of being smothered, and it overshadows everything else as I stagger away from Jared.

"But we lied. We can't just change our minds. They'll know."

"No, they won't," Jared reasons. "You had memory loss. You just got your memory back."

I can sense the edges of hysteria at the thoughts of going to the Gardaí after lying.

"You never lied to them, Layla. At the time you gave your statement, you didn't know." Jared speaks as if he read my mind.

"What about you? Are you okay with lying?"

Jared's smile is quick, and it drips with a silent story of hurt and pain. "Yeah, I'm good with lying to them."

My stomach coils as if I've swallowed something poisonous. I turn to try to find some of my footing, but Jared's arms circle me, and I'm against his solid chest.

"When we were kids, I rang them to help us," Jared whispers in my ear. "And they didn't." His voice is low, but his words are loud. Hot pain burns a path right down to my tattered soul. "I rang them so many times when he was—"

I turn in Jared's arms, and he lets me. I'm expecting to see a pair of dark eyes filled with unshed tears, but the only thing Jared's gaze is filled with is hardness. His arms drop to my waist, and I rest my hands on his chest. "So I'm okay with lying to them, Layla."

My anger is hanging on by a thread, and it snaps as I lean against Jared's chest. His heart thrashes wildly under my ear.

"I love you," I say on a whoosh of expelled air.

Jared presses a kiss to the crown of my head. "I love all of you."

When I glance up at Jared, his eyes are still hard. I reach up and touch his brow, tracing it with my finger. "Smile for me, Jared." My words are soaked in the pain that our past has coated us in.

His lips lift slightly.

"That's the best you can do for me?" I keep my hand over his pounding heart.

He focuses over my head, and when he glances back, his dimples make an appearance. I reach up on the tip of my toes and press a kiss to his lips. "Once we do this, I'll need to tell Evelyn and Carl." My shoulders sag at the thoughts of the conversation with Evelyn and Carl.

Jared releases me. "Okay. Are you ready to go now?"

"Yeah, let me grab my shoes." I find my tennis shoes and grab my bag and denim jacket. Jared waits patiently, and when I turn with everything in my hand, he stops me from leaving. His long fingers circle my wrist.

"I'll be with you every step of the way."

My heart *thump, thump, thumps* in my chest. "I know."

***

Jared keeps to his word and never leaves my side through the two-hour ordeal at the Gardaí station. By the time he drops me off at Carl and Evelyn's, I'm emotionally spent.

I let myself in with my own key, and Jared doesn't leave until I close the door and lean against it. I listen as his car pulls away, and my body is ready to sag. I don't want to crash in the hall. I take the stairs two at a time, not being able to reach my room quickly enough.

"What happened?" Evelyn stands on the landing with a pile of clean clothes in her arms. Her brows knit together as she moves toward me. I try to focus on the swish of her full-length tan skirt to stop the harrowing feeling that's consuming every inch of my fiber.

"Layla?" she questions, drawing me to her worried gaze. The tightening of her eyes should have been a warning for me to put her mind at rest, but I don't. Instead, I let the whole day's emotions pour from me. My tears have Evelyn dropping the clothes and embracing me, which makes me cry harder.

"Shh. It's okay, sweetheart." Evelyn's hand runs up and down my back in a soothing rhythm, but it doesn't stop the onslaught of emotions that pour from me. Today, everything that I've kept tucked away comes crashing down.

"What happened?" The strength in Evelyn's voice isn't the therapist I'm used to. It's more of what I imagine a fierce mother would sound like.

"You'll hate me, and I wouldn't blame you." I sniffle.

"What happened?"

I stiffen but don't turn at Carl's voice. I plead with Evelyn with my eyes.

"Just girl talk. It's fine." Evelyn gives a smile to Carl over my head. I don't want her to lie to him, but I appreciate it more than she will ever know. Carl would only get mad at Jared, and that's the last thing I want.

"I'll be downstairs," Carl says reluctantly. The stairs creak under his weight as he descends the stairs.

I wait alone with Evelyn, who wants an explanation. She releases me, and we walk to the room that we set up for meditation and where I do most of my therapy with Evelyn. It's a room I don't associate with pain and hurt, even though I've poured my heart and soul out in this room. No. It's a room of healing and love for me.

I focus on my surroundings to ground myself. The room is scarcely furnished, but that's the point. It isn't a big room, but it feels spacious.

The clever arrangement of the furniture and the use of light colors make it appear large. The walls are painted in a simple magnolia, while the wooden floor is glossed over in white paint. I curl up in my hanging chair that Carl had hung from the ceiling. The large circle is a safe space for me, a warm cocoon where Bert or Ronnie can't get me. Evelyn sits across from me on a large wicker chair that has several floral throws strewn across the back.

I slip off my shoes and let them fall on the shaggy cream rug that covers most of the wooden floor before tucking my bare feet under me. Evelyn lights her incense that sits on a wicker-style table. I always love the smell and find it relaxes me, but not today.

"I could never hate you, Layla." Evelyn's smile is as soft as fresh whipped cream, making me want to smile too. Her kindness always steals a bit of my fear at times like this.

"I know who shot me. I lied about it."

She shifts in her seat, moving forward. Her fingers tap her leg, and she nods several times. "Who?"

Who doesn't really matter. "Chester. I babysat for his girlfriend a few nights before the shooting, and we had words. He wasn't happy I was minding his child."

Evelyn sits forward. "Do you think he shot you because of that?"

Everything feels tight: my dress, my chest, the lies. Lies that won't stop. "No, I don't. I think it was a coincidence that I met him before he robbed Jared's home and shot me." I try to find some resolve before I shatter. Tears make paths down my cheeks. "I'm sorry I lied."

"Did you lie because you were afraid?"

I nod. It's easier than using my words.

"I have a confession," Evelyn says as she reaches to pick up the lighter that she used to light the incense. "I didn't like Jared. I never wanted you to find him."

Her words carve more pain into me, and I find myself pulling my floral cushion to my chest. I blink several times. I kind of knew this, but her saying it really brings it home. "But," she continues, "I tracked him down years ago. I've known where he was all this time."

A bitter taste pools in my mouth. The gash that my past carved into my soul reopens all over again.

Evelyn's eyes glaze with unshed tears. "I keep waiting for you to fully blossom in your life, but I knew something was holding you back. So..." The smile she wears rips a strip of anger from me. She tilts her head and blinks, tears falling. "I packed up our lives and dropped you across Ireland so you could hopefully find your peace."

Evelyn wipes her face with both hands before rubbing them together. "Ever since we arrived here, I've kept waiting for you to come alive again." She swallows all her tears. "You do, Layla. You come alive around Jared, and I'm so sorry I kept you from him all that time."

Her words cause tears to pour soundlessly down my face. She's telling me what I already knew, what I've been trying to explain. We aren't unhealthy together. I swipe the tears away.

"I'm sorry I've been so hard on him. I'm sorry I've been so hard on you." She holds her head high, trying to hide the fact that her apology is taking far more out of her than she's willing to admit.

She lied to me. I lied to her. We both did it to protect the other, yet all we seem to have done is cause each other pain.

"Layla." Evelyn sits forward, joining her hands together. "I was afraid I might have made the wrong judgment call to bring you here. I was afraid it would open new wounds too widely."

"Since I've had Jared back in my life, I realize what I've always been missing. Him." The confession makes my heart squeeze. I pick at my nails. "He's the same person." I don't look up at Evelyn. I don't like how those words make me feel. "He's hiding something from me."

"Okay, let's start with what you think he could be hiding." Evelyn is now very much in therapist mode, and I shift slightly, wondering if I really want to go down this road with her. But I need to. I can't let it keep spinning around in my mind. And frankly, I have no one else to talk to.

"He carries a lot of anger." I chew my lip.

"Did you talk to Jared about it?" Evelyn tilts her head, and I suppress a smile. It's a tell that she's uncomfortable with what I'm saying, but she's trying to stay in the moment.

"He's never angry toward me." I put her mind at rest before I continue. "He's angry at everyone else." I let my legs hang out of the chair.

"He's violent at times." My words are low as I think of Kieran. I hate telling Evelyn, but I can't seem to let that knowledge go.

"Layla. I have raised you for the last seven years of your life. You are my *daughter*, and I can see it in your eyes that something has happened. So you're going to tell me the *truth*." Evelyn's tone is fierce, and so much of that sentence has my head spinning.

She just called me her daughter.

"I kissed Kieran and Jared saw it. He attacked Kieran," I admit.

A slow smile transforms Evelyn's face. "He was jealous. Boys fight."

I want to tell her she wasn't there. She didn't see how he held Kieran under the water, or how he tried to buy a gun to shoot Bert. Jesus, the more I think about it, the more I realize that telling her all this is madness.

"Yeah, you're probably right." Outside the window, the sky has turned a deep crimson color, and I focus on the rays that scatter across the horizon from the setting sun. Thinking of Bert makes me think of Nelson. "I wish I had time with Nelson before he died. I wish I had gotten to talk to him." I look back at Evelyn.

Her eyes flash with knowledge before she speaks. "We actually got more word about Nelson. I was able to dig around, and we found out his cause of death."

I grip my foot and pull it up onto the chair, waiting.

"I'm so sorry, Layla. Nelson took his own life."

The room spirals, and my chest constricts as I repeat Evelyn's words. "Nelson took his own life."

"I'm afraid so, sweetheart." Evelyn nods several times.

Pain leaks from my eyes faster than I can think. "He was, what?" I blink but my vision doesn't clear as I produce more tears at a brutal rate. "Eighteen, Nineteen?"

"I'm not sure, love."

I blink Evelyn into focus. "Why?"

Evelyn shrugs, her fingers tightening on the lighter. "No one knows."

All I can think is: I need to tell Jared.

We sit in silence for a long time, and I get lost in a pool of heartache and pain. The sky darkens when Evelyn finally speaks.

"How are you feeling?" Her voice snaps me back to the present.

"It's so weird. You know"—I frown at my own thoughts—"it makes sense. Even as a kid, Nelson always held such... anger, darkness, hurt." A chill slides across my skin and a whisper niggles at me. *Nelson isn't the only one who harbored such emotions.*

"It's a pity to see a young life taken. Grieve for him, Layla, but don't get swallowed up in his pain."

I nod. I have a habit of doing just that. "I won't."

My phone buzzes in my bag, and I don't need to look to know who it is. I get off the chair and rummage through my purse.

"I'll be out in a minute," I say to Jared before ending the call and facing Evelyn.

She rises and holds out her arms. "I'm so proud of you."

I step into her embrace, and her warmth seeps into my soul. The heaviness I feel starts to lift, and I forgot how powerful Evelyn's hugs are. "I love you, Evelyn."

"I love you too, Layla."

I break the embrace. "Once Chester is arrested, I'll come home."

"Carl and I would really like that." Evelyn's eyes burn so brightly with happiness, and I give her one final hug before putting on my shoes and gathering my bag and jacket, and some strength. This will be all over soon, I tell myself.

CHAPTER SIXTEEN

JARED

"WHERE ARE THE PAINTINGS?" my father shouts through the phone.

I lift my head and glance up at Layla's window before answering him. "Safe." My one word has him growling through the phone.

"Jay, this is no time for your smartness. Where are they?"

I'm tempted to hang up, when I see movement close to the front door. I just rang Layla to tell her I'm outside.

I look at the phone. "Layla remembers who shot her, so we reported it to the Gardaí like good citizens. So the paintings are in their rightful place."

I had to call in another favor with Warren O'Reagan. He hasn't told me what it will cost, but I'm sure it won't be cheap. He had his men move the paintings into Chester's home before I took Layla to the Gardaí station.

"I'm sure by now Chester has been arrested, and we will be receiving a phone call to say our artwork has been recovered."

My father breathes heavily. "I'll speak to you when you get home." He has absolutely no gratitude for what I've done.

Layla steps out of Evelyn and Carl's house, and she wraps her arms around her waist.

"Yeah, see you then." I hang up. I have no intention of going home. The closer Layla gets to my car, the clearer she becomes. She's been crying. Layla doesn't look at me as she walks around the car and gets in. Evelyn stands at the door and waves. I don't wave back until I know what's happened and why Layla was crying.

"What happened? Did she upset you?"

Layla's gaze is drawn to Evelyn, and her hand rises as she gives a small wave. "No."

I turn the keys in the ignition and pull away from Layla's home.

"She knew where you were all this time." Layla's voice hitches with upset. "She always knew," Layla repeats.

I also knew this. My father already told me. When I don't answer, Layla's eyes widen.

"Why aren't you saying anything? I thought you would be cursing her?"

Her analysis is fair. "My father told me when you first arrived that Evelyn was aware of where I lived. I just didn't believe it."

"You didn't think to tell me?"

The sensation that rises inside me has me gripping my hands on the steering wheel. "My father lies a lot, so I didn't know what to believe."

Layla lets out a long breath and slumps lower in the seat. "I told her about Chester as well. So, no more secrets."

When my gaze meets Layla's, I have this need to know what she isn't saying. It scorches itself on my skin; it's angry.

I push it aside and focus on driving. "I want to show you something," I say.

Layla sits up straight and grips the overhead handle.

We arrive in town, which is quiet at this hour of the night. Nervousness isn't an emotion I'm accustomed to, but that's what has me dragging my hands through my hair several times. I do it enough to garner Layla's attention. She raises a brow.

"Are you okay?" She turns in her seat.

"Yes. Stop worrying," I say and it's funny how sure and confident I sound, when really my insides churn uncomfortably.

I approach the empty gym and pull up close to the door. I take out the set of keys that Rex gave me.

"A gym?" Layla dips her head and stares out the windshield.

"Come on." I get out of the car, and Layla does the same.

I open the front door and lock it behind us. Flicking on all the overhead lights, Layla looks at me shyly over her shoulder, and automatically, I reach out and take her hand.

"This is where I practice with Rex." My heart thumps rapidly in my chest. It's not a big deal. It *shouldn't* be a big deal, but really, it is. It's a part of me that I've never shared with anyone I've cared for, and I want to share it with Layla.

I let my fingers leave the safety of Layla's hand and slide my fingers up her wrist, stopping on her rapid heartbeat.

My fingers trail from her wrist, and I walk toward the ring. I get in it and turn so I'm facing Layla. "This is where the magic happens." I grin.

She smiles.

Layla tucks her hands behind her back, and I'm waiting for her to walk to me, but she makes her way to a large glass case instead. "I'm assuming some of these trophies are yours?"

The teasing in her voice has me jumping down from the ring. The moment my feet touch the ground, she glances at me. I love how she swallows as I walk toward her. She makes me feel far more powerful than I am. I don't stand beside her but stop right behind her and inhale her scent.

"A few," I say and brush her hair over one shoulder. I meet her gaze in the glass.

"I don't think I could watch you getting hit." She chews her lip.

I laugh and she turns. I have to take a step back to give her some room. "It's a good thing, then, that I don't get hit."

"Cocky." She's fighting a grin.

I take her hand and lead her to the boxing area. "I'll show you how skilled I am." I grip her waist and lift her until she's standing on the edge of the ring. I climb up and hold the rope so she can enter.

"It's so much bigger when you're up here." Layla walks around.

"Everyone says that."

Layla tuts and heat scorches her cheeks.

I dance slowly from foot to foot. The action is automatic once I enter a ring. "When I'm here, everything fades away. It's only me and Rex. Or me and my opponent. Nothing else."

Layla's fingers flutter rapidly along the sides of her pink dress as she nods. "Like me with gardening."

I stop shifting from foot to foot. "Like you with gardening," I repeat before walking to her and capturing her chin in my hand.

"Teach me some moves." Layla's gaze dances along my mouth.

I release her. "I won't go easy on you," I warn as I step back.

Her laugh is infectious and twists my gut. Fuck me, she's gorgeous. "I won't go easy on you either."

"Let's dance, Layla Masters." I can't stop the stupid smile that crosses my face as I bounce on my feet and hold my fists close to my face.

Layla mimics my actions, and she looks so fucking cute. I shift closer to her, and she strikes. Her small fists impact my arm.

"Easy there, tiger," I say.

She barks a laugh and drops her hands. "Shut up. I'm not made of muscle like some people."

I drop my hands from my face. "I'll gladly show you all my muscles."

Her eyes dance with excitement, and I clear the space between us, done playing. I capture her mouth with mine. Her lips are soft and warm, and I devour her. My cock grows, and I wrap an arm around Layla's waist, dragging her small frame against mine. Her breath hitches. My hand easily slides down until I cup her perfectly round ass. Her hands grip my shoulders, and

I lift her, wanting her closer. She automatically wraps her legs around my waist as I push my tongue deeper into her mouth. I move us to the padded corner of the ring. I let her slide down so I can press my cock against her core.

"I want you to touch me." Layla arches her body impatiently against mine. My blood roars in my ears, and I'm hanging on by a thread. It breaks as I trail my fingers under her dress. She holds her breath at the contact and exhales loudly as I push her panties aside and slide my fingers slowly between her folds.

Layla's hands dig into my shoulders, and she tries to bury her head in my chest.

"Look at me."

She does as I remove my finger before pushing it inside her again. I gather some of her wetness and withdraw my finger only to rub it along her clit in long, tantalizing strides. My cock presses painfully against my jeans. I lean my forehead against Layla's as I withdraw my fingers and fix her dress back into place.

As much as I want Layla right now, I don't want to give Rex a show.

"I don't want you to stop." The confession from Layla's pretty mouth tests my willpower.

"I don't want to stop either." I bring my wet fingers to my mouth and taste the sweetness of Layla.

Her eyes widen, and the excitement I recognize in her gaze has me taking her hand. "Let's go home."

She doesn't answer, but her fingers tighten around my hand. I turn off all the lights and lock up before we leave.

The moment we're in the car, I can't help myself as I reach out and grip Layla by the back of the neck, dragging her to me.

"I want to fuck you." I press a kiss between each word.

Layla's breath grows harsh. "I want that too."

I turn the ignition and try to keep to the speed limit.

Layla chews on her bottom lip, and I don't want to give her time to think. I don't want her to change her mind. I run my hand under her dress. Her legs part easily for me, and she shimmies down on the seat, giving me access to her folds.

My finger sinks inside her, and her pussy coils tightly around my fingers. My cock twitches. I extract my finger to run the wetness along her folds before pushing two fingers inside her.

She's gripping the door, and I'm contemplating pulling over and taking her here and now. I would, I fucking would, only I remind myself she's a virgin.

When I extract my hand to shift gears, I press the two fingers that had been buried in her against my lips.

"You taste so sweet." Just like I knew she would.

Layla appears dazed as she sits up and fixes her dress. The gates to my home appear, and this time when I glance at Layla, the nerves are back as she wrings her hands repeatedly in her lap.

I try to grapple for control as I pull into the garage. "We don't have to have sex, Layla."

I stop the car and turn it off.

Layla makes no reply at first. "I want to." Her soft reply has me looking at her.

"Good." Because I didn't think I could deliver on the no-sex part.

Layla gets out first, and I fix my erection before getting out and following her into the house. I take her hand automatically and steer her toward my room.

The intensity to have Layla rises rapidly as I get my bedroom door open. I rotate the key once she's in and turn toward her.

She surprises me when she springs forward and slams her mouth on mine. I don't need a second longer to respond, pulling her small body harshly against mine.

I kiss her back as I guide us to the bed. I lie her down, her blonde hair sprawling around her head like a halo. I step back because I've envisioned this a million times. "You look just like I pictured you would," I admit.

I reach down and run my hands up Layla's bare legs and grip her panties as I drag them down slowly. I pull off her tennis shoes and socks, then toss them so they join her panties on the floor.

"Are you sure about this?" I ask for the final time.

She swallows but nods. "Yes, I want this."

I crawl onto the bed and bury my head between her legs. Licking her juices from my fingers was nice, but drinking from the source has my hard-on painfully pushing against my jeans. I reach down and open my belt and jeans, trying to give my cock some relief. My tongue slides between her folds, and I lap up her wetness.

She's ready for me. Coming up, I take both of Layla's hands and sit her up so I can pull the dress over her head. Once her bra is off, I throw her clothes on the floor. She tries to cover herself up.

"Don't. You're perfect." I get off the bed, and she obediently places her hands along her side. "Perfection."

Every curve, every freckle on her stomach, the scar on her leg—it's all perfect. It's all Layla.

I pull off my shirt and love when Layla swallows. My jeans and boxers come next, and my cock rages.

I take the strip of condoms from the drawer and rip one open.

"Spread your legs for me," I command as I roll on the condom with a clenched jaw. I want to bury myself inside her, but I know I need to pace myself. She's a virgin.

Once again, Layla does as I ask and spreads her legs. I get back up on the bed and stroke my erection. Her body tenses, and I reach out and run my hand along her stomach, which she sucks in on impact.

"You need to relax," I say, though I know the words are pointless.

I direct my cock to her entrance, and it takes every ounce of resilience not to slam myself inside her. I inch in and allow my body to lower slightly. With my hands on either side of her head, I focus on her face. I don't want to miss one second of taking her virginity. Layla was made just for me.

She rears her head, trying to press her lips against mine, but I don't allow it. "I want to watch you."

I slide a little deeper, her pussy painfully tight around my cock, and Layla tries to press her legs together, but that's not possible as I shift my thighs from side to side, stopping her and pushing my cock a little deeper.

Discomfort on her tightening features has me pulling out slightly before moving back in just a bit. I try to keep the rhythm, and soon it pays off as Layla groans in pleasure. I move slightly faster but not deeper. Layla's hands grip the bedding beneath her, and her head lolls to the side in pleasure. When her eyes flutter closed, I'm ready to tell her to look at me, but she does on her own. I push a bit deeper, wanting to fill every single inch of her sweet, perfect pussy.

"Oh, God." Her groan has my control slipping, and I propel further into her. Her hiss gives me back some of that control, and I slip a bit back out but keep a steady pace for her.

Her breasts swell under my chest; her nipples are hard and brush against me. My balls are full as I struggle to keep control. The thought of pulling out crosses my mind until she groans again in pleasure.

I give in and push all the way in. Her body stills, and her hands slam down on my shoulders. I quickly cover her mouth with mine and pull out only to fill her again. It takes a few strokes before she starts to relax under me. Her fingers don't dig as painfully into my shoulder, and she lets me slip my tongue into her mouth as I move faster. It's not enough for me, but I think I've taken enough from her.

Breaking the kiss, I continue the steady pace, and her eyes widen before her head thrashes to the side. I watch as Layla reaches a height, her hands digging into my shoulders before she comes all over my cock.

CHAPTER SEVENTEEN

LAYLA

I'M NO LONGER A virgin.

"Did you come?" I ask breathlessly. Jared is still inside me. The strain on his face tells me he didn't, which disappoints me.

"What I witnessed was better than coming." He presses a soft kiss to my lips before he pulls out of me with such gentleness. I'm still sore and bite down on my lip so I don't hiss. He's watching me too carefully. "You will be sore for a few days."

I'm tempted to cover myself, but I don't. Jared rolls the condom off his very large cock, which I can't believe fit inside me, and leaves to dispose of it in the bathroom. I sit up on my elbows and marvel at how perfect every single inch of him is.

He's naked apart from the key that dangles around his neck. When he's out of sight, I sit up and pull the blanket around my naked and sore body. Everything about this was perfect. For such a large guy, he was so tender, so careful, so open.

Jared steps out of the bathroom. He's pulled on a pair of sweatpants, but I can still appreciate him bare chested.

I can see his dimples are out as he leans against the doorframe, smiling at me.

It's hard to stay still under his scrutiny.

"I'll have to marry you now." His words are said so offhandedly.

Only for his smile, I would think he was serious. "And why is that, Master Jay?"

He leaves the doorframe quickly and marches toward me. The bed dips under his weight. "Don't 'Master Jay' me." He grabs my waist, and I'm rolling backward on the bed until I'm under Jared. "I've taken your virginity, so I think it's best we get married."

This time, he isn't smiling. I'm waiting for him to laugh or tell me he's joking, but he doesn't.

"I don't think it works that way, Jared."

He clears his throat and sits up, giving me some space. "What if it did? Would you say yes?"

"I'm nineteen." That's the best answer I can give him. The idea of marrying Jared elates me, but we're too young, even if at times I feel like I've lived several lives in my short time on earth.

He's not satisfied; his mouth forms a thin line before he smiles. "It doesn't matter. You're mine no matter what. It's only a matter of time before I marry you." He steals a kiss and some of my breath, and sanity flees with it.

Having Jared forever is a dream come true.

He's watching me, and a sudden explosion of love erupts and takes over everything. "God, I love you."

His eyes are light, like they hold the foundations of what life truly is, the fundamentals of what makes us human. It boils down to the one thing always: Love.

"I love you, Layla." He moves closer. His fingers circle my ankle before he opens them and runs them along my calf. They dance across my scar; his touch stitches my wound a little tighter.

His gaze flashes with a touch of anger before it vanishes, and his fingers skim higher. I reach out and press my hand over his chest. I love the feel of it under my touch.

My fingers shift until I pick up the key. He freezes, and my gaze snaps to him as I drop the key. "Sorry."

He clears his throat while his brows drag down. "No, it's only a key."

I pick the key back up. "It's pretty." I smile at him before focusing on the small carvings. "What does it open? A safe?"

"My heart."

I laugh and drop the key before pressing my hand against his racing heart. I shift closer and lean in. Jared licks his bottom lip, and I capture his tongue before he pulls it back into his mouth. A knock on the door has us separating.

"I'll get rid of them." Jared presses a kiss to my forehead before getting off the bed. I tug the blankets tighter around me.

Jared doesn't open the door fully. "William."

"Master Jay." William's voice floats into the room. Jared closes the door and turns, holding a piece of paper, which he opens.

"It's good news." He finishes reading before walking back to me. "Chester has been arrested."

"That's fantastic." My shoulder burns at the reminder, and I reach up and touch the place where I was shot.

Jared rejoins me on the bed. "You don't have to worry anymore."

"Neither do you," I say because I'm not seeing the joy I feel displayed on Jared's features. He's still tense.

"Our artwork was recovered too," he adds.

"That's good, right?"

Jared forces a smile, but it's all wrong on his handsome face. "Of course, Layla."

I reach out and take his hand in mine. "Then why don't you look happy?" I tilt my head as I ask.

"I'll be happy when he's rotting behind bars."

I agree with Jared on this. I hope I never hear Chester's name again. "Evelyn and Carl will be so happy. I can go home soon." Even as I say it, I don't feel the excitement the words should bring me.

"Home?" Jared's eyes pool with darkness.

Adrenaline shoots through my body, and I have no idea what to do with it. I slide off the bed, only for Jared to stop me. His arm circles my waist, and he pulls me back into his chest. "Maybe after the court case."

We both know there's no need for me to stay here any longer. I glance down at Jared's hand as it rests on my abdomen. "That makes sense."

Jared brushes a kiss to my cheek before pressing his face to mine. "Perfect sense."

I grin, but my smile soon dwindles as I think of Evelyn's excitement to have me home. That leads my mind to Nelson. I still haven't told Jared about how Nelson died.

It doesn't feel like the right time, but I'm not sure there ever will be a right time.

"I found out how Nelson died." I place my hand over Jared's. My focus is on the black ink tattoo on his wrist.

I'm waiting for him to ask me how, but when he doesn't, I give in. "He took his own life." Anger pools heavily in my mouth, and when I swallow, it settles with an empty thud in the pit of my stomach.

"This is when I need you to say something."

Jared presses a brash kiss to my cheek, then he releases me and he's off the bed. I spin, trying to understand what's going on.

"What do you want me to say?" He opens a drawer and pulls out a dark T-shirt before putting it on.

Every muscle in my body tightens to a breaking point. "Anything." I squeeze between my numb lips.

"I hope he rests in peace." Jared squeezes the bridge of his nose. "I'm tired. Why don't we get some sleep?" Jared turns his back on me and takes out another T-shirt. "Let it go, Layla."

I close my mouth and swallow my confusion. He seems more put together and not as scattered as he displayed only moments ago.

I'm not letting it go, but for now, I'll let it rest. I pull on the T-shirt and Jared lifts me before settling my head on the pillows. Without words, he drags the blanket over us and pulls me into his chest.

This close to him, he can't conceal what he doesn't want me to see. He's upset. The news has him shaken, and maybe he needs time to process it. I press a kiss to his chin before placing another on his lips.

"Good night." I have no idea how I'm going to sleep in Jared's arms. Everything about him was designed to wake me up.

"Good night." He holds me tighter, and for a while, we both pretend to be asleep until we finally aren't pretending anymore.

***

I'm tempted to run my finger along the bridge of his nose and then hold his nose, cutting off the air. I used to do this when we were kids, and he would wake up gasping for breath. It was hilarious. I'm half laughing as I reach out. His hand rises, and long fingers circle my wrist.

"Don't even think about it." He speaks with his eyes closed.

"How did you know?" I pull my hand back.

Jared opens one eye. "You're breathing and laughing all over me." Both eyes are open now, and I can sense him pulling away, retreating from me, and I don't understand.

My hand flutters to his chest. "I'm going to take a bath." I don't know how to seduce anyone, so I try again. "Your bathtub is huge."

He grins, and I see a small sparkle of interest. "Do you want me to run a bath for you?"

I'm not sure if my intentions are getting across. "No, I can do that." I roll out of the bed.

"Or I could get Kerry to do it for you," Jared offers.

I wave him off as I walk to the bathroom. "It's okay."

His bathroom is twice the size of mine, and the black-and-white theme carries on from his bedroom into here. The bathtub sits in the center of the room. The clawed-foot tub isn't a regular size; this one is so much bigger. I start to fill it and add some bubbles before opening up some cabinets in my search for towels. I find a stack and set them on the vanity table. I've only a T-shirt to strip off, so I keep it on as I step into the tub and sit on the edge. I watch the bubbles multiply as the water rises.

When the water reaches past my calf, I pull off the T-shirt but don't sink into the tub.

"I want to draw you." Jared's voice is rough.

I glance at him over my shoulder. My heart thumps in my chest, and I do the only thing I can think of, which is to sink into the tub. I move over to the taps and turn off the water. "Maybe you can later."

Jared steps into the bathroom, and I swallow with excitement as he pulls down his trousers. He never put on boxers, so his cock is on full display and he's aroused. Jared stops at the vanity and takes out a condom. He opens it while looking at me. Once he has the condom out, he rolls it onto his cock before giving it too long, slow strokes. My hand floats along the top of the water, moving bubbles aside.

Jared pulls off his shirt and discards it before stepping up to the tub. "You aren't very subtle."

My cheeks heat, but I don't shy away. "I'm only learning. I've never tried to seduce a man before." Jared gets into the bath, and having him naked beside me sends my heart racing. "Good. I'd hate to have to kill anyone." His remark is laced with a serious note I try to ignore.

I tilt my head and narrow my eyes. "Don't say things like that."

Jared sinks into the water and reaches for me. "I mean it. If anyone ever touched you"—he twirls a lock of my hair around his finger—"I'd kill them."

Jared pulls on my hair, dragging my face closer to his mouth. "This time, I get to fuck you."

Jared's hand cups the back of my head as he pushes me back into the water. Fear has me gripping the sides. My head thuds against the bathtub, and my grip loosens on the edge. His hands feel rough as they leave my hair and part my legs. Jared moves quickly and fills the space between them. The water sloshes across the tub and onto the floor at his quick movement.

I'm not ready for his entry, so when he pushes himself inside me in one controlled motion, I gasp, but I don't have a second to recover before he pulls out and slides inside me again. Water sloshes onto the floor at each jerk. Jared's head is buried in my neck. His arms grip the side of the tub, his muscles coiling and straining as he uses pulls his body into mine repeatedly. The burn and soreness steals my breath, but soon there's a nugget of pleasure that grows with each stroke.

The strength and awe of what's building inside me has me reaching out and gripping his forearms. I don't know if I want him to stop or continue. A part of me doesn't think I have a choice as he continues moving over my body, each jerk faster and harder than the one before. Air nips my legs as the water continues to slosh out. I'm aware of everything, down to Jared's hair that brushes my cheek, and his breathing that whooshes in my ear. Blood pounds in my ears, and each time Jared pumps into me, my head thuds on the bathtub while taking me to a new height. My body starts to quiver as Jared groans in my ear. His movements grow quicker, and there's a violence in his motion that has me sinking my nails into his forearms.

It's too much.

It's not enough.

His pumps become brutal against my body and my pleasure ebbs.

"You are mine. All of you," he declares and my arousal jumps. My hands leave his arm, and I give into him fully, spreading my legs as far as possible. I take the pain with the pleasure, but his words are the ribbon that ties the gift. I'm throbbing and squirming, and Jared has lost any semblance of control as he sinks fully into me. My heart has leapt into my throat at the unexpected orgasm that steals the air from my lungs before slamming into me with a force that has me trying to throw my head back.

Jared's movements are frantic before they cease with the cry of his own release.

CHAPTER EIGHTEEN

JARED

Anger leeches on to me, and no matter what I do, I can't seem to shake it off. Layla holds my hand, looking perfect in my letterman jacket. My mind keeps skipping to Nelson. It shouldn't. I shouldn't give two fucks what happened to him. His death had nothing to do with me. Yet, the voice that whispers in the back of my mind tells me his death had everything to do with me, because I know why he took his life.

"You okay?" Layla's wide, innocent eyes stare up at me. I reach out and touch her cheek. I don't ever want that innocence to leave her. She's pure and I'm tainted.

"Yeah," I answer while glancing over her shoulder at Alex, Abby, and Caroline, who walk toward us, linked arm in arm.

Perfect. I know exactly where to direct all my fucking anger.

Mark and Warren get out of their cars and walk toward us too. Layla tenses, and her shoulders curl forward like she's trying to make herself smaller. I want to hide her from them. I don't want them to have as much as one more second to hurt her in any shape or form.

"I love your jacket." Caroline steps up close to Layla, and I step between them, blocking her from Caroline. Caroline skips back away from me.

"You like older men," I say to Alex, wearing a grin.

Her lips drag down as she shrugs her shoulders and gives a short laugh. "Is that like a question?"

I want to grip her neck, but I laugh too. Layla tries to wriggle her fingers out of my hand, but I don't allow it. "No. It's not a question, Alex." My voice deadpans.

"Why so serious, Jay?" Caroline asks while unlinking herself from Alex.

"I don't know, Caroline." I allow my lips to turn up. "Maybe because Alex has been blowing my father."

Abby chokes before she goes into a coughing fit. Finally, Alex is affected. Her cheeks deepen in color. Warren sneers behind me, and Layla attempts to pull her hand out of mine again, but I don't allow it. I tighten my hold. I'm sure Layla wants to run off right about now. This would be uncomfortable for her, but I want her to witness me tear Alex down.

"I mean, I know your blow jobs are good, but my old man? Really?" I sneer.

"Stop it," Alex grits through her teeth. Her gaze fills with tears. Tears that I intend to spill in front of everyone. Other students are filing into the school, and it's a perfect opportunity. I release Layla's hand and turn, climbing to stand on the hood of my car.

"What are you doing?" Alex's panic is perfection.

"Have you heard, folks?" I shout and some students stop, while others make their way toward us. "Alex and my father are at it like rabbits." Laughter and gasps shoot out from the crowd.

Alex's face is taut with pure fear. I don't look at Layla; I keep my focus on Alex. "I even have the footage to back it up. You want to say anything to that, Alex?" I'm keeping my voice loud.

"Please stop!" she begs.

I jump down off the hood of the car and land beside her. "I haven't even fucking started."

"Jared." Layla's voice is to my left, and I know if I look at her, I'll break. I remind myself this is for her.

"You are pathetic," I say to Alex.

Tears stream down her face.

"Lying about your parents' divorce? Pathetic. Lies, that's all you ever tell." I lean in closer as she cries. "You were right when you said no one likes you."

"Jared." Layla's voice is stronger, but it doesn't matter. The damage is done as Alex barrels past me and through the crowd, screaming for everyone to get out of her way. Abby and Caroline don't follow her, and I feel nothing but disgust for them.

I finally look at Layla. Her chest rises and falls rapidly, and her cheeks have lost all color. Her mouth opens and closes while I reach out to take her hand. She doesn't pull away. I salute Warren, and Mark has his back to me before he chases after Alex. The crowd parts for me and Layla as I walk us up to the school.

"She won't bother you again."

Layla pulls her hand out of mine. "Jared. That was cruel."

I can't stop the smile that springs to my face. "That's not cruel Layla. That's justice. She got what was coming to her. "

Layla's brows drag down. "It didn't have to be by you."

"No, that's where you're wrong. It had to be by me. That's the only way she'll learn."

Layla gives a bitter laugh. "I forgot you're king of the school."

I step closer to Layla and tilt my head. "Don't get like that with me. I did it for you."

Layla folds her arms across her chest. "You shouldn't have." Her focus leaves me, and I follow her line of sight to Ashley. The moment Ashley's gaze clashes with mine, she runs off.

Smart.

"She won't talk to me," Layla whispers, and while she's half-distracted, I clear the distance between us and capture her face in my hands.

"I love you. That's all that matters." I press a kiss to her mouth, which is still dragged down. When we break the kiss, her frown isn't as severe.

"I love you, too."

I kiss her again, and when she smiles, I start to walk while holding her hand. "Of course you do. I am, after all, king of the school," I tease.

Layla isn't ready to joke. I walk her to class, and I don't leave until her lecture starts. I depart to find Warren. He's outside, making out with a girl. I don't have to ask how he passes his classes. The same way I do: money.

Money talks. Or in our case, gets us good grades and out of class.

Warren breaks the kiss and takes a piece of gum out of his mouth. "I think this is yours, love," he says, holding it out to the girl. She giggles and takes the gum, putting it back in her mouth. Warren notices me. "I might let you go down on me later." He winks at her before walking to me.

"Real Casanova," I say when he falls into step beside me.

"I'd say you're a heartbreaker, but I think you fucking smashed Alex's into oblivion. Remind me not to piss you off." Warren takes out his cigarettes and lighter.

"She had it coming." I defend my actions.

Warren lights up the cigarette. "Was she really fucking your dad?"

"Yeah." I stuff my hands in my jeans pockets.

"Is she good at giving blow jobs?" Warren asks.

I grin as I imagine Alex being propositioned by Warren. She'd run. He wouldn't be good enough for her. "Not bad," I answer.

"Might try her some time," Warren says.

I don't tell him that's not likely, but I honestly don't care if Alex blows the whole school.

"So Chester got arrested, and the paintings were recovered," he says.

I step out onto the lawn. "How did you get him to come home?" That's the part I can't piece together. Why did Chester make such a quick reappearance when my PI couldn't find him?

"You don't want to know." Warren raises a brow while he grins.

I face him. "I do." I'm fucking serious.

"Okay." Warren takes a drag of his cigarette. "We used bait to draw him out." Warren flicks the cigarette across the lawn.

Bait? I want to ask, but the wheels in my head start to turn. What could they have used?

"His son." Warren fills in the blanks.

My gut twists. Not the fucking kid. "I paid you to find Chester, not bring his kid into this."

Warren's demeanor changes, and he steps up to me. It's a clear reminder of who he is, but I don't back down from him. "I got the job done. A thank you would be nice. And the kid is fine."

I scratch my neck. "Thanks."

Warren flashes a quick grin. "So, does that mean I can cancel the other job?"

It takes me a minute to think about the other job. "No. I still want him dead. Now we have a time and place. After his court case, have someone there to take him out. I'm pushing for it next week, so it should be a quick trial."

Warren grins. "Is that why you flushed him out? So you could clip him at the courthouse? I like the way you think, Jay. Ever think of becoming a criminal, call me."

I laugh. "I'm flattered."

"We don't let people into our circle, so you should be."

I'm ready to answer Warren when I spot my mother standing at my car. "Fuck's sake. I'll catch you later." I fist-bump Warren before walking over to her to see what she wants.

"Do I need to call security?" I practically shout at her.

She spins around, and my body seems to bend toward her like it recognizes her as my mother.

"Jared. I just want a moment."

I stop at the hood of my car and lean against it. Folding my arms across my chest, I raise a brow. "Your time has already started." I shouldn't be entertaining her, but I still have some pent-up anger I need to get rid of. "Start speaking, Maura."

She doesn't like that I used her name. "I couldn't come by the house again, as he changed the code on the gate."

"I'm sorry. Do you want the new code? I can't understand why he would lock you out." Sarcasm drips from every word.

My mother steps closer. "It's not safe here," she whispers.

I lean in. "Then leave," I whisper back.

"Jared, all he wants is your money." My mother holds my stare.

I nod and unfold my arms. "It's always about money, isn't it?"

Color leaks out of her cheeks. "Sadly, yes."

"What if I don't want the money? Have you ever thought of that?" I push off my car and tower over my mother. "Stay away from me." I give my warning and turn to get into my car.

"The problem isn't if you want the money or not, Jared. The problem is *he* wants it, and at any cost." Her voice rises with emotion.

I unlock my car, and I'm ready to climb in. I'm hesitant with my next words, but they beg to be voiced. "I had a dream that I was about six and Dad was on the bathroom floor. He'd cut his wrists, and I was standing in his blood."

I pause and wait for her to say something, but she doesn't. I turn to face her, and tears stream down her face.

"I tried to hide you after that. I was terrified for you."

I grit my teeth and tighten my jaw. "See, this is the fucking thing. Nothing you say makes sense. And I know you're full of shit."

She sniffles and wipes falling tears from her eyes. "I'm trying to warn you."

"Leave me alone."

I get into the car and start the engine, but my mother stands at the window.

"Just promise me you won't sign anything."

I'm staring into her watery eyes. I don't answer her as I push my foot to the floor and drive home. I need to see my father's wrists. I need to see if all of this is in my head or if it happened. I don't recall him having scars, but I need to put my mind at rest, once and for all.

CHAPTER NINETEEN

LAYLA

One of Jared's security drops me back to his home, as Jared was 'caught up.' I wasn't too sure what that meant. Kerry, Andrea, and Amanda are waiting for me when I arrive home from school. I politely dismiss them with the promise I'll eat the food that was laid out for me.

I walk to the window where the table and small chairs are nestled. It's an odd feeling not having Jared at my side. I'm so used to his company that I find myself calling him.

Music floats in the background when he answers. He turns the volume down, but not before I catch a note. "What are you listening to?" I ask.

"Florence and the Machine."

My lips tug up. "I wouldn't have pictured you as a Florence fan." I pick up one half of the sandwich and look to see what it is. A chicken salad sandwich.

"What kind of music would you have pictured, then?"

"Maybe like techno or something," I say, placing the food back down on the plate.

My answer elects a soft laugh from Jared. "Nah. Not my thing. So, I hope you are eating?"

I sit down and open the can of soda. It crackles close to the phone. "Satisfied?"

"That's not food, Layla."

I chew my lip. "I'm just about to put on a horror show if you want to join me." I want to ask why he didn't come home with me, but I also need to give him some space.

"Yeah? Since when do you watch horrors? Remember that one time Nelson put on the advertisement for Freddy Kruger and you lost it?" Jared sounds like he's smiling.

I try to overlook my heightened heart rate at Nelson's name, but I'm also glad that Jared is speaking about him.

"That wasn't funny, Jared. I had nightmares for years."

"We're going to watch it one day. You have to conquer your fears."

I snort at the stupidity. "Sure. Keep thinking that."

"We are. It's a promise."

I groan, sitting back in the chair, but a part of me is excited about the future promise. Not the movie, but knowing we get to spend more time with each other. That this won't end between us.

I can hear Jared's gritty laugh, and an image of his smiling face and dimples fills my mind. I pick up the sandwich and take a bite. "So..."

Silence drags out. "So..." Jared says, and I get the feeling he knows I'm curious about where he is. "I'm on my way home. My father sent me to pick up some paperwork for him," he finally says. "Like he doesn't have a million flunkies to do it for him."

"You don't need to explain yourself."

"I know, but I wanted to. I'll be home soon."

I nod but remember he can't see me. "Okay."

I hang up, and the overwhelming level of relief at the thought of Jared coming home hits me hard and fast. I take another bite of the sandwich mechanically and sip my soda as I wait for him to arrive home.

A knock at the door has me rising from the chair, but I don't get far as the door opens. My hands immediately go to my back as Jared's father steps in.

"Am I okay to enter?" he asks.

I want to point out that he already has, but I force a smile. "Of course, Mr—"

He holds up his index finger in warning.

"Athar," I finish.

He smiles. "Are you settling in okay?"

He glances around my room, and I find myself doing the same. "I have more than I could possibly ever need."

He nods his head. "I'm sure it's a huge difference for you. But it's a lifestyle that most of us can get used to."

An uncomfortable silence falls around the room, and somewhere in the deepest part of my mind, I know he isn't here to be friendly. The thought startles me, and I find my shoulders growing stiffer.

"Jared has been so kind." The words fall flat. I'm at a loss for what to say.

"Jared is reckless with money, but"—his fingers flutter in front of him—"that's not why I'm here."

Once again, I'm at a loss for words, but this time I don't reach for filler conversation.

Athar closes the door behind him. "Jared's mother has tried to contact him on more than one occasion."

"I didn't know." I don't like the idea of being trapped in a room with Athar. My own thoughts shock me.

"I know you didn't. Jared is private." Athar smiles kindly at me, but the smile carries an undercurrent that scrapes against my flesh.

"Is there something I can do?" I ask.

Athar exhales loudly. "Actually, there is. But you won't like it, Layla Masters."

I don't like him using my full name. I'm glancing at the door, hoping Jared arrives at any second. Athar follows my line of sight. "He's not coming. I sent him on an errand so we could have some time to talk."

The room grows tighter by the second.

"I think this will be easier if I show you." Athar walks to the door and opens it. "It won't take long."

He leaves and I stand for a moment, wondering what to do. Then my feet start to clear the space, and I'm following Jared's father out into the hall and up the stairs.

"Jared is a sweet kid with a very loving streak. But at times, that love turns obsessive." Athar glances at me. "It becomes unhealthy, and that triggers a darkness in him."

"A darkness?" I ask as we step up onto the landing where I was shot.

"Yes, Layla. A darkness." He stops walking and faces me. "Do you know what my son asked me when he came home today?"

I shake my head.

"He wanted to see my wrists. He was looking for scars because he believes I tried to kill myself when he was a kid."

Now I'm looking for scars on Athar's wrists.

Athar laughs, but it's not humorous as he lifts the sleeves of his jacket.

Embarrassment at being caught scorches my cheeks.

"No marks."

He's right, there are none, but I'm getting more and more confused by the second. "I'm sorry, Athar, but what does this have to do with me?"

He nods. "Let me show you." We continue walking as Athar fixes the sleeves of his jacket. He pauses outside the door that's always locked, the one I wondered what it held. Jared said it was storage.

"The key my son wears around his neck is for this room."

My heart roars, and when he opens the door, a part of me wants to turn and run. I'm not prepared for what I step into.

Athar flicks on the light, and I gasp as the blood roars and crashes against my eardrums.

My mind is taking in all the drawings, but I don't think I'm processing it. I'm cold as I step into the chaotic room.

"Jared is obsessed with you. I understand what you both went through as kids, but when he first came here, we couldn't stop this." His father moves his hand around the room.

There isn't an inch that isn't covered with my face. It's all too much. My legs buckle, and I reach out to steady myself.

Athar takes my arm. "I'm sorry, Layla. I didn't want to show you this. But I also need you to understand that Jared isn't well. A few years ago, Jared finally locked this room, and we witnessed him getting better." Athar stops talking.

My vision blurs. "Until I resurfaced," I finish.

He nods. "It's not just the drawings. He thinks I'm trying to get his money. He even accused me of sleeping with Alex, a friend of his."

Oh, God. It wasn't true about Alex? He humiliated her at school.

"I fear my son is in far more trouble than I thought."

I face Athar. "What do you mean?"

"I don't want to worry you."

My fingers sink into Athar's arm. "Please. If I can help..."

"He's been seen with Warren O'Reagan."

I nod. "That's his friend."

"Warren O'Reagan is in the Mafia, and my son has been transferring money to him. I don't know why. I was hoping you would."

This keeps getting worse by the second. "I don't know," I admit. I need to sit.

"If we don't find out what he's up to, he may end up in trouble." Athar's voice is filled with doom.

I release his arm.

"Ask him," I say. "Jared won't lie."

Athar looks at me like I'm stupid. "He might tell you, but he won't tell me. Right now, he thinks I'm the enemy." Athar glances around the room. "We need to keep this between us."

I can't deceive Jared. "I don't think I can do that."

"If you love him, you will." Athar holds out his arm. "We'd better go before he returns."

I leave the room in a daze.

I don't have a moment to recover before Athar starts to hurry. He's on his phone, and then in a flash, he puts it away. "He's home. I hope you can help me, Layla. I want to make sure my son is safe, and you are the person he trusts the most these days."

I nod as my heart pounds. Athar squeezes my shoulder before leaving me alone.

I'm on the second floor when Jared appears. Fear curls in my stomach. I try to shake it off, but I wonder how well I know him.

He pauses, and his smile falls from his face. "What's wrong?" He's looking past me.

"I was just remembering." The lie has me wrapping my arms around my waist.

Jared zones in on me.

"The shooting," I finish and continue down the stairs. My heart beats rapidly as I approach Jared.

He moves to the center of the steps, blocking me. "Are you sure that's all?"

"Is it not enough?" I ask and sniffle. I need space. I need to think.

"Jesus. Of course, Layla." He grips my forearms and gently rubs them. "You shouldn't be up here."

I drop my gaze to the floor. "I just think I need to lie down." I manage to wriggle out of his grasp. He's heavy on my heels, and I try not to run, but I don't know why I'm feeling panicked.

"Don't you want to watch the movie?" Jared asks from behind me.

I reach the ground floor. "Maybe later." I'm expecting him to leave me, but he follows me to my room. Kerry is at the door.

"Could you get me some Tylenol? I have a headache," I explain. Kerry departs to get me the tablets.

"What made you go up there?" Jared asks.

"I was bored." I shrug, but I can't make eye contact when I finally look up at him as he's watching me. God, I hate lying to him, but all I have to think about is that room. I swallow. "I won't be going back up there," I say.

"Chester will be behind bars soon, Layla. Right now, he's in custody. You have nothing to fear." Jared steps closer to me, and I try not to flinch. I know he would never hurt me.

"What about the gun? What if Chester tells them?" I ask. Why isn't that important anymore?

"I don't think anyone will believe him."

"You did before," I point out.

Jared takes another step closer. "Yes, but that was before he was caught with all our stolen paintings."

Did he even steal them?

My head hurts too much.

Kerry arrives back and pauses in the door. I hold out my hand for the tablets and water as she enters. "I'm going to lie down," I tell Kerry.

"Shall I draw the curtains?" she asks.

"Please, Kerry," I say as I drink down the painkillers. When I empty the glass, I look at Jared.

"I'll let you get some rest. If you need me, I'll just be next door." That didn't sound comforting. I nod and wait until he and Kerry are gone before locking the door. My vision wavers, and I cover my mouth with my hands as I start to cry.

CHAPTER TWENTY

LAYLA

THE MORNING COMES TOO soon. I'm tired, and my eyes feel grainy. I scrub my face, hoping to bring some life back into it. I look so much paler than I usually do. Getting dressed for class, I ignore the knock on my door and the soft words from Kerry. I tie my hair up in a high ponytail and try to center myself. Today at school, I'm going to ask Warren about Jared.

Every time I think of everything that Athar told me last night, my head spins. So, one thing at a time. I don't want Jared to get into trouble, so finding out what he and Warren are up to is what I'm going to focus on today.

The knock at my bedroom door again has me taking one final look around my room before I open it.

"Good morning," Kerry says. "Your breakfast is ready in the dining room with Master Jay and his father."

Breakfast with Jared and his father. My chest tightens as I leave the room and make my way to the dining room. My heart betrays me as I look at Jared. His dimples appear, and he stands when I enter.

"How are you feeling?" His concern has guilt haunting me.

"Better." I steady my breathing as I walk to the table.

Athar lowers his newspaper. "Good morning, Layla."

"Good morning, Athar."

Jared pulls out a chair for me beside him. A stack of pancakes and a steaming cup of tea are waiting for me. "Thank you." My heart pounds in my chest, and I don't reach for the knife and fork. Instead, I place my hands on my lap to make sure they're steady.

"Jared was telling me you had a bad headache. Pesky things, they are." Athar eats a spoonful of his cereal.

"I'm all better now," I say as I decide my hands are steady enough to pick up my knife and fork. I eat while Jared's presence beside me has my nerves jangled. He's watching me, and each time our gazes clash, I want to cave in and just ask him what's going on. I want to ask about the secret room. I want to ask why he's hiding so much from me. I look away before he can see the hurt in my eyes.

I keep my mouth full so I don't have to talk. Athar returns to reading his morning paper.

"We'd better get going," Jared says.

I'm so happy to be released from the table. I take a large gulp of tea, and when I look at Jared, he's grinning.

"That headache sure worked up an appetite."

I place my knife and fork on my plate and thank Athar for breakfast before following Jared to the garage. When we're about to get in the car, Jared stops, and with the keys in his hands, he tilts his head.

"You okay?" His brow draws down, and he rattles the keys.

"Yeah, I'm fine." I widen my eyes before forcing a smile and getting into the car.

Once again, I'm struggling to remain calm and silent with the knowledge I have. I don't think I'll make it to the end of the day. I keep stealing glances at Jared, and all I want to do is crack and confess to what I know.

But I stay strong, and when we reach the school, there's no time for chatting, as my class is about to start. Jared walks me to class, and he looks troubled. I hate that I've put that look on his face, but once I find out what he and Warren are up to, maybe I can help in some way.

Yeah, maybe.

***

Lunchtime arrives, and Jared is waiting for me outside my third class. It's warm, so everyone has opted to eat outside. Jared hands me a sandwich and a plastic disposable cup that's filled with tea. A girl I recognize from the beach party gives me a quick smile.

"Hi. I think I know you." She points at me.

"Yeah, I know you from Mark's beach party," I say. I notice that both Mark and Alex aren't sitting with us on the lawn. But Warren is. He's right beside the girl from the beach party. He's lying back on his elbows staring up at the sky. Jared's leg brushes against mine.

The girl smiles widely, and silver sparkles in her mouth from her tongue ring. "Sally." She gives a quick wave. "I vaguely remember you. I think I was drinking more than I was serving."

I smile at her. "Yeah, well, I didn't fare too well either, so..."

Sally smiles before looking back at Warren. She nudges his leg. Warren stops staring at the sky and focuses on Sally.

"What?" he asks.

"You're quiet." She's still smiling. Her tongue flicks out, and she licks her lips.

"Are you bored? I can give you something to keep you occupied." Warren sits forward, and Sally leans further into him.

"Maybe later." She kisses him before getting up and waving at me. "Nice meeting you again."

"You too, Sally," I say, realizing I never told her my name. She leaves, and I don't turn to Abby and Caroline, who sit a few feet away from us.

"Could you get me a soda?" I ask Jared sweetly. He doesn't question me, and I feel so bad when he presses a kiss to the crown of my head before getting up.

"Sure, no problem."

I nibble on the sandwich and look to make sure Jared is out of earshot. I know I don't have much time.

"You and Jared are close," I start, leaning toward Warren.

Warren sits up and both brows rise while a ghost of a smile plays on his lips.

"I know something is going on between the two of you," I continue as my heart races.

"If you're worried I'm going to steal him"—he raises both hands—"I can assure you, he's all yours." His grin holds humor.

My heart pounds heavier in my chest, and I glance toward the college before speaking to Warren.

"Is he in some sort of trouble?" I ask. "I love him, and I can't bear to think about anything happening to him."

Warren's smile leaves his face, and he moves closer. I'm holding my breath. He's going to tell me what's going on.

"Do you know who I am?" he starts.

"I don't care who you are. All I know is that something is going on, and I want to know what."

More amusement flashes across Warren's face. He looks over my shoulder. "I think you're asking the wrong person." He lies back, placing his hands under his head.

I'm confused until a can of soda appears in front of me. My gaze is drawn to the black ink band around Jared's wrists. How much did he hear?

I reach up and take the can. "Thank you," I whisper and keep my fingers tight around it. I don't open the can as Jared sits back down. Once I gather some courage, I finally look at him.

His gaze looks troubled, and when he glances at Warren, anger tightens his features.

"I was asking Warren about Sally," I lie.

Jared picks at the grass—well, tearing it is more accurate.

"She just seems so nice," I continue and I know I need to shut up.

Warren remains lying back, sunbathing, doing nothing to help me.

Jared's eyes appear almost black. "Aren't you going to drink your soda?" he asks.

I feel like I've been caught conspiring against him. My heart hurts, and I reach out and touch his hand. "Thank you for getting me this," I say.

His features soften slightly.

Ashley freezes when our gazes meet, and she's ready to run off. We haven't talked in a long time, and right now, I want to avoid all of Jared's questions, so I quickly get up.

"I'll be back in a minute." I walk quickly.

"Ashley," I call.

She doesn't stop, but I know she hears me. "Ashley." I catch up to her, and she finally stops walking. "You've been avoiding me."

"I've just had a lot on my mind," she says, but she doesn't have that normal Ashley attitude I've become accustomed to.

"Me too," I admit. How I wish I could talk to someone about all this.

"You look tired," Ashley says, and she reaches out and briefly touches my arm.

"Yeah, rough day yesterday."

Ashley raises a sharp eyebrow, encouraging me to continue. The action makes me smile. It's so like her.

"Honestly, I don't want to talk about it. So tell me all about Nicco. He's worth talking about."

Ashley smiles like the proud mother she is, and it's so nice just to chat with her. "Before we start talking about my adorable son"—her huge smile is contagious, and my lips rise—"I want to talk about the night you babysat."

Both our smiles fade. I nod, letting her continue.

Ashley looks nervous as she chews her lip. "So, you know Chester's Nicco's father."

I want to ask if that happened in a drunken moment, but I remain silent and find myself reaching up and touching my shoulder.

Guilt fills Ashley's gaze, and now I wonder if that's why she's been avoiding me.

"Chester and I have been off and on since we were kids. But it's over for good now, so his coming over the other night wasn't something I thought would happen. And finding out what he did to you..." She rubs the back of her neck, pain radiating from her gaze. "I didn't think he would be capable of such violence."

"It's fine, Ashley. Honestly. Chester is going to be locked away, and I think that's good for everyone."

Ashley frowns.

"Seriously, we are good. And it won't put me off babysitting Nicco," I say, and Ashley smiles at me.

I take a peek at where Jared was sitting with Warren, but he's no longer there. Neither is Warren. *Shit. I should have kept an eye on them.* Someone I don't want to see is making their way toward us.

"What's wrong?" Ashley asks, turning around before facing me again. "Oh, God. I heard what happened with her and Jared."

Alex's long hair is done in braids that fall down her back. She looks fabulous today, just as she always does, though I hate admitting that.

Her dark leather pants look like they're painted on, but she has the figure to wear them, and she paired them with a small green tank top, which showcases her ample bust. When she reaches us, she looks at me. "I was wondering if I could have a word."

Ashley tuts while rolling her eyes, and I sink my heels into the ground. "Don't start, Alex," Ashley tells her. "Seriously, Layla doesn't want to hear it."

Oh, that's harsh, and there is a moment of vulnerability on Alex's face, but she covers it up. A sharpness enters her features.

Alex doesn't respond to Ashley. "Fine, I'll say my piece here. I've been friends with Jay for years, and we've never had a bad word between us." Alex shakes out her shoulders. "Until you arrived. But I get it, and I'm willing to forgive you."

Forgive me? I want to ask for what. I don't need any grief from Alex. I'm scanning the area again for Jared and Warren, but they're nowhere in sight.

"I'm trying to fix things here, Layla. You could at least answer me."

"I don't know what you want, Alex." I finally focus on her. "I think you need to talk to Jared. Not me."

Alex doesn't like my answer, her lips pulling into a thin line, but she brushes her hair back off her shoulder. "I'll let him know we've patched things up."

I'm too distracted to really care. "Okay," I reply.

"Can we chat later?" I reach out and touch Ashley's arm.

She frowns but nods. "Yeah, of course."

I don't wait around but head to the parking lot. I call Jared's phone, but it goes to voicemail.

Shit.

CHAPTER TWENTY-ONE

LAYLA

THE REST OF THE day drags, and when classes end, Jared is nowhere in sight. William is waiting for me in the parking lot. Jared's car is gone.

Without a word, I climb into the back, and William closes the door behind me. On the way home, I call Evelyn after seeing a few missed calls from her.

"I've been trying to call you all day," she says, but her voice is light, telling me it isn't urgent.

"I left my phone on silent in my locker."

"Carl and I have been invited to a dinner for a charity. I just wanted to make sure you weren't coming home. I didn't want you to arrive and us not to be there."

I buckle my belt. "No, I've got loads of homework. Go enjoy yourself. You guys deserve it."

Evelyn's laughter is warm, trickling through the phone and settling on my shoulders. "I'm looking forward to it. So how is college?" Evelyn asks, and we chat easily as William drives me back to Jared's. The call ends on a nice note, and I'm smiling into the phone long after Evelyn hangs up.

The car stops, and it's my cue to remove my seat belt. I thank William as I enter the house. I stop by Jared's room, but he isn't there. I consider checking his drawers, but I won't invade his privacy like that.

No, instead you quiz his friends. The voice in my head mocks me as I make my way to my room.

I change into yoga pants and a gray T-shirt before letting my hair down. I massage my temples as I walk barefoot around the room. I've gone the wrong way about everything. Maybe I should have just asked Jared. I try to focus on my studies but find I'm checking my phone every ten minutes. The handle of my door rattles, and I climb off the bed as the door opens.

I take in a sharp breath.

"What happened?" The cut over Jared's eye looks pretty bad, and he has a bruised cheek to go with it. My heart thumps in my chest with worry.

Jared's lip twitches, and his cut eyebrow rises, only to drop back quickly. The pain is apparent.

I fold my arms across my chest as he closes the door behind him. He throws me a sidelong look and passes me before sitting down on my bed. I pivot so I'm facing him.

"Well, are you going to answer me?" I ask once a few more seconds have passed.

Jared starts to get up.

"Jared, sit down," I demand. His surprise at my tone lights up his eyes, but he does as I say. I'm a little surprised by my tone too, so I add, "Please" before getting a damp cloth from my bathroom. I return, bringing over one of the chairs and pulling it close to Jared. He accommodates me by spreading out his long legs on either side of my chair. I wasn't thinking about how intimate this position would be until now.

I dab the cut over his eye with the cloth. I have to pull my chair closer to him in order to reach. My heart picks up, and I flicker my gaze to Jared, who's observing me the whole time.

"This is going to sting," I tell him, and he nods, not speaking or taking his eyes off me. I can feel a slight tremor enter my hands. Guilt weighs heavily on my shoulders. Reaching out with my free hand, I hold his face. As I lean in, I can smell him, the uniqueness that is Jared. He closes his eyes just before I dab the cut. He doesn't flinch.

"Am I hurting you?" I ask, pausing. I just want to make sure.

"No." His one word sounds different, his tone deeper. He keeps his eyes closed as I wipe the cut.

"What happened?" I ask again, and he glances up at me. I bite my lip as I give a final dab, wishing he kept his eyes closed. The deep brown of his eyes makes me feel jittery. I lean away. The distance is minimal, but it's enough for me to get my bearings. Thankfully, the cut isn't deep.

"I got into a fight."

"Really? I would have never guessed." My sarcastic remark has his lips twitching. I don't find this funny. Jared reaches over and takes my free hand in his, entwining our fingers together. Looking down at our hands, I take in his damaged knuckles.

"Layla, I'm fine," Jared says, but my throat is tightening.

"Who did you fight with?" I ask. My suspicions are growing that it was Warren. I hope I'm wrong.

Jared's eyes darken, and he looks away. "Warren, and he deserved it," he finally says, looking back at me. I don't have to ask why. This is because I was talking to him.

"Stay still," I tell him while removing my hand from his. I need to get ointment for his cut. I leave him and find a first-aid kit in the bathroom. When I return, Jared hasn't moved. This time, he doesn't close his eyes. He watches me, and I nearly get ointment in his eye because he's making me so nervous. His breath brushes my neck, moving down the *V* of my T-shirt. Heat spreads up my neck and to my cheeks.

When I lean back, I focus on getting a Q-tip and antiseptic for his knuckles. My eyes dart to him as I get them ready. He's once again tracking every movement I make. When I sit back and take one of his large hands into my lap, he stretches out his fingers for me.

"It was a small fight."

I snort while dabbing the broken skin. He hisses, and I stop.

"Don't stop. It's fine," he says, so I continue. I don't want to hurt him, but if his cuts aren't cleaned, they could get infected.

"We're cool with each other," Jared continues.

I stop what I'm doing and narrow my eyes at him. "After you hit him?"

Jared's eyes darken once again. "Yes." He's serious, and I don't know what's worse: that he beat him up or that he still spoke to him after.

We're quiet as I finish his hands, and I realize that the bruise on his cheek isn't bad.

"Any more bruises or cuts?" I ask.

The corner of his mouth turns up. "Unfortunately not." His grin grows.

I don't smile. "What does that even mean?" *He wanted someone to hurt him?*

He quickly entwines our fingers together, making me look at him. "Layla, it was a joke." He dips his head, forcing me to look up at him.

"I'm not laughing, Jared."

"You're so gentle. I meant that I wish I had more wounds for you to clean."

The tips of my ears burn at the compliment. I don't feel I deserve it. "Oh. Okay then."

A small awkward laugh escapes my lips, and Jared's gaze flickers to them before returning to my eyes. He smiles with dimples and all.

My heart slows, along with my frantic thoughts. "You need to promise me no more fighting."

"It was only a bit of a scuffle. Seriously, stop worrying."

I raise a brow at him. *A scuffle?* I play with the Q-tip.

"So how bad does Warren look?" I ask as I wonder just how bad it is compared to Jared's face.

He gives me a guarded look. "Same as I do." The shrug he gives doesn't match his tone and look.

"You said no one ever gets a hit on you," I say and wish that it were still true. Seeing Jared injured hurts far worse than I ever expected it to.

"He's Warren O'Reagan. I had to let him get in a few hits."

"This isn't funny," I repeat and get up, only to have Jared grip my wrists.

His expression hardens. "What were you asking him?"

"About Sally," I lie and it falls flat.

He takes a deep breath, and I slowly lift my gaze until our eyes meet.

"Why are you lying to me?" Jared reaches out and touches my face. "You don't have to lie to me, Layla."

He's killing me. I swallow the lump in my throat and stare into his eyes. "I asked Warren what you two were up to." My pulse spikes as I speak.

His gaze is guarded.

"Are you in trouble?" I ask.

Jared stares at me as his hand leaves my face. "I'm only trying to help, Jared."

"You should have just asked me."

My chest burns with embarrassment. My mind is in a frenzy, trying to figure out how much I messed up.

His gaze bores into mine. "I would have told you." His serious tone has me nodding. I feel so far out of my depth right now. Our gazes are locked, and I think my chest is going to explode.

My lips part as I think of what I want to say.

A flash of uncertainty passes through his features.

"Then tell me, what dealings do you have with Warren O'Reagan?"

Jared reaches out and takes my hands before pulling me back into the chair I was previously sitting in. His legs clamp on either side of me, and I feel trapped. I think that's his intention.

He would never hurt me. I repeat the reminder in order to stay calm.

"First, tell me why you're asking." Jared shifts closer to the edge of the bed. If I leaned in slightly, our foreheads would touch. His hands trail along my arms until his fingers rest on my wrist. I glance down. His thumb strokes the tender flesh.

"Your heart is beating so fast, Layla."

I try to pull my hands back, and when Jared doesn't release them, I glare at him. "Let me go."

"Why? Are you afraid that I can tell when you're lying?"

I yank my hands again. "You think this is normal?"

He releases me before running his fingers through his hair.

"Your father said you made several large transactions to Warren O'Reagan and that you might be in a lot of trouble." My mouth keeps moving. "He said I'm the only person you trust."

Jared leans back, and the weight of my words pushes down on his wide shoulders. I hate the effect I'm having on him.

"You and my father were talking about me?" Hurt flashes in Jared's gaze.

"Yes. He showed me the room." I can't hold his stare. My gaze dances to the key that's hidden under his shirt. "He wanted me to help find out what you and Warren were up to."

"Anything else?" Jared growls.

"He said you're in contact with your mother and that you aren't..." I glance at Jared. The weight of a freight train slams into me. "Well," I finish.

I want to run and hide, but I keep my head high.

"Well?" Jared questions.

"He said you came home and checked his wrists for scars. He said that you believe he tried to take his life."

Jared exhales and rubs his mouth roughly. "So you had no headache last night? Just like you didn't have one the day you went dress shopping with Alex?"

I hate how disappointed he is. The urge to run again is choking, but I remain where I am.

"I think I avoid confrontation," I answer.

A ghost of a smile graces Jared's mouth. I don't know how he can smile right now. "I asked Warren what you two were talking about. He wouldn't tell me, but he said he liked you and thought you were very brave."

That sets me back.

"I told him you were the bravest person I know." Jared looks proud, then he tilts his head. "Then we got into a fight."

Jared reaches out but pauses before taking my hands. "You should have come to me, Layla."

"I'm sorry." I'm the one who takes Jared's hands in mine. I don't entwine our fingers, but I do something he did to me only moments ago. I run my middle and index finger along his wrist, feeling for his steady heartbeat.

His brow rises, and he grins. He doesn't stop me but holds still.

"Why did you send Warren money?" I ask.

"When Chester broke in and shot you, my father made it look like a burglary. He had William hide some of our artwork. Before we went to the Gardaí station, I hired Warren to put the artwork in Chester's house."

I hear the words, but I'm so focused on the steady beat of Jared's heart under my fingers that it's hard for them to register. "That's it? That's your dealings with him?"

"No." Jared leans closer. "You don't need to know all this, Layla."

"I beg to differ, Jared."

He nods. "I also needed him to flush Chester out so the Gardaí could capture him. I paid a PI, but he had no luck."

I want to smile. I want to rejoice that it's not that bad. Why did my mind go to drugs? I feared Jared getting involved with the Mafia.

"Is Warren actually Mafia?"

Jared grins. "Yes. He's the real deal."

I let that sink in. "Your father said you weren't well. What exactly did he mean?"

Jared's heart beats a bit faster under my fingers, yet he doesn't pull away.

"He thinks I'm obsessed with you." Jared pulls his wrists out of my fingers. "Maybe I am." He reaches up and cups my cheek. I lean into his touch. "The room was a place I could think of you, draw you. He didn't like it."

"I asked you about the key around your neck." I trail off. It doesn't really matter.

Jared surprises me when he pulls me onto his lap, my legs falling on either side of him. I wrap my arms around his neck. "I told you it was the key to my heart. I didn't lie."

My heart beats wildly.

"Any other questions?"

I focus on his lips and inhale the scent of him. I want to kiss him, but I also don't feel completely satisfied. He's giving me an answer for everything, but his gaze tells me there's so much more.

I lean my forehead against his. "Your mother. Tell me about her."

Jared tenses, and I know I've finally hit a sore spot.

"She put me in the foster system. What more can I say?"

I reach up and trace the outline of Jared's mouth. "I know this sounds horrible, but I'm glad she did. I'm glad I had you." I look at Jared. "I survived because of you, Jared, and I'm sorry for not being honest with you about your dad."

"He had no right going to you." Jared's tongue flicks out, and he licks my thumb.

"He was concerned." I start to defend Athar, but after speaking to Jared, I don't feel as unstable as his father made me feel.

"I'm not so sure," Jared says.

I lift my fingers from Jared's mouth and trace the outline of his brow. The one that isn't cut. "You might need stitches," I say.

He grins, raising the bruise on his cheek. "There is only one way to heal me."

I meet his gaze. "And what's that?"

"A kiss."

My lips touch his, and all the fear and anxiety that had built up seems to pour out of me, and I shuffle closer to Jared's solid body.

Jared's damaged hands roam across my ass, and when he pulls me heavily against him, his erection presses into my core. I push him back, and without a second's hesitation, Jared lies back and I straddle him. He makes me feel powerful with how he's looking at me. Awe and pleasure mix together in the depths of his eyes.

When I bend my head to press a kiss to his lips, his hands circle my wrists, and he drags them against his chest. "Don't ever lie to me again."

I swallow at the visible anger in his gaze.

I nod, but that acknowledgment doesn't seem like enough for Jared. "I won't."

He takes some pressure off my wrists before pulling me down on top of him. Our mouths smash together. His tongue enters my mouth, and I'm out of control as I give over to the need to have him.

I give a startled cry as his hands move under my shirt and wiggle their way under my bra. His fingers knead and squeeze my breasts, and I'm not ready for the flood of wetness that pools between my legs.

Jared moves quickly, and I find him on top of me while I stare up at him. His hands roam across my upper body. I do nothing but lie there and close my eyes. When his hands leave my skin, I open my eyes to find Jared removing his clothes. I'm kicking off my own shoes and socks as he walks naked and erect to the drawer. I've removed the rest of my clothes when he returns with a condom on.

My heart pounds as I think of the bath and how conflicting it felt. As Jared climbs back onto the bed, that conflicting feeling flees. He grips my legs and pulls my body hard against his. He's so much bigger than me, and his body smothers mine while he supports his upper body on his elbows. His flesh is warm against mine as his hands grip my thighs and direct my core to his cock. I hold my breath as I wait for the pain, but it doesn't come as Jared dips only the tip inside me. I close my eyes at the perfect feeling as he moves in slowly before pulling out.

"Look at me."

I do as Jared commands, and it's like an out-of-body experience as I stare into the dark abyss of his eyes. He moves with a perfect rhythm in and out of me, getting deeper when I'm stretched to take it. It's perfect, and I reach up to touch his bruised cheek.

"I love you."

Jared pauses before he turns his face and presses a kiss to the inside of my hand. "I love you too, Layla."

We stare into each other's eyes as Jared continues to move smoothly inside me. I can sense the build, but I don't want it to end.

I close my eyes but open them when Jared reminds me to keep looking at him.

His face tightens as he, too, closes in on what we both seek, and I stop holding back. My hands reach out and grip his shoulders as he speeds up inside me, and the thoughts of Jared coming inside me have me moving my hips along with him.

"Oh, fuck." He groans and I move my hips faster. He mimics my speed, and I know I can't hold on much longer.

Jared pumps harder. His features strain just as I reach a height before I come, and he joins me in ecstasy.

CHAPTER TWENTY-TWO

JARED

IT'S THE MORNING OF the court case. We only found out last night that it would be held today. My father's legal team had worked tirelessly to pull this off, and I'm impressed at the speed they did it in.

Layla stands in front of the mirror, fixing her black suit jacket. She's been doing the same thing for the last ten minutes. I loosen the collar of my shirt. I'll close the top two buttons before we leave the house.

"I wish you didn't have to do this, but my father has assured me the proceedings will be quick." I reach out and touch Layla's shoulder. She lays her hand on top of mine.

"I'm the only one who can identify him." Layla turns, and my hand falls away from her. "It will be quick, like ripping off a Band-Aid."

My father promised that Layla would be on the stand for only a few moments, and I have to believe him. I have no choice. But I'm still fuming with him for being a colossal asshole. Showing Layla the room and trying to turn her against me is something I'm not willing to forgive or forget.

Layla reaches up and touches my cut brow gently. "You're frowning." She forces her lips into a smile.

"I just want this over with." I'm antsy as I think of what will happen after the court case. Warren said the sniper would be in place. I'm assuming he'll be in one of the surrounding buildings. I consider calling it off, but as I stand here in front of Layla, I know I'm making the right decision. Chester deserves to die. The callousness with which he shot Layla point-blank can't go unpunished.

"Me too," Layla confesses.

Layla is quiet as we gather the last of our belongings. Carl and Evelyn are going to meet us at the courthouse. My father wants to drive us, but I don't want to be in his presence, so I drive myself and Layla to Navan Court-house. The courtyard we pull into doesn't have many cars. We're early. The traffic was light this morning, which I hadn't expected. Normally, it's busy with primary school commuters.

Evelyn and Carl are sitting in Carl's Mercedes across from us. Evelyn nods at me before she bends down and sits back up.

"You just have to identify him, and that's it." I grip Layla's hand. If I could do it for her, I would. I fucking hate that she has to take the stand.

Layla nods. "It will be over quickly."

"Like ripping off a Band-Aid." I repeat her earlier words and get a gen-uine smile out of her. Evelyn gets out of the car, and Carl follows behind. Layla lifts our joined hands and presses a kiss to mine before releasing it.

"I'm going to say hi to Evelyn and Carl." Layla speaks as she removes her seat belt and scoops her bag up off the floor.

"I'll be with you in a minute." I move the rearview mirror and button up my shirt, then I straighten my tie.

Layla gets out and closes the door. Carl waves at me, and I salute him before fixing the mirror and gathering my phone and keys. I'm tempted to text Warren to make sure everything is in place, but he hasn't let me down yet. Even after our fistfight, he said it changed nothing between us. He smiled and licked blood off his lip before declaring he hadn't enjoyed a fight like that in a while. I'm tempted to touch my brow, but I focus on getting out of the car, trusting that Warren will keep his word.

Walking around the hood, I lock the car before I join Layla, Evelyn, and Carl.

"That's a nasty cut you have," Evelyn says, eyeing my face. She wraps an arm around Layla's shoulder, pulling her closer. I'm beginning to think that Evelyn doesn't see how overprotective she is when it comes to Layla. But, I'm glad for it today. I think Layla needs a mother's touch.

"A friendly boxing match." I touch my cut brow like it doesn't sting like a bitch.

Evelyn raises both brows. "I wouldn't like to see if it was unfriendly."

Carl steps forward and holds out his hand. "Great seeing you again."

I take his hand and shake it. "You too, Carl." He's actually a decent man who is good to Layla.

My father arrives. He pulls his car next to mine and smiles at us all. I don't smile back, and Layla seems to stiffen. I wouldn't have been surprised if he arrived in his helicopter, but I'm also glad he didn't make a spectacle of himself.

"We should go in." Evelyn speaks to Layla.

"Go ahead. I'll be there in a minute," I say to Layla.

Layla is sandwiched between Carl and Evelyn as they walk to the courthouse. My father approaches, and I don't let him fall into step beside me.

"Where is your legal team?" I ask as he trails behind me.

"Inside." My father grips my arm, stopping me from walking. "We need to look united, son."

I step closer to my father. "Take your hand off me."

He does and uncertainty has his gaze darting around the space. I'm sure he's wondering who is watching.

"Stay out of my way," I warn as I turn and make my way into the courthouse. My father's legal team stands together with files pressed tightly against their chests. They laugh and chat. Their suits cost more than some of the cars in the parking lot. I approach them, and they fall silent.

"I want Layla's questioning kept short and to the point," I remind them. "If anyone drags it out…" I let my threat hang over their heads as I meet each of them with a hard gaze.

"They already know this, Jay." My father steps up beside me. "My men will do a great job."

"I don't care what happens. Just make sure Layla isn't on the stand long," I say again before pushing my hands into my trouser pockets. Having my hands trapped stops me from poking them in the chest to drive my words home.

"We will. We think we can get the maximum sentence of ten years."

My father looks proud as his solicitor speaks up. I don't care if Chester walks out of here a free man. As long as he leaves this courthouse to give the sniper his moment to take him out, that's all that matters to me. Nothing else.

Layla is inside the main courtroom. She's at the front, with Evelyn and Carl two seats behind. I join her. Opening my suit jacket, I sit down.

"How are you?" I ask.

Her complexion is stark white. I reach for her hand and squeeze her fingers before looking over my shoulder as my father's legal team makes their way to us.

"Water off a duck's back," Layla whispers under her breath.

A few more people are in the courtroom. I spot Ashley at the back. She's not looking around and is focused on a device in her hands. My father speaks to random people as he makes his way slowly to us. He thinks he's a local celebrity. A lull falls around the room as Chester arrives in chains. Two Gardaí escort him in. His solicitor isn't far behind.

I'm waiting for the judge to arrive so this can be quick. Judge Berwick has been paid handsomely to make this an open-and-shut case. He will rule in whatever way my father's legal team deems fit.

Judge Berwick arrives out onto his stage, and everyone rises. I release Layla's hand and look over at Chester. He's grinning at me, and rage has me facing forward before I do something fucking stupid like dashing across the room and plummeting my fist into his face. He thinks he'll get away with this.

It takes a lot of force to keep me facing forward. The case starts, and after the details are delivered from both sides, Layla is called to the stand. My father's legal team keeps to their word, and the questioning is over promptly. Layla points at Chester, declaring he is the one who shot her. She's released from the stand. She walks back to me, her gaze locked on the floor.

I don't care about all the rest of the jargon. The doctors, Inspector Reilly, and William all take the stand. Time ticks away painfully slow, and it still takes another twenty minutes before Chester's ruling is handed down. He gets the maximum sentence. Ten years.

He pulls against his handcuffs, the force rocking the two Gardaí on either side of him. It's my turn to grin as I take pleasure in Chester's outburst as he's dragged past me.

I take Layla's hand and wait a few minutes as Chester is pulled from the courtroom. "I'm so proud of you," I whisper into her ear.

"It's over." She smiles up at me. There's more relief on her face than anything else. Evelyn and Carl hug Layla.

"You did so well." Evelyn presses a kiss on Layla's forehead.

I'm trying to stay present with them, but I'm waiting for a gunshot. I'm waiting to hear the wails of panic. I'm waiting, but nothing happens. I wonder if the gun will have a silencer or if we'll hear the bang.

We continue leaving as more people arrive in the courtroom for the next case to be heard. The crowd is far larger than what we had. Outside, the air feels tight, or maybe it's me. Between the crowd and the cars, there's an undercurrent that has me tempted to look up at the surrounding buildings.

Chester is closing in on the Gardaí car. They open the door to the back of the squad car.

My chest tightens as I fear that Warren lied to me. Layla speaks to Evelyn about the ruling, and I'm half listening as I watch Chester. This can't be happening. Warren lied to me.

A scream starts off to our right, and on instinct, I reach for Layla and drag her behind me. She squeals in surprise, and I keep my hand clamped on her forearm as I watch through the gaps in the crowd.

A man with his face hooded approaches Chester, the gun in his hand raised. Both Gardaí extract stun guns. The edge of the crowd notices the gunman, and more people join in panicked screams. The tasers are useless weapons, but the Gardaí don't get to fire them, as the gunman empties a round of bullets into Chester's head. Each loud bang of the gun seems violent.

Pop. Pop. Pop.

The screams and chaos that ensue are numbing. I still have Layla behind me when running people slam into me. A burly gentleman crashes into my shoulder hard, and it's enough to make me move as I drag Layla for cover behind a car. She's not screaming or crying like most people. She's staring at me with a look of pure horror in her eyes.

"Stay down," I warn her as I stand up to see the gunman being taken to the ground by the power of two stun guns. He's disarmed and cuffed in seconds, but the screams continue as Chester's body is visible to everyone. Blood pools around the crown of his head, and my mind goes back to the moment with my father.

I can see him so clearly in my mind, blood pooling from his sliced wrists. I stood in it, confused and terrified, until my mother took me from the room.

"Where is she?" Evelyn's hysterical screech pulls me back to the present, back to the chaos of the moment.

"She's here." My voice is stable, and Evelyn's running toward me. She falls to her knees behind the car and grabs Layla, who's sitting quietly in a complete state of shock. Carl pulls off his tie, and as everyone starts to calm down, there's a void that's filled with soft cries and low whispers.

"Layla. Baby, talk to me." Evelyn brushes Layla's hair away from her face.

"I'm okay." Layla's words are breathy as she blinks as if she's just waking up.

Sirens wail in the distance, and I continue to watch everything unfold as more Gardaí cars and an ambulance arrive on site. I don't take my eyes off the damage I did. Not until they lift Chester onto a stretcher. A white sheet covers him, and it soaks up his blood as they place the stretcher in the back of the ambulance and close the doors.

The area is cordoned off with red-and-white tape. A white sheet is erected in seconds and forensics arrive. The gunman's weapon is collected, and I curse Warren, wondering what kind of donkey he hired to take out Chester. I didn't expect someone to shoot him point-blank in the head.

My attention is drawn to Layla as she finally stands. She still wears a dazed look as she looks around the space. "Ashley," Layla says with anguish twisting her features.

Layla moves from behind the car even against Evelyn's cries.

"The gunman is gone." Carl tries to reassure his wife, but I follow Layla as she goes to Ashley and pulls her into her arms. I'm a few feet away and decide I'm close enough to keep an eye on Layla.

My father steps up beside me, and I wish he didn't look so unaffected. "One less to feed in prison. I'm sure they can think of better ways to spend our tax money. Maybe fix some of the potholes on the Monalty road."

"Why are you speaking to me?" I face my father and open the top two buttons of my shirt before loosening my tie.

"Are you still sulking? I got him put away for ten years for you and Layla," he says with pride.

"I got him put down for good," I whisper.

My father's features grow slack. "You." His gaze travels to the pool of blood that's still partially visible under the white sheeting. "This is what you were doing with Warren O'Reagan."

My father looks around the courtyard. "How foolish of you. How foolish of you both." He walks away looking haunted.

I'm still left shocked that Chester was shot at such close range, and the shooter is now in custody. This could go very wrong. For Warren, maybe. I take a second look around the space before I approach Layla.

"I think we should go." I shove my hands into my pockets so I don't reach out and touch her.

"I'm not leaving her." Layla widens her gaze at me while she keeps an arm around a sobbing Ashley's shoulder.

"Do you have anyone to take you home?" I ask Ashley and try to keep my irritation at bay.

Ashley sniffles and looks up like it's the first time she's seen me. "I'll find a way."

"No. We'll drop you home." Layla smiles kindly at Ashley, who nods in acceptance.

I'm left with Ashley as Layla goes over to Carl and Evelyn. I'm expecting Ashley to change her mind and grab a taxi, but she stays close to me with her arms folded across her chest. Her head is bowed as she waits for Layla to return.

"Are you ready?" I ask Layla when she walks back to us.

"Yes. Let's go." Layla takes Ashley's arm, and they walk in front of me. We pass the spot where Chester was shot. Most people have given their statements about what happened, and just when I think we'll get away, we're stopped by two Gardaí.

I feel the color drain from my face even as I tell myself to remain calm.

CHAPTER TWENTY-THREE

JARED

THE GARDAÍ ASK US about what we saw. Ashley and Layla go first, and by the time it's my turn to answer questions, I'm more controlled. We're told they may have future questions for us, but for now, we can leave.

"I could get a taxi," Ashley says from the back seat. I think it's a great idea, but Layla doesn't.

"Don't be silly. We don't mind." Layla glances at Ashley in the rearview mirror.

"How are you? I mean..." Ashley trails off.

"I'm fine. I don't think anyone is walking away unaffected." Layla meets my gaze.

"Take the next left," Ashley says, her voice distant.

I can't wait to have her out of my car. My skin feels tight, and I reach up to unbutton my shirt but remember it's already opened.

With my foot pressed on the brake, I drop down a gear, indicate, and take the next left.

"He came out of nowhere," Ashley says, her shock still lingering.

"I just heard the bang." Layla wrings her hands in her lap.

I want to say that he deserved to die, but I don't think my words would be appreciated. A large stone archway greets us as I drive into the park.

"Number seven," Layla says. To think she babysat here, and Chester had belittled her, makes me want to get away from this place.

I pull up at the designated parking spot, but I don't kill the engine.

"Will you come in?" Ashley asks.

No. I'm waiting for Layla to say no.

"We would love to." Layla unbuckles her belt, and I'm hoping Ashley will give us a moment, but she sits in the back waiting for Layla.

I switch off the ignition and join them outside.

Layla nods her head at me and gives me a small smile. It softens the edges of her tense features. I relax and take her hand. If this is helping Layla, then I'll go in and make small talk.

Ashley goes ahead of us to the trailer, and we follow behind.

"Hi. How is my little man?" Ashley's voice has shed any earlier upset.

"He's good. You're back early." A young girl's voice floats out the door.

I release Layla's hand so she can go in first, and I follow her. The trailer is small and creaks as we all step in. A young girl, maybe fourteen, is sitting on the floor cross-legged, playing with a baby. I move around them and sit down on the settee.

"Jessie, you are the best," Ashley pays the young girl, who gets up shyly. She doesn't speak to me or Layla but says her goodbyes to Ashley and the baby.

"Isn't he adorable?" Layla whispers to me as she joins the baby on the floor.

Ashley takes off her jacket and folds it in front of her. She's watching Layla play with the baby on the floor.

"I had the most horrible thought."

Layla looks up at Ashley, who's sitting back on her heels as she waits for Ashley to continue.

"I'm glad he died when Nicco wasn't around. Imagine if he had been here and someone shot him. Or hurt Nicco." Tears roll down Ashley's face.

"I know it's a horrible thought, but…" She cries into her hands, and Layla gets up and hugs her.

Nicco plays with his small blocks on the floor, a smile on his chubby face. He has no idea that his father is dead, or that he will never see him again.

I reach up to open my shirt buttons, but my fingers touch the flesh of my neck. I want to ask if anyone else feels hot. Ashley keeps crying, and the baby keeps playing.

I stand, needing air. "I'm going outside."

Layla still holds Ashley but nods her head to me in acknowledgment.

The air outside takes away a small amount of the tightness in my chest, but not enough. I keep looking back at the door, hoping Layla will hurry up and come out.

I take out my phone, tempted to ring Warren and ask him what the fuck had happened. Shooting someone at point-blank range isn't what I paid for. The shooter is in custody, and he's hardly going to keep quiet. I rub my hands down my face when the door opens, and Layla sticks her head out. She glances to either side, and when she looks at me, she steps out.

"Can you come in for a second?"

No.

I step away from my car and jog to Layla. "What's wrong?"

"Ashley is throwing up," Layla opens the door wider. "Will you just stay with Nicco?"

I've never sat with a baby in my life. "Yeah."

"Thank you." Her gratitude runs deeply into her words. I reenter the trailer, and she disappears under an arch, leaving me with Nicco.

He's still playing, still giggling as he attempts to stack blocks. I sit down on the settee, and he notices me. His smile wobbles, and I can tell he's going to cry.

"It's okay." I slowly join him on the floor and stack the blocks for him. "I'm just stacking blocks. No need to cry." I speak while I dismantle the tower of blocks before building it up again. I look at Nicco, who's watching me.

I hold out a block to him. His chubby hands try to take it, but it tumbles to the floor, and he laughs.

"You like that?" I ask and stack two blocks together. I flick them and they tumble down, making Nicco laugh again.

"Okay, I see," I say as I repeat building a tower and knocking it down. My objective is to make Nicco laugh, and I achieve it every time. I'm smiling at him when Ashley and Layla step into the room.

Layla wears a look I've never seen before. I immediately get up.

"Thanks for everything." Ashley folds her arms as she speaks to Layla. "I think I'll go lie down."

"Are you sure you don't want us to stay with Nicco?"

As cute as the kid is, I don't want to be here any longer.

"No, I'll take him with me." Ashley uncrosses her arm and rubs Layla's arm. "I'll text later."

I head for the door and let them say their goodbyes. I hate the guilt that swirls inside me, dragging every justified thought with it. I took a father from a child.

I get into the car and watch Layla as she pulls the trailer door shut behind her. She can't seem to help putting people before herself. Layla gets into the car, and once her door is closed, she leans across and presses a kiss to my cheek. "Thank you for doing that for me."

What would she think if she knew I ordered the kill on Chester?

I start the car. "No problem."

I pull out of the trailer park.

"She's had so much happen lately. My heart breaks for her," Layla says.

"You've had a lot happen to you, too," I remind her.

"I know. But I can't help but wonder if you're responsible."

I tighten my hold on the steering wheel as my heart pounds in my chest. "What do you mean?" I glance at Layla.

She's pissed; her small features tighten. There is no fucking way she could know that I got Chester shot, and even so, I don't think she would be pissed. I think she would be demanding for me to drop her back to Evelyn and Carl's.

"Lucas and Sam. They lost their scholarships. Please, Jared, tell me that wasn't you."

My fingers relax on the steering wheel.

"Oh my God. It was," Layla declares. "How could you?"

"Very easily, actually," I mumble and regret it as Layla turns in her seat, only to have the seat belt restrict her.

"Calm down," I say, not wanting her to hurt herself.

"I can't believe you could do such a thing."

"You're in shock and have had a tough day—"

Layla cuts off my words. "No, Jared. What you did to those boys is wrong. That's all they had. They can't afford to educate themselves." Disgust is evident in Layla's words.

I slow down as we reach the gates to my home. They open slowly.

"I promised Evelyn I'd ring her when I get back to your house to let her know I'm safe," Layla explains as she takes her phone out of her bag.

"I'll have Lucas and Sam reinstated," I say while I put the car into gear and drive up toward the house.

"Promise me." Layla's voice is soft.

I pull into the garage and turn off the engine before facing Layla. "I promise you."

She presses a kiss to my cheek. "Thank you."

I nod. "Ring Evelyn. I'll give you a minute," I say, getting out of the car.

I enter the empty kitchen. I'm not sure who I was expecting to see, but it seems emptier than normal. I take out my phone and text Warren.

We need to talk.

I can't stop picturing Nicco sitting on the floor of the trailer, smiling and stacking blocks. Why did I have to see him? Was it to make me feel like I had actually done something wrong? I hate how much it's eating me up.

"Evelyn is going to lie down," Layla says as she enters the kitchen. "I think today took a lot out of everyone." She puts her handbag on the counter and shakes her head. "Can you believe he's dead? That someone just walked right up to him and shot him?"

Layla's brows pull down, and she continues to shake her head. "I know what I saw, but it's so hard to accept."

"I know." I walk to Layla, and she folds in my arms.

"Why are people so evil?" Layla asks.

"I don't know," I respond as my phone vibrates in my pocket. I slip it out as I hold Layla and read the content over her head. It's Warren.

Yeah, I heard. Meet you at KC?

"I have to leave for an hour."

Layla leaves my arms and looks up at me. "Why?"

I reach out and touch her face. "I have to go to the school to speak to the dean."

"For Lucas and Sam?" A ghost of a smile starts on her face.

"Yes. I'll make it right," I promise her, and it's worth it as she smiles. "I won't be long." I press another kiss to her forehead, then I text Warren back, letting him know I'm on my way.

***

The level of guilt that churns in my system has me pushing my foot to the floor as I speed down the road. Killing Chester didn't give me the happiness I thought it would. I'm left with nothing but regret and guilt for taking a child's father from him. Maybe because I grew up without mine. Bert was the closest thing I had as a father, and he was a piss-poor excuse for one. I'm starting to realize that killing Bert won't give me any happiness, either.

I'm trying to stay in control, even as my system flashes warnings telling me that I'm overwhelmed. I take a sharp right onto the college grounds and pull up beside Warren. I unlock the passenger door, and he climbs in. He's wearing a shiner. I accept the fist bump.

I don't say anything but wait for him to start.

"No matter what, you aren't getting a refund." Warren lights up a cigarette. "Not that you need it."

"He walked up to Chester and shot him in the fucking face," I blurt out.

"I heard it was some show, and you had a front-row seat." Warren rolls down the window and flicks out his ashes.

"Are you fucking serious?" I'm trying to keep the anger at bay. Why am I feeling like this?

"That wasn't my guy, Jay," Warren says. "My sniper was on the roof and never got to take the shot. But he did show up for the job, so no refunds."

I slump back in the seat. "I didn't kill Chester," I say to the roof of the car.

"I heard it was a revenge killing. The guy who did it got paid well, and he won't be in prison for long. He's part of a rival gang." Warren claps me on the arm, startling me. "You didn't even have to hire anyone in the end."

He has no idea what all this means to me. "Yeah," I answer.

He inhales a few drags of his cigarette before throwing it out the window, then he laughs. "You must think we're amateurs to shoot someone at close range."

I'm shaking my head, but my mind has left this conversation. I didn't kill Chester. It wasn't my fault. "I thought it odd," I say offhandedly.

"How is Layla?" Warren asks.

That gets my fucking attention, and when I look at him, he grins. "I'm not going to touch your woman."

"I'd hate to have to really beat you up," I say. "You know I held back." The truth tumbles from my mouth. Maybe realizing I didn't kill Chester is giving me some courage.

"I know. But next time, don't." Warren holds out his fist.

"Next time?" I question.

He sneers while tapping my fist with his. "We're good?" he asks.

"Yeah, we're good."

He gets out of the car, and I'm ready to leave but remember my promise to Layla. It doesn't take long with the dean, and the boys will be reinstated by the end of the day. I'm feeling lighter with each step I take to my car, only to stop halfway down the path.

What the actual fuck?

My mother is waiting by my car again.

"I'm not in the mood, Maura," I say as I start walking again.

"I was hoping I could show you something," she says.

"Keep hoping and wishing, because I've somewhere to be." I unlock my car.

"Please. Just give me a lift, and I'll leave you alone."

Maybe it's the day's events that have me considering it. "A lift to where?"

"If I told you, you wouldn't believe me."

Fuck it.

"No. You're pissing me off again." I get into the car, done with her shit.

"To the graveyard." She knocks on the passenger side. "I promise, you do this and I'll leave you alone."

She's holding my gaze. The graveyard is only on the outskirts of town. I want to ask her who's buried there, but instead, I pop the lock and she quickly climbs in.

"Thank you so much," she says.

"You'll leave me alone after this? No more showing up at my home or school?"

She nods. "Yes."

I start the car and leave the school grounds while texting Layla, telling her I'll be home in a few minutes. I don't like her being alone.

"You shouldn't be on the phone while driving," Maura says.

"I never said you could talk." I put my phone away.

"The memory you had as a boy of your father in the bathroom? That was real."

I narrow my eyes at Maura. "Fucking stop. I checked his wrists. There isn't a blemish on them. So stop fucking lying. Now shut up, or I'll drop you off on the side of the road." My threat should have her going silent, but it doesn't.

"He's not your father. He's your uncle."

I jam on the breaks. "Get out."

"Listen to me. He's your uncle. Your father had an identical twin. And when your father took his life, your uncle took his place."

I'm sitting in my car listening to this crackpot. I exhale loudly and try to remain calm. "Get out." I speak low.

"He did it for the money, Jared. But he didn't know that when either I or your father died, everything went to you. Nothing can be transferred until you're twenty-two. That's what he'll ask you to sign in a week. It's not so you can inherit everything. It's so you will transfer everything back to him. Your father made it in his will. We both did."

My heart roars in my ears, and I don't know what to make of my mother's words. "Why did you put me in the foster system?" I ask.

"To hide you. To keep you safe from him. I feared he might kill you."

I face my mother. "Why not take me with you?"

"We had to separate." My mother reaches for my hand. "You have no idea what he is capable of."

"I have no idea what you're capable of. Right now, Maura, this sounds like a crock of shit." I pretend that her words have no effect on me, but sadly, they do.

"I can show you your father's grave."

"Get out of my car." I rub my temples like I can dispel the confusion her words are causing.

"William knows the truth. He's always looked out for you."

"If he's my uncle, how could he pose as my father? What about social security?" I'm asking questions, but I really feel that money can get you anything.

"I don't know how he convinced the child protective services to hand you over. I just know he did."

She's pleading with her eyes, and I want to believe her, but it's too farfetched. Yet, my gut won't settle. Nothing in me will settle, and I know I won't either until I have the truth.

"This is my final time telling you this, Maura. Get out of my car."

Tears stream down her face, and she finally unbuckles her belt. "Just talk to William" are her departing words as she gets out of the car.

CHAPTER TWENTY-FOUR

LAYLA

JARED TEXTED SAYING HE would be home in a few minutes. That was two hours ago. I've changed out of my court clothes and swapped them for yoga pants and an oversized green sweater. After slipping on my tennis shoes, I leave my room and knock on Jared's bedroom door before entering. No one is here. His bed is made; his room immaculate.

I leave and make my way through the large hallway. Kerry smiles at me as she passes. "Anything I can do for you?"

"Have you seen Jared?" I ask.

Her smile slowly fades. "No. Shall I look for him?"

I wave her off. "No, thanks. That's okay, Kerry."

The kitchen is empty, and I check the garage. I'm surprised when I spot the BMW that Jared has been driving since his own car is at the garage for repair. I close the garage door and return to the house. I find my feet moving toward the staircase, but I pause on the first step. If he is up there, maybe I should give him some space.

I take my foot off the step and walk down the opposite hall. I haven't explored this side of the house. The doors that line either side of the wall are numerous.

"What do you want?" Jared's words are spoken harshly—a sharpness I'm sure would be visible on his face if I could see him.

I step closer to the half-open door.

"Just a minute of your time, son." Athar says the word 'son' as if he's leaning into it. I don't know him very well, but I can imagine his lips tightening around the word.

I push the door open more and see Jared's back is to me. His hands hang on either side of him, and his shoulders seem tense. Athar has his back to me, too, so I feel safe in my position as I watch them. I should announce that I'm here, but something holds me back.

"I have some paperwork I thought we could sign today, as my solicitor sent it over before the court case."

Jared snorts, his hands rolling into fists. "Is this for my inheritance?"

"Yes." Athar turns and sees me. His gaze hardens, and I try to move out of his line of sight, but it's too late. Jared turns, and I'm ready to explain why I'm standing here listening.

"Layla, come on in."

I take a hesitant step into the room. "I was worried about you," I say.

It's awkward as I walk across the floor to Jared.

"Don't you think it best to let Layla rest while we talk business?" Athar says as he walks to a large desk that dominates the space.

I'm ready to run from the room. I'd gladly give them space, but Jared shakes his head.

"Actually, I'd like Layla here."

Athar narrows his eyes briefly before relaxing back into his seat. "Very well." He opens a folder on his desk and takes out some paperwork. "I'm sure Layla will want to celebrate also."

Jared steps toward his father's desk.

"Celebrate what?" I ask.

"Why, Jared's inheritance."

I grow uncomfortable. "Only if Jared wants me here," I say and try not to pull at my sweater.

"I do." Jared speaks with his back to me as he picks up the paperwork. "If you had asked me to sign this a few hours ago, I would have been asking for a pen. But…" Jared places the paperwork on the desk. "I don't think I'm ready for the business."

"Nonsense. You are ready. You're my son." Athar stands with his shoulders back, and I get that feeling like I'm intruding on a tender moment. I glance away and take in the rows of bookshelves that are mounted to the wall.

Jared exhales loudly. "No, I'm not."

I take a peek as Jared slides the paperwork back to his father. Athar's lips form an angry, thin line, and color soaks into his cheeks.

"I want you to have it, son. Sign today, sign tomorrow. It won't matter. It will be yours. You don't have to start work straight away. I understand there will be a transition period."

"What if it's already mine?" Jared asks and his words are low, deadly.

Athar flinches, and I startle as the door opens behind me. William arrives carrying a file in his hand. Or maybe it's a large envelope.

"What do you want, William?" Athar bites. I've never heard him raise his voice before.

I wrap my arms around my waist. I want Jared to just sign the papers so we can leave.

"I was a loyal servant of Brian's," William starts. "He was a good man. I knew one day the truth would come out, and I swore to Maura that I would be here to bring the secrets into the light."

"What are you spouting on about?" Athar stands up from his chair, but he's visibly shaken. I have no idea what's going on.

"There was so much I couldn't piece together. Like the memory of my father dying in the bathroom."

"Not this again." Athar moves around the desk.

"You will listen to me." Jared's roar has my heart stalling in my chest. I think even the air stills with fear.

Athar pauses, the color draining from his face.

"My father is dead. And you are an imposter." Jared's words leave me reeling.

"Prove it." Athar stands straight, with his shoulders back.

William steps closer and hands Jared a file.

"At school, one of my friends asked Warren O'Reagan about his uncle's once owning the castle." Jared paces as he speaks. "I mean, I knew it was ours, so when Warren said they still owned it, I was surprised."

Jared stops moving as he faces his father. "I asked Warren about it today, and he told me that the O'Reagan's forged documents for you." Jared fires the file at Athar. It hits his chest, and pages flutter to the floor.

Anger flushes Athar's skin, and I take a step back.

"You didn't care about what Warren and I were up to. You were worried I might get close enough for him to tell me all about your seedy dealings." Jared takes a step toward Athar with his fists tightened.

"What about you? You had Chester shot. How will people feel when they know the lunatic you are?" Athar looks at me. "How will Layla feel?"

I take another step back, and I'm shaking my head. Jared turns, and his gaze is so full of anger that it halts my steps.

"No. You wouldn't do that to Chester." I'm praying that this isn't true.

Jared deflates immediately. "No, I didn't."

My head spins as Jared looks back to his father. "What happened to Chester was from a rival gang."

"Lies," Athar shouts and he's a drowning man.

Jared steps around Athar and picks up the documents that Athar wanted him to sign only moments ago. "What are these papers for?"

Athar doesn't answer. I'm holding my breath, and when Jared launches himself at Athar, I'm frozen as his fist slams into his father's face. William rushes forward to stop Jared, but Jared swings and sends William sailing back onto the ground.

I race to William to help him up. "Are you okay?" I ask.

William nods his head. I turn to Jared, who has Athar on the ground, and his fist smashes into Athar's face.

"Did you kill my father?" Jared roars, but even if Athar wanted to answer, Jared doesn't give him the opportunity.

"Stop it." I get up off the floor and run to Jared. "Stop it."

His violence pours out of him, and this isn't the boy I remember. My heart seems to shatter as I watch Jared lose himself in the rage that is powering him. I saw it with Kieran, and now I see it again with Jared and his father. I grip Jared's arm.

"What's going on? This isn't you. You're not violent." He doesn't look at me but stares down at Athar, who is bleeding from his mouth and nose.

"He's not my father."

I'm starting to see that nothing is what it seemed here. "I believe you."

His head whips up, a muscle tightening in his jaw.

"But the rage, it's making you into something you're not," I say.

He snorts with anger and releases Athar, who groans on the floor. "You have no idea."

Snakes coil in my stomach at his words. The silence that follows is deafening.

"What aren't you telling me?" I finally say it out loud and can feel the full extent of Jared's stare on me. But I can't look away from him, and fear has me trying to claw my words back. I'm going to lose him. He looks like a man possessed as he pulls at his shirt. His hands touch his neck, and I reach out to him. "What's happening?"

"Nothing."

His one word has tears running down my face.

Everything.

I cling to the moment as my heart bounces around in my chest.

"You're lying." My words have him jumping off the floor.

"I can't fucking breathe." Jared walks to William. "Don't let him out of your sight. The Gardaí are on their way," Jared tells William, who nods.

Before I can react, Jared starts to run from the room. He never runs or hides from me. My legs propel me forward, and I'm chasing after Jared.

"Talk to me!" I scream at him as he runs for the front door. He glances at me over his shoulder, and I've never seen such fear in someone's eyes. Jared pauses as he opens the front door to the onslaught of rain. I'm waiting for him to stop, but he runs out into the pounding rain. I don't pause and ignore the rain.

"What aren't you telling me?" I scream at his back. Jared freezes.

"What aren't you telling me?" I demand again. Jared stands still, breathing heavily in the rain. Something about his stance reminds me of a cornered animal.

"Today, I feel like I don't even know you."

Rain falls heavier; each drop feels so full and cold as I wait for Jared to answer.

"You know me."

I'm shaking my head as he speaks. "Not all of you. Not that person in there. You are so angry. Jesus. I've seen it before with Kieran." I turn away, my clothes soaked right through.

I don't fully understand what took place in his home with Athar, but something made me feel this isn't really about that. I think I've been avoiding the truth for a long time.

"Fine. I'll tell you," Jared whispers.

I hear him and my soul shivers. I'm finally going to find out.

CHAPTER TWENTY-FIVE

LAYLA

Jared's chest rises and falls rapidly. "He's not my father."

I'm shaking my head. "You know what I'm asking."

I wasn't asking about Athar or anything else. I'm finally asking why Jared, who was always a peacekeeper while we were growing up, has turned into someone who is so violent. I recognize pain, and maybe I was too scared of the answer before. Maybe I'm at a breaking point with everything that has happened. Maybe I'm tired of turning a blind eye.

"I used to go into your room at night to steal your sweater," I say. "Why was Bert leaving your room?" It was a memory from when I was a child, yet the image of Bert coming out of Jared's bedroom always haunted me. Tears mix with rain, and I want to scream into the air.

"Bert hurt me too." The whispered words have me moving closer to Jared, in case I miss one word. He's staring at the ground, his fists clenched. I stop moving when he looks up at me. I've often heard the phrase that there's a storm brewing in someone's eyes, but I never understood the meaning until right now, looking at Jared.

His irises dilate, consuming the brown and turning them black. Anger flashes, then a sparkle of gold splashes across them. The brown lightens until all the color is gone, and only sadness, hurt, and pain are left. Some part of me knows he's been hurt in a way no one ever should be.

My eyes burn as I stare at Jared. Swallowing, I swipe at droplets of rain on my cheek. Jared's hair darkens as the rain continues to pelt down on top of us.

"Like he hurt me?" I ask. The tension that enters Jared's frame is at a snapping point, and some part of me wants him to snap. I want him to crumble and let it all out.

His jaw clenches as he works a muscle in his jaw. He speaks through his teeth. Each word is ground out. "No, not like he hurt you, Layla."

I nod, not sure why I am. He looks away again, his shoulders slumping, crumbling, and I take another step toward him. I'm terrified of what he might say but terrified that he won't say anything either.

The rain falls with more weight, and the volume soaks both of us, but Jared doesn't seem to notice. He's stuck in his own turmoil. I take a final step and stand in front of him.

"Jared."

His head springs up. His eyes are haunted by whatever memory he's having. Something tells me not to touch him, and I listen to the voice.

"Nobody knew." Jared speaks with furrowed brows. "I made sure no one knew."

I'm nodding again, swallowing my fear. My stomach has been twisting and diving since I chased after him. From the moment he had paused at the front door, I felt the dread dripping down my spine. I shiver, not only from the rain but also from the look on Jared's face. The pain inside me is like nothing I've ever known.

"What did he do?" I ask, and my heart plummets.

He doesn't answer me. "Did he touch you?" I whisper, wanting him to tell me that I'm crazy. That I'm wrong.

But he nods, not looking at me.

The ground shifts under my feet, and Jared reaches out, grabbing me around the waist, stopping me from hitting the ground. Pain roars through me, blocking out sound briefly before it comes crashing back.

"Now you know all of me," he says with an emptiness in his voice.

That is more frightening than anything I've ever heard before. My mind races with so many questions. Like, why didn't he tell someone? How long did it go on? Oh God, how far did it go?

I want to bawl for him, for Jared. I want to kill Bert. I hated him before, but now, thinking of what he did to Jared...

The things I wanted to do to him before now seem like nothing. Knowing what I know now, I want him to suffer. I feel sick. My heart pounds at the injustice, but I know Jared and right now, looking at him, he needs me. He still holds me, his grip solid, and I reach up, taking his face in my hands.

"I love you, Jared. All. Of. You." My lips touch his cold and stiff ones, but after a moment, he kisses me back. The agony of knowing he's hurting feels so real, and I want a morphine drip to stop the pain. How must he feel?

Blue and red lights catch droplets of rain before they expand, and the world is blanketed in the lights of the Gardaí car that makes its way up the driveway.

The front door is still open, and William is standing, watching us, and I wonder how much he heard.

"Jay McGivney?" A Ban-Gardaí walks toward us. Holding her hat down over her head like it might keep her dry. Her waterproof clothes shine with the falling rain.

I'm not sure how aware Jared is of his surroundings.

"The man you want is in the house," William calls from the front door.

The second Gardaí joins the Ban-Gardaí, and they follow William inside.

They all disappear through the curtain of rain. I entwine my fingers with Jared's, but he pulls against me.

"What are you doing?" he asks, and I stop tugging.

"Please, trust me?" I say.

He nods and I kiss him softly on the lips before resuming our walk toward the house. William left the front door open. Commotion down the hall has Jared pulling his hand out of mine.

"This is ludicrous," Athar yells.

"Athar McGivney, you're being arrested for identity theft, fraud offenses, and embezzlement. You are not obliged to say anything unless you wish to do so, but whatever you say will be taken down in writing and may be given in evidence."

Handcuffs are placed around Athar's wrists, and it's all starting to sink in that this man isn't Jared's father. Athar pulls against his cuffs as he approaches us, and I find myself stepping in front of Jared.

"You won't get away with this," he snarls.

"All they have to do is a blood test. Everyone will know the truth of who you are." Jared's words are flat.

Athar is taken from the house by the Ban-Gardaí. The Gardaí stops in front of us.

"How long have you been standing out in the rain? You're soaked." The Gardaí looks from me to Jared. When I glance back at Jared, he looks so haunted and dazed. I don't want any more questions fired at him. He's been through enough.

"I lost my purse. We were looking for it," I say. The lights bounce around the foyer, and I just want the Gardaí to leave.

Maybe he senses it as he looks at Jared. "We'll be in touch." He leaves and William closes the door behind him.

The cold settles fast and hard.

"I'll get you some towels," William says while walking away, and it gives me a moment with Jared.

He stuffs his hands into the pockets of his jeans as water drips off him.

William returns, handing me a stack of towels.

"Thank you, William." I hold them to my chest.

"If you need anything else…" William doesn't finish his sentence but takes a worrying glance at Jared before leaving us alone.

"I think you should go home." Some emotion has entered Jared's words.

I'm shaking my head, already expecting this from him. "I need you." I allow the pain to enter my voice. It works like I knew it would, and I don't feel guilty.

Jared reaches out, and I hand him a towel. He starts to dry himself off.

"I should go to the Gardaí station." Jared speaks as he pulls off his shirt.

I'm shaking my head as I grab my hair and pat it between the towels. "Jared, you can face all that tomorrow. Tonight, I need you."

We dry in silence, and when Jared reaches for me, I grip his hand while my emotions skyrocket. It's like all his pain is transferred in that small touch. We walk to his room, and with each step, his features continue to tighten.

Once we're in his room, Jared strips off the rest of his clothes. He's standing still, holding the key in his hand. He's lost in his thoughts, and pain tears through me as tears roll down his face. I'm frozen, broken, as my chest threatens to cave in. Jared takes the key from around his neck and places it on the top of the chest of drawers. He half looks at me before going to his walk-in wardrobe. With him out of sight, my heart palpitates, and I take quick, deep breaths.

Don't cry, Layla. Don't cry, I chant in my head. Yet tears escape, and I wipe them away quickly as Jared returns dressed in sweatpants and a T-shirt. He hands me sweatpants and a T-shirt as well.

"Thank you." I take them and strip off my wet clothes. I don't bother with the sweatpants but change into the oversized top that floats to my knees. I towel-dry my hair and comb it out with my fingers as Jared walks around his room, scrubbing his face every few minutes. He won't look at me, and when I catch glimpses, his eyes are red and puffy.

I wipe my own tears as I climb up onto his bed. "Get in," I tell him, pulling the blankets back.

Jared stuffs his hands into his pockets. He seems to be considering it, and my heart pounds. I don't want him to be alone tonight, but it's there in his eyes that he wants to leave or send me away.

"Please," I whisper.

His brows furrow. I win. He walks to the bed and lies down beside me. I sit beside him while pulling the blankets up to his knees.

"I remember the first time I told Evelyn about what happened to me. It was the most terrifying thing ever. When she came back the next day, I wanted her to leave. I wanted to take my words back because by saying it, it became real." I touch Jared's face. "But it healed a part of me. It was a small part, but it was a start."

Jared's eyes glisten, and a silent tear runs down the side of his face, and I die a little inside but remain still.

"I won't run from you, Layla. I was afraid you might run from me." His honest words stab at me, and my eyes and throat burn. My body has never felt so taut, so hell-bent on snapping. All the tension is at the breaking point.

"I love you. I'm here for the good and bad. Always." I kiss him gently on the lips before lying down beside him.

Deep circles darken under his haunted eyes, and I rub his cheek, letting my hand trail into his hair. The exhaustion has his eyelashes touching his cheeks. I caress his hair until his breathing evens out, and I know he's asleep.

***

I barely sleep, and every time Jared moves, I wake up, afraid he'll leave. But he sleeps the whole night through. His breathing isn't as even now, telling me he's waking up. I pull my arms tight against my body, and he stares at me. A smile spreads across his face, his arm reaching out until he captures me around the waist. A small squeal escapes my lips as he pulls me to him and buries his head in the crook of my neck.

"I could smell you," he says, his warm breath causing goose bumps to break out along my skin. It isn't the reception I expected, but for just this moment, I won't complain. His nibbles on my neck have me choking a laugh.

"Good morning." Brown eyes still half-closed with sleep stare at me as a lazy smile hangs from his lips. His tongue flicks out to moisten them.

"Good morning." I lean in and kiss him, his eyes widening before closing as he deepens the kiss.

A knock on the bedroom door has us breaking apart. Jared wakes up fully and gets out of bed. The heaviness of last night returns with each step he takes. The transformation has his shoulders tensing.

"Good morning, William." As Jared speaks, he opens the door fully. Jared runs his hands through his hair.

"Master Jay. Breakfast is ready."

Jared nods. "We will be there in a moment." Jared doesn't close the door, and when William's gaze lands on me, I give him a half smile. He bows his head before leaving. Jared returns to the edge of the bed and reaches across to entwine our fingers together. I'm beginning to think he isn't aware of what he's doing. He just constantly needs to be touching me. I'm not complaining, but it's distracting.

"How did you sleep?" he asks.

"Good," I reply.

Jared rubs his jaw. "You look tired."

"So do you." I shuffle closer to him. "We need to talk about last night."

Jared releases my hand while running his fingers through his hair. "Not now. I need to eat first." He stands, not looking at me. I knew it would be a sensitive topic, but I don't want it ignored and buried again.

"I'm going to get dressed," I say to Jared, understanding that now isn't the time.

Jared goes to his walk-in wardrobe to get dressed, and I pause, tempted to follow him in there and make him face what he told me last night. But, I need to have patience. I leave him and go to my room. Kerry is standing outside the door.

"You can take the day off, Kerry," I say, knowing that the entire staff isn't necessary.

She folds her hands in front of her. "Are you sure?"

"Positive, and the same for Andrea and Amanda."

Kerry bows her head before leaving, and I dress mechanically, hating not being with Jared. I don't want him to flee. I dress in record time and make my way to the dining room. Jared is already there, and I sit across from him, where William places a full Irish breakfast in front of me.

"Thank you, William," I say.

"You are very welcome."

"I have to go to the Gardaí station this morning." Jared's plate is still full. He holds the knife and fork and pushes a sausage on his plate.

"After you eat," I say.

He forces a smile, but it's a shadow of what I'm used to.

"William will drive you to Evelyn and Carl's. You should spend some time with them today."

I'm already shaking my head. William hasn't left, but I don't hold back. "No, I'll wait here for you, Jared."

"I'll be gone most of the day, Layla. I have to go to the Gardaí and my solicitor." Jared's features soften. "I'll pick you up later. Please do this for me."

"Okay." I give in, knowing staying here all day isn't something I want to do, and I also know Jared needs to get his affairs in order.

Jared rises and walks around the table. He stops and presses a kiss on the crown of my head.

"Jared, we need to chat later," I remind him. I can't bear for him to shut me out.

"Yeah," he mumbles and then he's gone.

CHAPTER TWENTY-SIX

LAYLA

I DON'T LINGER AFTER Jared leaves, and William drops me home. I let myself in but stand staring at the door I closed behind me. My throat burns when I finally let what Jared told me sink in. My mind races through every memory, every moment, looking for signs, and the sad thing is, they were there. I cover the sob that forces its way up my throat. Bert had hit all of us—except Jared and Nelson. My heart pounds. Is that why Nelson killed himself? My eyes burn, and my vision wavers.

"Layla."

I squeeze my eyes shut when I hear Evelyn's voice. She's standing behind me, distraught and confused, and yet I don't know what to tell her. I try to push down my emotions. My face is still wet as I turn to her.

"Do you want to talk about it?" she asks softly, her head tilting to the side.

I pull down the sleeves of my top over my fingers. "Yes. But I can't."

She nods. "Did something happen between you and Jared?"

I wipe my nose with my sleeve. "No. Just something happened to him." My lip and voice tremble.

"Something you can't tell me," Evelyn says.

"No." My voice cracks, and then I'm in Evelyn's arms. Her hand rubs my hair like she's done for years. "I love him," I say.

"I know you do, sweetheart."

"I'm scared." This time, Evelyn makes me face her.

"Of what?" As Evelyn searches my face, her concern isn't coming from my therapist but from my mother.

"Of losing him again." Tears fall fast and hard. This time, I can't control them. Evelyn pulls me back into her arms.

"That boy loves you. He's not going anywhere."

I stop talking after that because that isn't what I meant. Evelyn, being the amazing mother she is, doesn't question me any further.

I take a shower before getting my phone out to text Jared, but I already have a message from him. My heart beats fast as I open the message. My stomach twists painfully. What if he's going to push me away?

I'm nearly done. Can I pick you up in an hour?

"Okay. Okay." I'm nodding as I speak out loud and write back: Okay.

This is a good sign. I get dressed in a long skirt, flip-flops, and a tank top. The day is already heating up. Tying my hair up, I arrive back downstairs. Evelyn is out in the backyard on our swing chair. The sliding door is open, and I step out into the hot day. Smoke billows around her, and the smell of cigarettes burns my nose. I've never seen Evelyn or Carl smoke; the minute Evelyn sees me, she drops her hand to her side, trying to hide the cigarette, but smoke still billows upwards.

"Since when do you smoke?" I ask, sitting beside her. She lifts the cigarette as if she's never seen it before, and I raise an eyebrow.

"Just sometimes," she says quickly before inhaling again. It's such a strange thing to see her do.

"What times call for a cigarette?" I ask, hating that I have worried her enough to smoke.

"Nothing for you to worry about." Her smile doesn't reach her eyes.

"I know you see me as a kid. But I'm here for you, too," I tell her.

Her eyes sparkle. "I don't see you as a kid, Layla." She rubs my face with her free hand. "You are a young woman, and I just hope I did enough." Her brows knit together. "That I made the right decisions along the way."

"Evelyn, you're the best mother ever," I tell her, and her tears fall, but she wipes them away quickly before inhaling her cigarette. Something tells me she's building herself up.

"When we found out that Nelson died, I did some digging," she says, then she throws the cigarette on the ground. Beads of sweat break out on my forehead.

"Ronnie came forward with information against Bert." Evelyn looks at me, and my heart pounds in my ears. I'm holding Evelyn's arm. I didn't realize I even moved.

"He abused Nelson," she says quietly. My lip trembles as I watch tears fall from Evelyn's eyes. "I have been your therapist for seven years, and I don't know how I missed this." And there it is: all her fear, all her guilt pouring out. All of it is unnecessary. She looks crushed as she glances up at me. "I'm so sorry."

I'm shaking my head, still holding on to her. "I wasn't... He didn't hurt me like that." Pain claws its way up my throat as I think of Jared. A part of me feels worse because it's Jared who has been hurt. My mind is conjuring up horrific scenes, and the worst part is, most likely, they're all real. I press my hand to my chest, trying to push the pain down.

"What he did to me has damaged me so much, Evelyn, but what he did to those boys..." Tears roll down my face. "I feel like when I think of Jared, I can't breathe." Anger has me clamping my teeth together as I cry. Evelyn moves closer, pulling me to her. No words are said as she rocks me, and I feel so selfish to grieve when I haven't suffered like the boys. Jared and Nelson did.

"I used to pray for Bert and Ronnie that they would stop hurting people." I sit back and wipe angrily at my face. "Now I hope they die a horrible and painful death."

"Shh." Evelyn's tears fall as she tries to settle me. I can feel hysteria tingeing my words, but speaking about it is letting out all the anger and upset.

We sit in each other's arms. Evelyn rubs my hair, but the worry around her eyes is gone with the knowledge that I wasn't harmed like that and that she didn't fail me. For me, I want to be strong when Jared picks me up. I want all the tears out so I can be his rock. I don't want him to hold me and soothe me. I want it to be about him.

When we finally let each other go, I'm still feeling tender, and by the drawn look on Evelyn's face, so is she.

"Jared's picking me up soon."

Evelyn nods at my words as she fixes my hair behind my ear.

"He had to go to the Gardaí station about Athar. He isn't Jared's father. He's his uncle, pretending to be his father."

I'm not sure how much more Evelyn can take. I'm not sure how much any of us can take, but I tell her everything that happened at Jared's.

"Athar seemed so nice, so considerate of Jared." Evelyn shakes her head. "I can't believe he's not his father. I'm shocked."

"It will take a long time to sink in," I say.

"Carl and I are here for both of you. You and Jared."

"Thank you, Evelyn," I whisper, closing my eyes tight just for a moment. Her words mean everything to me.

Jared was abused. How did I not notice? How did so many social workers that checked up on us not notice? Then again, I hid my own abuse so I wouldn't be separated from Jared. He was all I'd ever known; he was my safe feeling in a dangerous place. Now, the knowledge that it was far darker than I ever could have imagined leaves me feeling lost.

"If Jared needs to talk." Evelyn trails off at the look of horror on my face. "Not me, but I have lots of contacts."

I relax. I don't want my boyfriend telling my mother all his secrets and pain.

"Thanks." I manage a smile. My phone vibrates in my pocket, and I pull it out.

I'm outside.

It's from Jared. My stomach feels empty. Like that horrible, empty feeling you get when you go to bed without dinner and each hunger pain wakes you up. I get up off the swinging bench, pushing down another childhood memory.

"Jared's outside."

Evelyn gets up and hugs me tightly.

"Please don't forget that we're here for both of you," she tells me.

It eases my anxiety a bit, knowing that we aren't alone.

I quickly wash my face and grab my bag. Jared is parked in the drive, his head bowed as he looks at something in his hands. Closing the front door, he looks up. Against the horror of what is happening, I smile, knowing that everything will be alright. I have Jared, after all.

The smile that spreads across his face has me walking faster toward the car. His brown eyes never leave me, and I know there and then that I'm the luckiest person in the world.

Climbing in, I don't give him a second but take his face in my hands and kiss him. My life has been hard, his life has been harder, but I want the past to remain the past and focus on the future. It won't just be my future, but my and Jared's.

"I love you," I whisper against his lips.

His eyes flicker up to mine, his breath brushing my lips. "I love you too, Layla."

I smile into our next kiss, which is soft and short.

We drive in a silence that isn't awkward. I'm mentally preparing myself for what will come next. Maybe he is, too. Jared drives to the beach where the party took place. The day is warm, and when we pull up, we get out without saying anything. I know walking and talking about such a heavy topic will be easier than sitting in a tin can. Jared walks around the car and entwines our fingers together. There's a brief moment when a look passes between us. It's like we're both in agreement that we can do this. That we have to do this.

We remove our shoes and walk along the shoreline. Waves brush against my feet. The feel of water and sand is making me feel more grounded.

"Are you okay?" I start it off with a stupid question, but one that opens up the large black stage to its first victim. Jared, never one to hide, smiles at me. I wonder if he knows how brave he is.

"I am. I've sorted out a lot with Athar, but it won't happen overnight. It will take time." He says this as his free hand rubs the back of his neck.

"You're amazing. You know that?" I tell him.

His lips tug slightly as he narrows his eyes. "No, but I could get used to hearing that."

"Great. You're going to hear it every day, forever."

His smile grows as he tugs on my hand. "You always make me feel better." His words are delivered with a pull to my heart, and silence falls between us again. Pain tears at my heart every time I think of him being hurt. I stop walking, wanting to look at him.

"What can I do?" I ask.

His jaw tightens, but he doesn't shy away from me. "Just be here, be patient."

"Always."

Jared starts to walk again. "I was terrified to tell you, but I knew I had to."

I'm staring at Jared in awe. He is amazing. He is perfect.

He is mine.

"Thank you for trusting me." We stop again, and Jared moves closer, sending my heart pounding. The effect he has on me is frightening at times, and the way he looks at me now, like I'm the most important person in the world, has my breaths coming in short puffs.

"You're the only person I trust. You always have been." Jared's arm snakes around my waist as he pulls me into his arms.

I close my eyes and inhale deeply. I love him so much. The more we talk, the more I love him.

"What happens now?" I ask against his chest, staring out at the ocean.

"Right now? Like this second?" I can hear the laugh in his voice, and I smile into his chest.

"Don't be a smartass," I say, leaning back from him as his dimples appear.

"It's cute when you swear," he says before planting a kiss on my nose.

I wiggle my nose, and he laughs. "'Ass' isn't a curse," I declare.

"It's still cute." We smile at each other as the waves break at our feet.

"We'll be fine." Jared's words are said with such assurance that I believe him.

"Of course we will. We have each other."

EPILOGUE

LAYLA

I'D LIKE TO SAY we walked off into the sunset like I've seen in so many movies, but that's not what happened. We continued to grow and heal together. People say time is a great healer, and it is. But no wound ever fully heals. I think you just learn to live with your demons. They have a special corner in your head. A corner they stick to most of the time.

The court case against Bert arrives, and I take the stand, telling the world what I endured at the hands of Bert and Ronnie. It's hard. It's emotional. But I have Jared, Carl, Evelyn, and even Ashley to support me, which means so much. Rex and Jared's mother joined us too.

I've never been prouder than when Jared walks up the aisle to take the stand; I've also never been so terrified.

"I'm so proud of you," I tell Jared once we have a second alone. It's the first day of court, and we have a few more to go. We weren't the only children in Bert and Ronnie's care. The court has a lot of different witnesses to listen to. I just hated the fact that we had to see Bert and Ronnie again. I didn't look at them directly, but I could feel their eyes on me as I took the stand.

"Who's hungry?" Evelyn asks, and Ashley speaks first.

"I'm starving. Where are we going?"

I smile at her.

"There's a small café down the street," Jared's mother announces, and we all agree that will be fine. Evelyn and Carl walk beside me as Jared holds my hand. Maura walks in front of us, with Ashley and Rex following behind us. We're an odd group. But this is us.

These are the people that are important to us, and the ones that will help us through it. I squeeze Jared's hand, three quick times. It's a signal we've started doing when we can't talk. *We'll be okay*—that's what we're saying to each other. I smile when he squeezes my hand back.

Yeah, everything will be okay.

***

WANT TO READ MORE BOOKS LIKE THIS ONE FROM VI CARTER?

CHECK OUT A DEADLY OBSESSION DUET AND MORE BOXSETS HERE

Sign up to my newsletter if you want to be notified about my new releases. HERE

ACKNOWLEDGEMENTS

I'M VERY LUCKY TO have such amazing readers and Beta Readers. I want to thank the following people who worked with me on this book.

Developmental Editor: Amanda Cuff

Editor: Sherry Schafer

Proofreader: Michele Rolfe

Blurb was written by: Tami Thomason

Beta Readers

Amanda Sheridan

Laura Riley

Lucy Korth

Tami Thomason

Ashley Wheelock

Annas Book Nook

Other thanks:

Tom Korth

About The Author

WHEN VI CARTER ISN'T writing dark romance books, you can find her reading her favorite authors, baking, taking photos, or watching Netflix.

Married with three children, Vi divides her time between motherhood and all the other hats she wears as an Author.

Social Media Links for Vi Carter

Website

Facebook Reader Group

Facebook Author Page

www.ingramcontent.com/pod-product-compliance
Lightning Source LLC
Chambersburg PA
CBHW060725190726
48285CB00001B/69